K IS IN TROUBLE

K IS IN

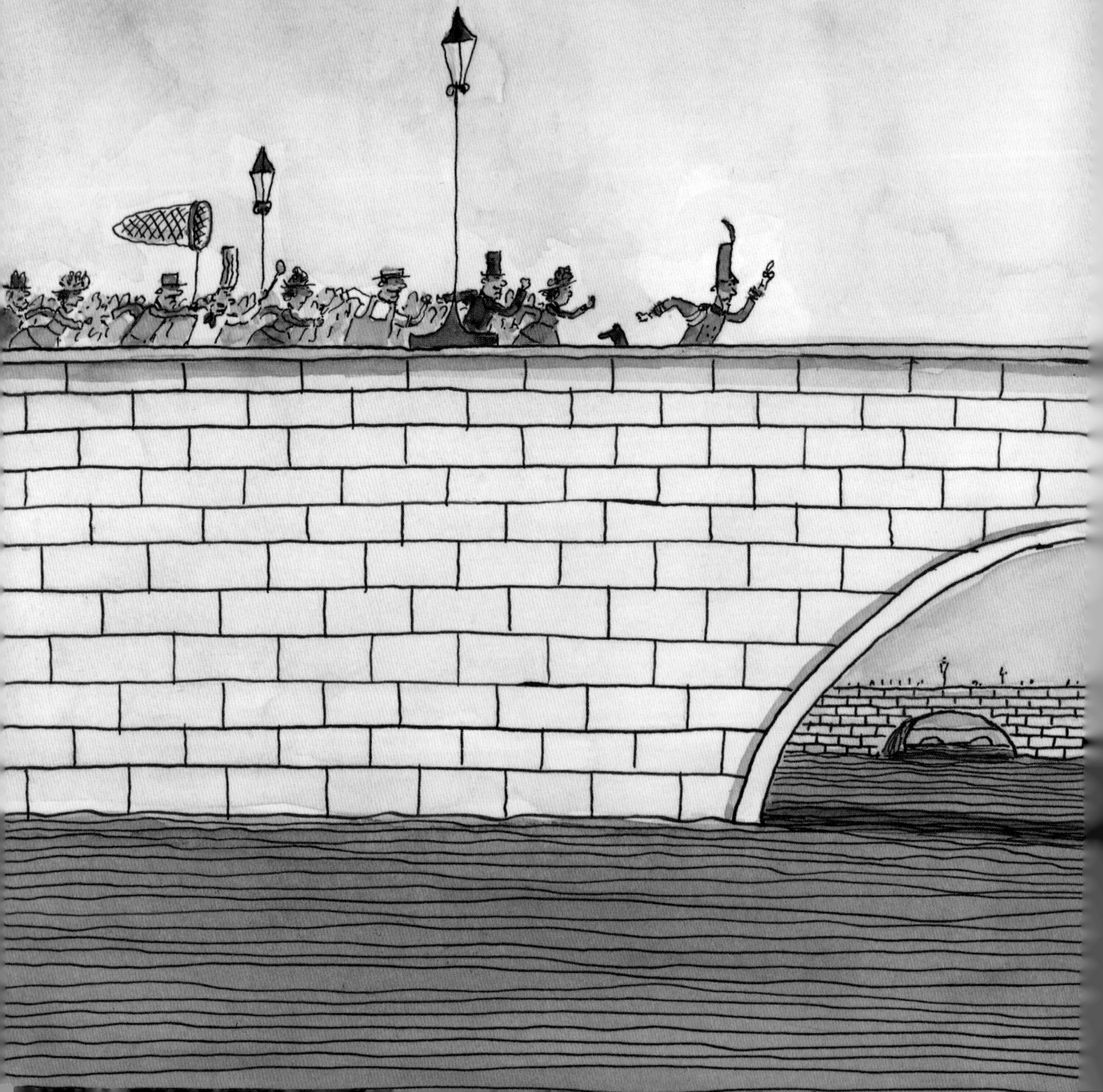

TROUBLE

GARY CLEMENT

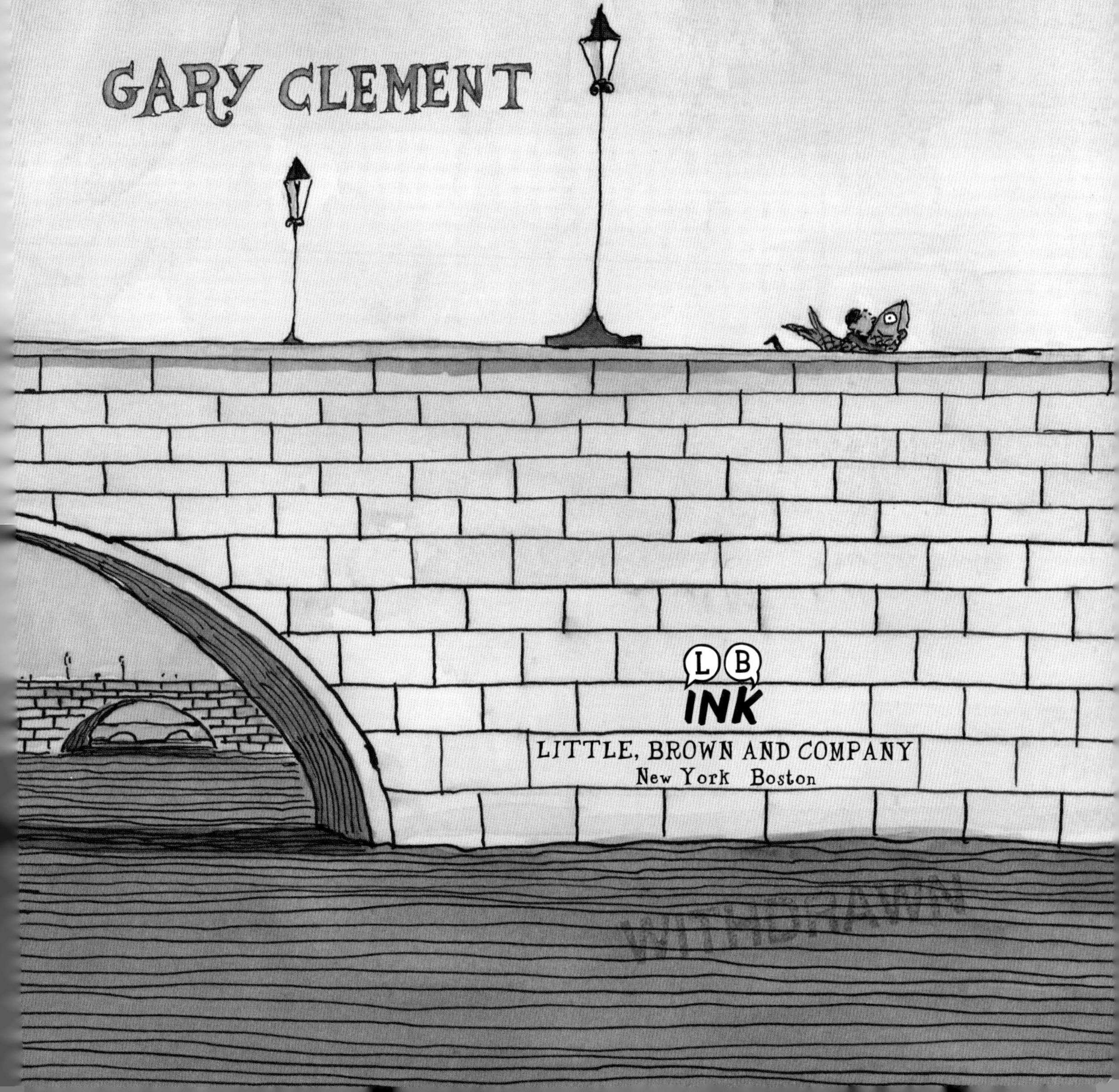

LB INK
LITTLE, BROWN AND COMPANY
New York Boston

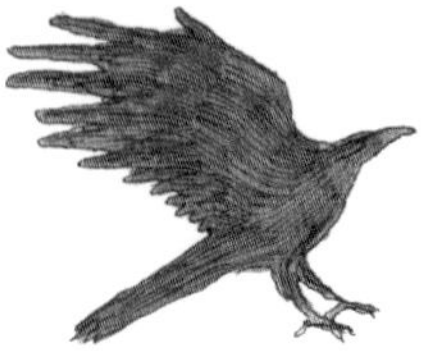

About This Book

The illustrations for this book were done in pen and ink with gouache on Fabriano paper. This book was edited by Andrea Colvin and designed by Megan McLaughlin. The production was supervised by Bernadette Flinn, and the production editor was Lindsay Walter-Greaney. The text was set in KafkABC.

 • Little, Brown Ink Hachette Book Group 1290 Avenue of the Americas, New York, NY 10104 • Visit us at LBYR.com • First Edition: January 2024 • Little, Brown Ink is an imprint of Little, Brown and Company. The Little, Brown Ink name and logo are trademarks of Hachette Book Group, Inc. • The publisher is not responsible for websites (or their content) that are not owned by the publisher. • Little, Brown and Company books may be purchased in bulk for business, educational, or promotional use. For information, please contact your local bookseller or the Hachette Book Group Special Markets Department at special.markets@hbgusa.com. • Library of Congress Cataloging-in-Publication Data Names: Clement, Gary, author, illustrator. | Clement, Gary, illustrator. • Title: K is in trouble / Gary Clement. • Description: First edition. | New York : Little, Brown and Company, 2024. | Summary: "K tries to get through his days, but is beset by talking fish, absurd adults, flocks of destructive crows, and detention" —Provided by publisher. Identifiers: LCCN 2023010469 | ISBN 9780316468527 (hardcover) | ISBN 9780316468602 (paperback) | ISBN 9780316468633 (ebook) • Subjects: CYAC: Graphic novels. | Family life—Fiction. | Schools—Fiction. | LCGFT: Graphic novels. • Classification: LCC PZ7.7.C5723 Kab 2024 | DDC 741.5/973—dc23/eng/20230413 • LC record available at https://lccn.loc.gov/2023010469 • ISBNs: 978-0-316-46852-7 (hardcover), 978-0-316-46860-2 (paperback), 978-0-316-46863-3 (ebook), 978-0-316-56608-7 (ebook), 978-0-316-56607-0 (ebook) • PRINTED IN CHINA • 1010

Hardcover: 10 9 8 7 6 5 4 3 2 1 • Paperback: 10 9 8 7 6 5 4 3 2 1

For G, S, and B.
With love and gratitude.

K IS
LATE

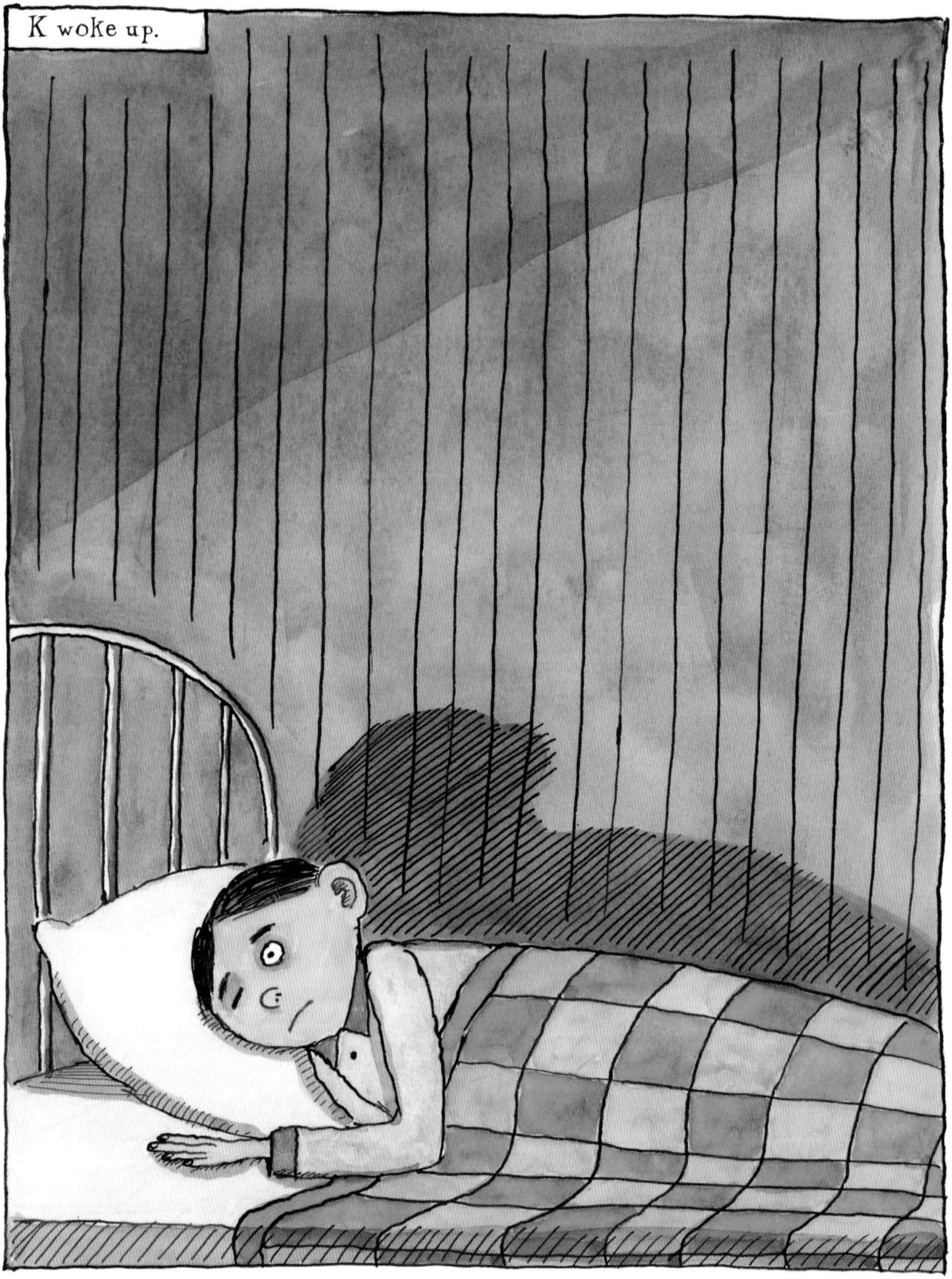
K woke up.

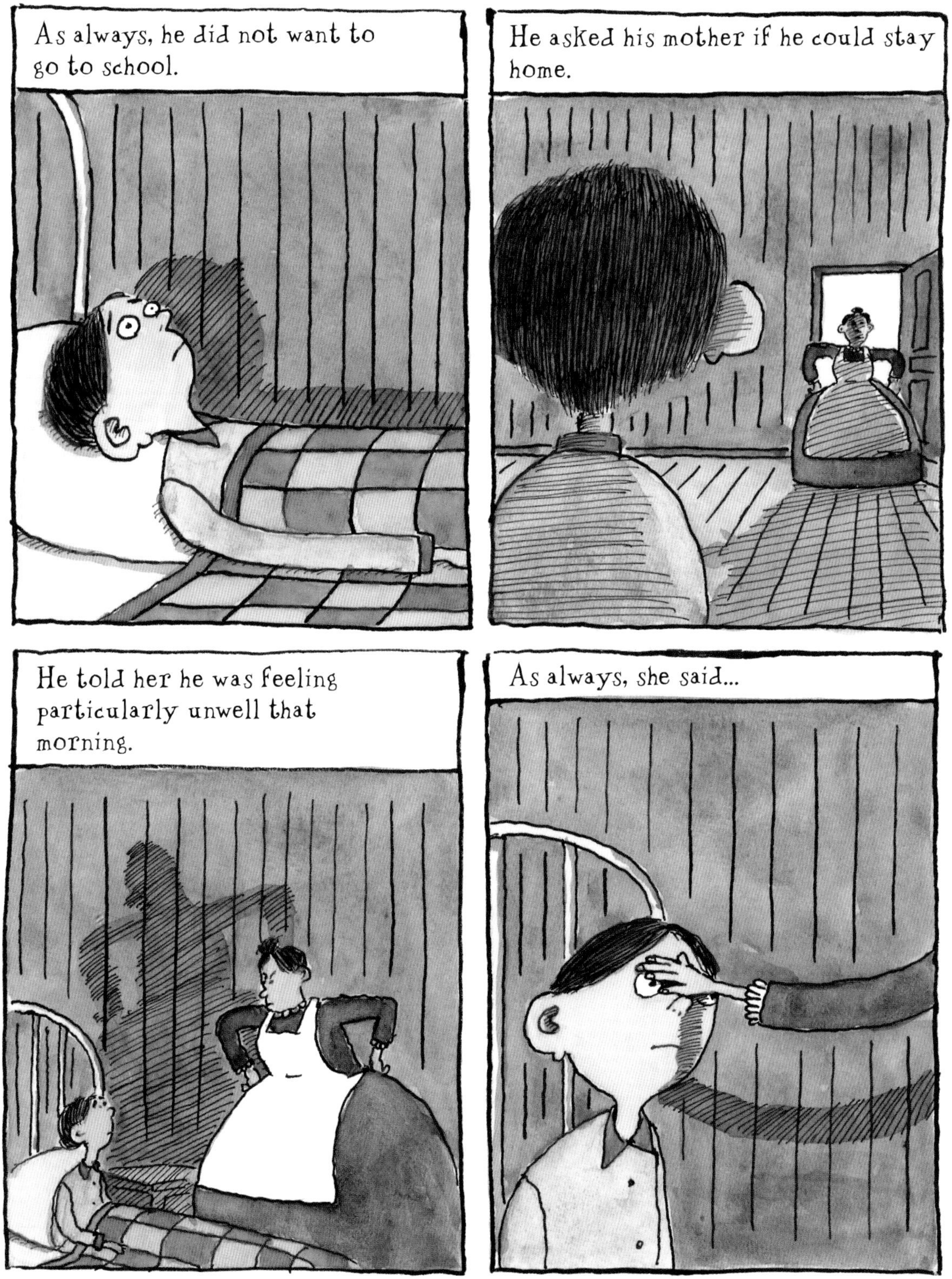
As always, he did not want to go to school.
He asked his mother if he could stay home.
He told her he was feeling particularly unwell that morning.
As always, she said...

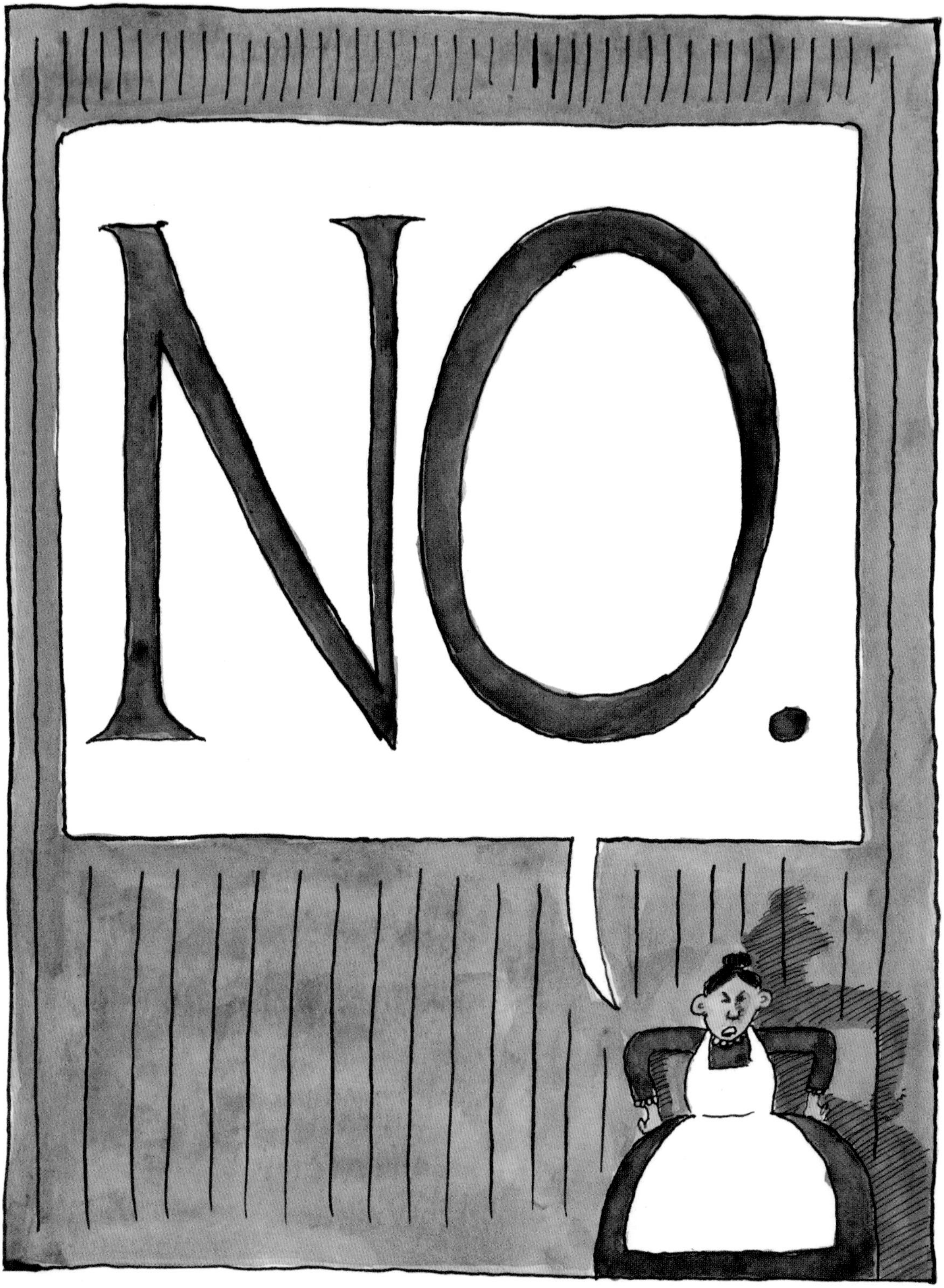
NO.

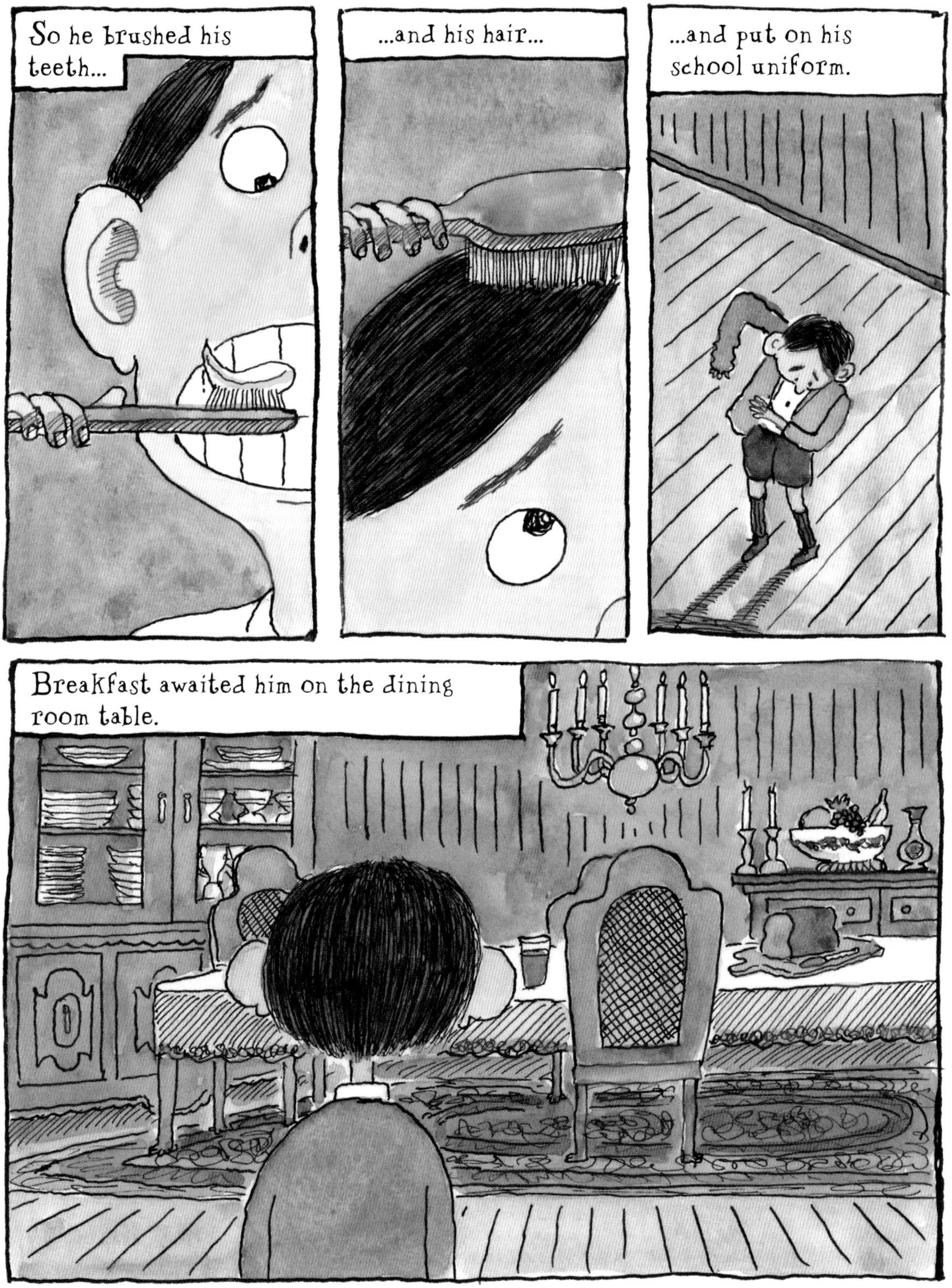
So he brushed his teeth...
...and his hair...
...and put on his school uniform.
Breakfast awaited him on the dining room table.

A loaf of dense black bread.

A soft-boiled egg.

A glass of prune juice.

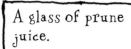

A bowl of grayish porridge.

A plate of sardines swimming in oil.

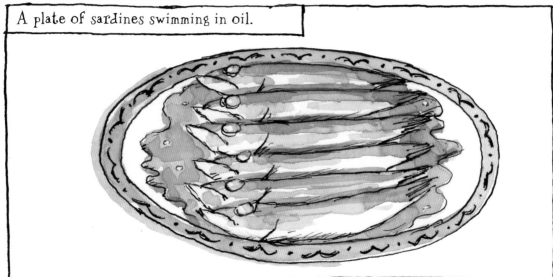

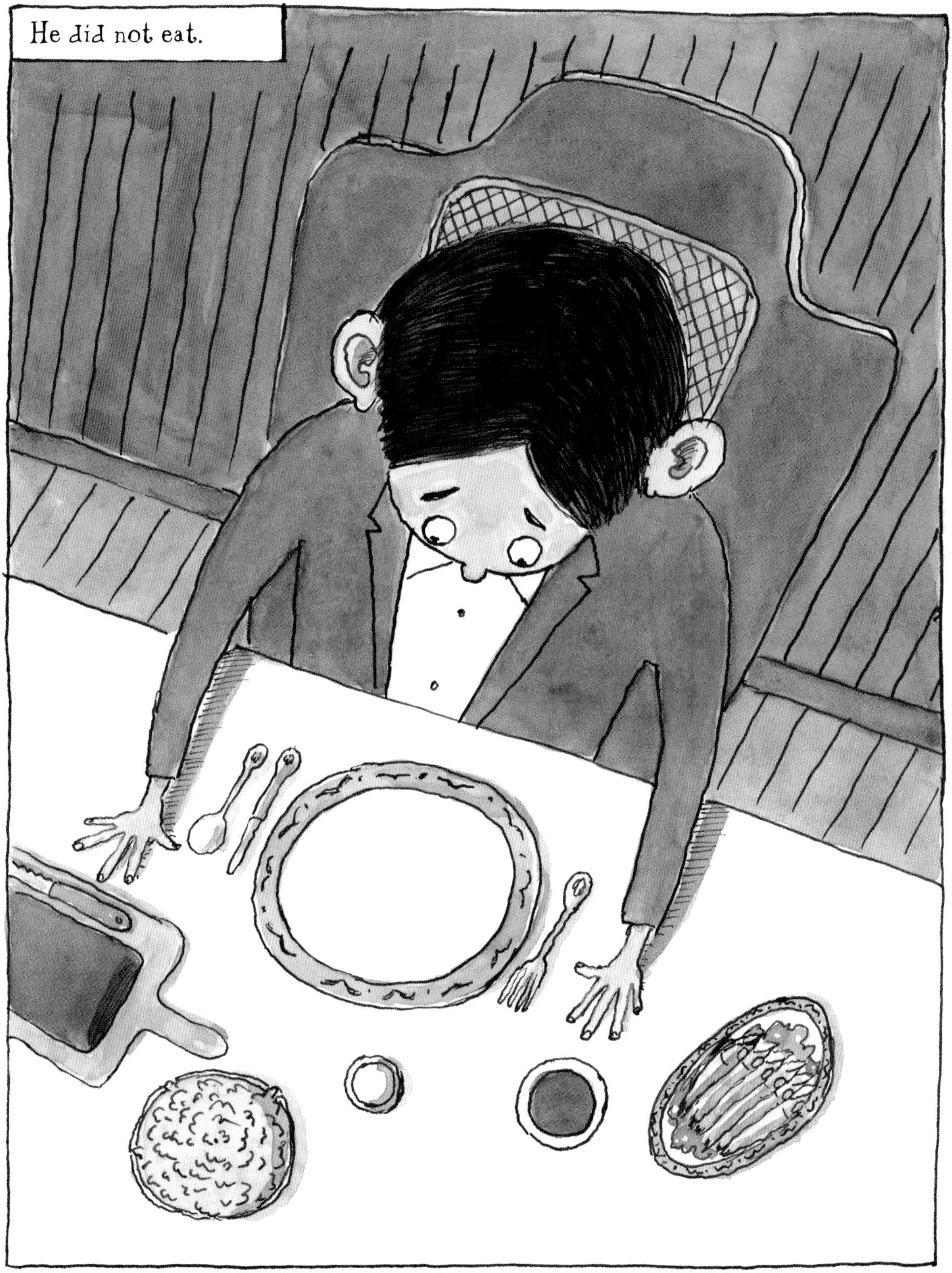
He did not eat.

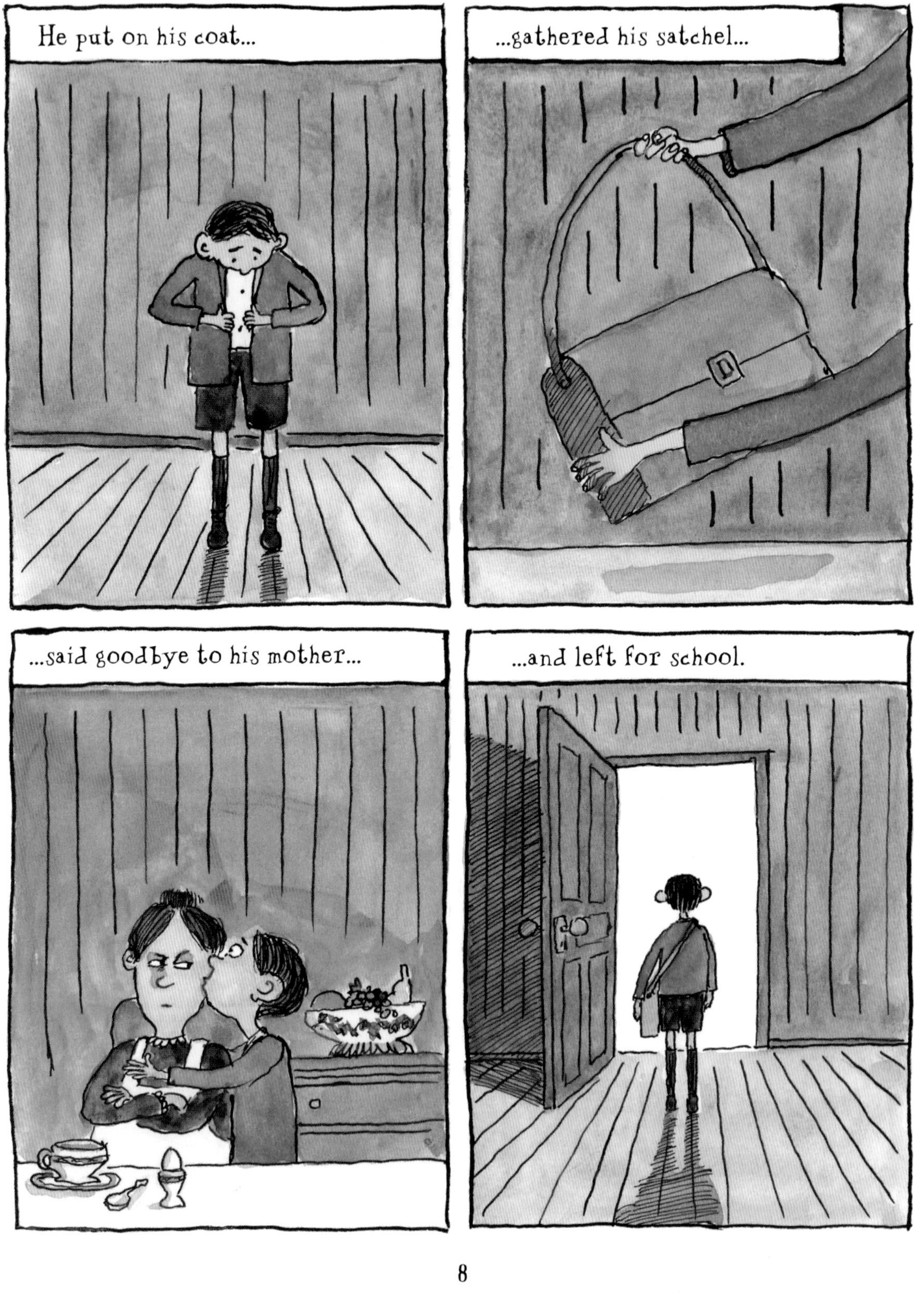
He put on his coat...
...gathered his satchel...
...said goodbye to his mother...
...and left for school.

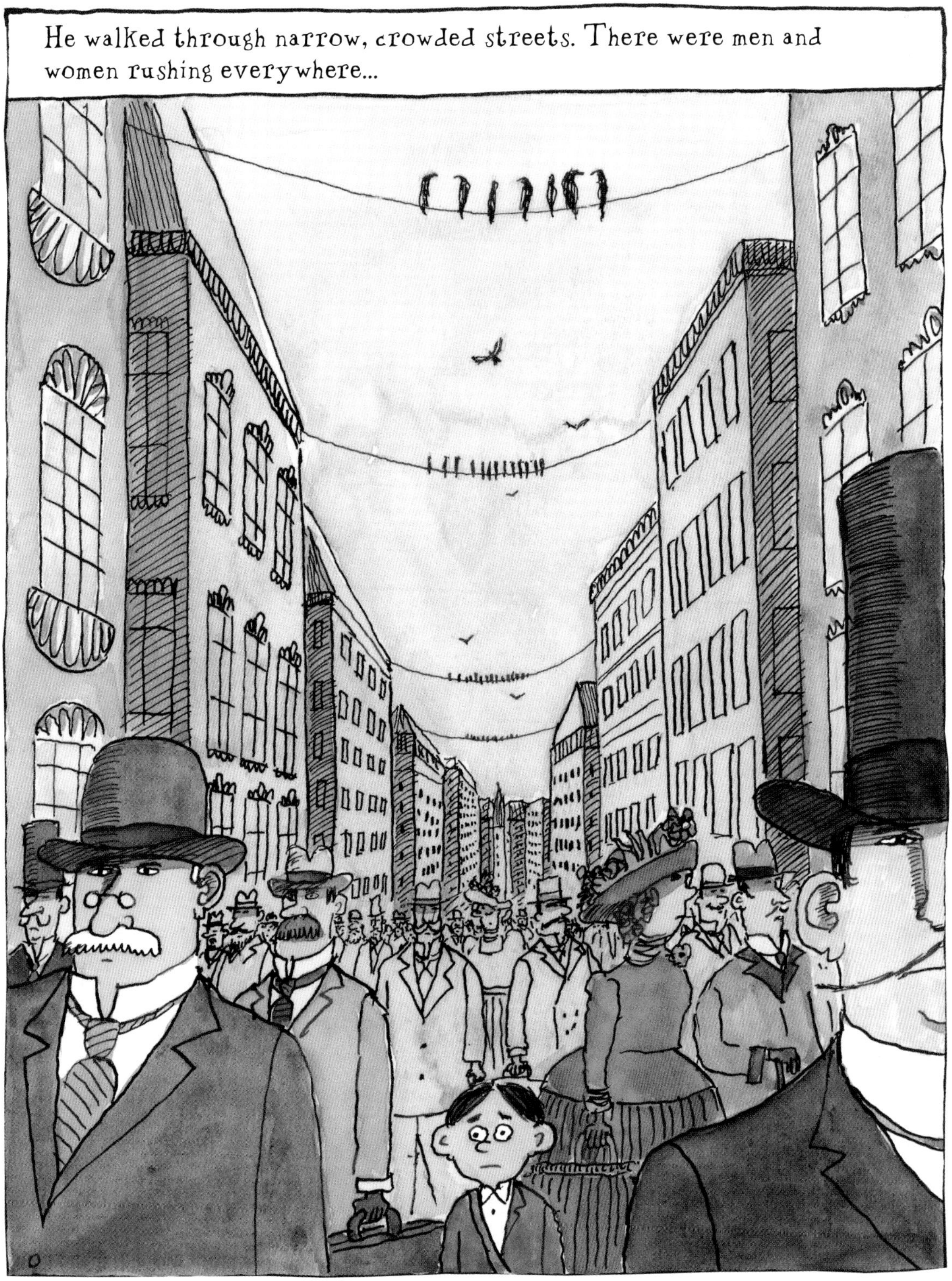
He walked through narrow, crowded streets. There were men and women rushing everywhere...

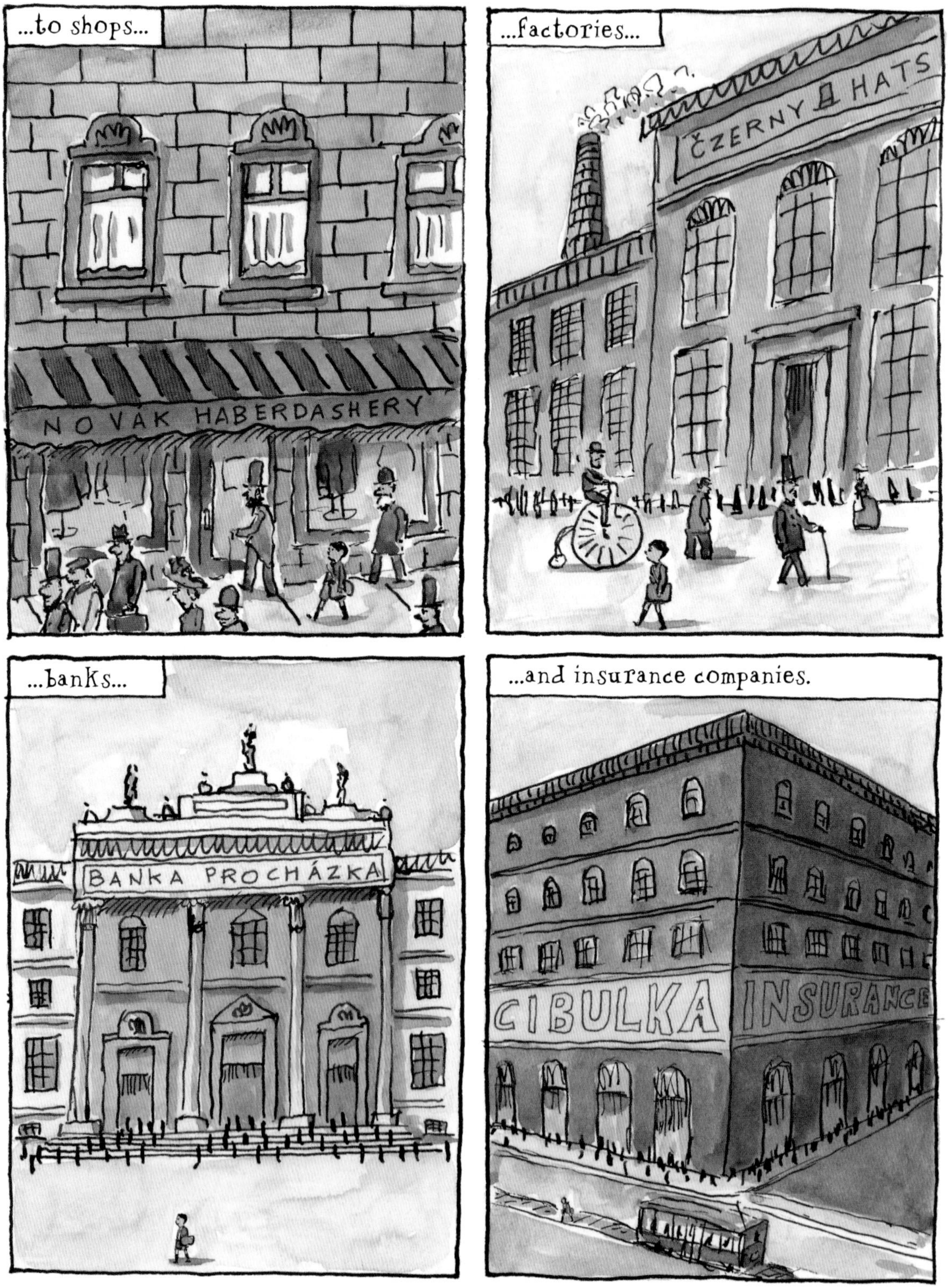

...to shops...
NOVÁK HABERDASHERY
...factories...
ČZERNY HATS
...banks...
BANKA PROCHÁZKA
...and insurance companies.
CIBULKA INSURANCE

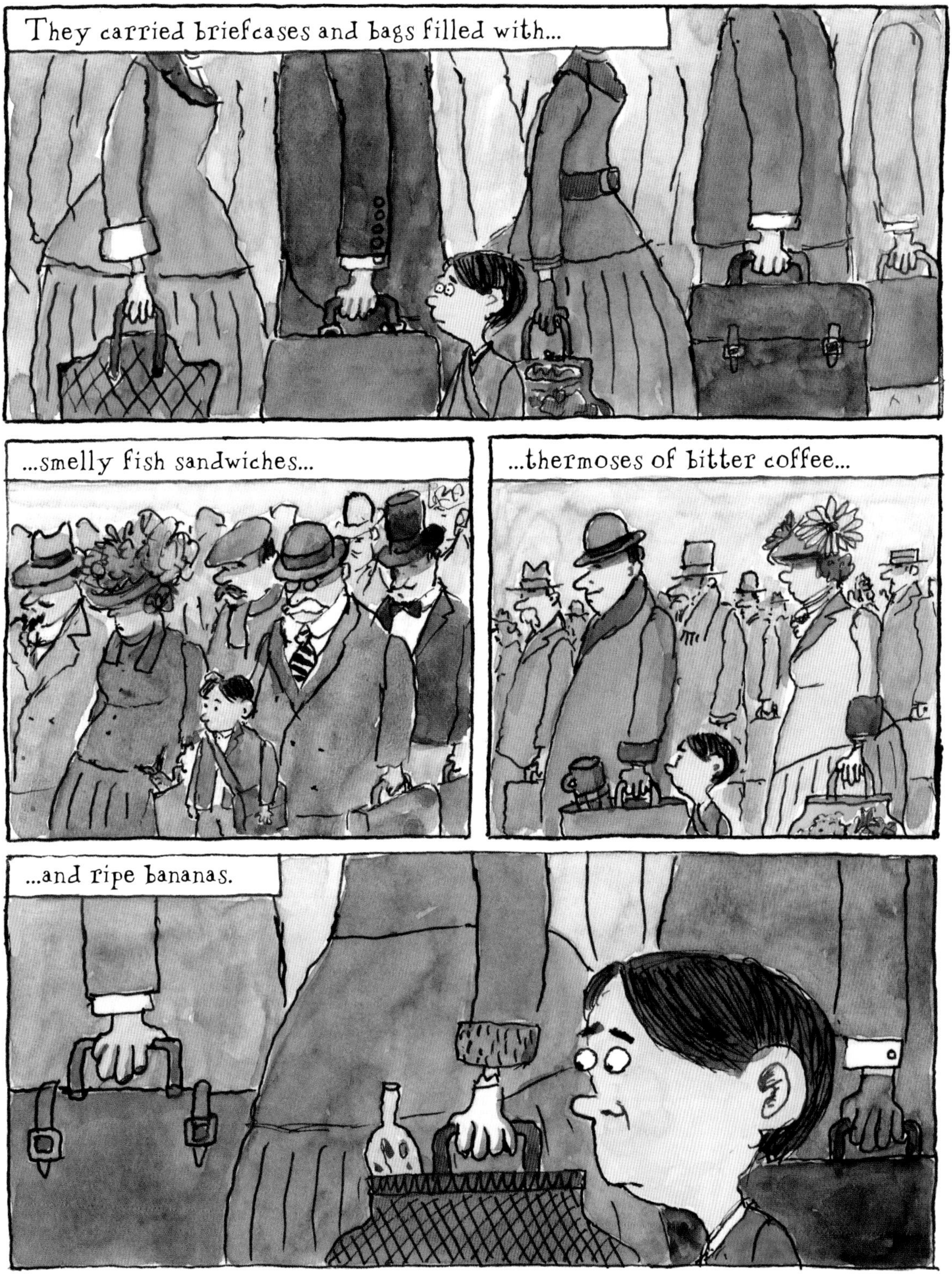
They carried briefcases and bags filled with...
...smelly fish sandwiches...
...thermoses of bitter coffee...
...and ripe bananas.

Sometimes people jostled him.

They never apologized.

Each step he took brought him closer to school.

He took small steps in order to delay his arrival.

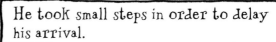

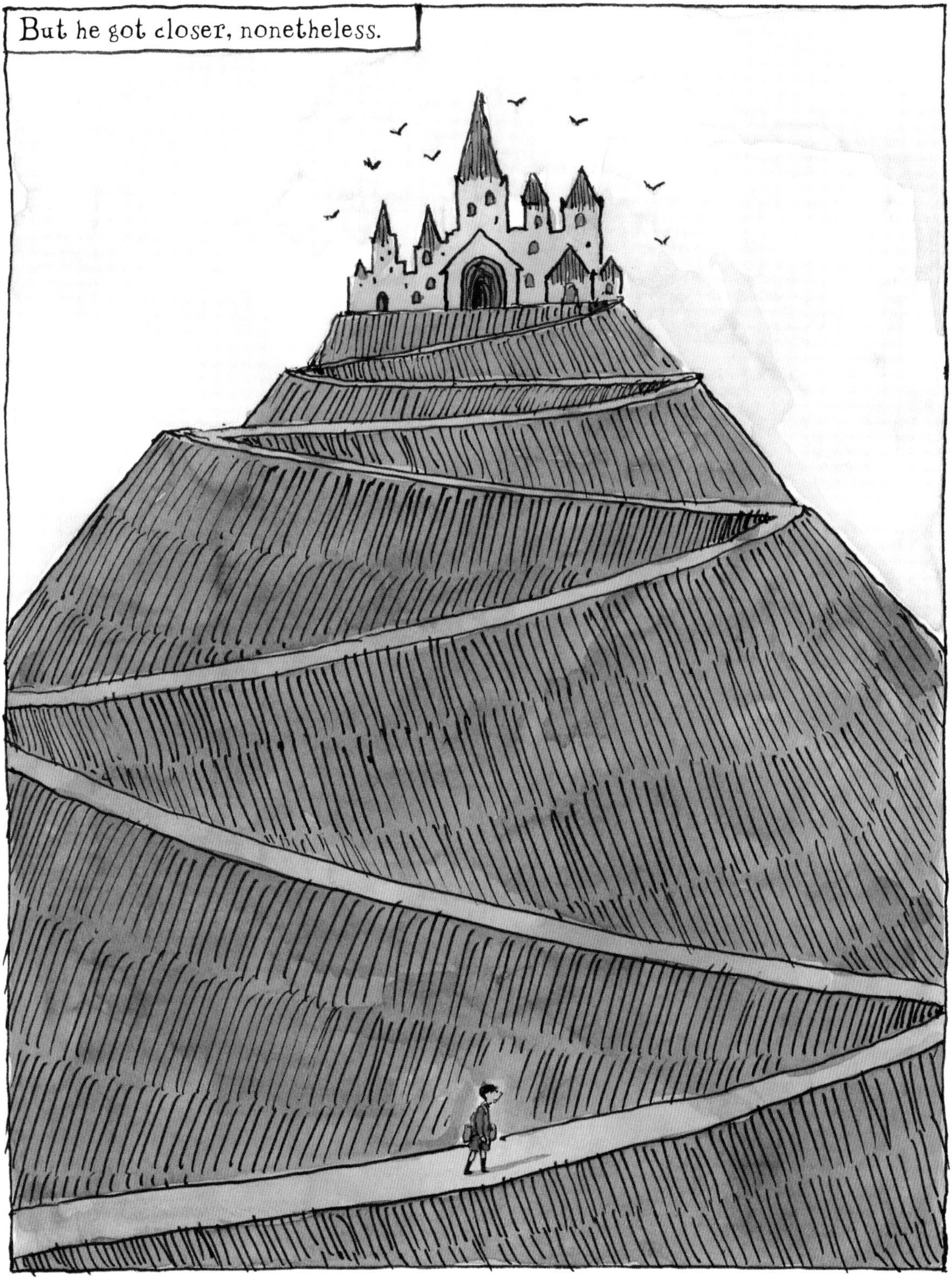
But he got closer, nonetheless.

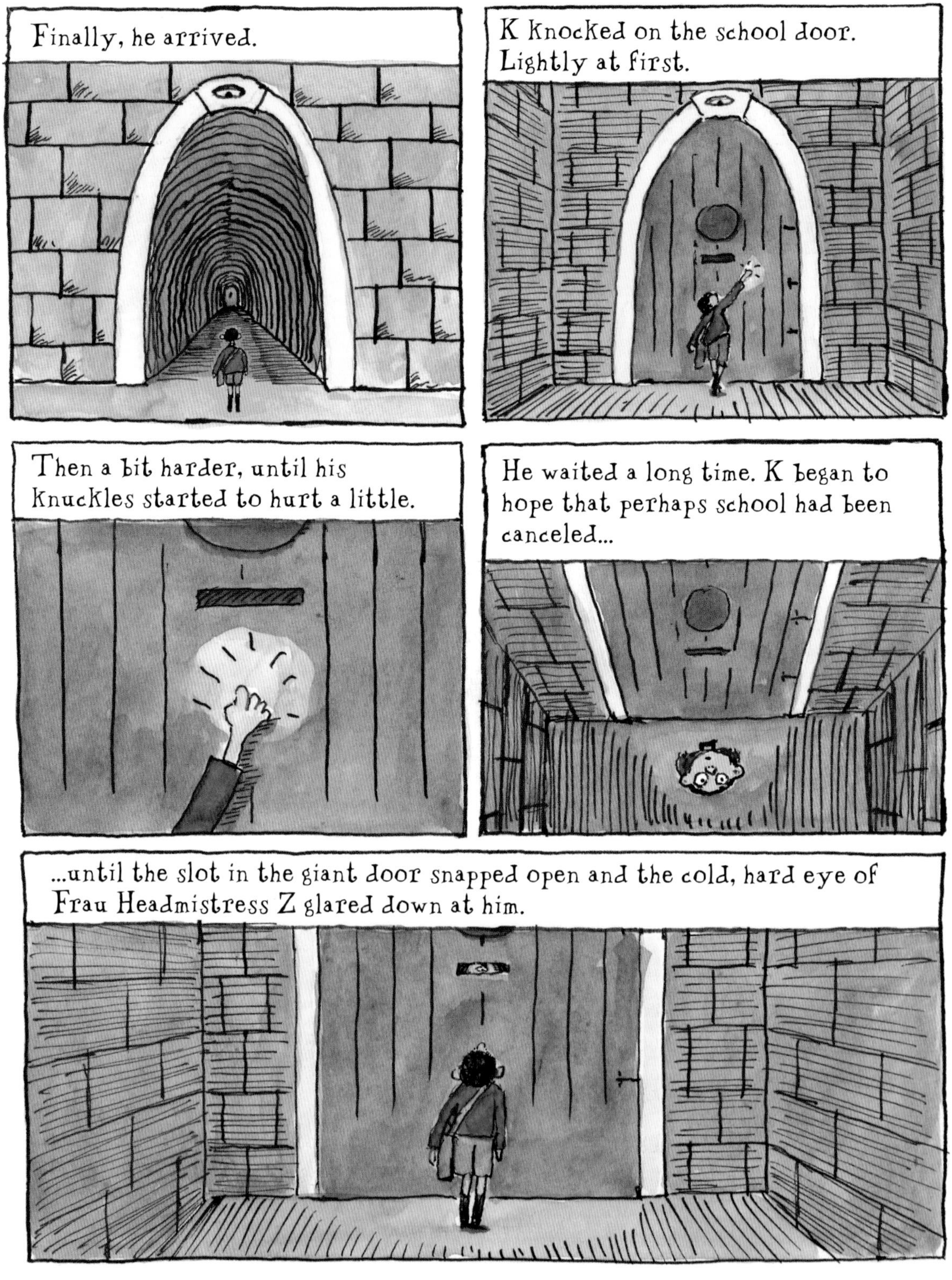
Finally, he arrived.
K knocked on the school door. Lightly at first.
Then a bit harder, until his knuckles started to hurt a little.
He waited a long time. K began to hope that perhaps school had been canceled...
...until the slot in the giant door snapped open and the cold, hard eye of Frau Headmistress Z glared down at him.

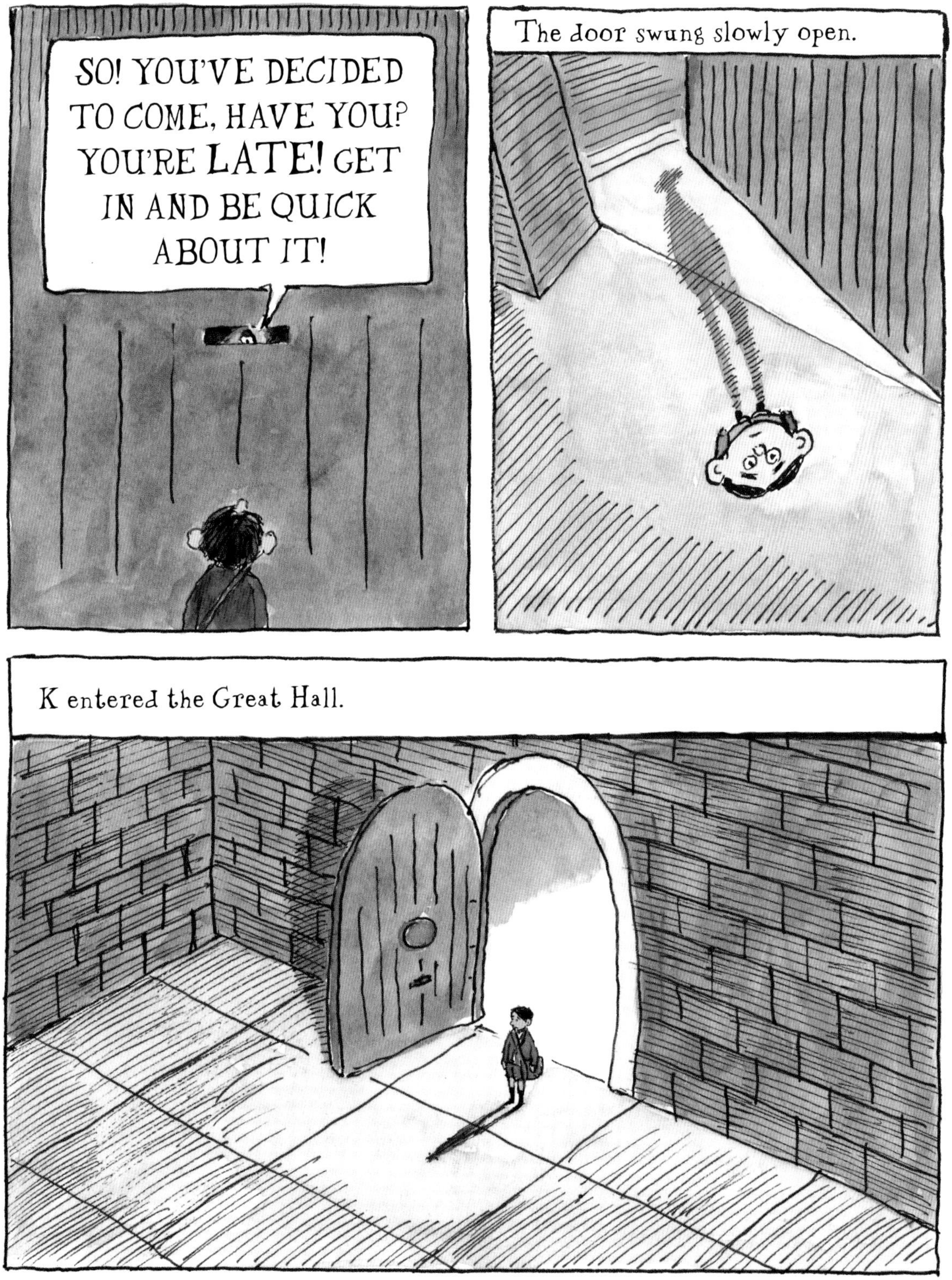
SO! YOU'VE DECIDED TO COME, HAVE YOU? YOU'RE LATE! GET IN AND BE QUICK ABOUT IT!
The door swung slowly open.
K entered the Great Hall.

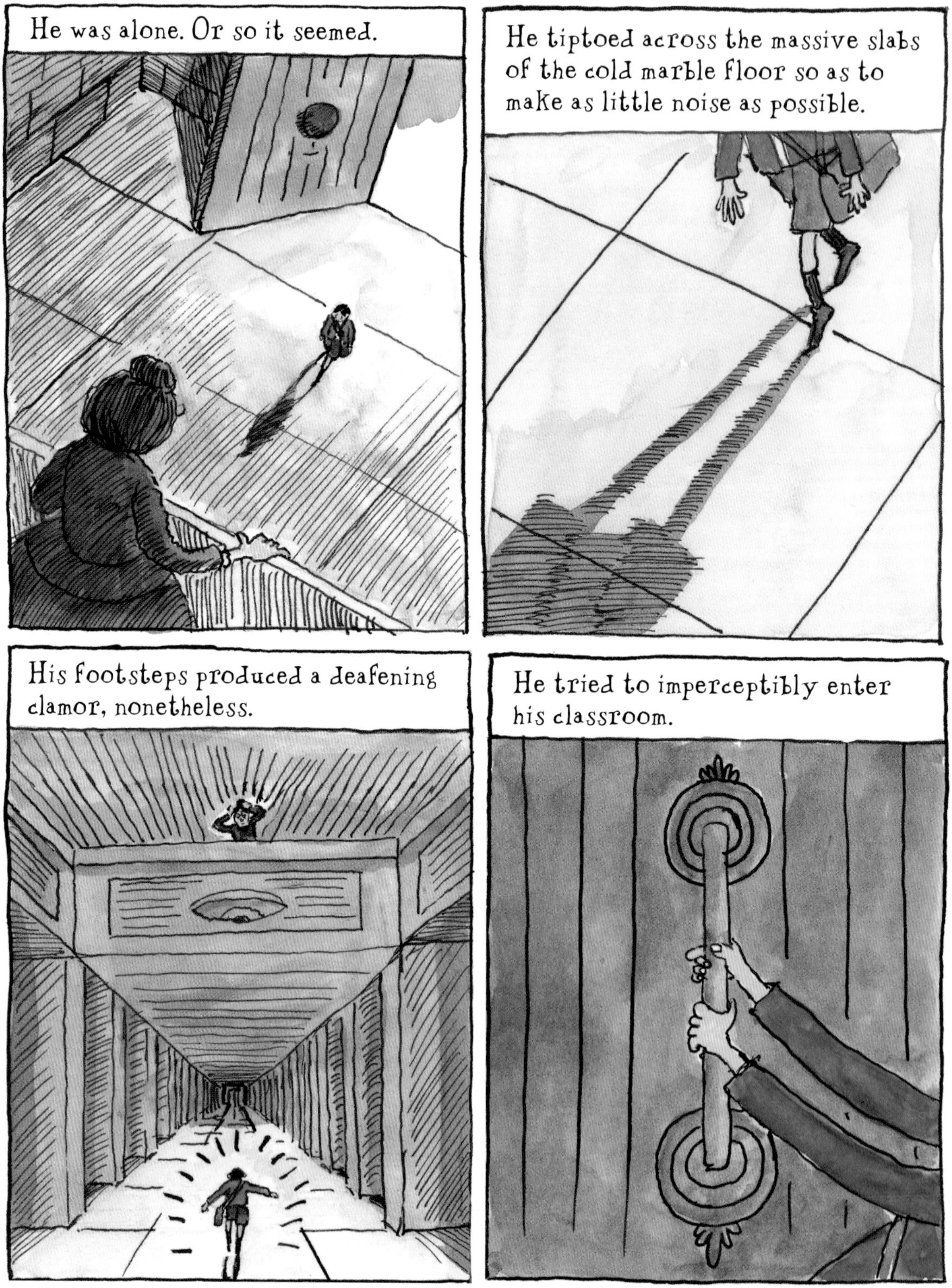
He was alone. Or so it seemed.
He tiptoed across the massive slabs of the cold marble floor so as to make as little noise as possible.
His footsteps produced a deafening clamor, nonetheless.
He tried to imperceptibly enter his classroom.

AH...SO GOOD OF YOU TO JOIN US, HERR K!

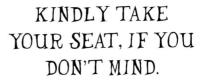

KINDLY TAKE YOUR SEAT, IF YOU DON'T MIND.

CAN I GET YOU ANYTHING?

PERHAPS A NICE, HOT CUP OF COCOA?

OR HOW ABOUT A PIECE OF FRESHLY BAKED SPONGE CAKE?

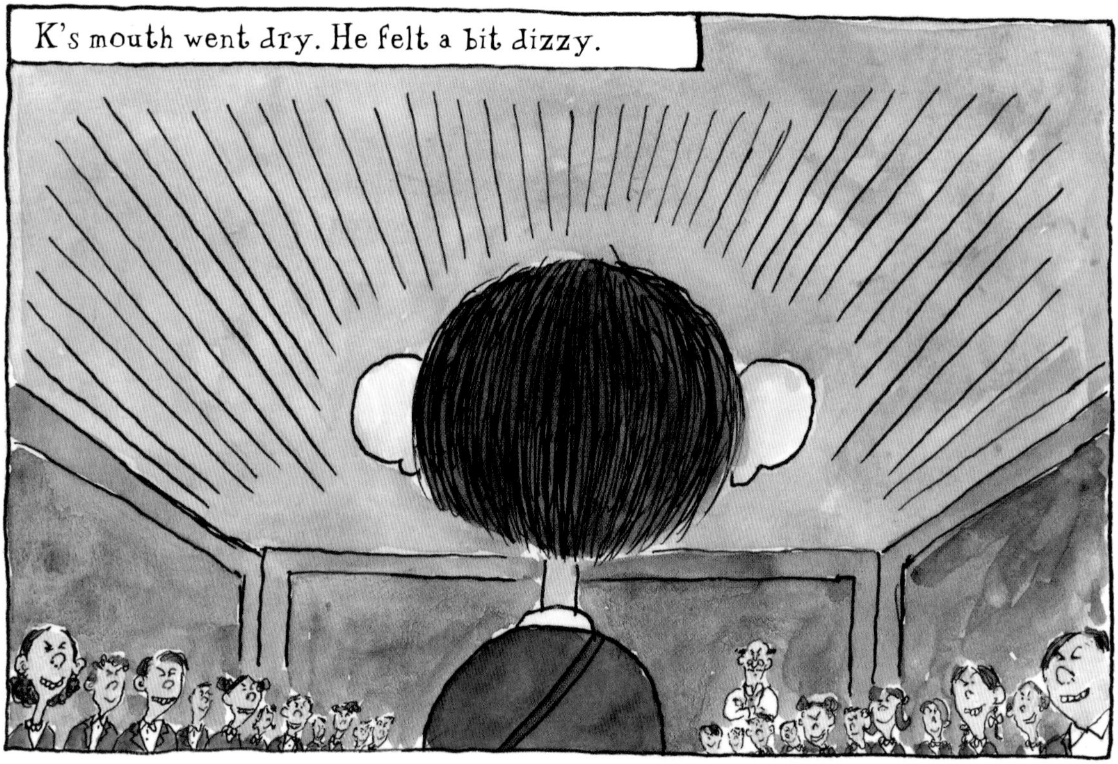
K's mouth went dry. He felt a bit dizzy.

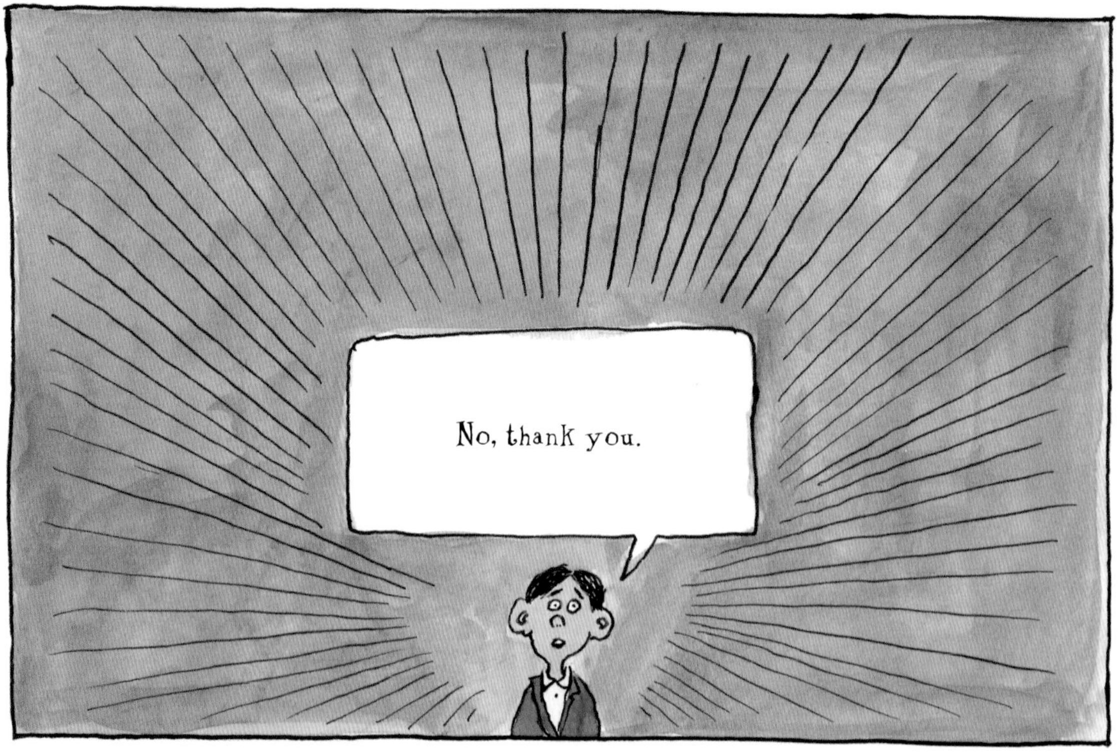
No, thank you.

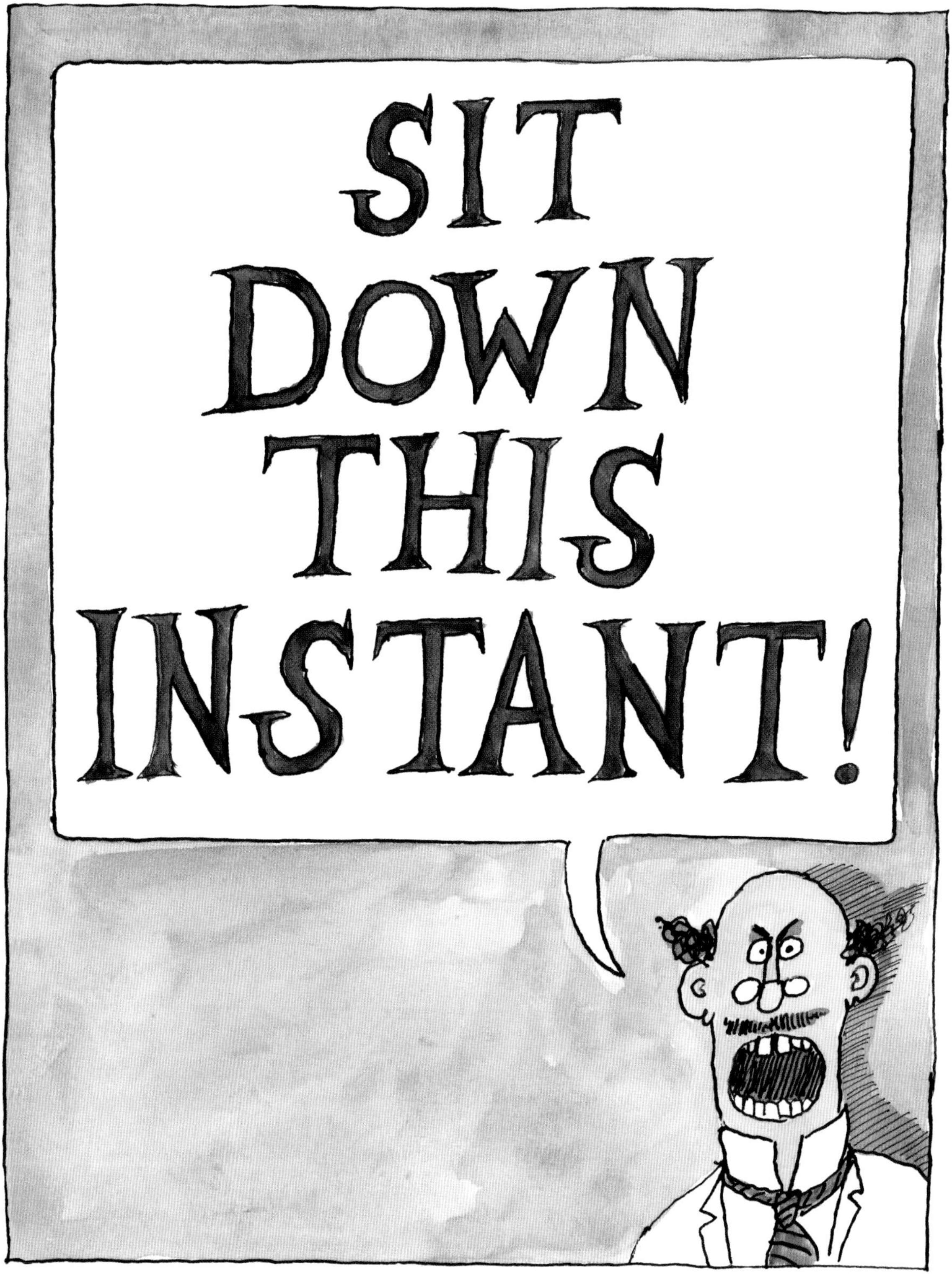
SIT DOWN THIS INSTANT!

K hurried to his seat as his classmates smirked and snickered.

Such impertinence.

The moment K settled into his chair, there was a sharp rap on the door as Frau Headmistress Z swooped in.

She pointed her long, bony finger directly at K.

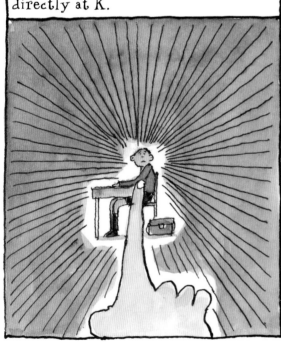

YOU...TO THE OFFICE. NOW!

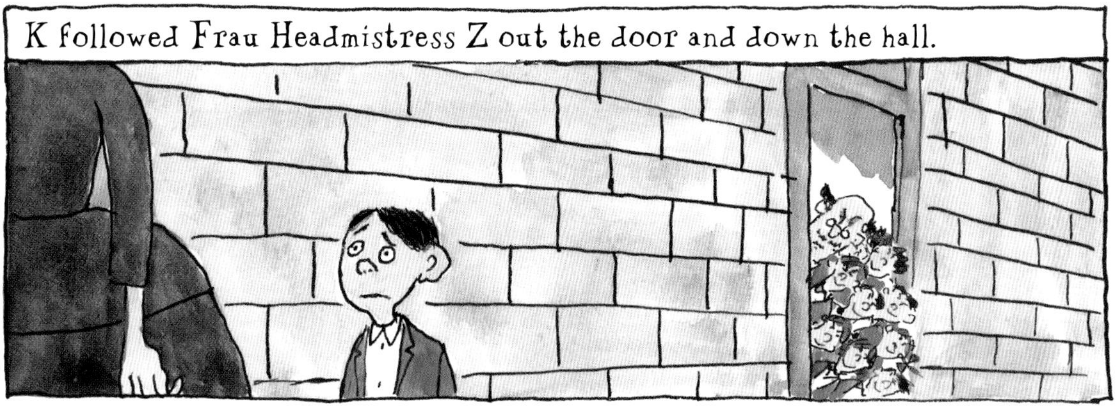
K followed Frau Headmistress Z out the door and down the hall.

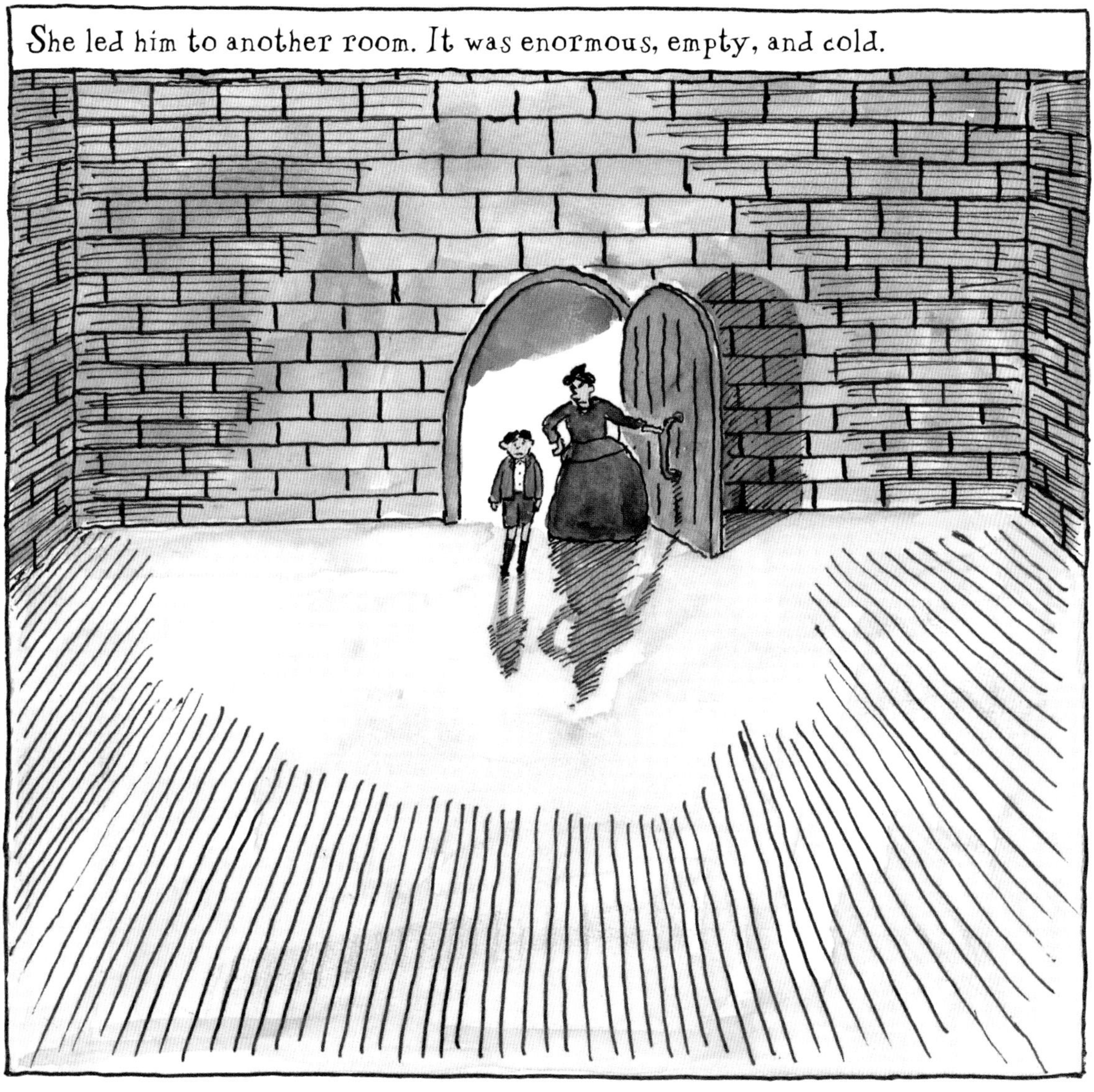
She led him to another room. It was enormous, empty, and cold.

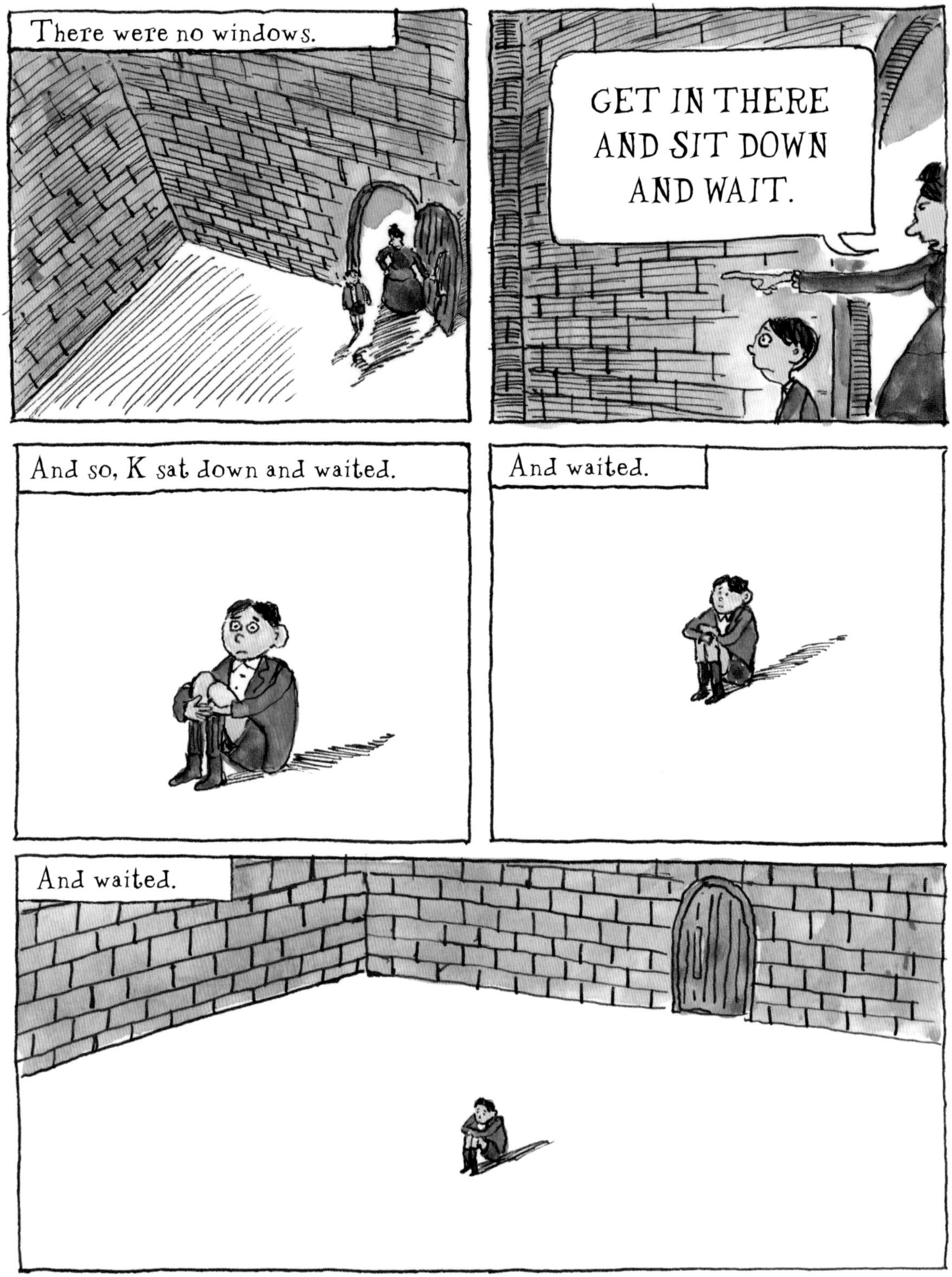
There were no windows.
GET IN THERE AND SIT DOWN AND WAIT.
And so, K sat down and waited.
And waited.
And waited.

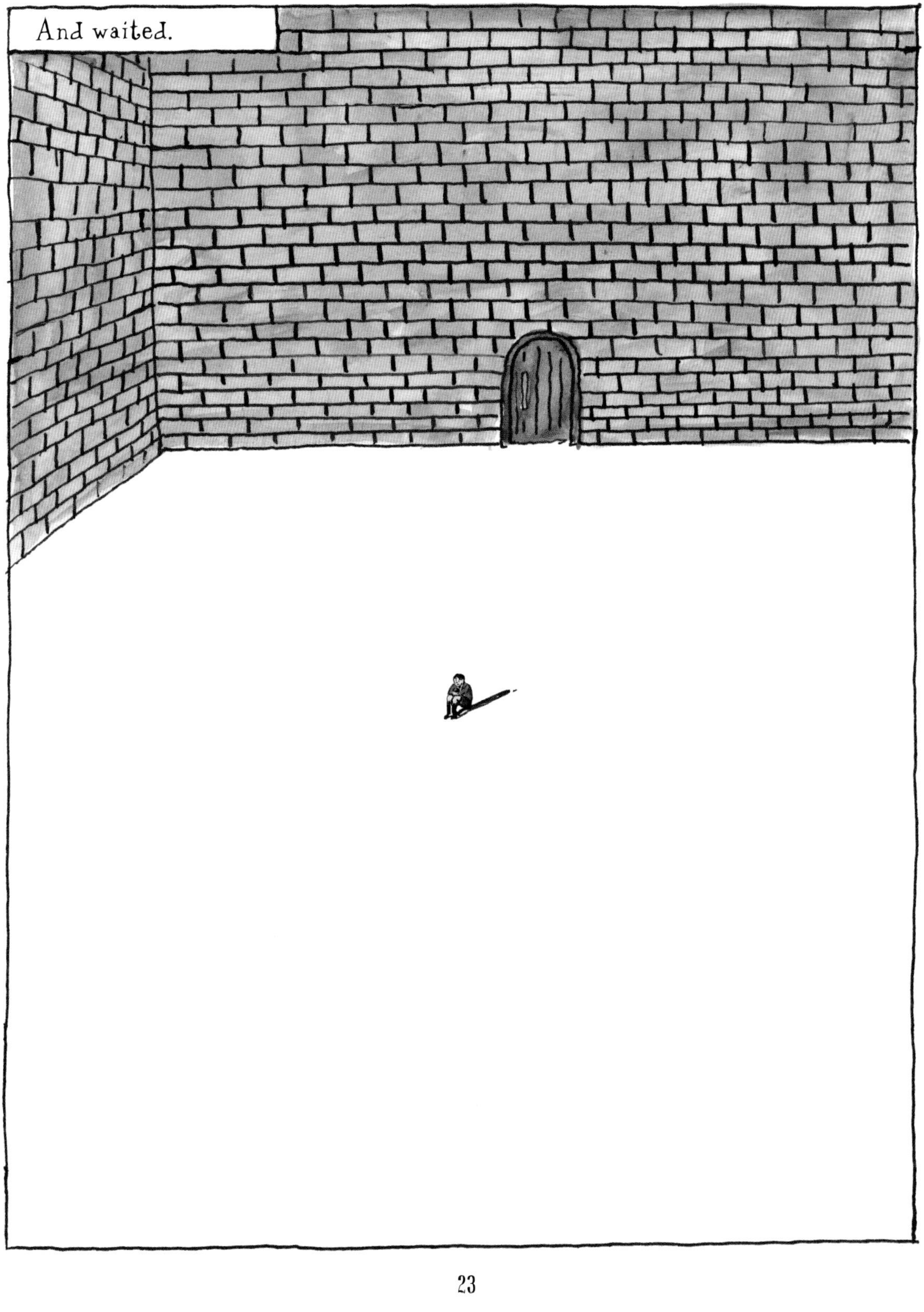
And waited.

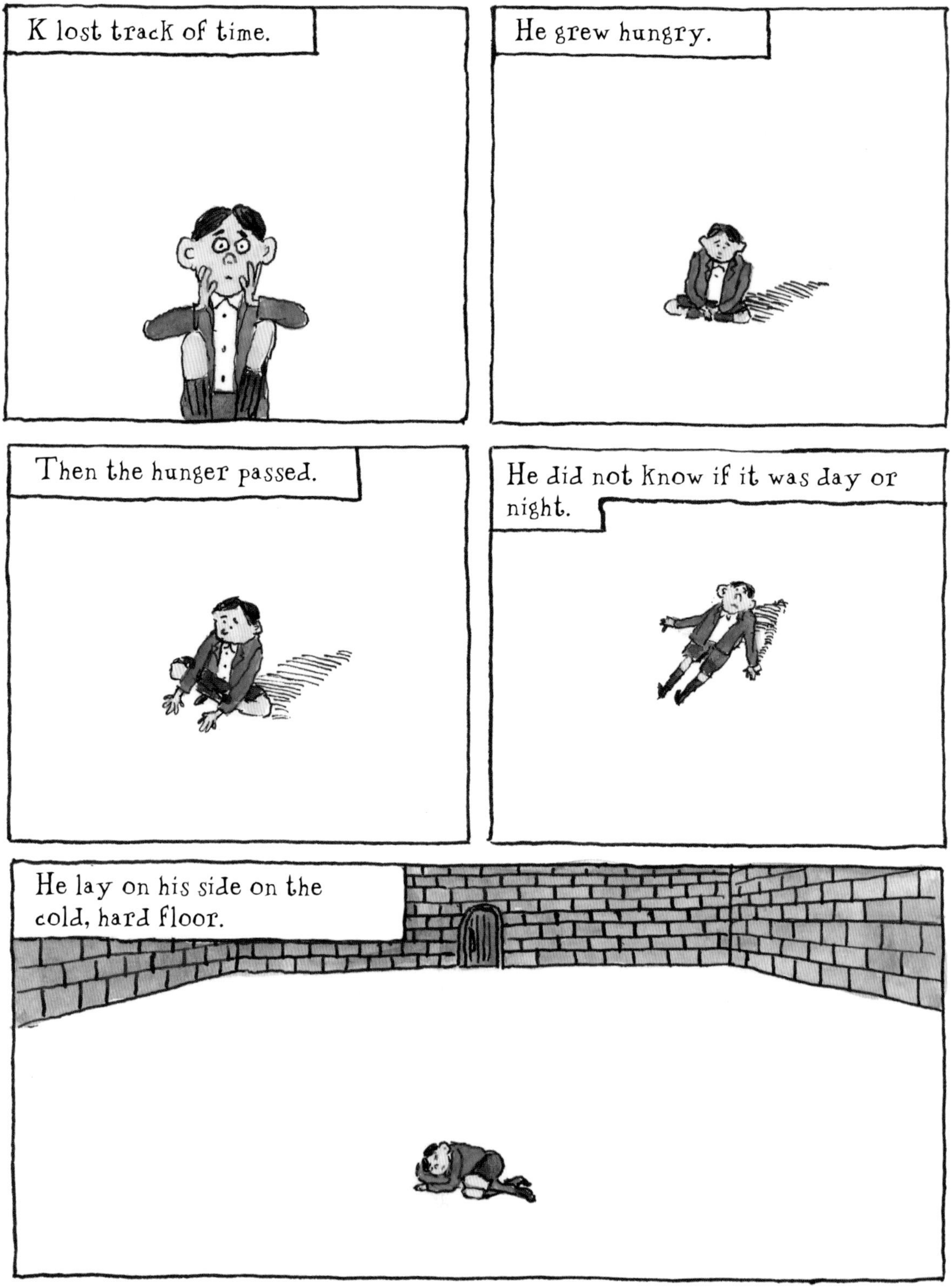
K lost track of time.
He grew hungry.
Then the hunger passed.
He did not know if it was day or night.
He lay on his side on the cold, hard floor.

He may have dozed for a while, but he could not be sure.

As his mind wandered from one thing to the next, he felt a soft tap on his nose.

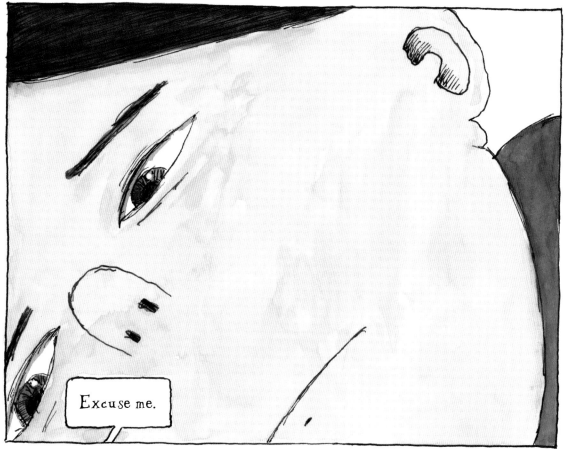

Excuse me.

There, in front of his face, was a small, brown beetle.

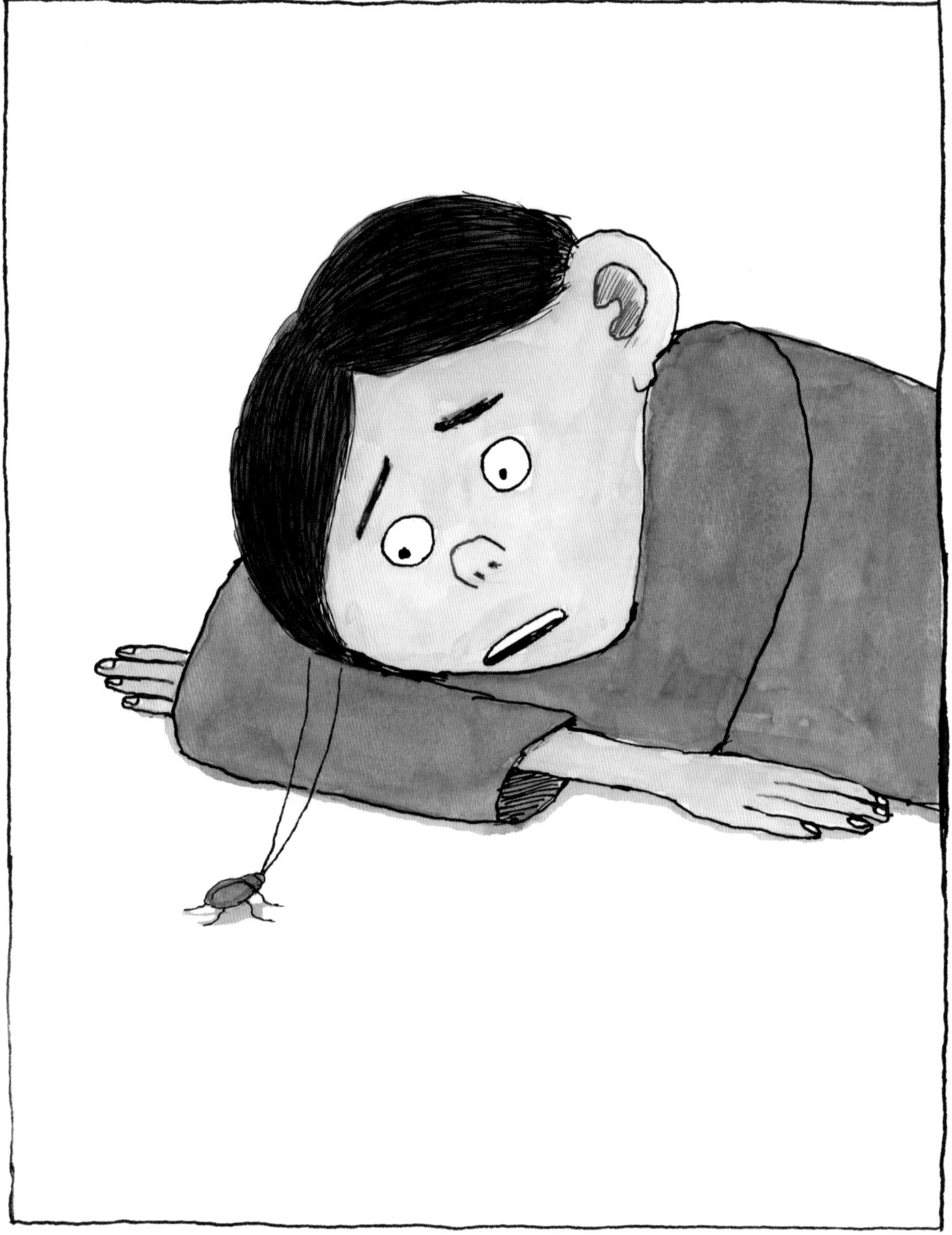

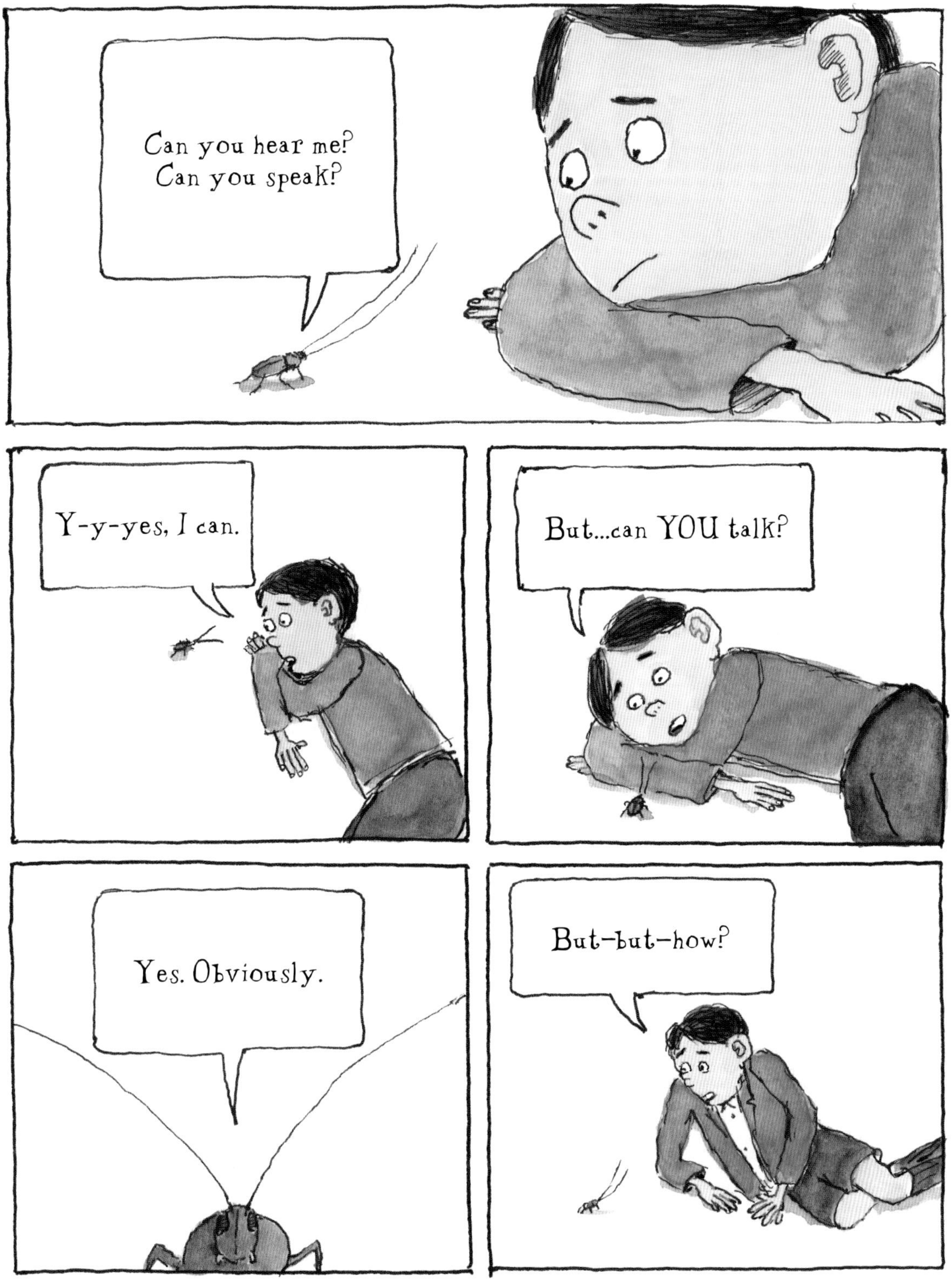
Can you hear me? Can you speak?
Y-y-yes, I can.
But...can YOU talk?
Yes. Obviously.
But-but-how?

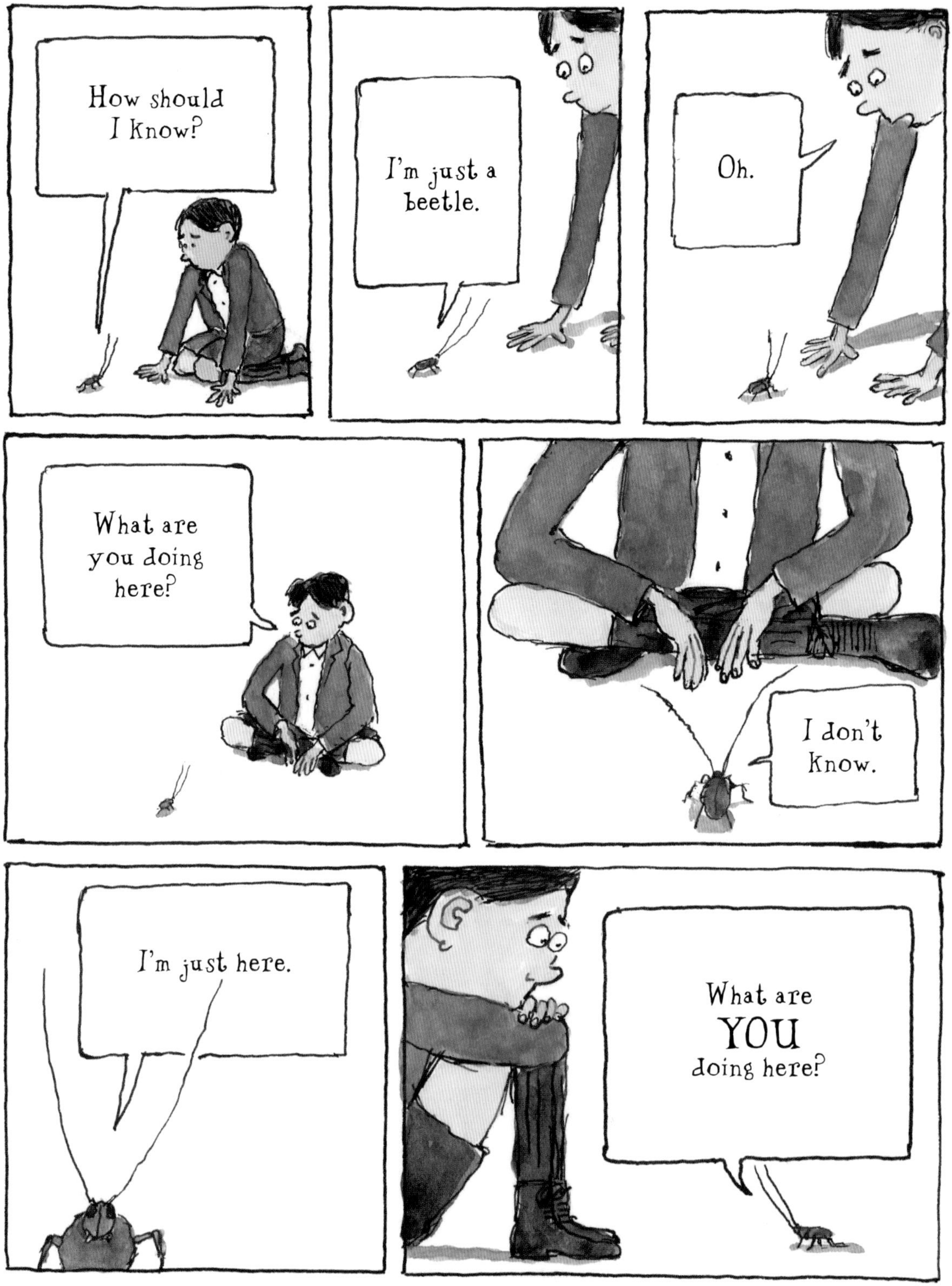
How should I know?
I'm just a beetle.
Oh.
What are you doing here?
I don't know.
I'm just here.
What are YOU doing here?

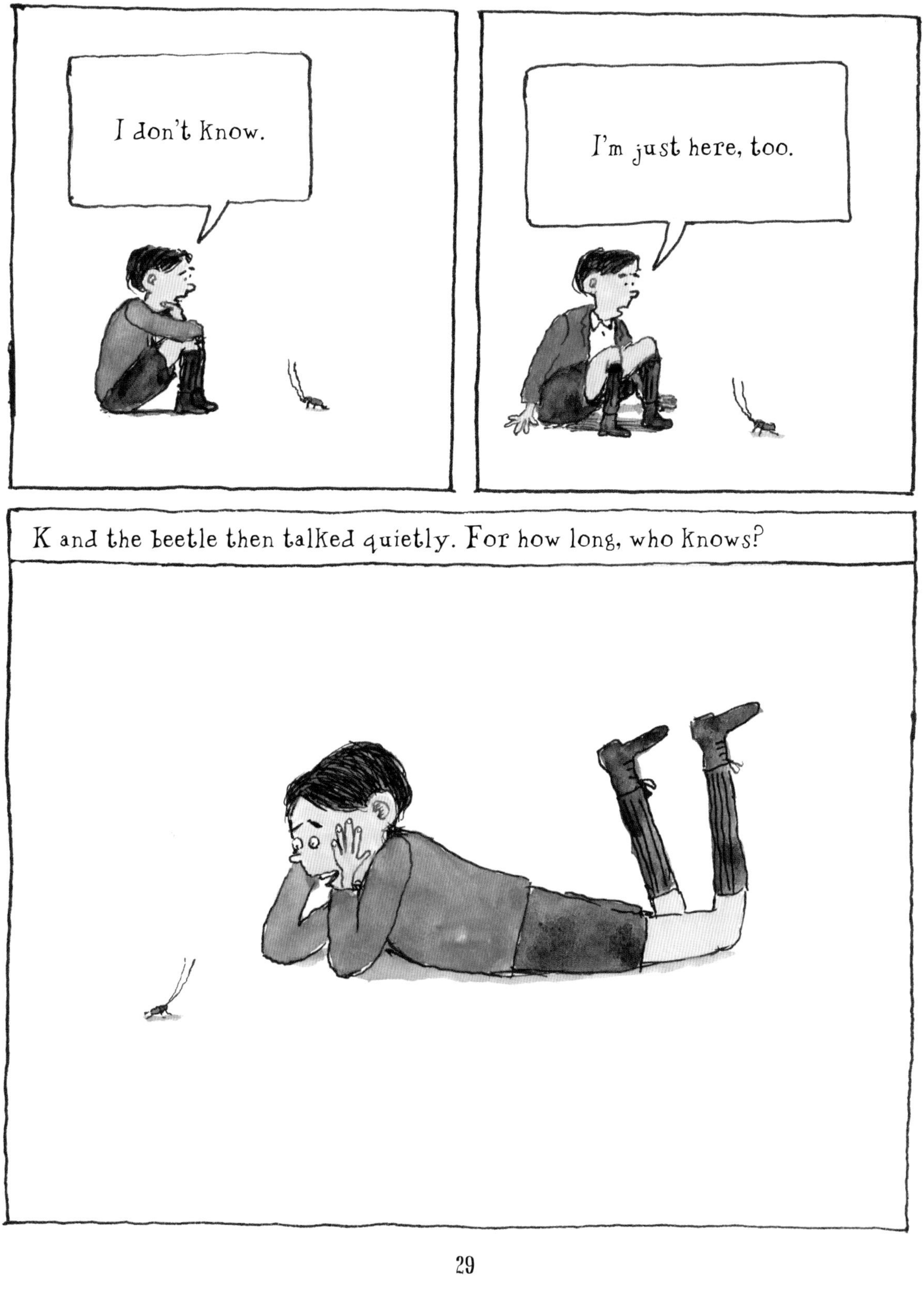
I don't know.
I'm just here, too.
K and the beetle then talked quietly. For how long, who knows?

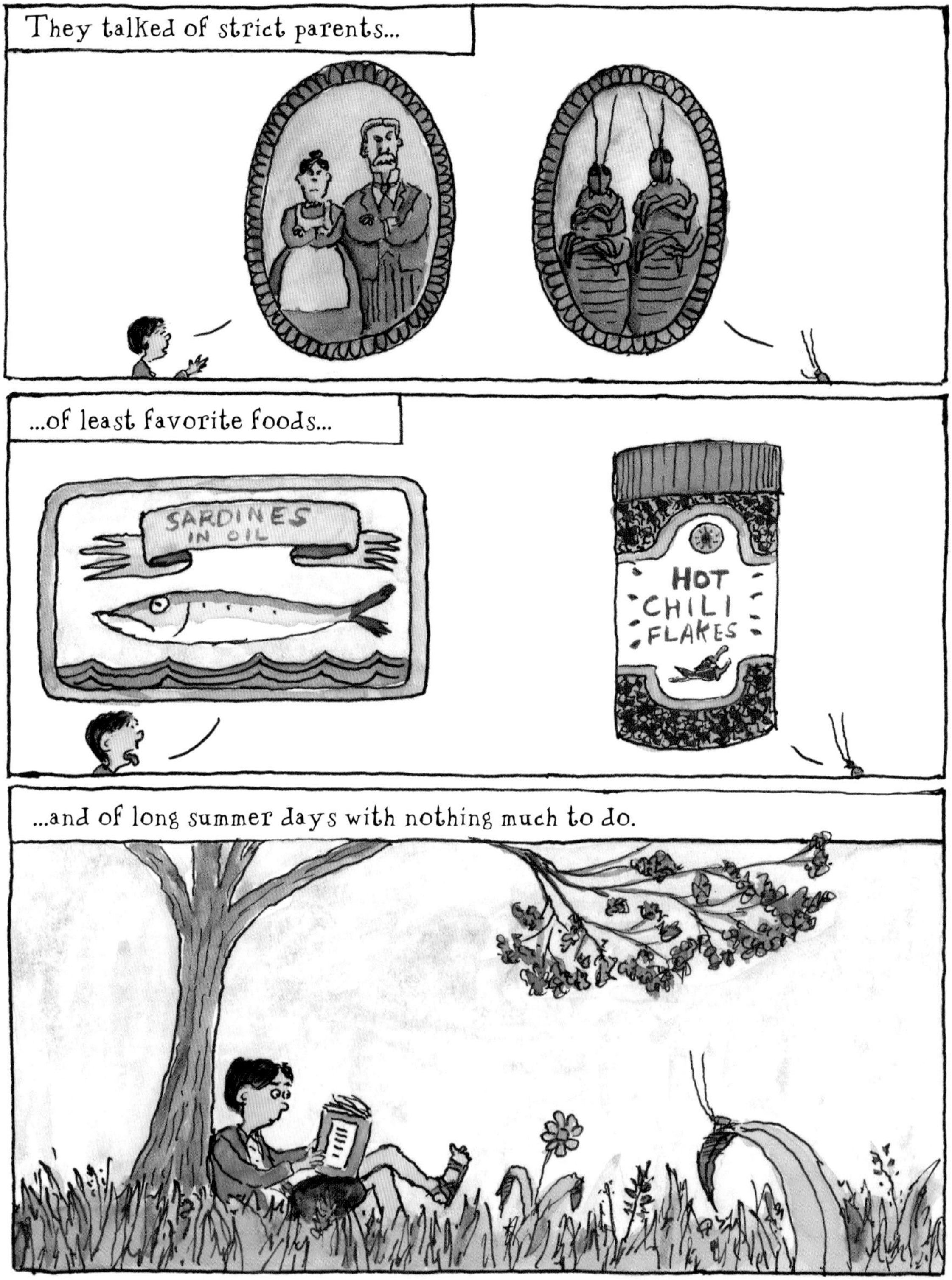
They talked of strict parents...
...of least favorite foods...
SARDINES IN OIL
HOT CHILI FLAKES
...and of long summer days with nothing much to do.

They talked about loneliness and about looking up at the stars on crisp winter nights and making wishes.

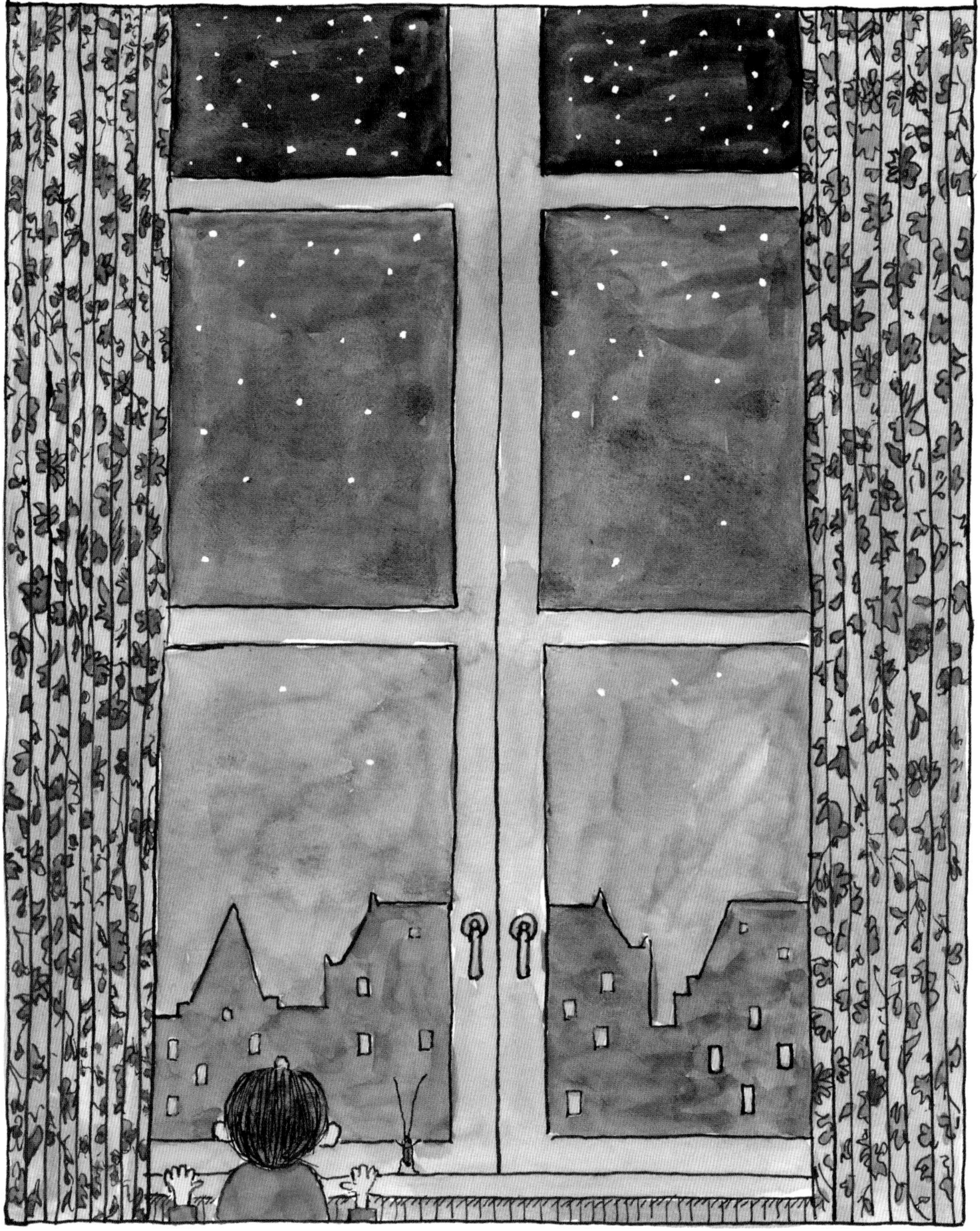

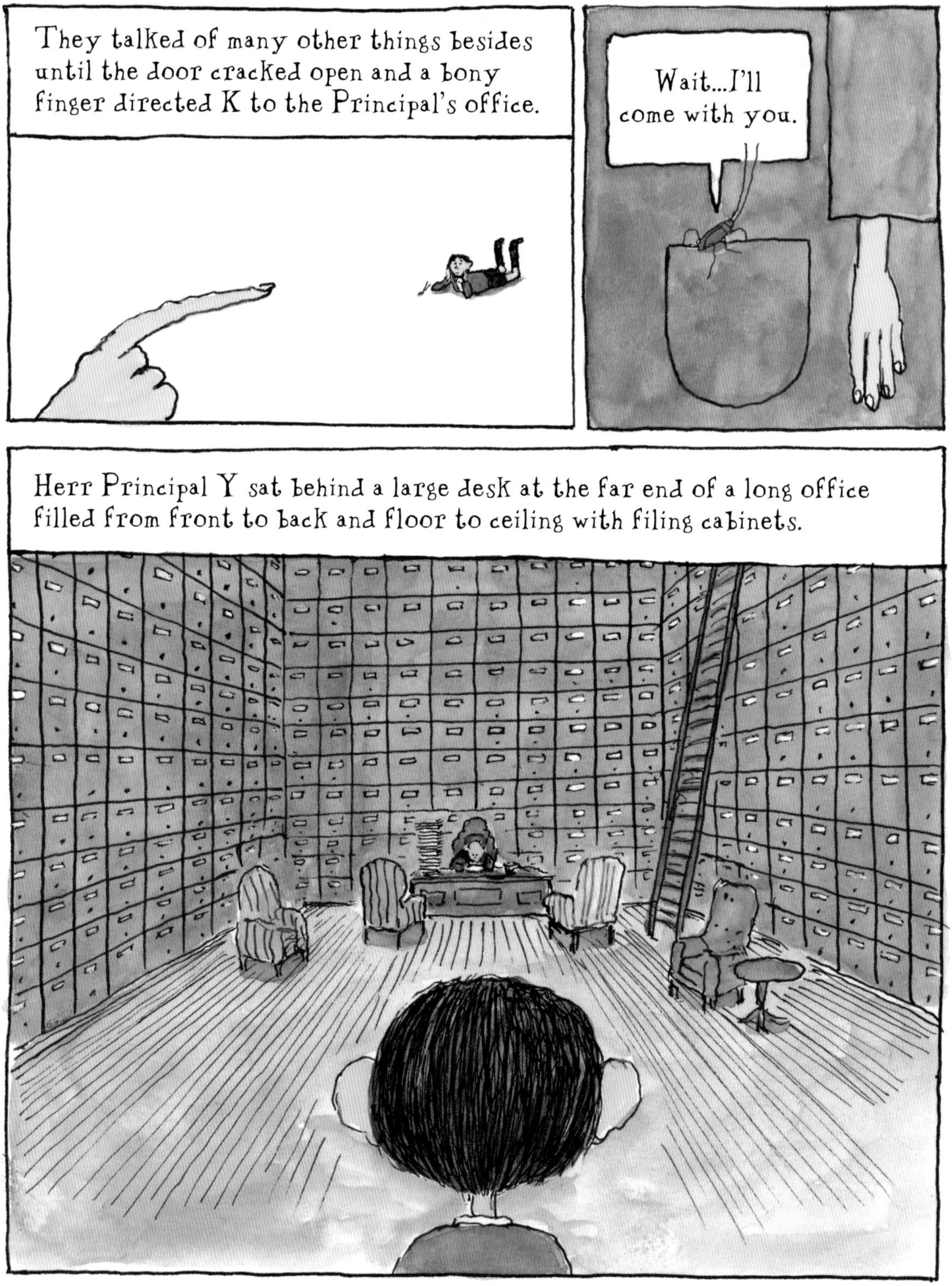
They talked of many other things besides until the door cracked open and a bony finger directed K to the Principal's office.
Wait...I'll come with you.
Herr Principal Y sat behind a large desk at the far end of a long office filled from front to back and floor to ceiling with filing cabinets.

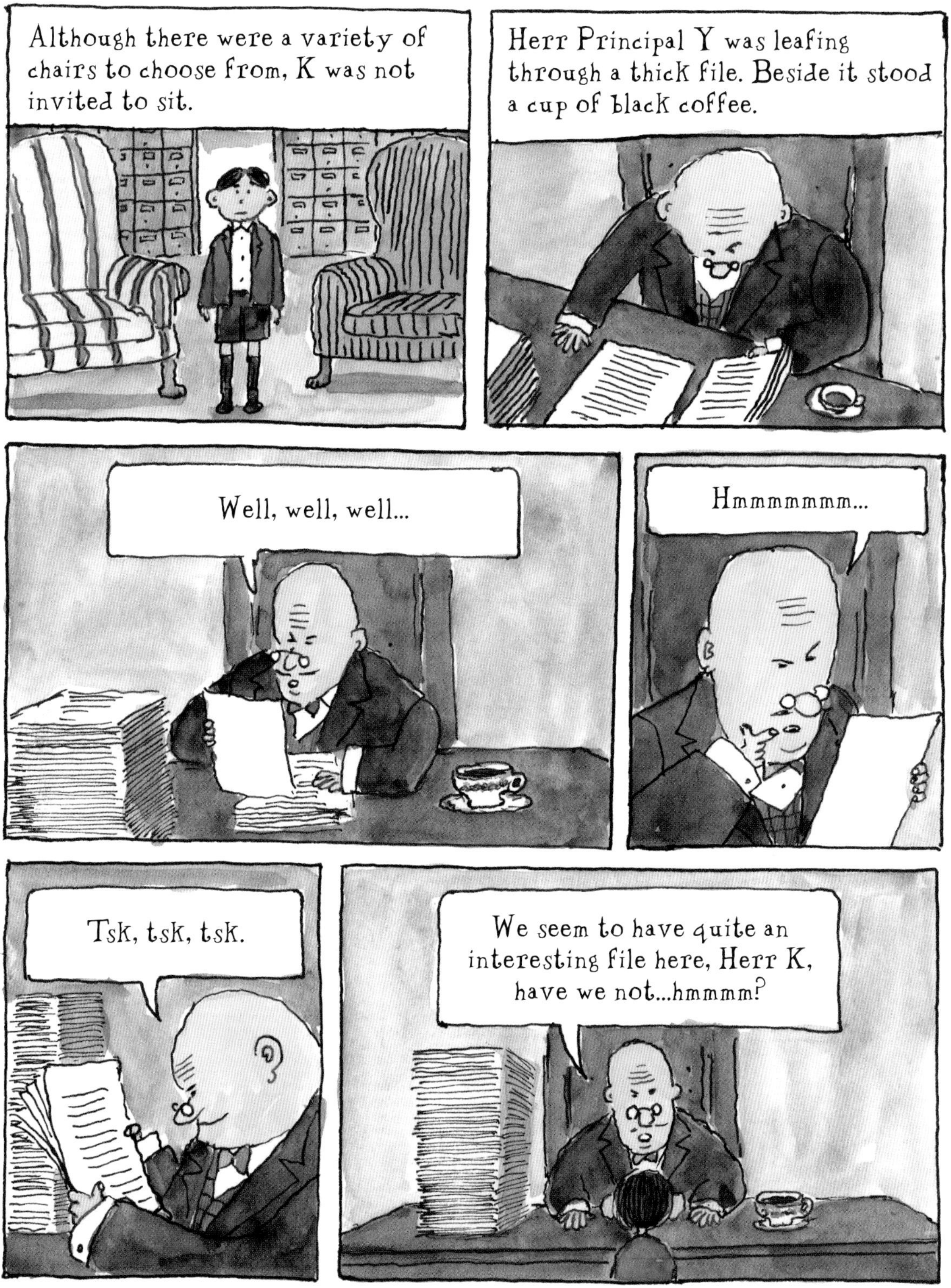
Although there were a variety of chairs to choose from, K was not invited to sit.
Herr Principal Y was leafing through a thick file. Beside it stood a cup of black coffee.
Well, well, well...
Hmmmmmmm...
Tsk, tsk, tsk.
We seem to have quite an interesting file here, Herr K, have we not...hmmmm?

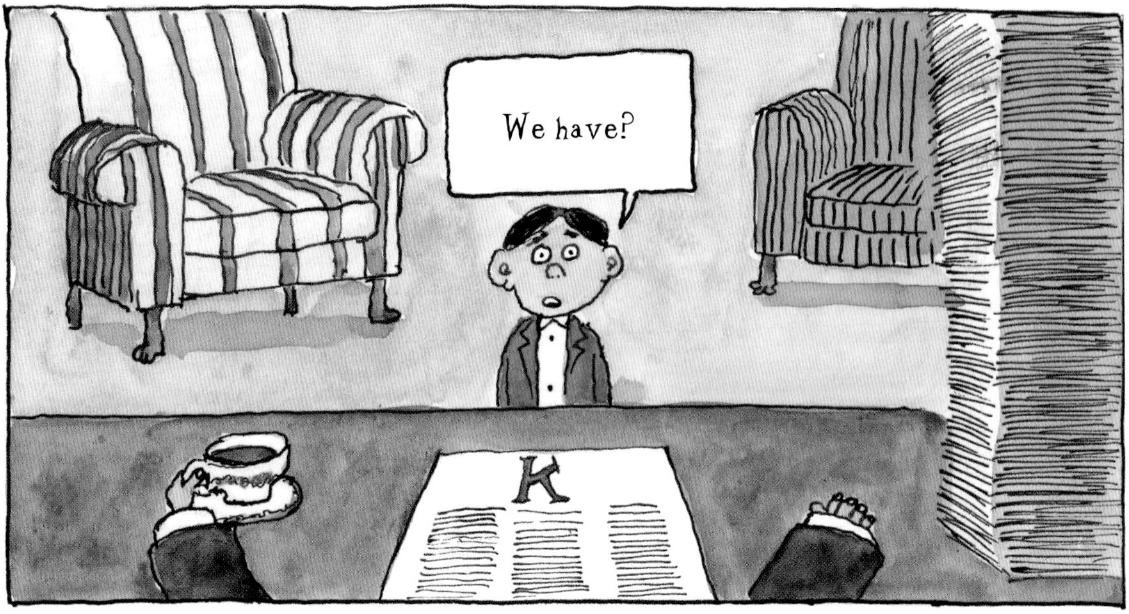
We have?
K

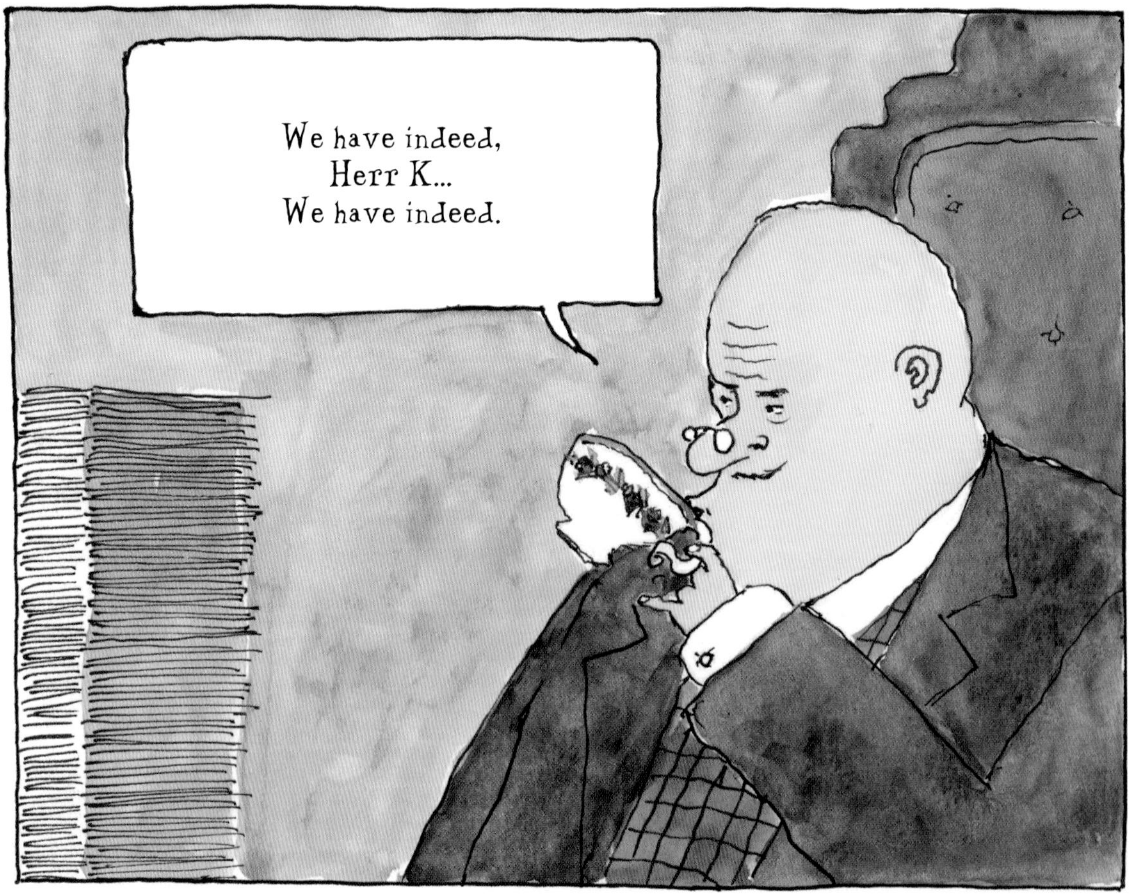
We have indeed,
Herr K...
We have indeed.

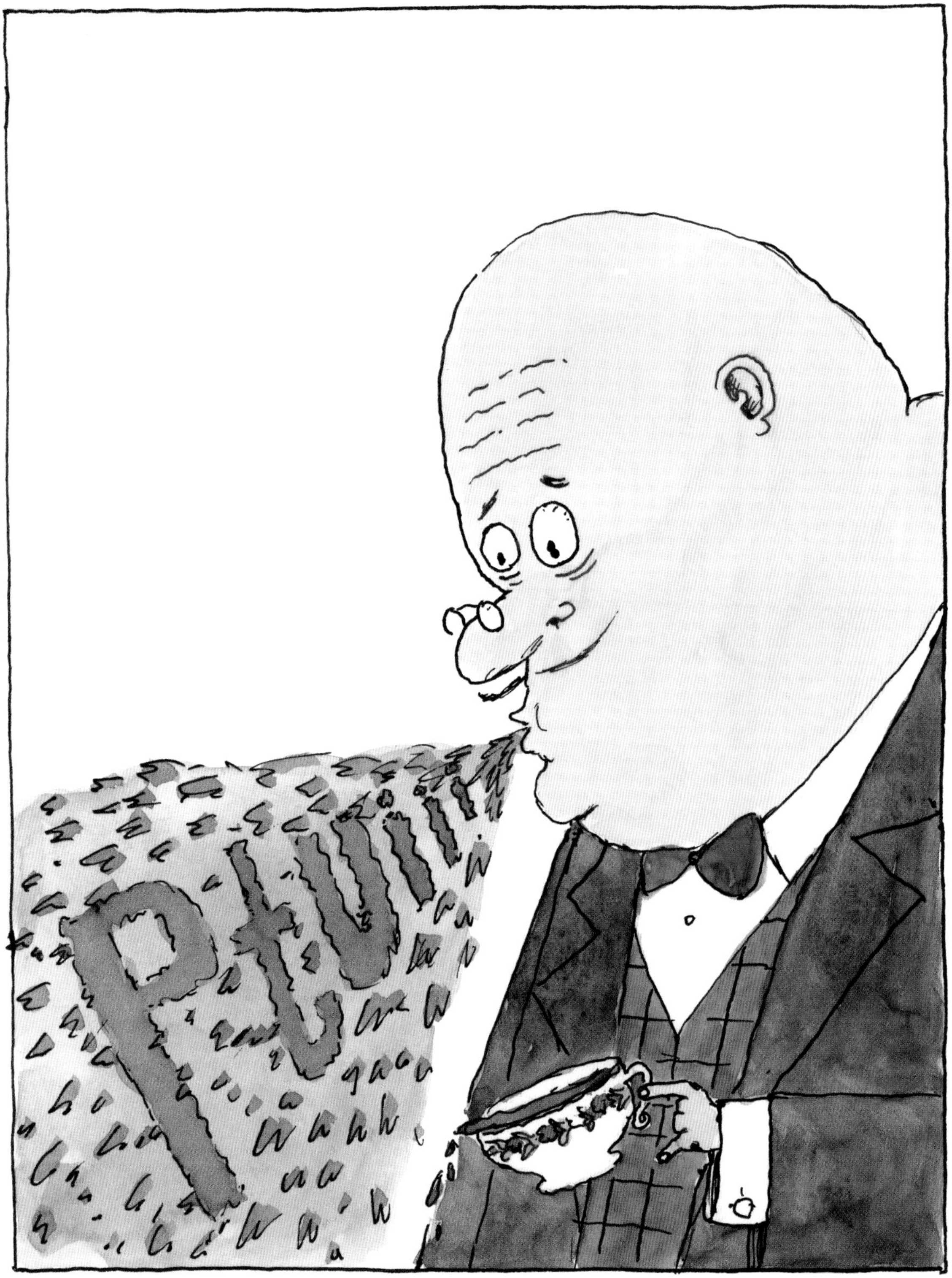
Ptui!!

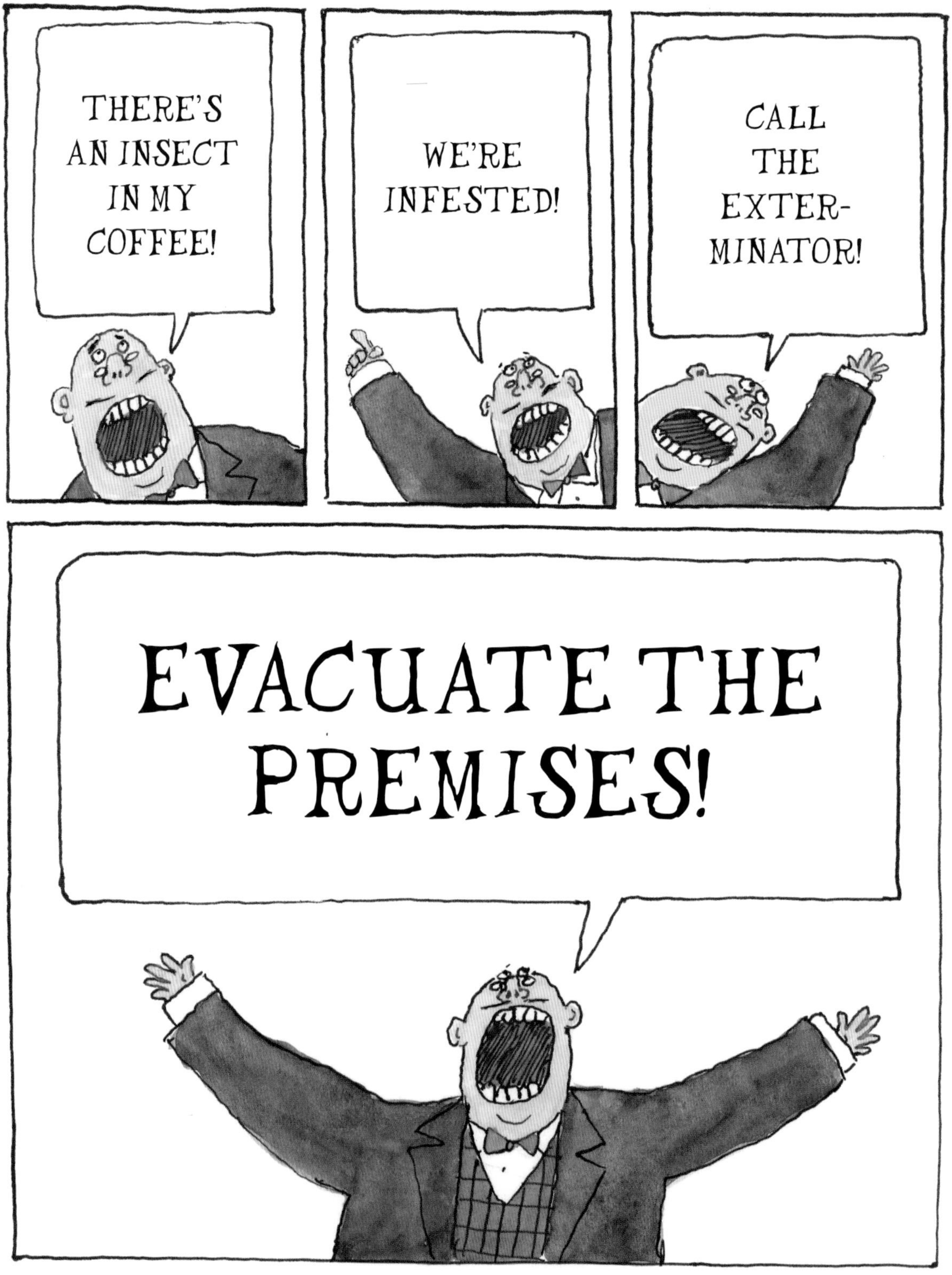
THERE'S AN INSECT IN MY COFFEE!
WE'RE INFESTED!
CALL THE EXTER-MINATOR!
EVACUATE THE PREMISES!

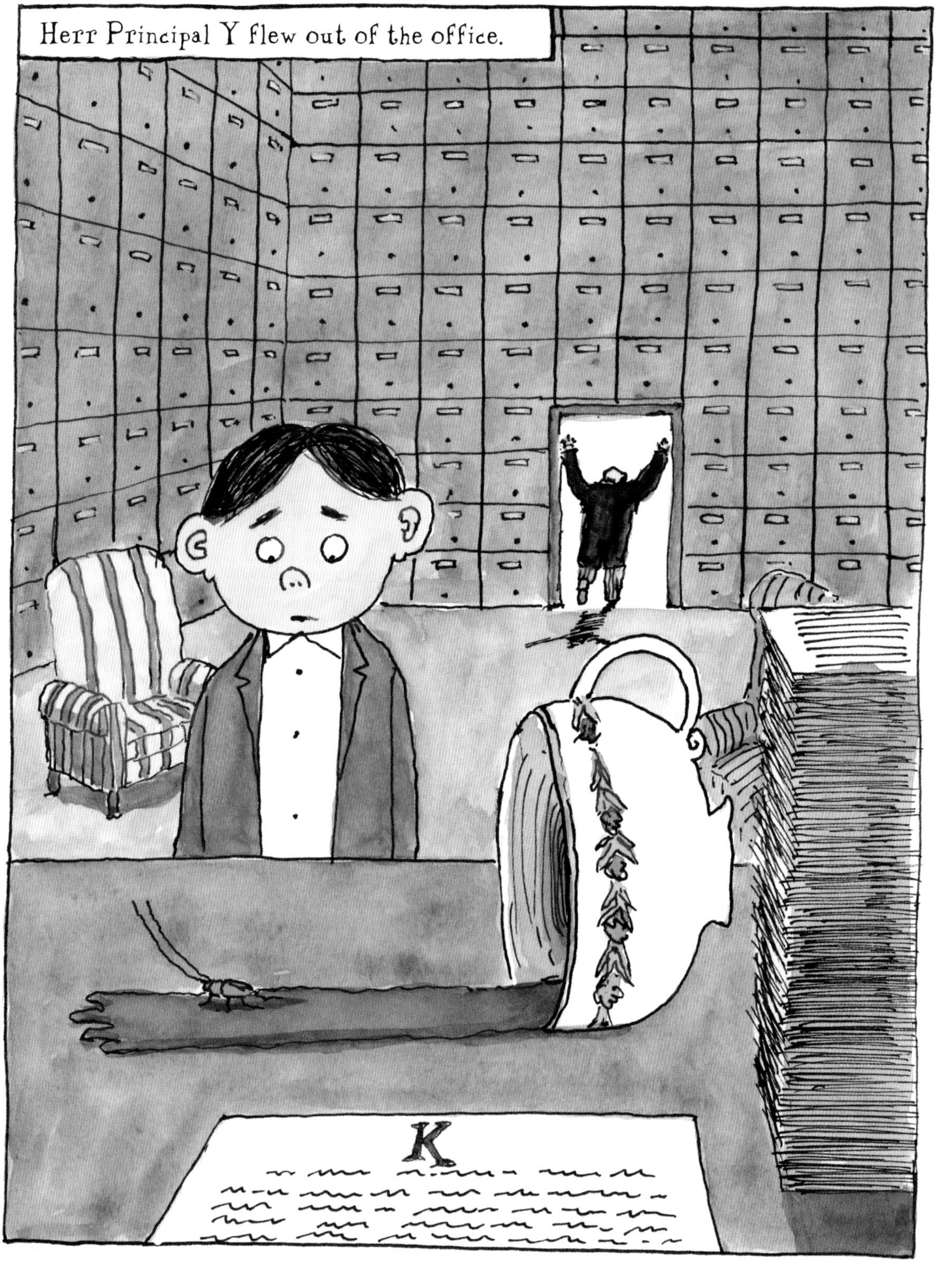
Herr Principal Y flew out of the office.
K

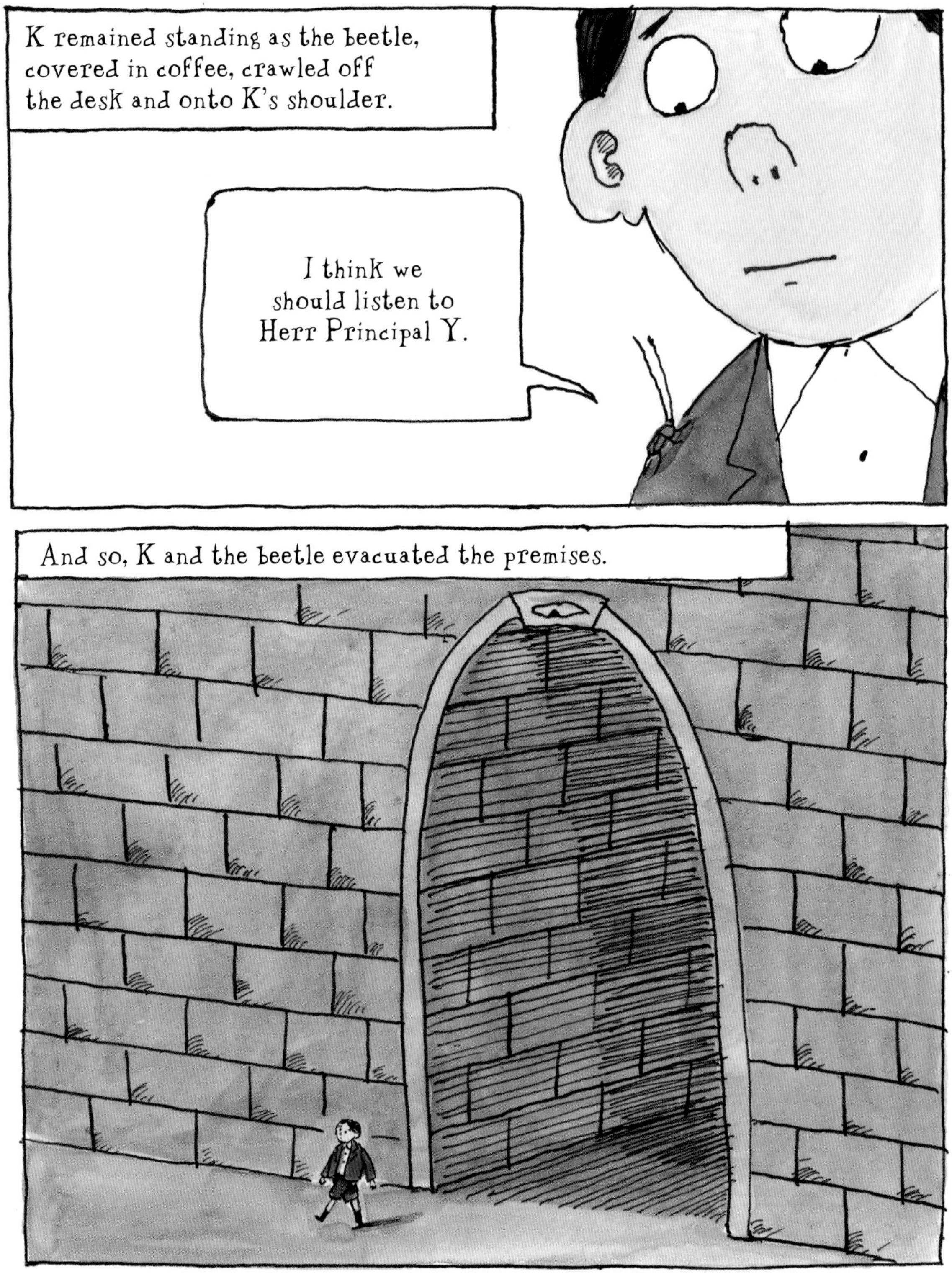
K remained standing as the beetle, covered in coffee, crawled off the desk and onto K's shoulder.
I think we should listen to Herr Principal Y.
And so, K and the beetle evacuated the premises.

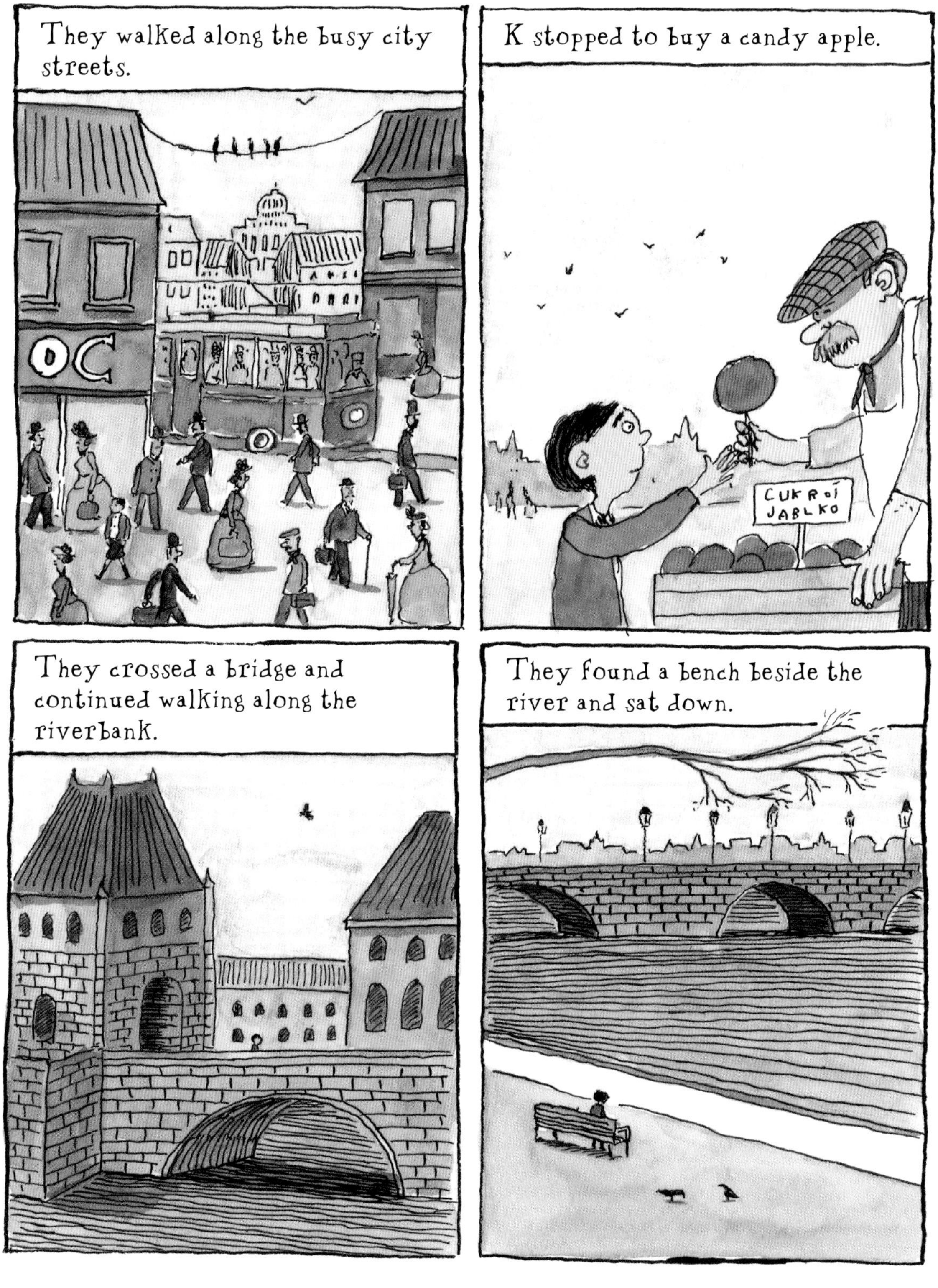
They walked along the busy city streets.
OC
K stopped to buy a candy apple.
CUKROÍ JABLKO
They crossed a bridge and continued walking along the riverbank.
They found a bench beside the river and sat down.

K broke off a piece of the candy apple and offered it to the beetle.

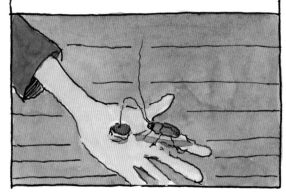

They ate in silence and watched the swans float by.

They sat for hours and hours...

...and talked and talked.

Together they observed weary workers trudging home from shops and factories, banks and insurance companies.

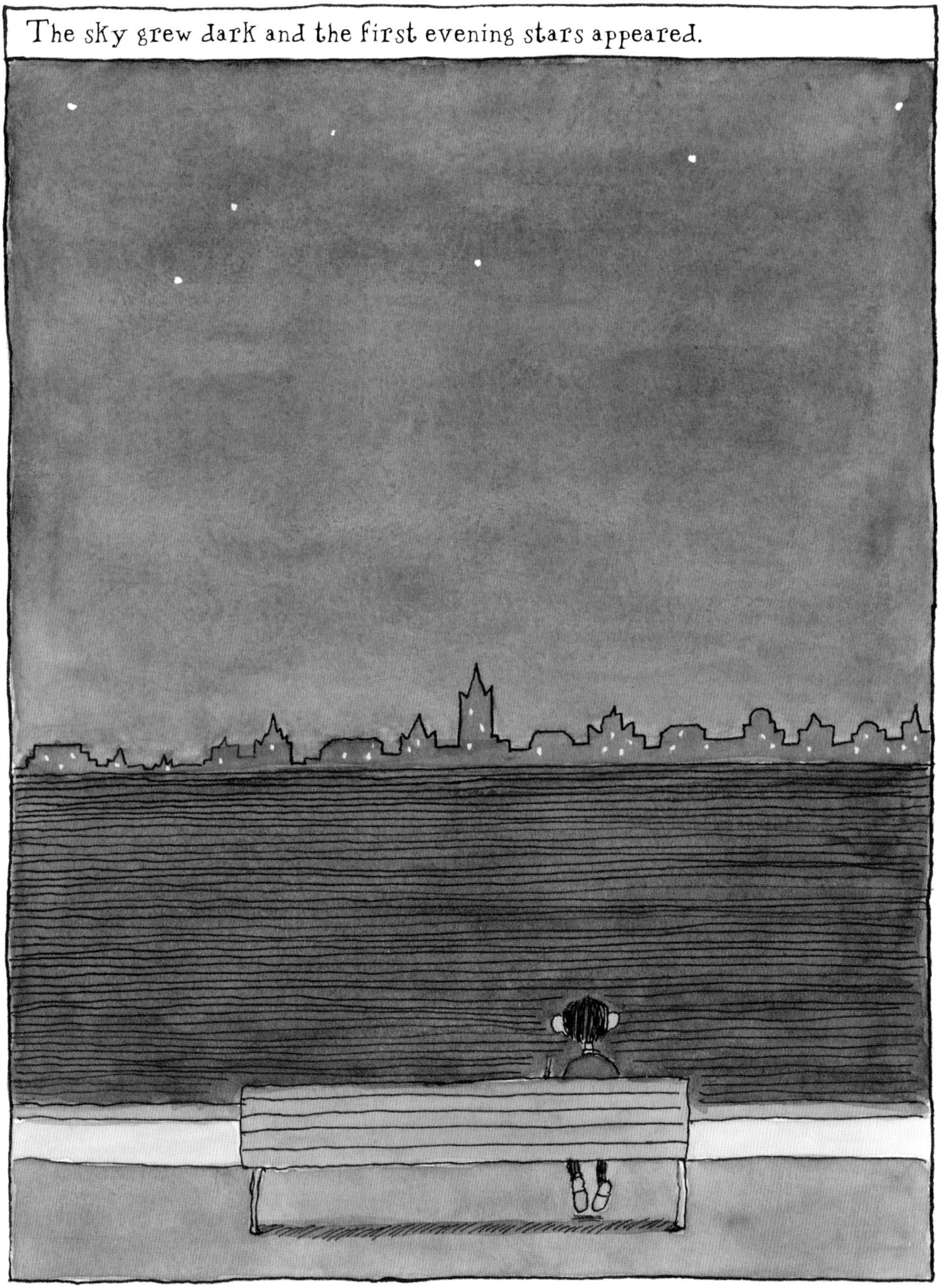
The sky grew dark and the first evening stars appeared.

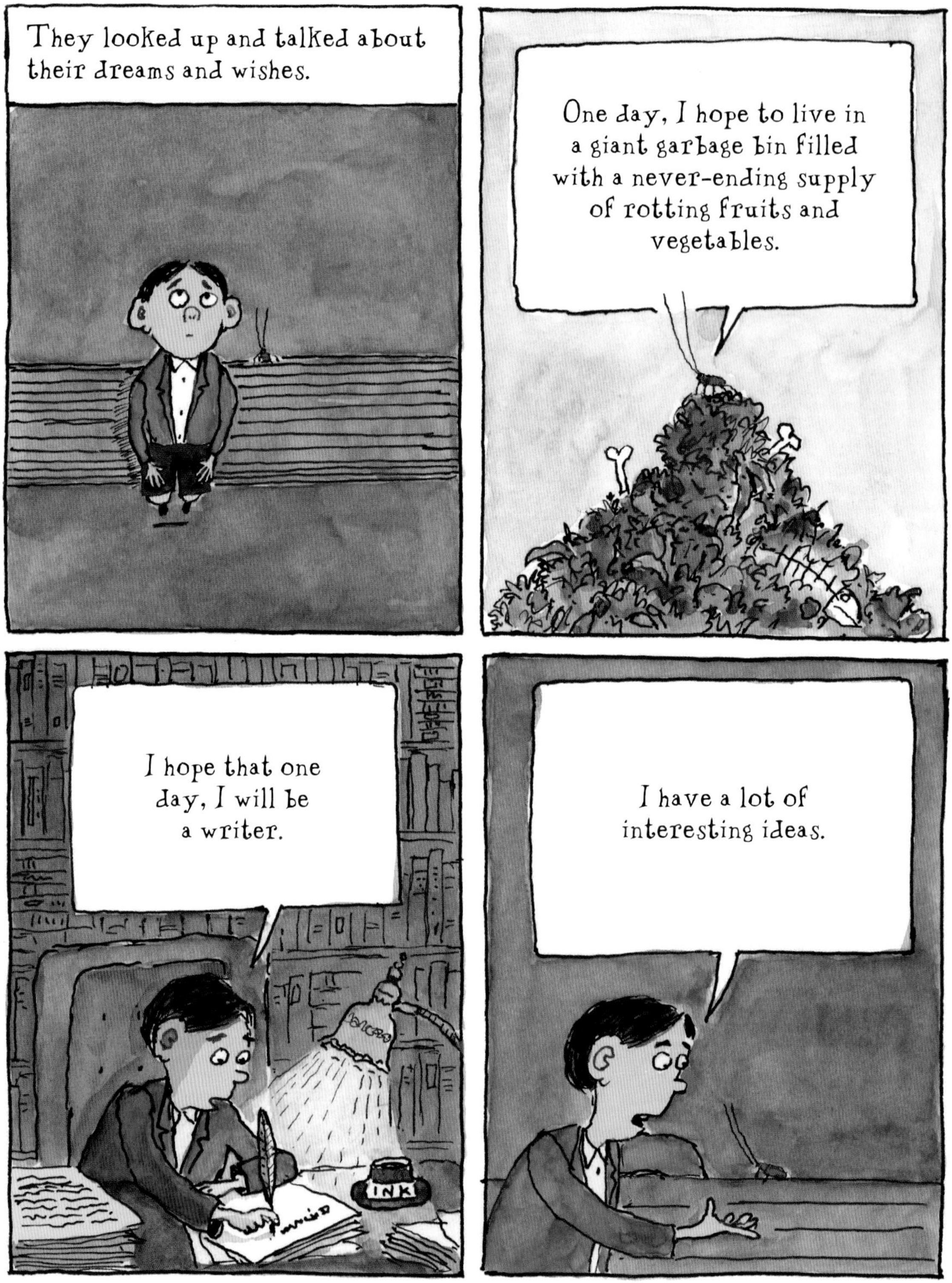
They looked up and talked about their dreams and wishes.
One day, I hope to live in a giant garbage bin filled with a never-ending supply of rotting fruits and vegetables.
I hope that one day, I will be a writer.
INK
I have a lot of interesting ideas.

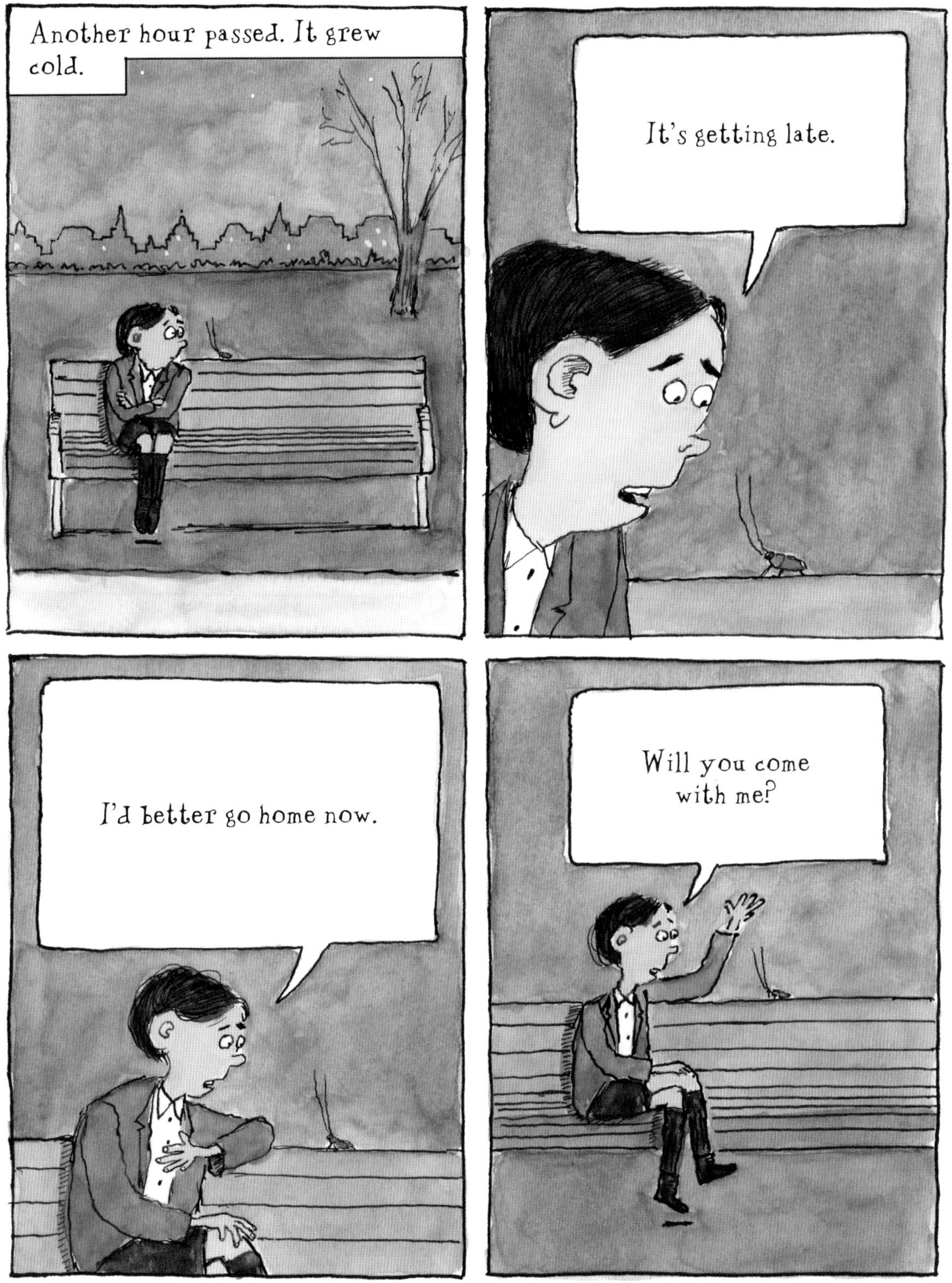
Another hour passed. It grew cold.
It's getting late.
I'd better go home now.
Will you come with me?

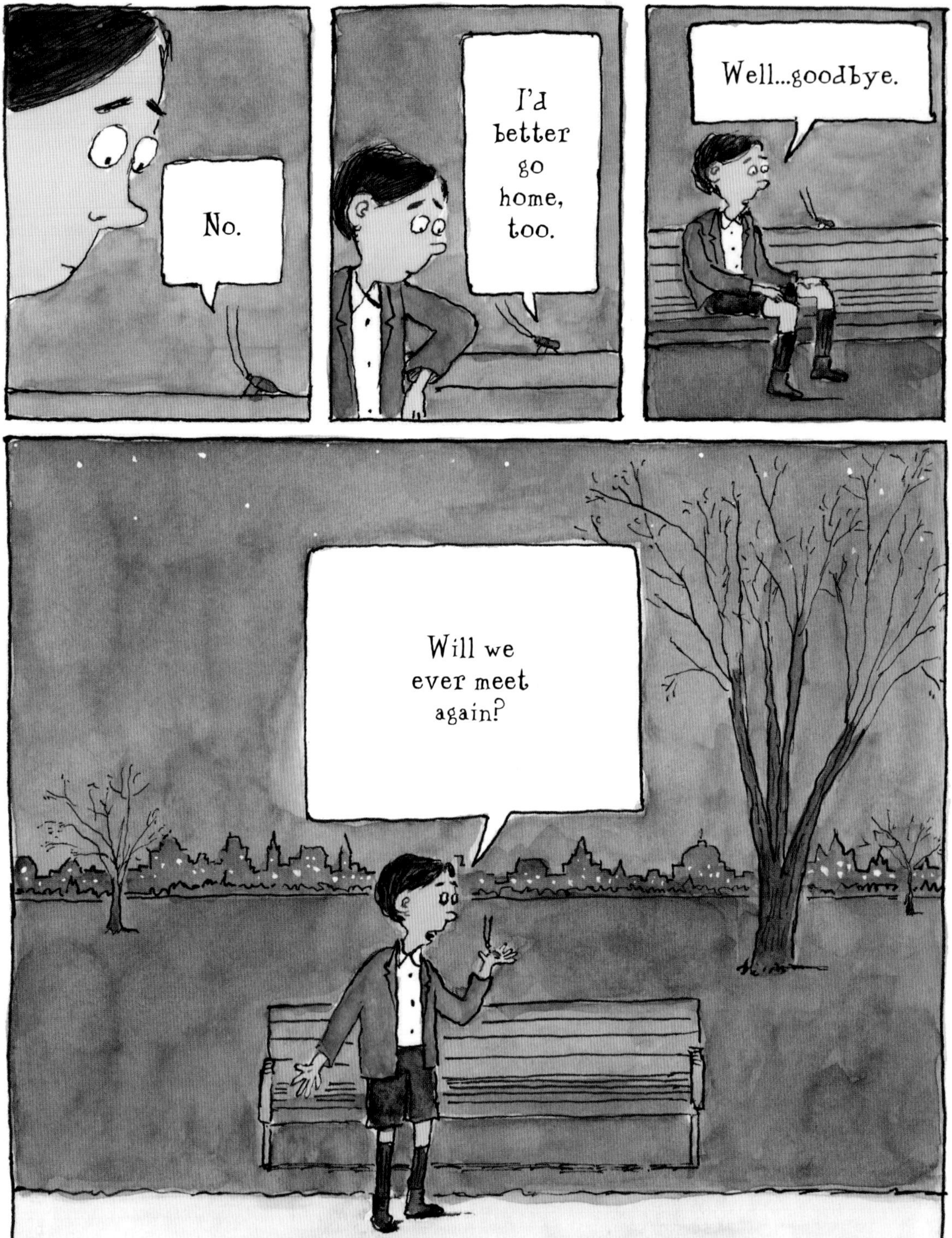
No.
I'd better go home, too.
Well...goodbye.
Will we ever meet again?

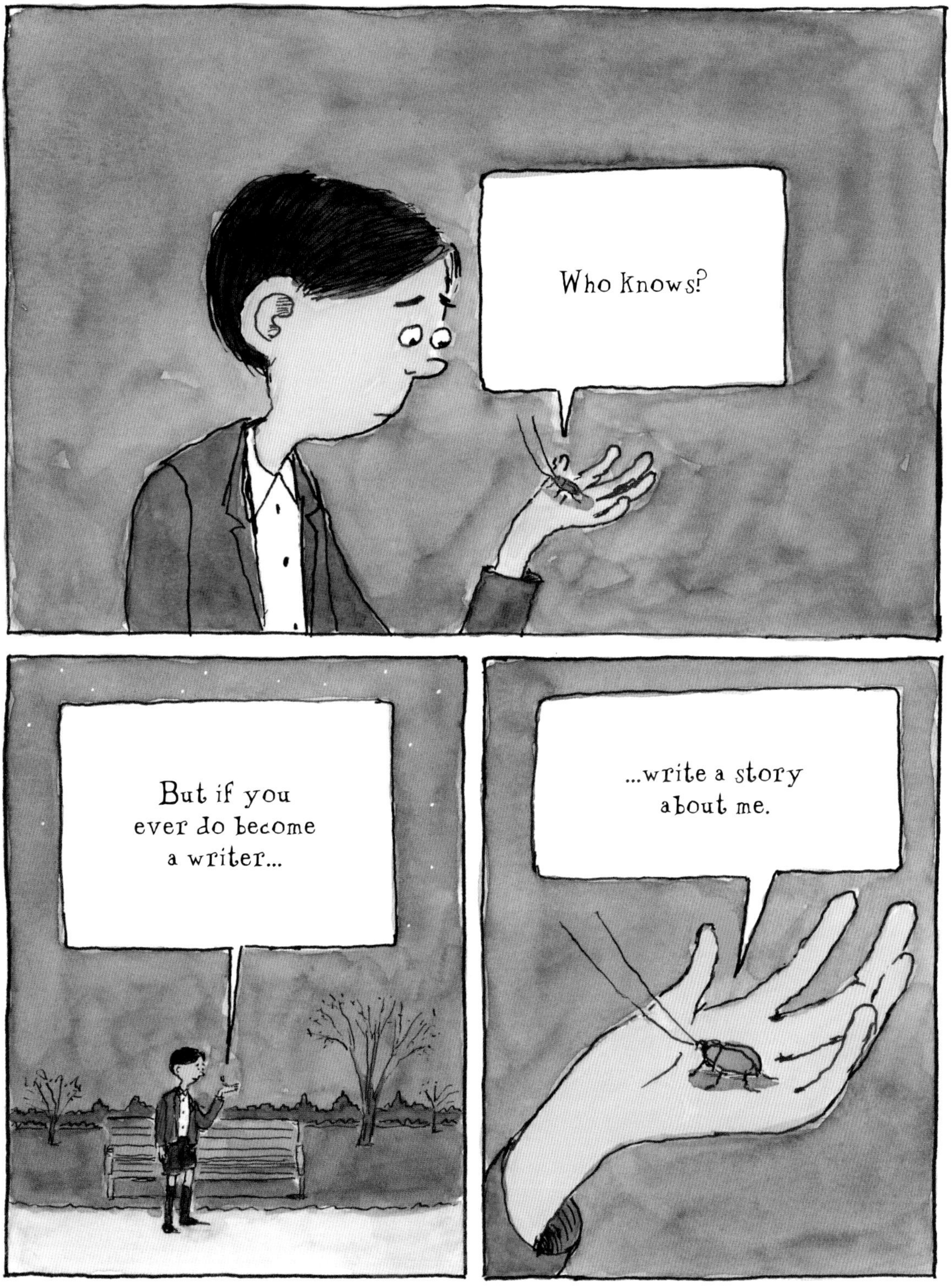
Who knows?
But if you ever do become a writer...
...write a story about me.

K promised that he would, and then they went their separate ways, each to their own home.

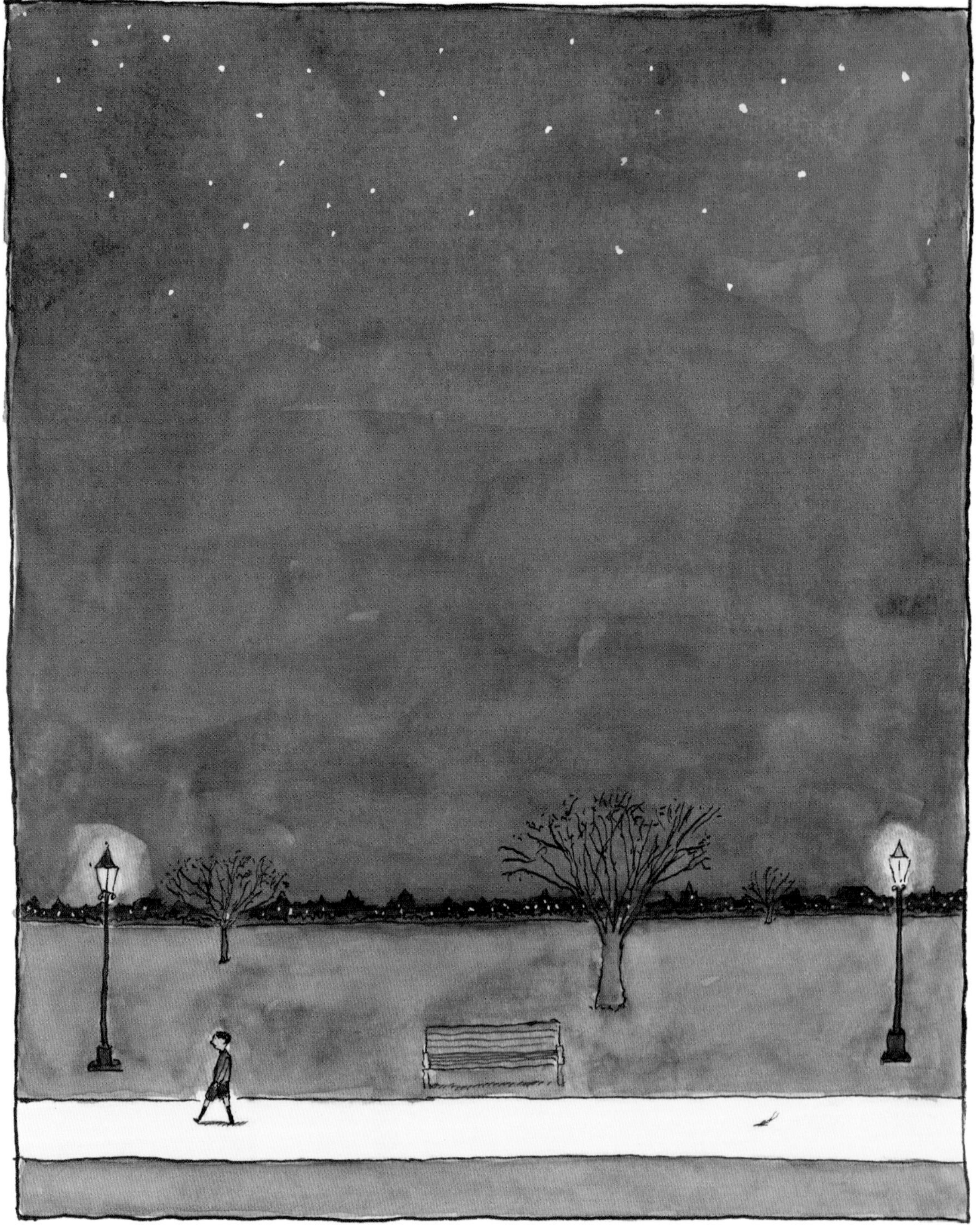

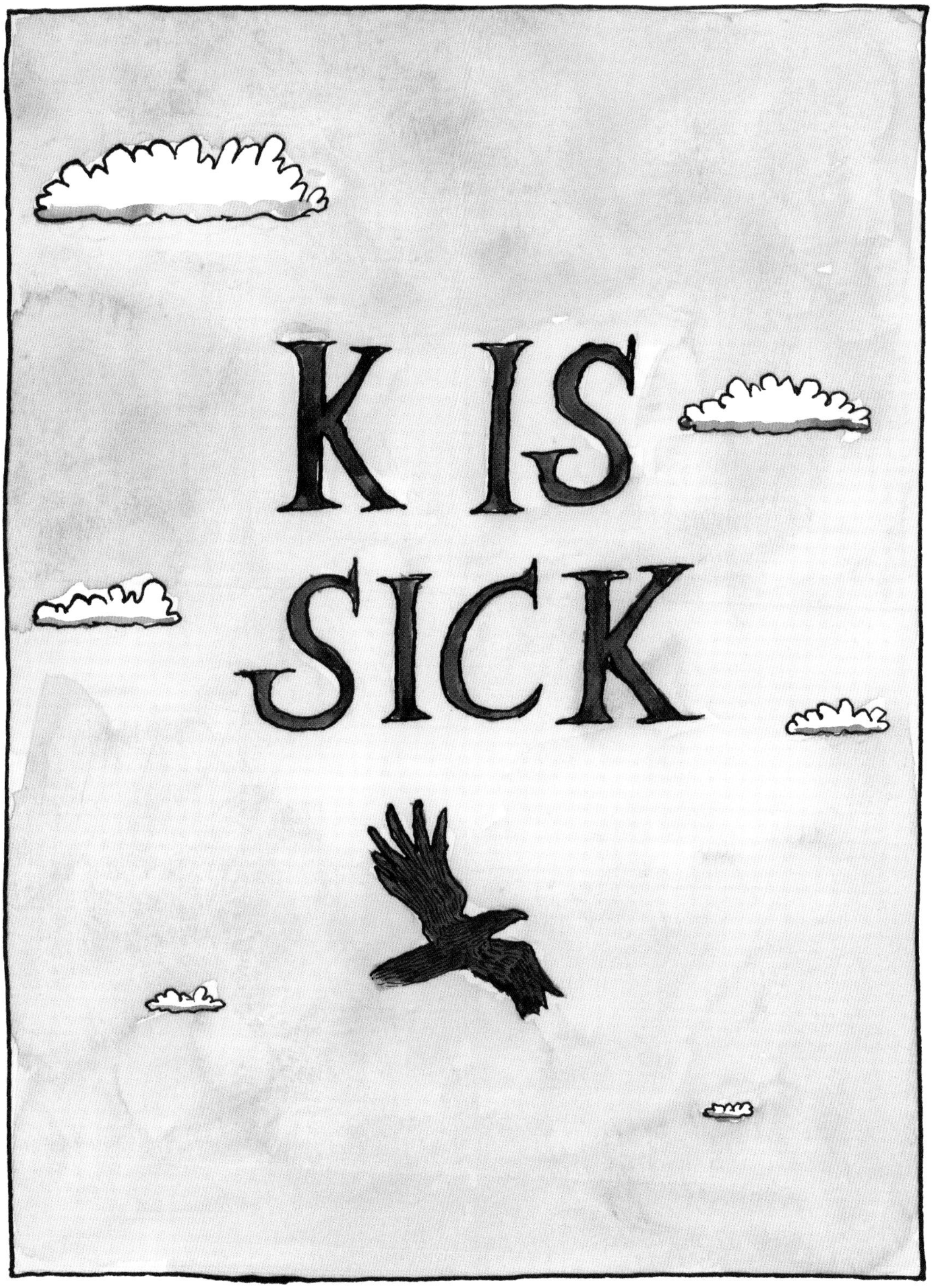
K IS
SICK

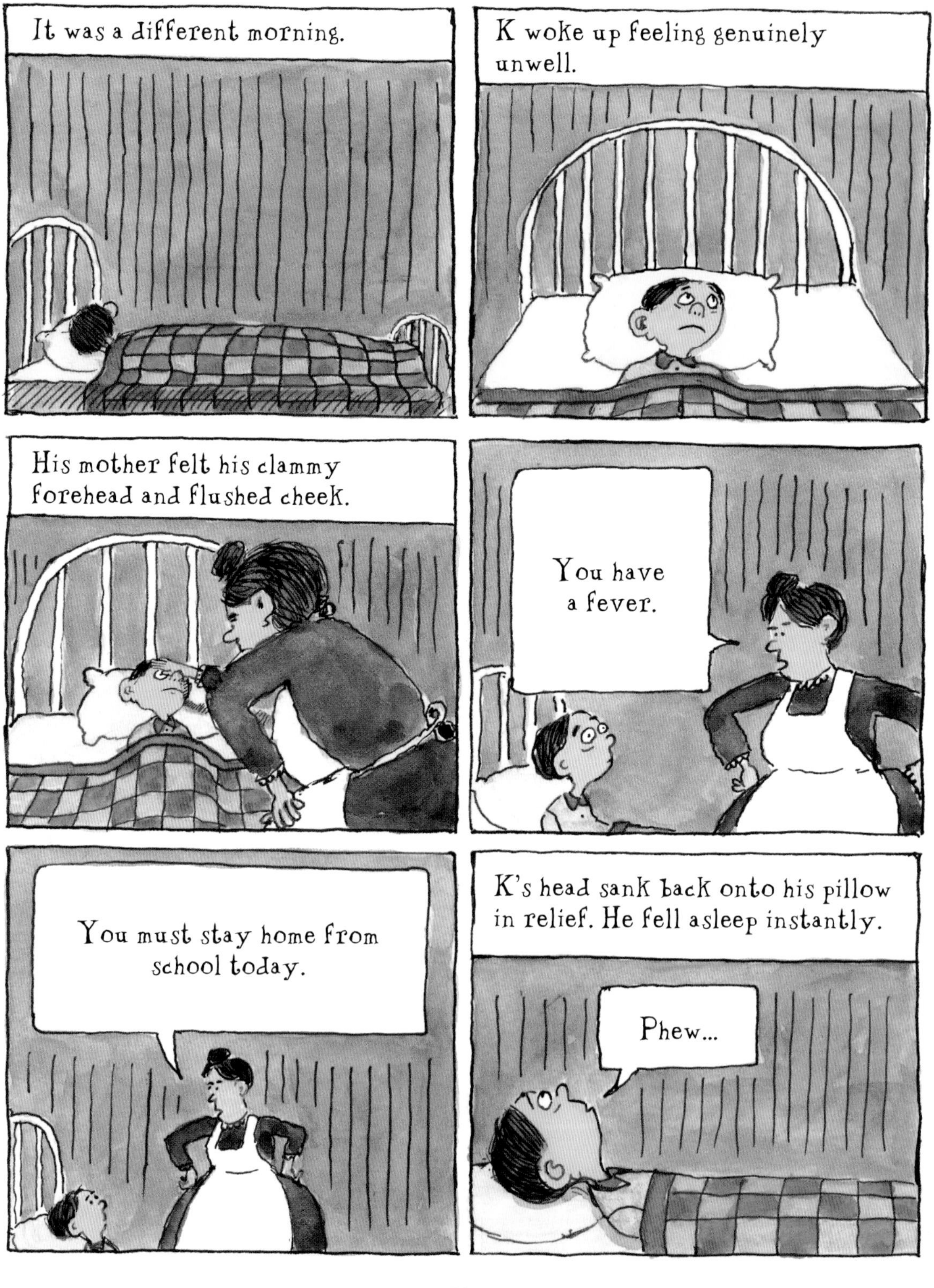
It was a different morning.
K woke up feeling genuinely unwell.
His mother felt his clammy forehead and flushed cheek.
You have a fever.
You must stay home from school today.
K's head sank back onto his pillow in relief. He fell asleep instantly.
Phew...

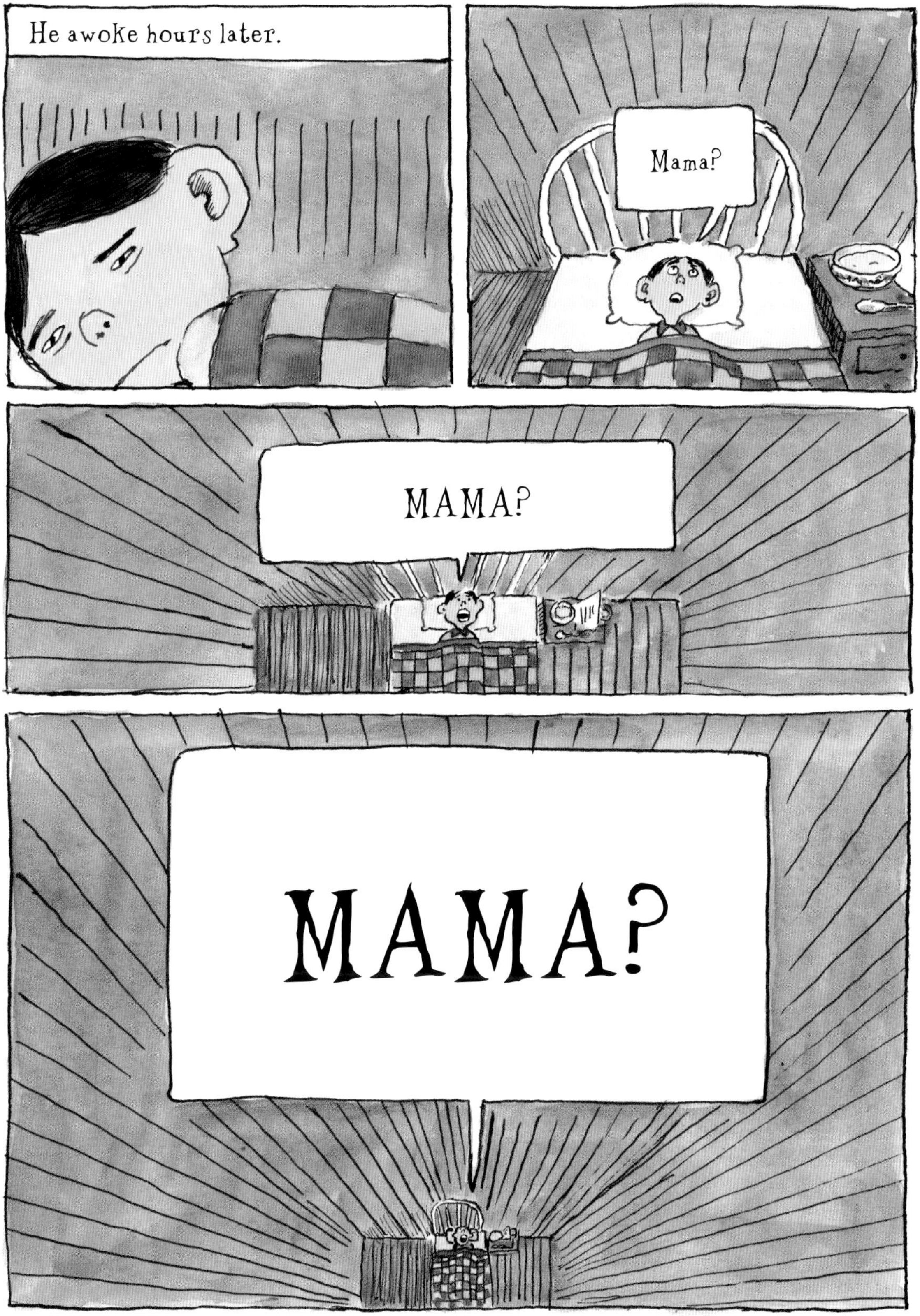
He awoke hours later.
Mama?
MAMA?
MAMA?

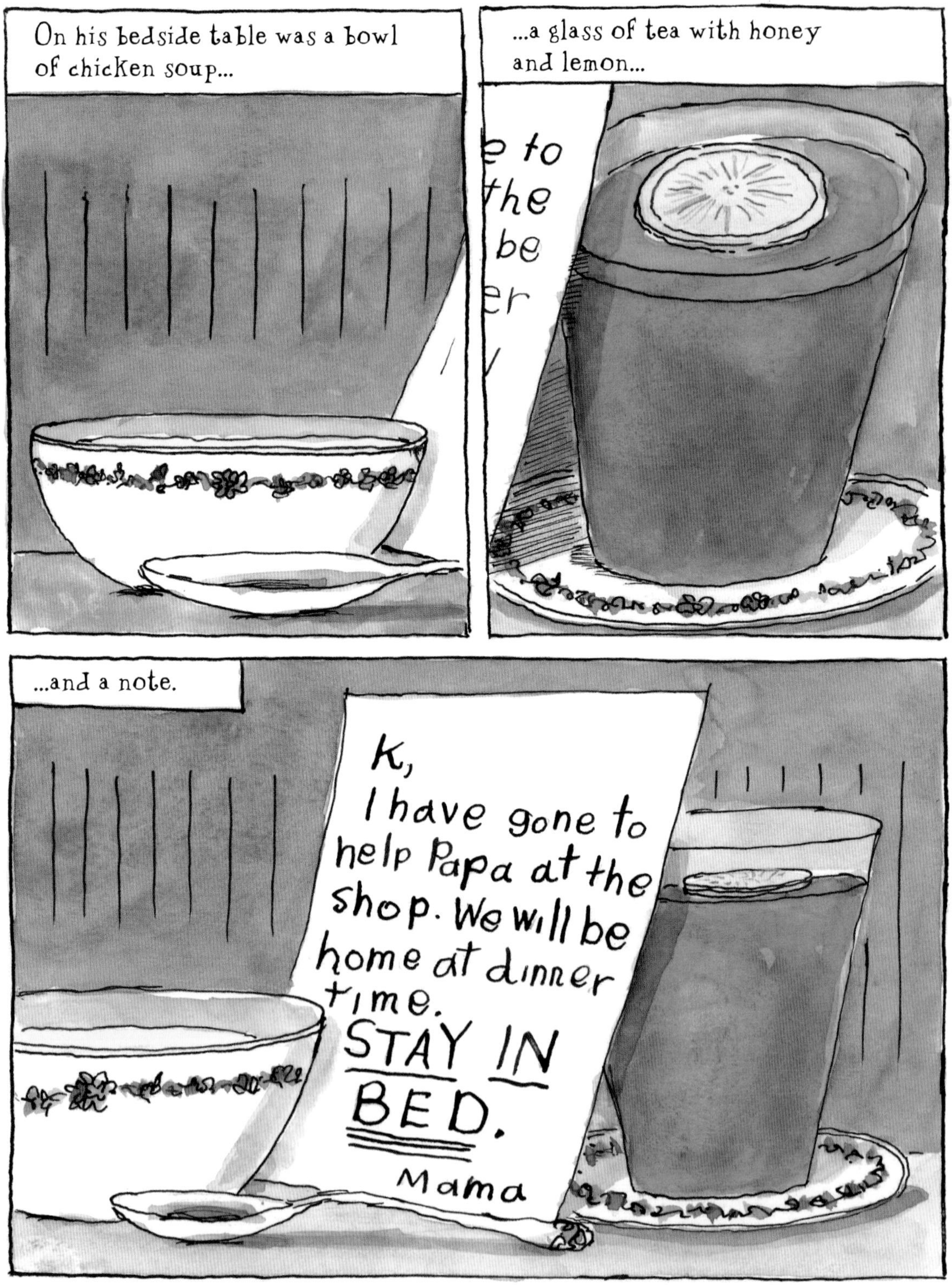
On his bedside table was a bowl of chicken soup...
...a glass of tea with honey and lemon...
...and a note.
K,
I have gone to help Papa at the shop. We will be home at dinner time.
STAY IN BED.
Mama

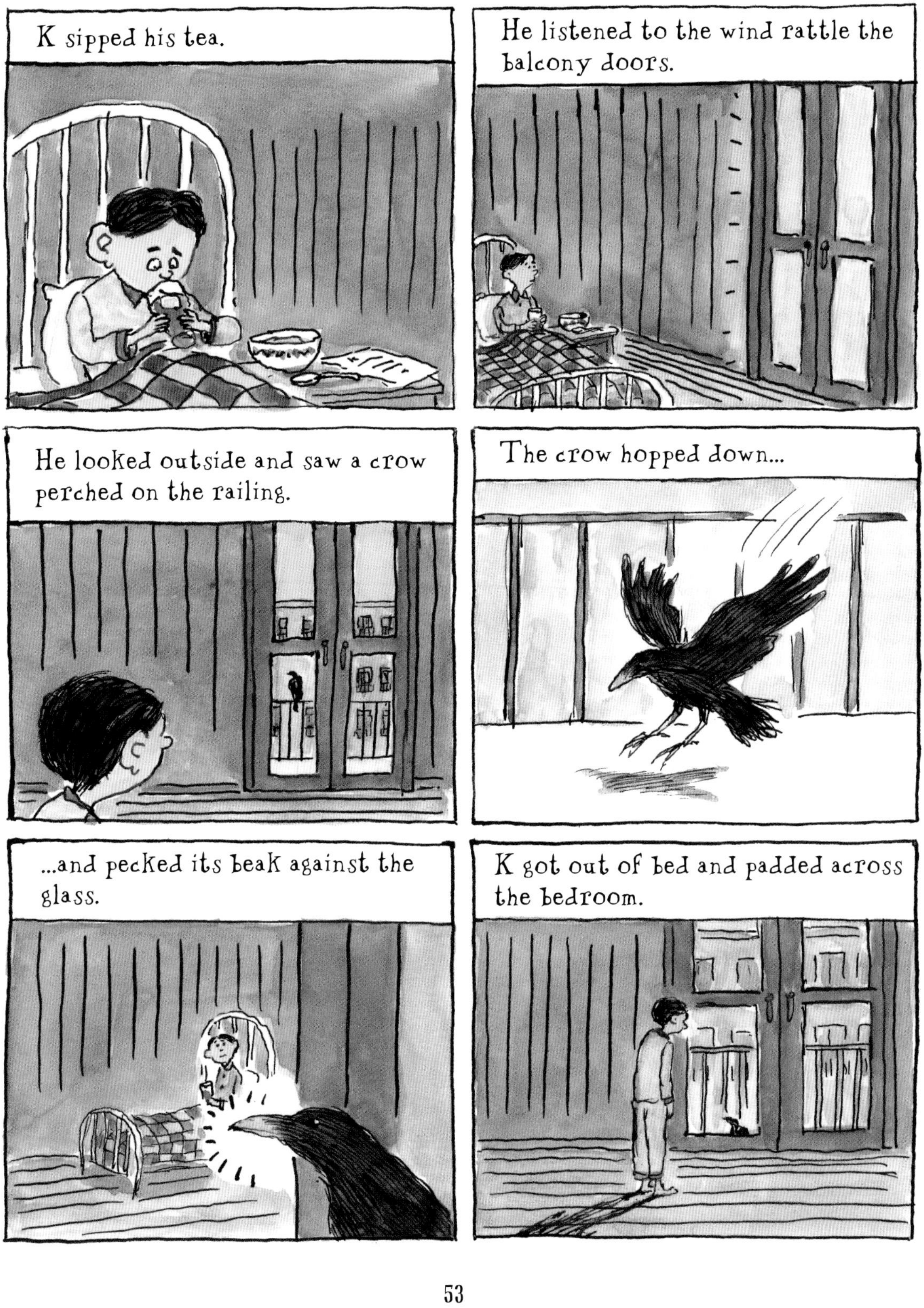
K sipped his tea.
He listened to the wind rattle the balcony doors.
He looked outside and saw a crow perched on the railing.
The crow hopped down...
...and pecked its beak against the glass.
K got out of bed and padded across the bedroom.

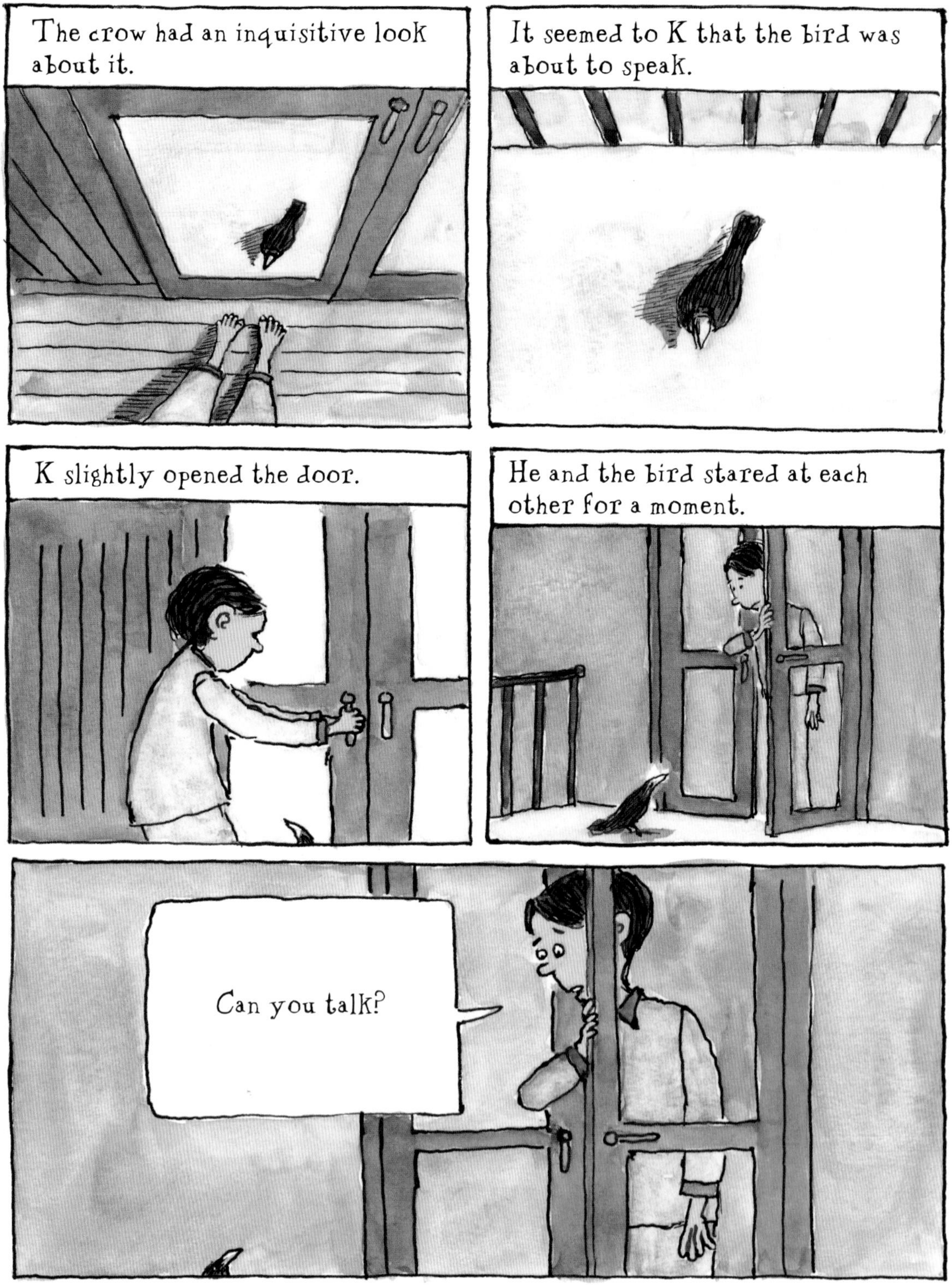
The crow had an inquisitive look about it.
It seemed to K that the bird was about to speak.
K slightly opened the door.
He and the bird stared at each other for a moment.
Can you talk?

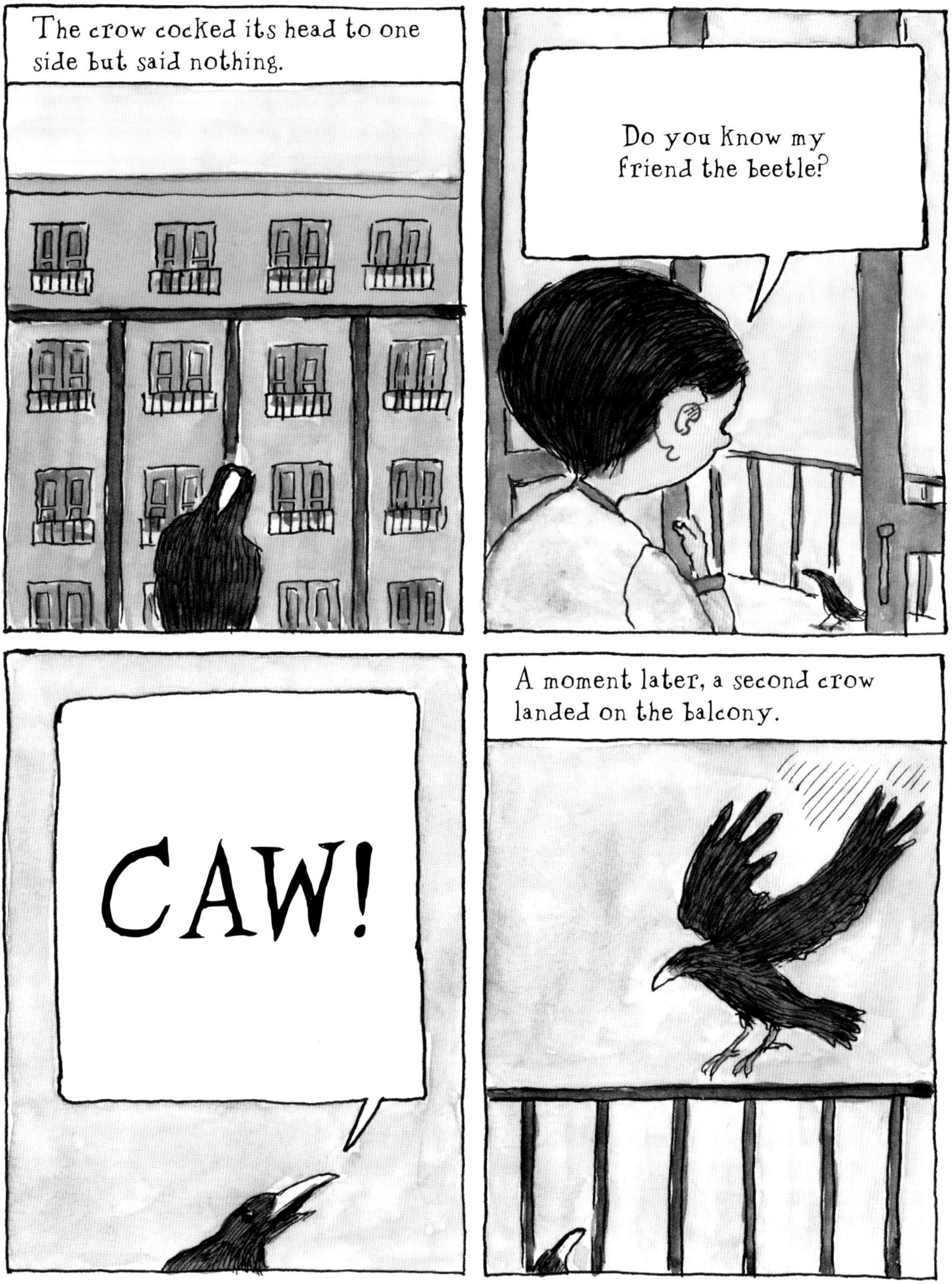
The crow cocked its head to one side but said nothing.
Do you know my friend the beetle?
CAW!
A moment later, a second crow landed on the balcony.

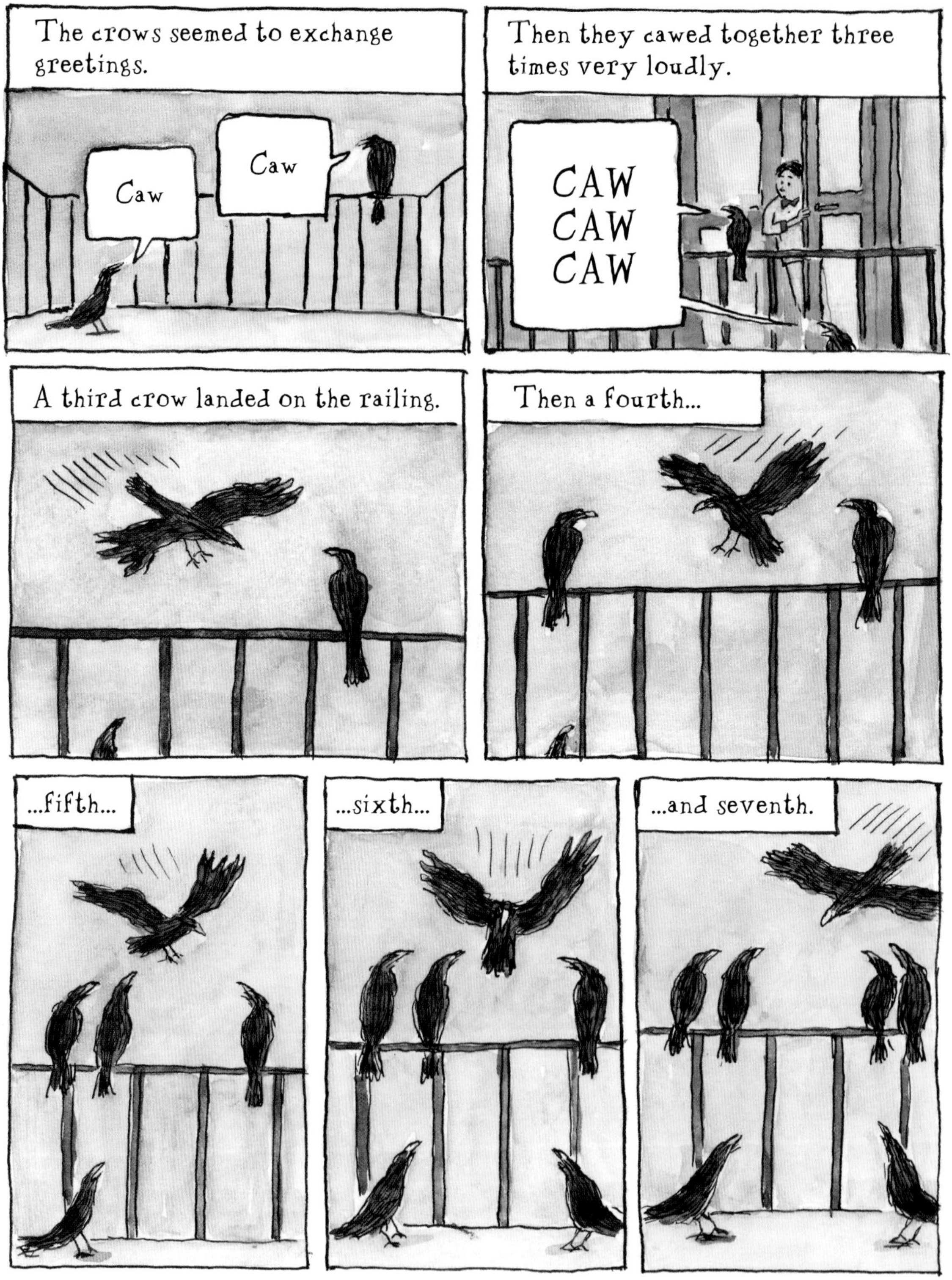
The crows seemed to exchange greetings.
Caw
Caw
Then they cawed together three times very loudly.
CAW CAW CAW
A third crow landed on the railing.
Then a fourth...
...fifth...
...sixth...
...and seventh.

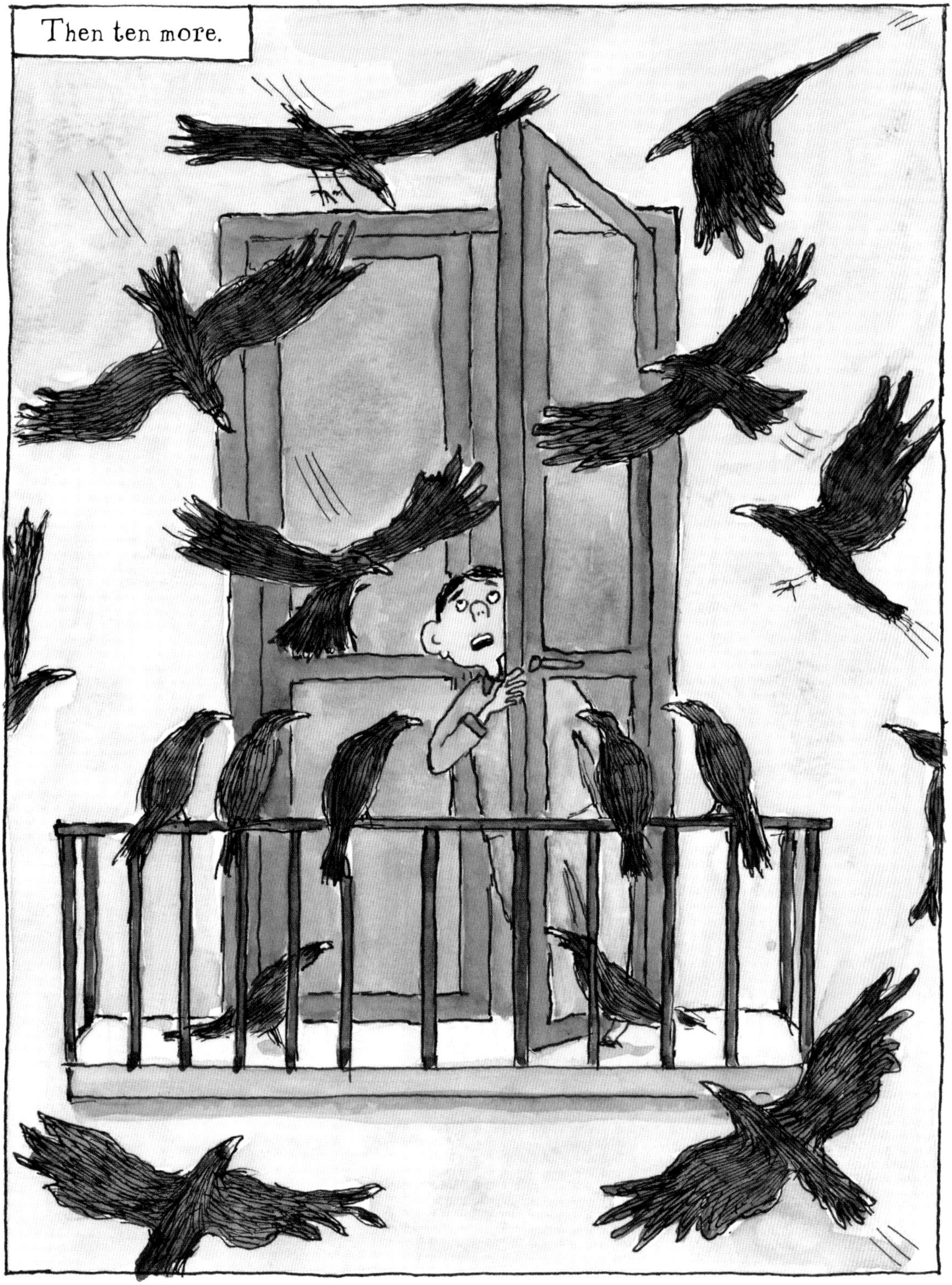
Then ten more.

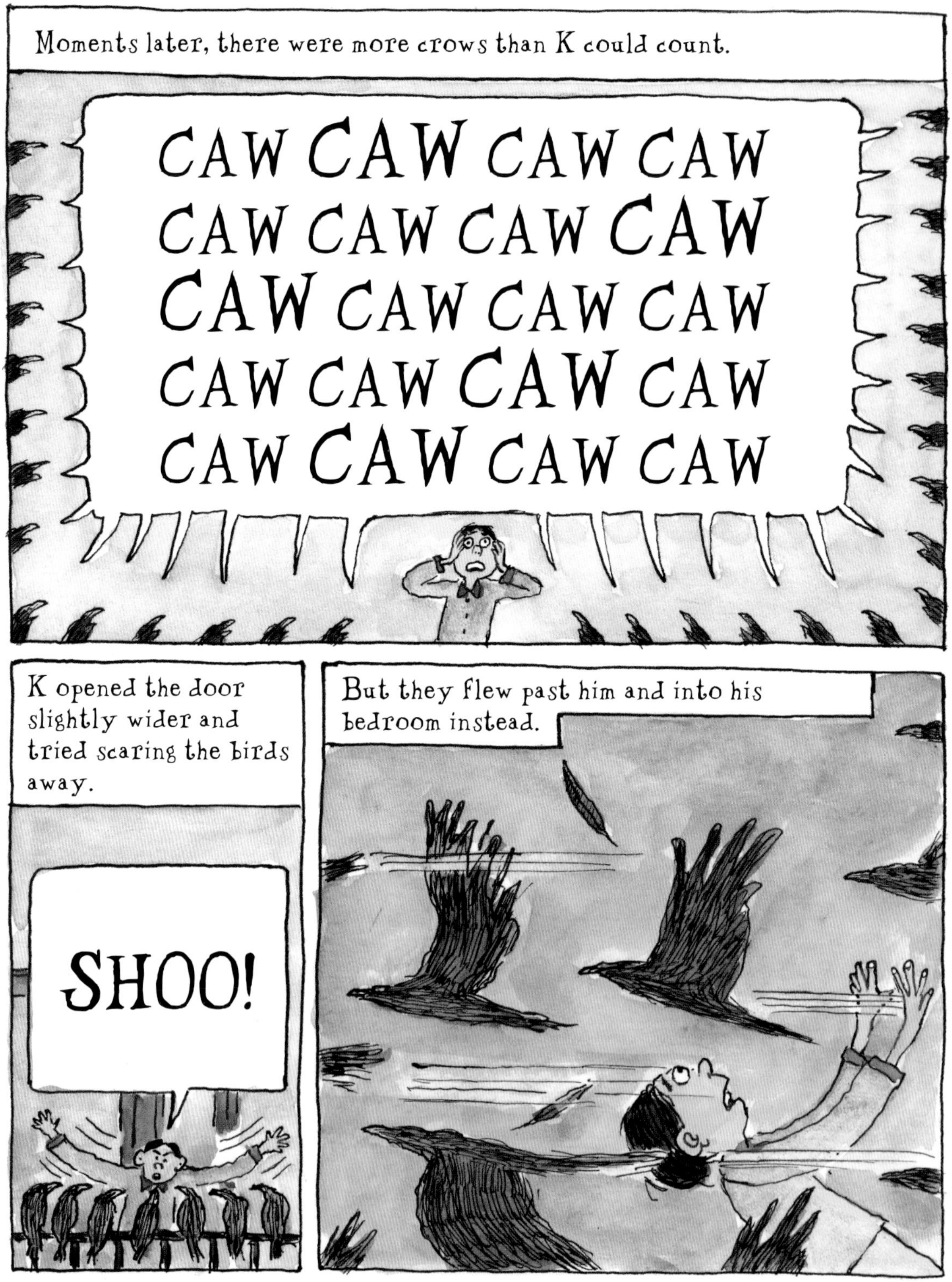

Moments later, there were more crows than K could count.
CAW CAW CAW CAW CAW CAW CAW CAW CAW CAW CAW CAW CAW CAW CAW CAW CAW CAW CAW CAW
K opened the door slightly wider and tried scaring the birds away.
SHOO!
But they flew past him and into his bedroom instead.

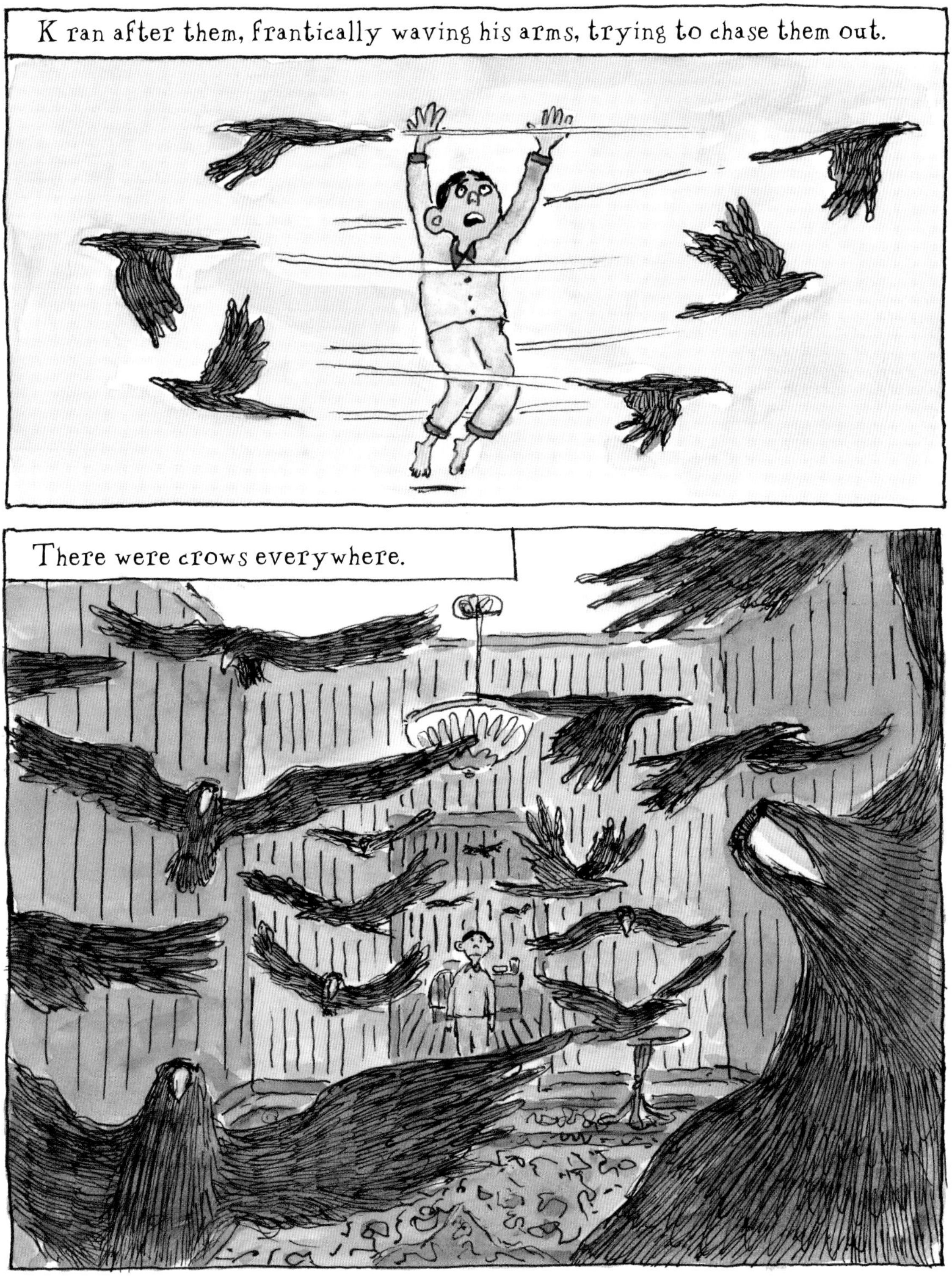
K ran after them, frantically waving his arms, trying to chase them out.
There were crows everywhere.

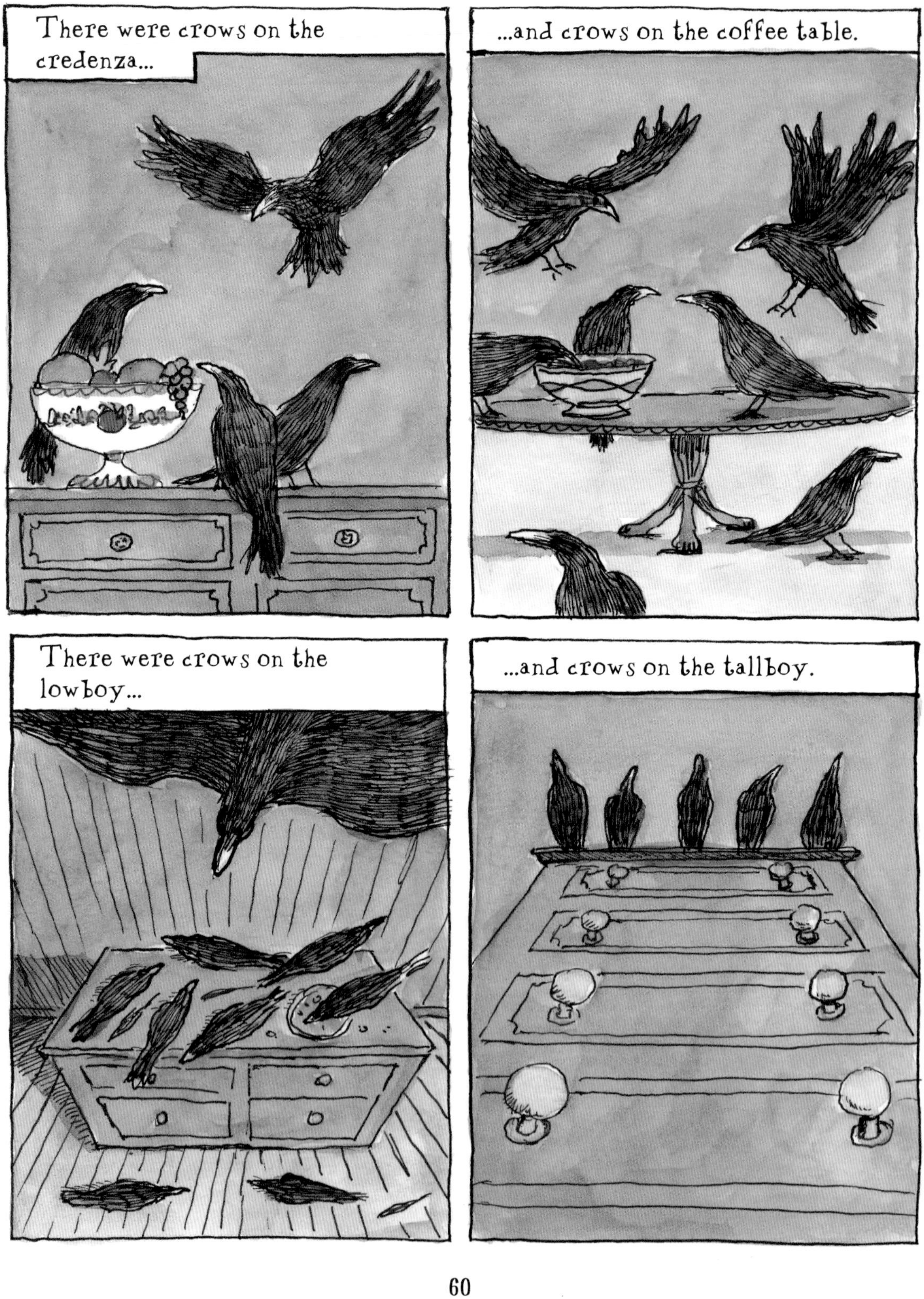
There were crows on the credenza...
...and crows on the coffee table.
There were crows on the lowboy...
...and crows on the tallboy.

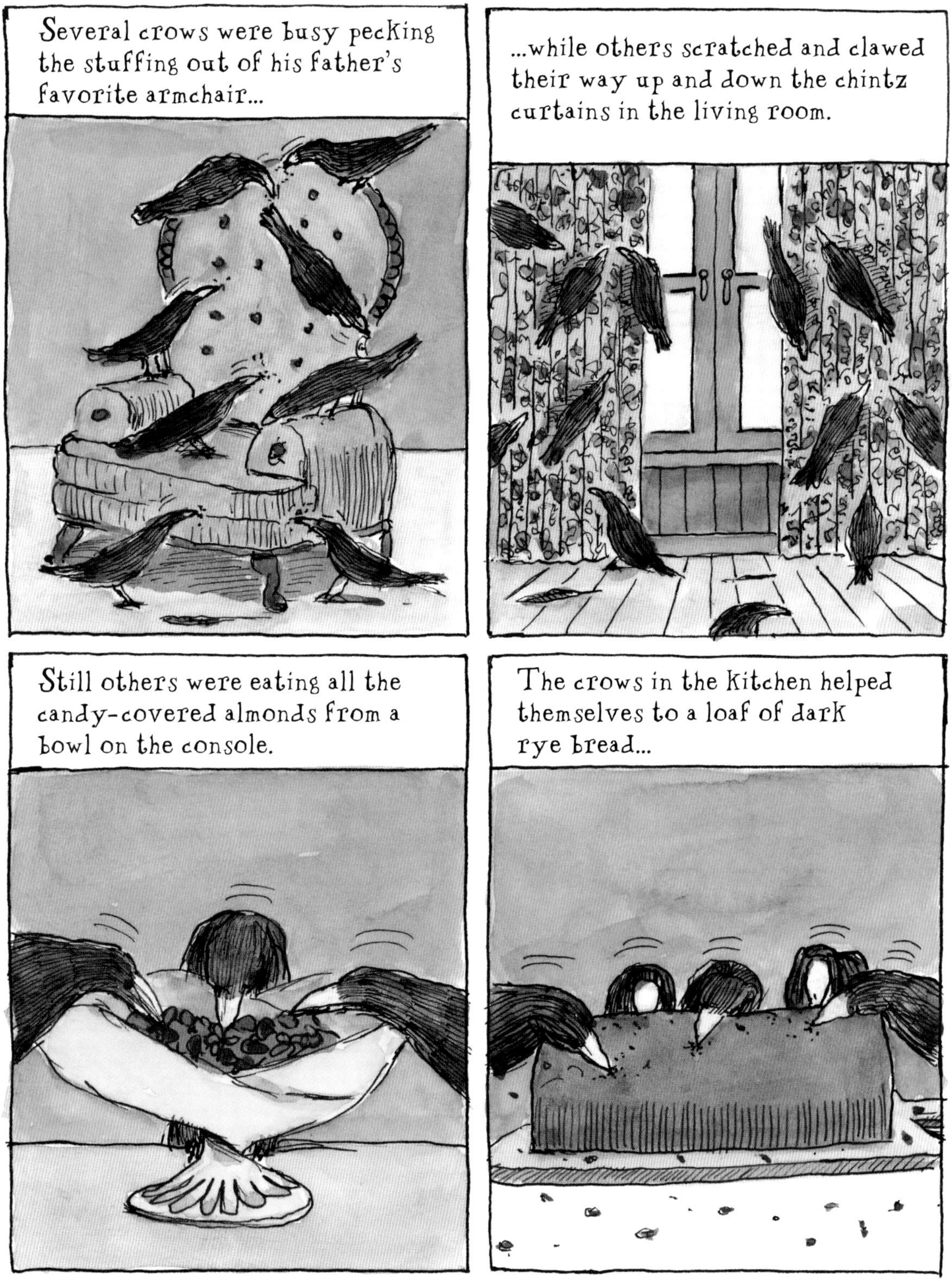
Several crows were busy pecking the stuffing out of his father's favorite armchair...
...while others scratched and clawed their way up and down the chintz curtains in the living room.
Still others were eating all the candy-covered almonds from a bowl on the console.
The crows in the kitchen helped themselves to a loaf of dark rye bread...

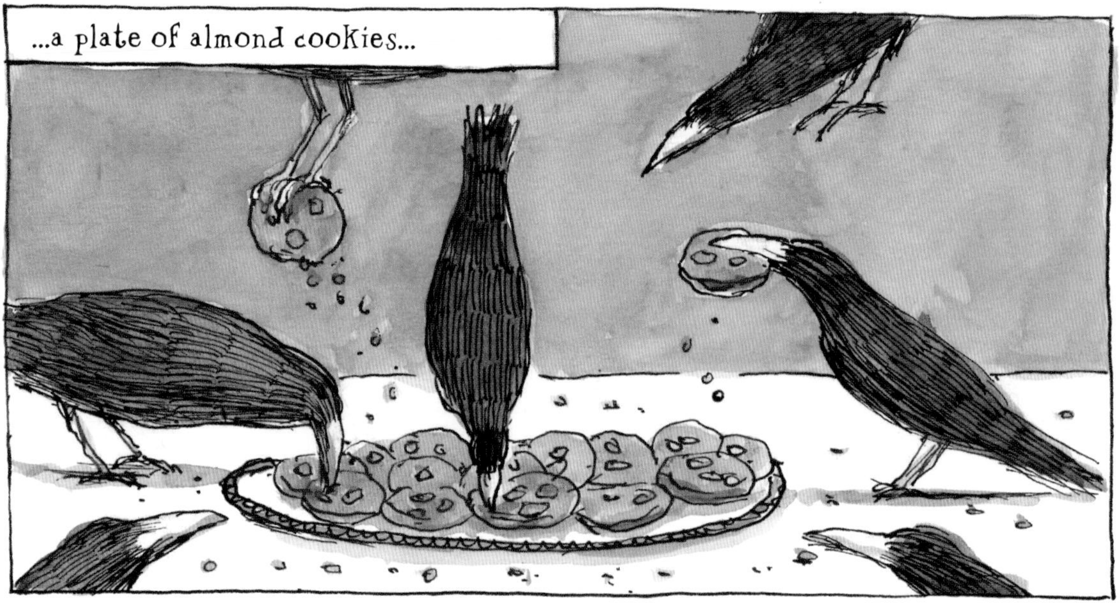
...a plate of almond cookies...

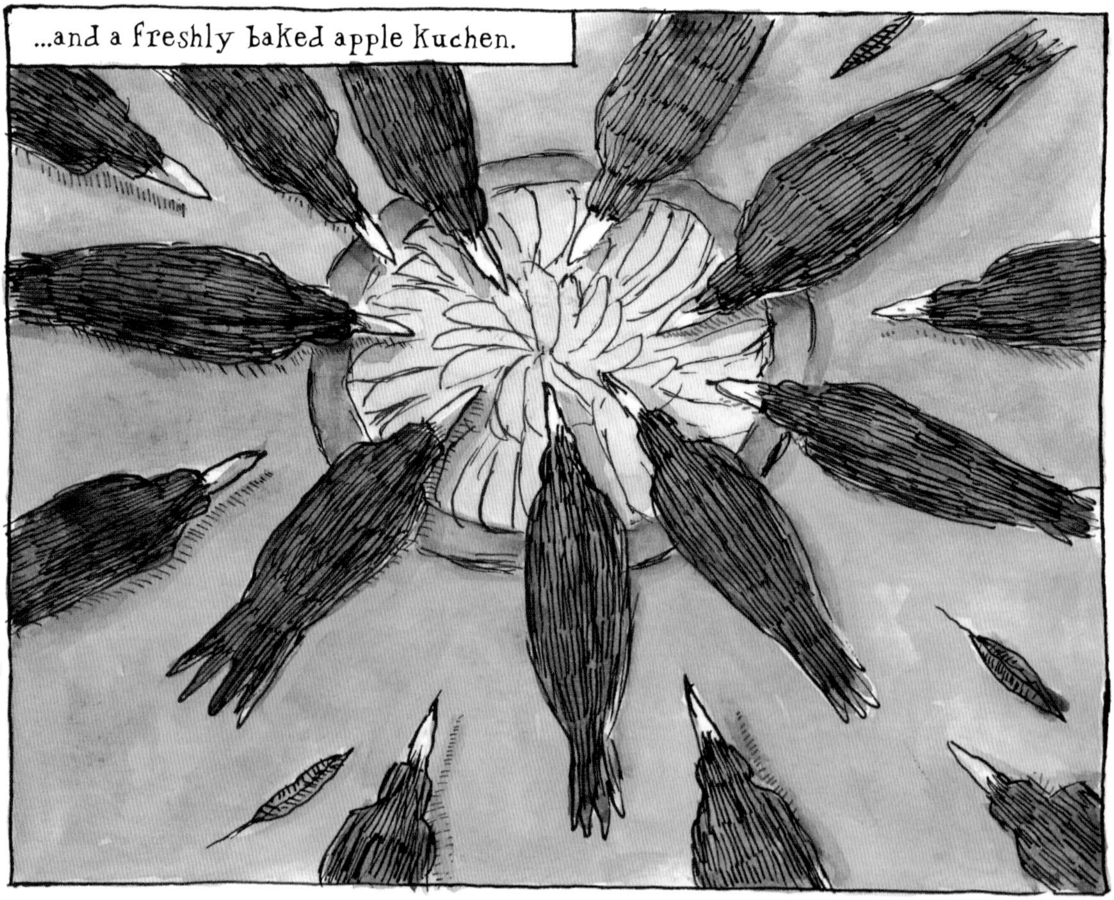
...and a freshly baked apple kuchen.

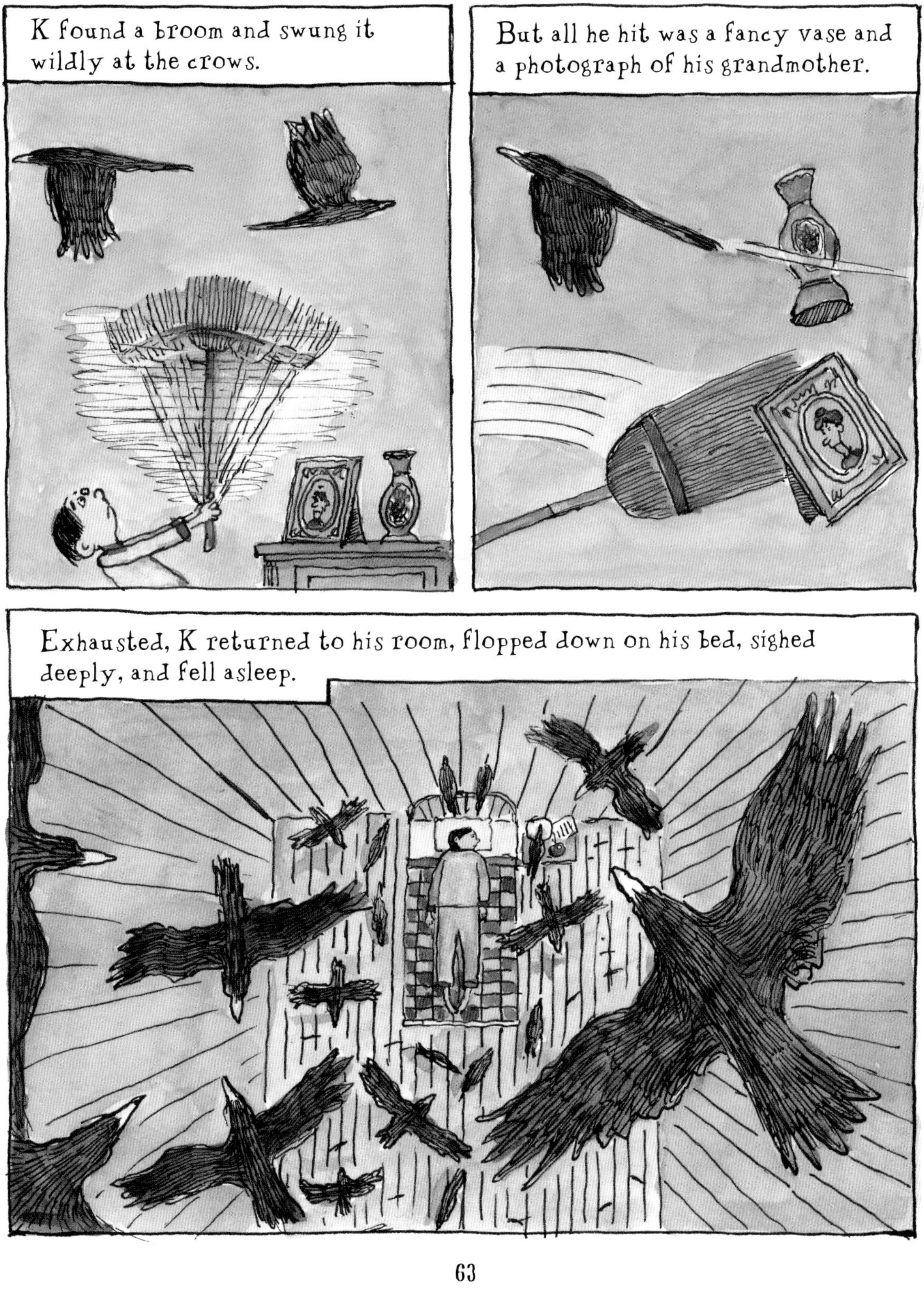
K found a broom and swung it wildly at the crows.
But all he hit was a fancy vase and a photograph of his grandmother.
Exhausted, K returned to his room, flopped down on his bed, sighed deeply, and fell asleep.

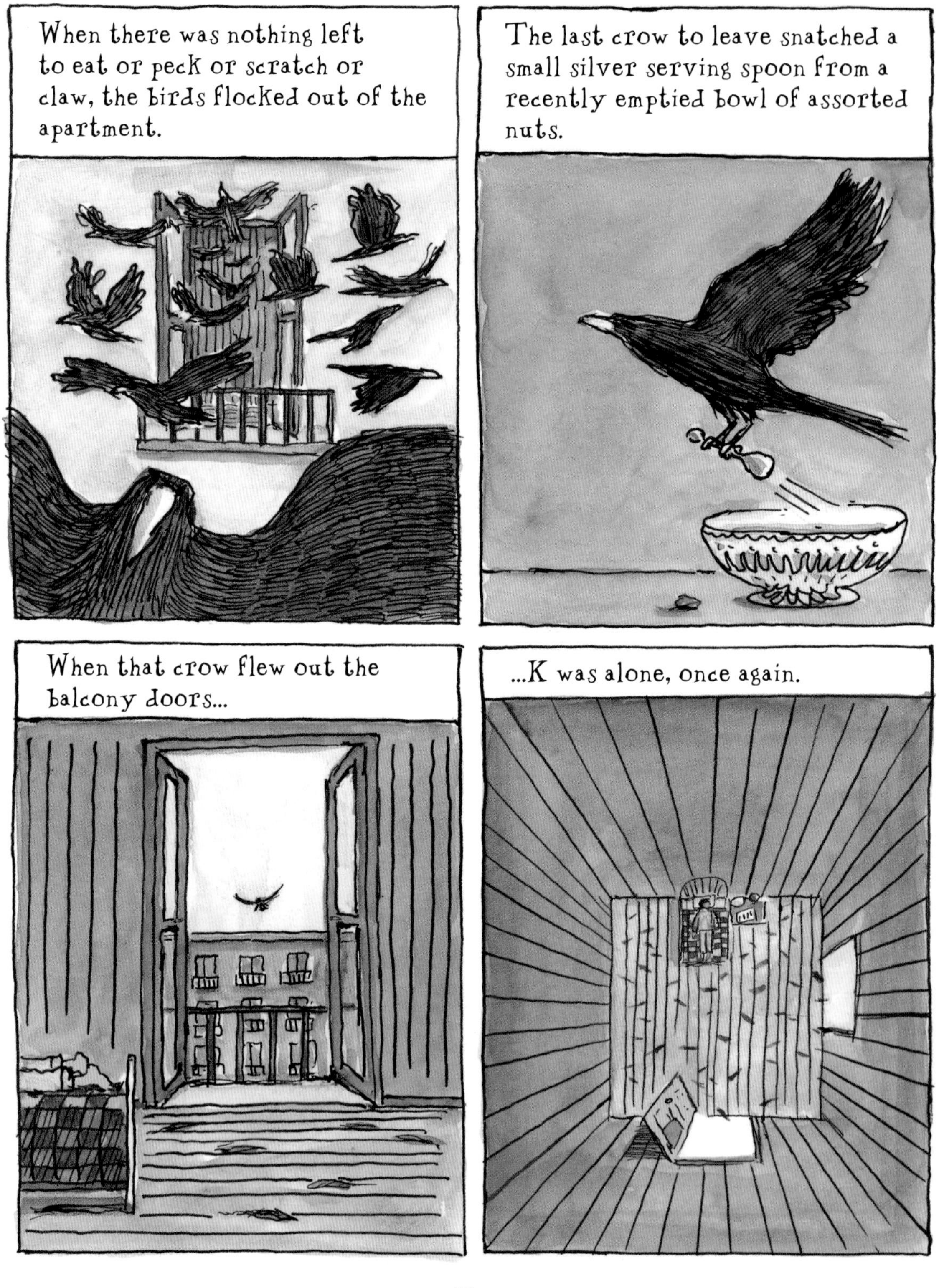
When there was nothing left to eat or peck or scratch or claw, the birds flocked out of the apartment.
The last crow to leave snatched a small silver serving spoon from a recently emptied bowl of assorted nuts.
When that crow flew out the balcony doors...
...K was alone, once again.

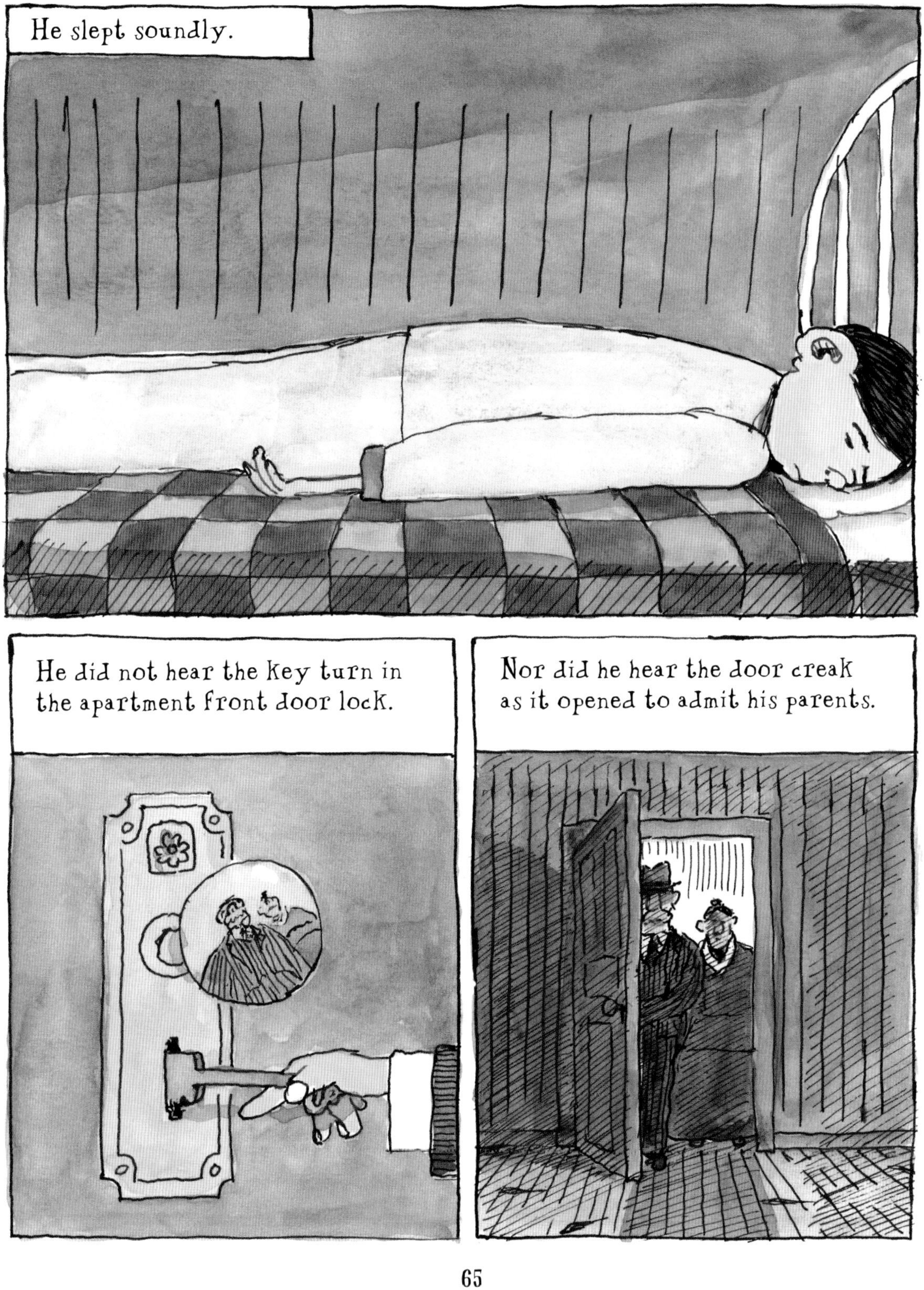
He slept soundly.
He did not hear the key turn in the apartment front door lock.
Nor did he hear the door creak as it opened to admit his parents.

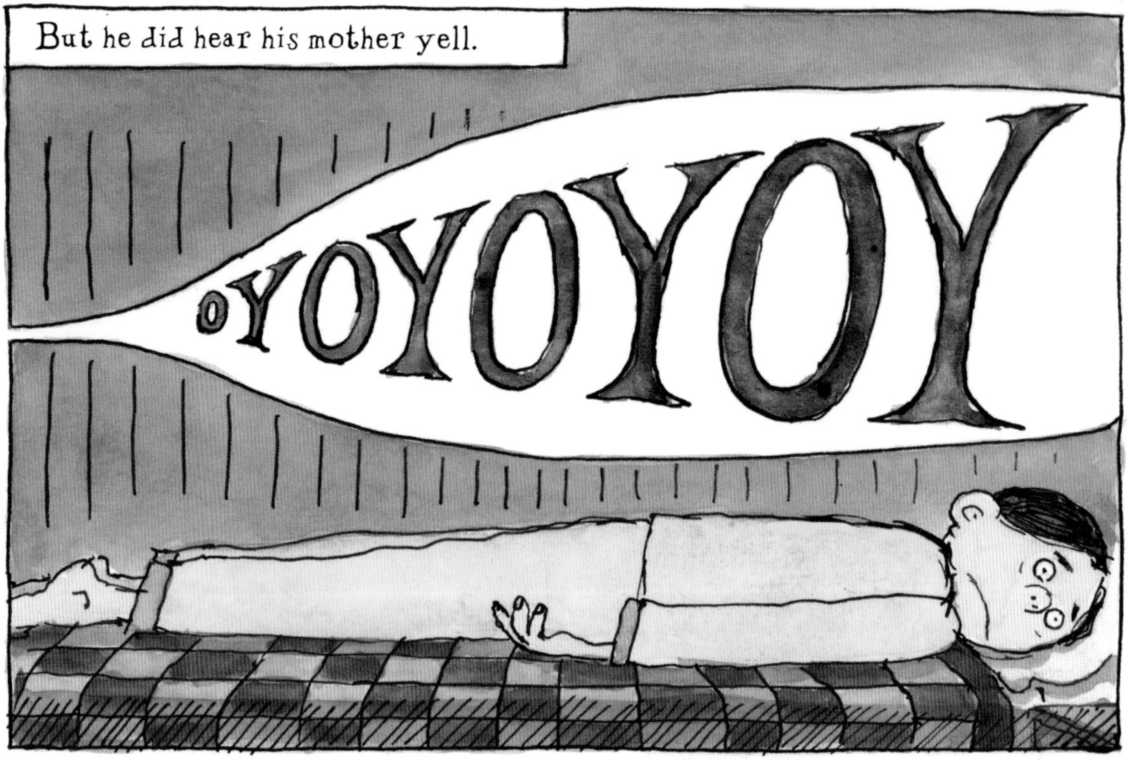
But he did hear his mother yell.
OYOYOYOY

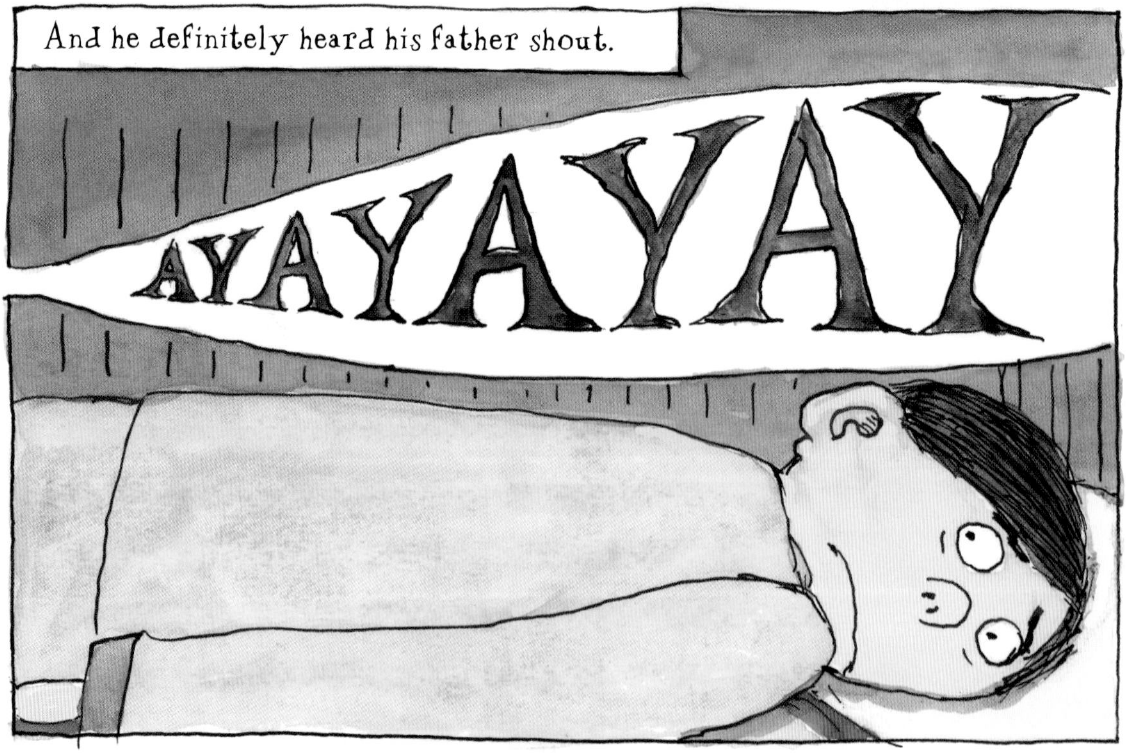
And he definitely heard his father shout.
AYAYAYAY

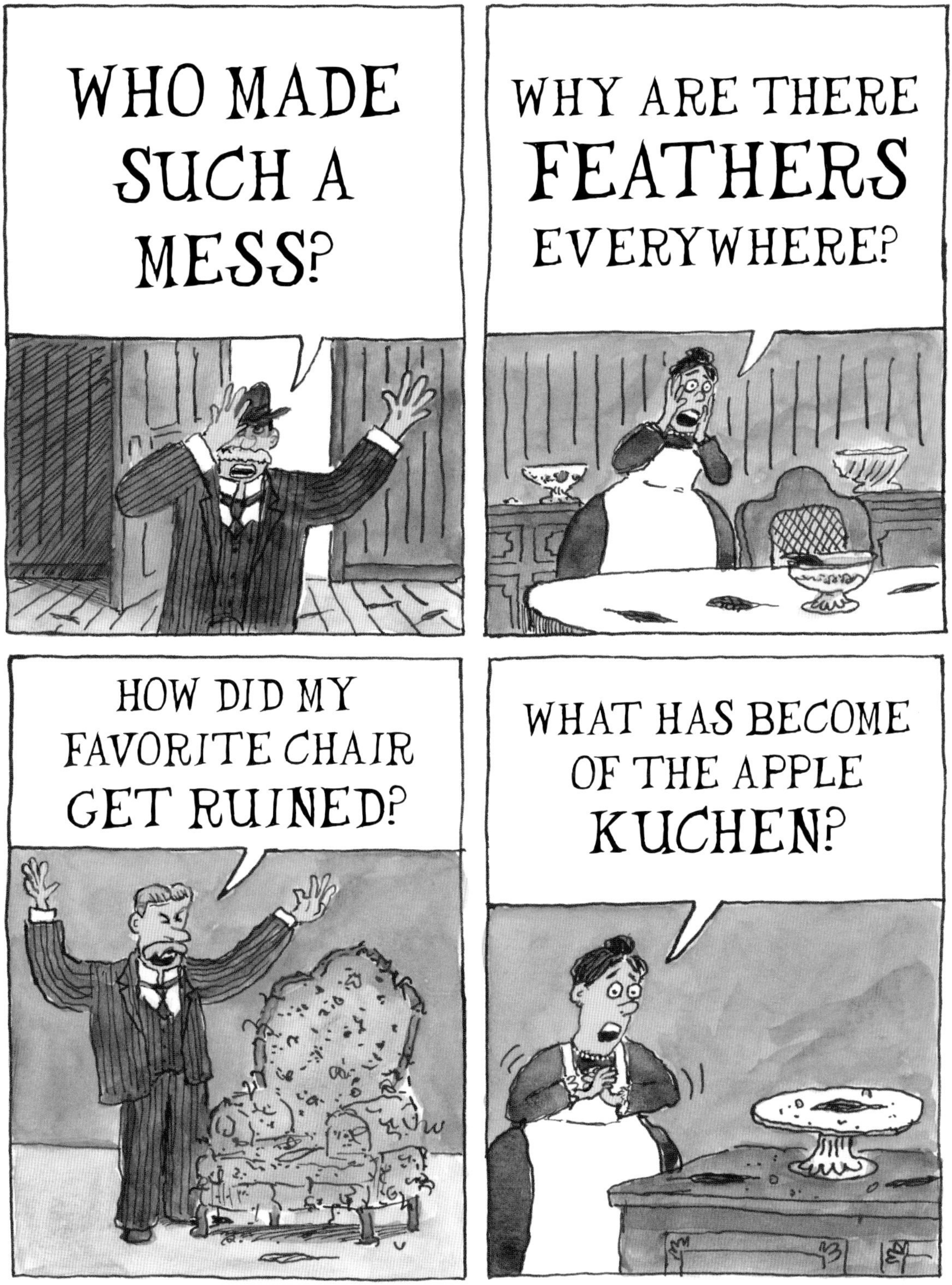
WHO MADE SUCH A MESS?
WHY ARE THERE FEATHERS EVERYWHERE?
HOW DID MY FAVORITE CHAIR GET RUINED?
WHAT HAS BECOME OF THE APPLE KUCHEN?

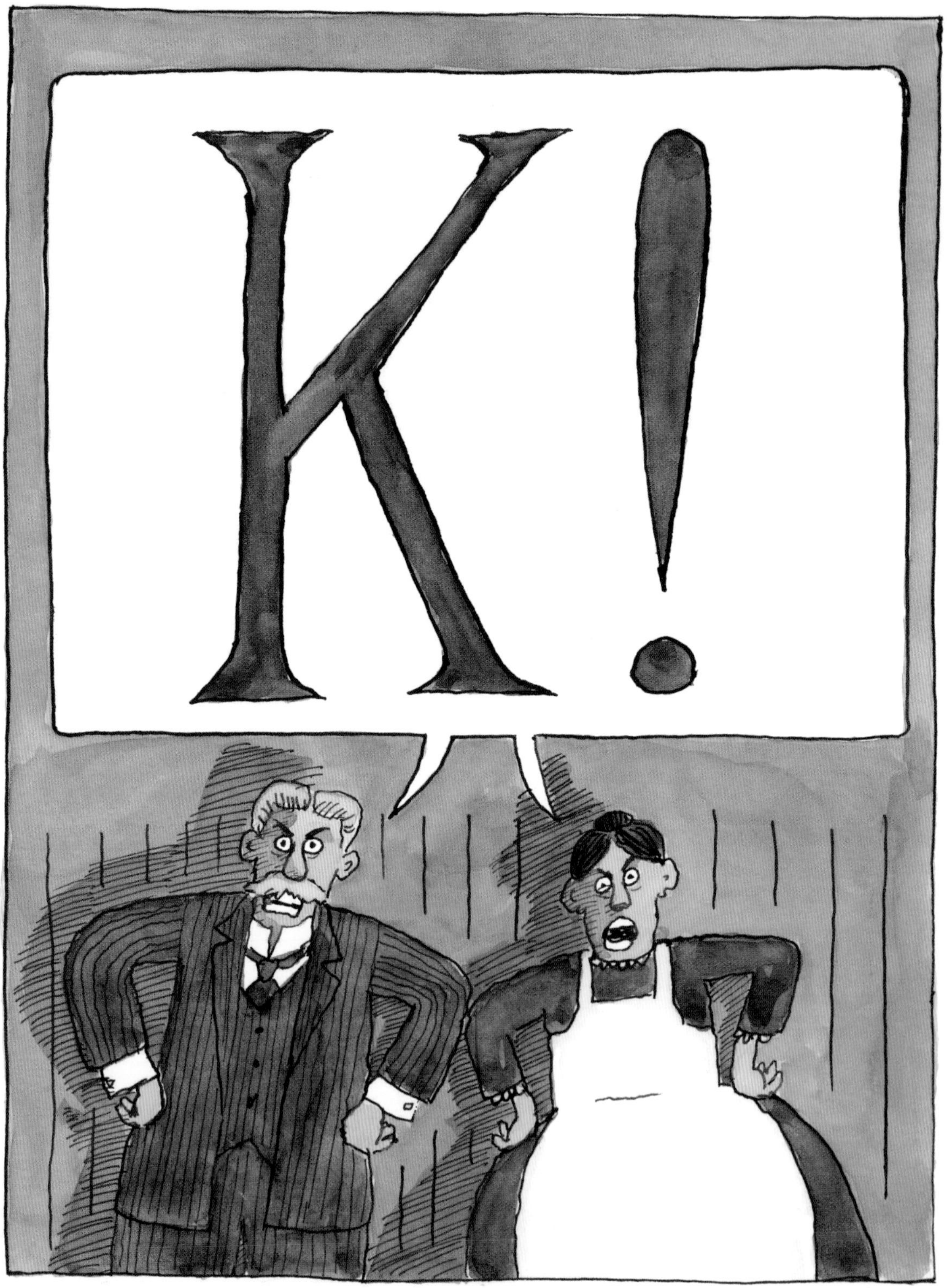
K!

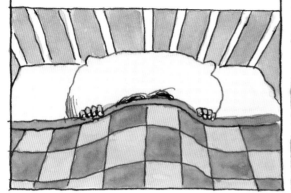

K slipped under the bedsheets and pulled them over his head.

WHAT HAPPENED, K?

I don't know.

I did just as your note said, Mama. I stayed in bed.

I slept all day, Papa.

I still feel quite unwell.

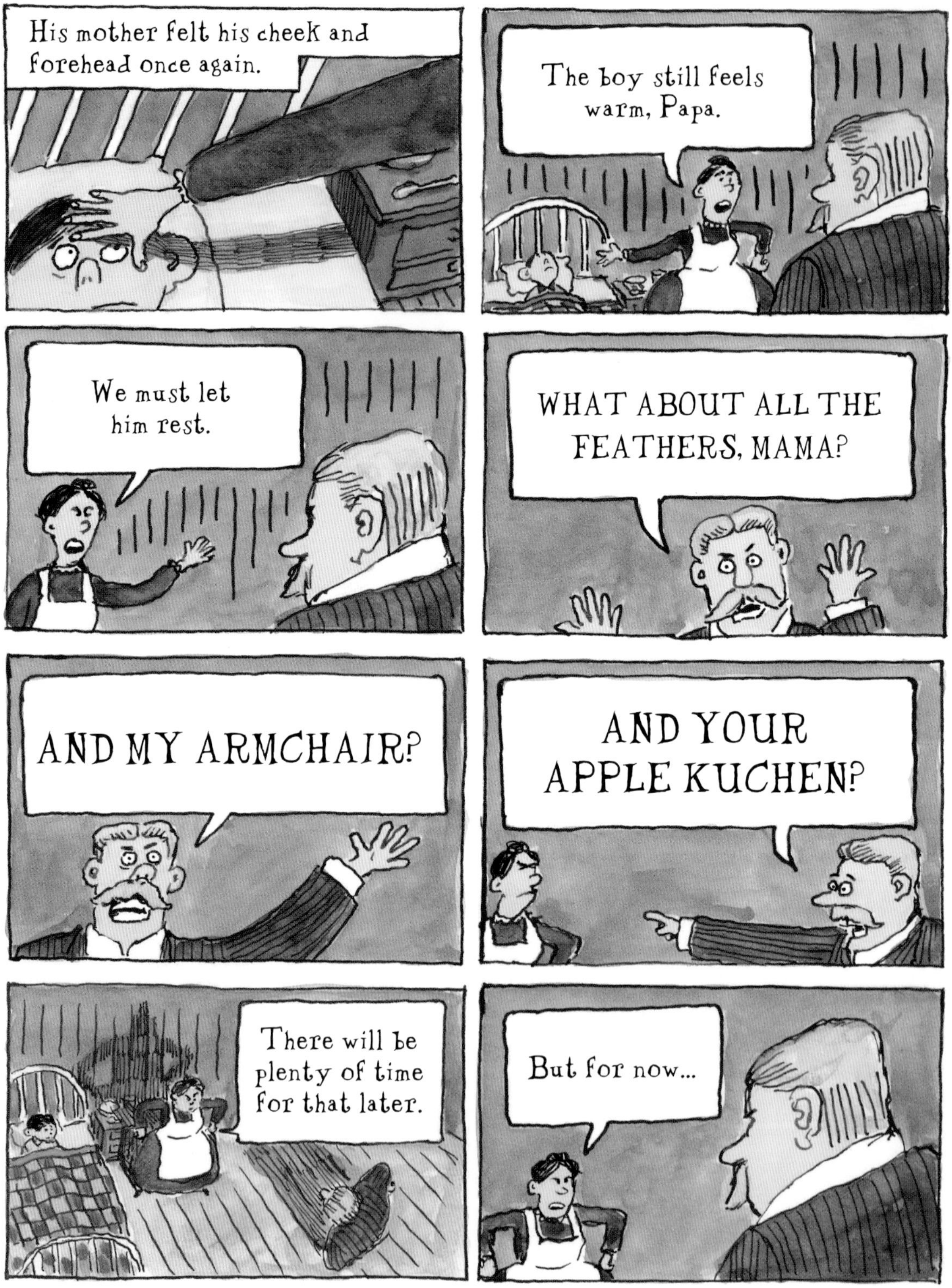
His mother felt his cheek and forehead once again.
The boy still feels warm, Papa.
We must let him rest.
WHAT ABOUT ALL THE FEATHERS, MAMA?
AND MY ARMCHAIR?
AND YOUR APPLE KUCHEN?
There will be plenty of time for that later.
But for now...

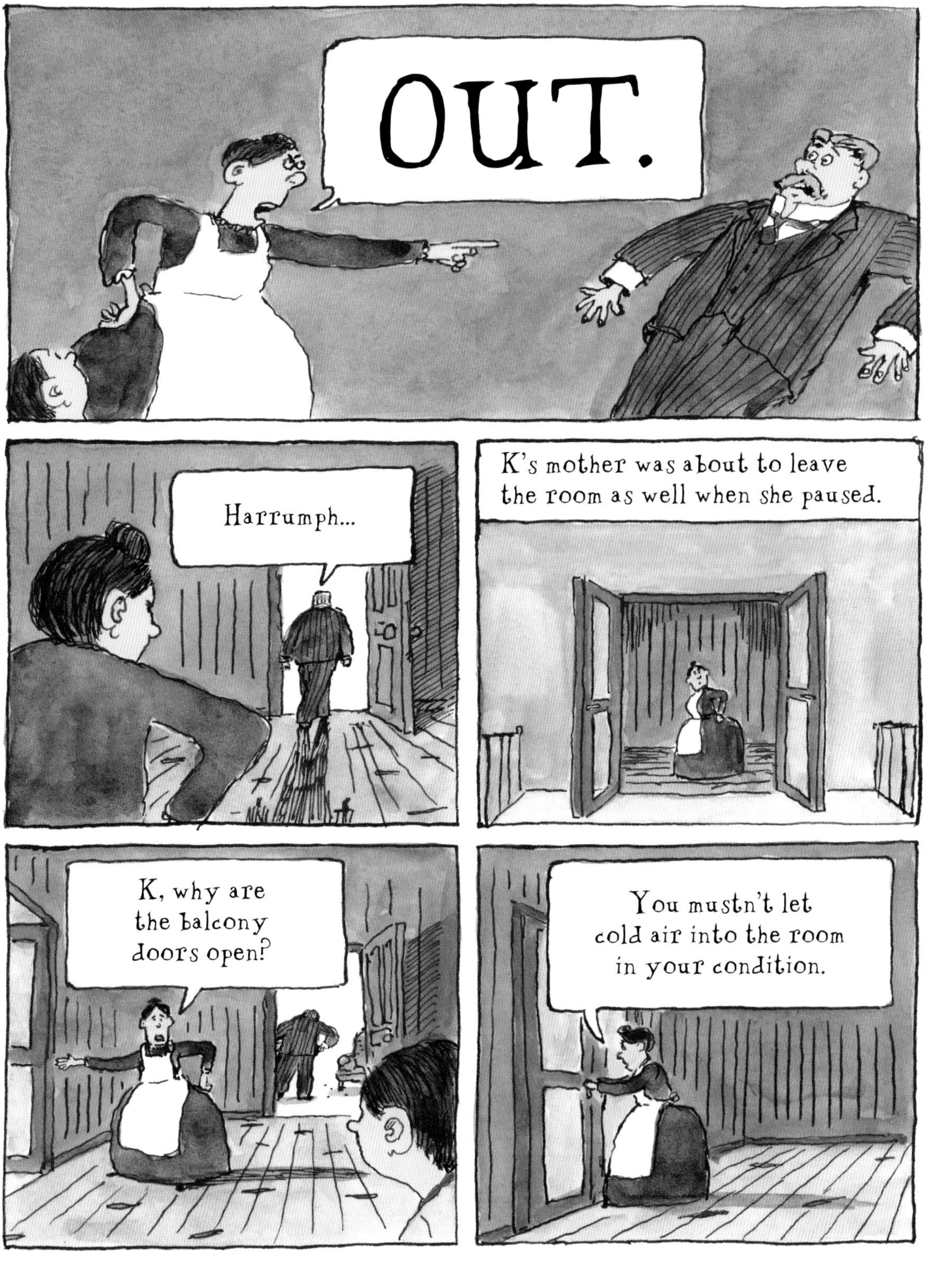
OUT.
Harrumph...
K's mother was about to leave the room as well when she paused.
K, why are the balcony doors open?
You mustn't let cold air into the room in your condition.

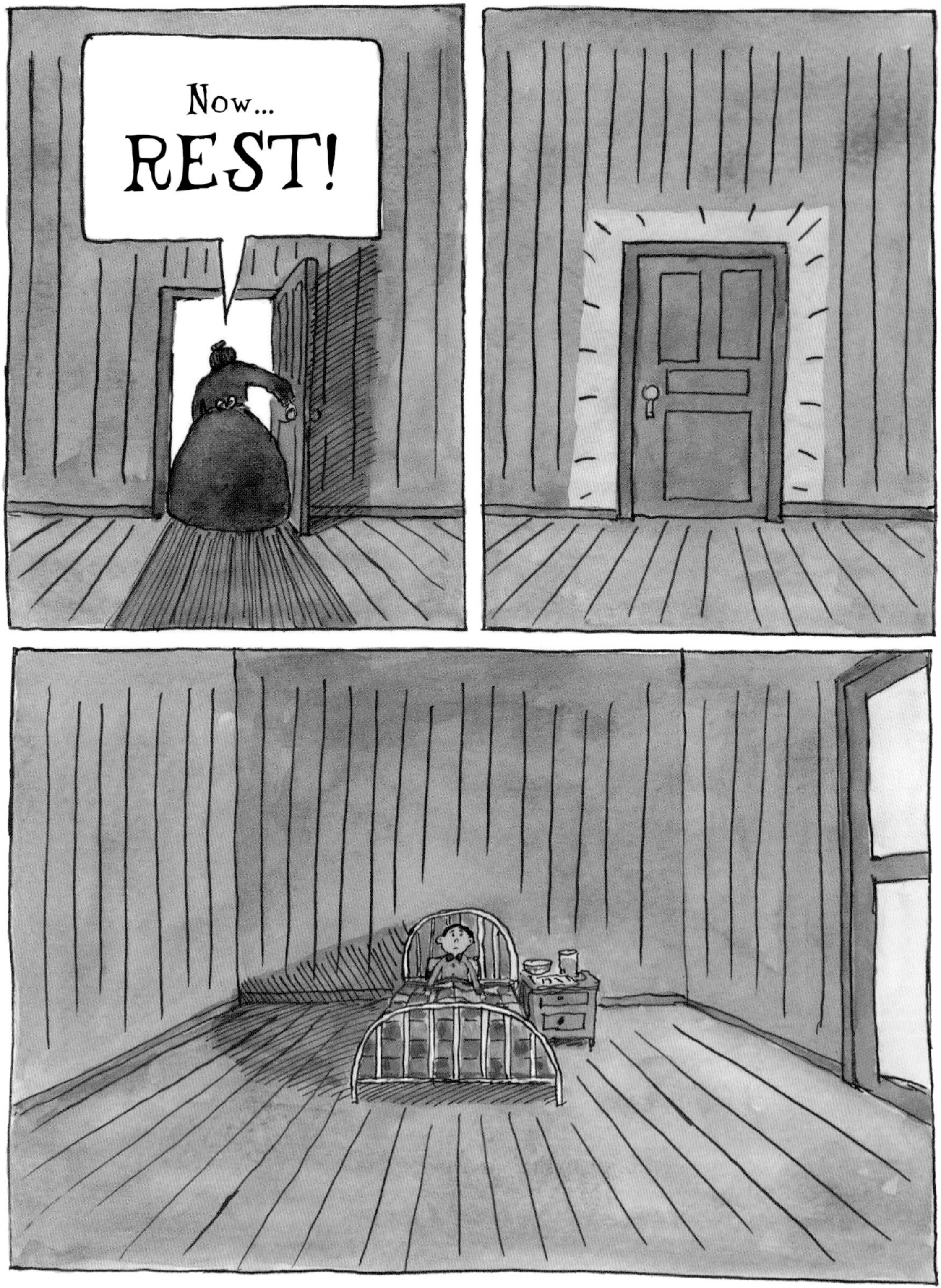
Now... REST!

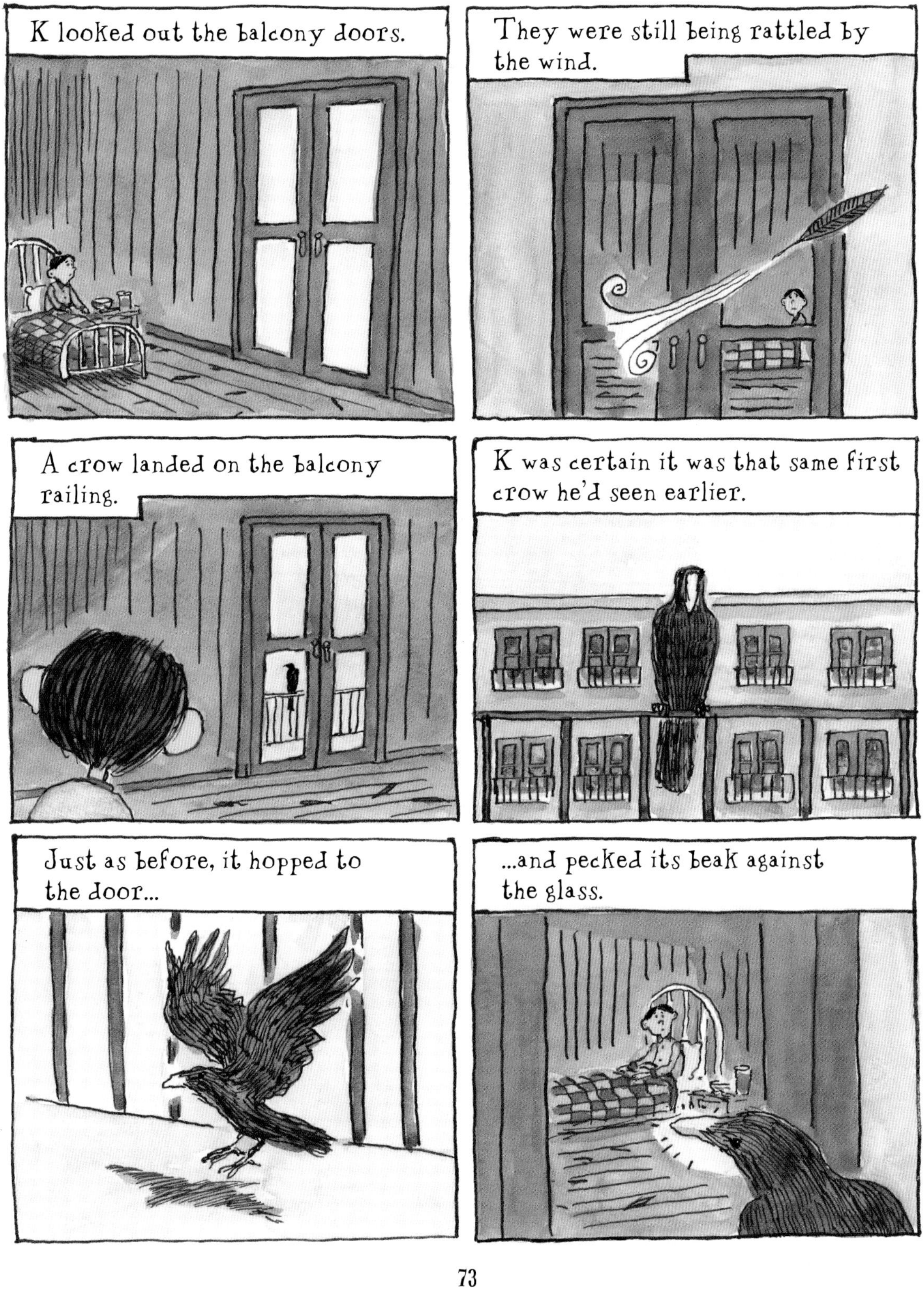
K looked out the balcony doors.
They were still being rattled by the wind.
A crow landed on the balcony railing.
K was certain it was that same first crow he'd seen earlier.
Just as before, it hopped to the door...
...and pecked its beak against the glass.

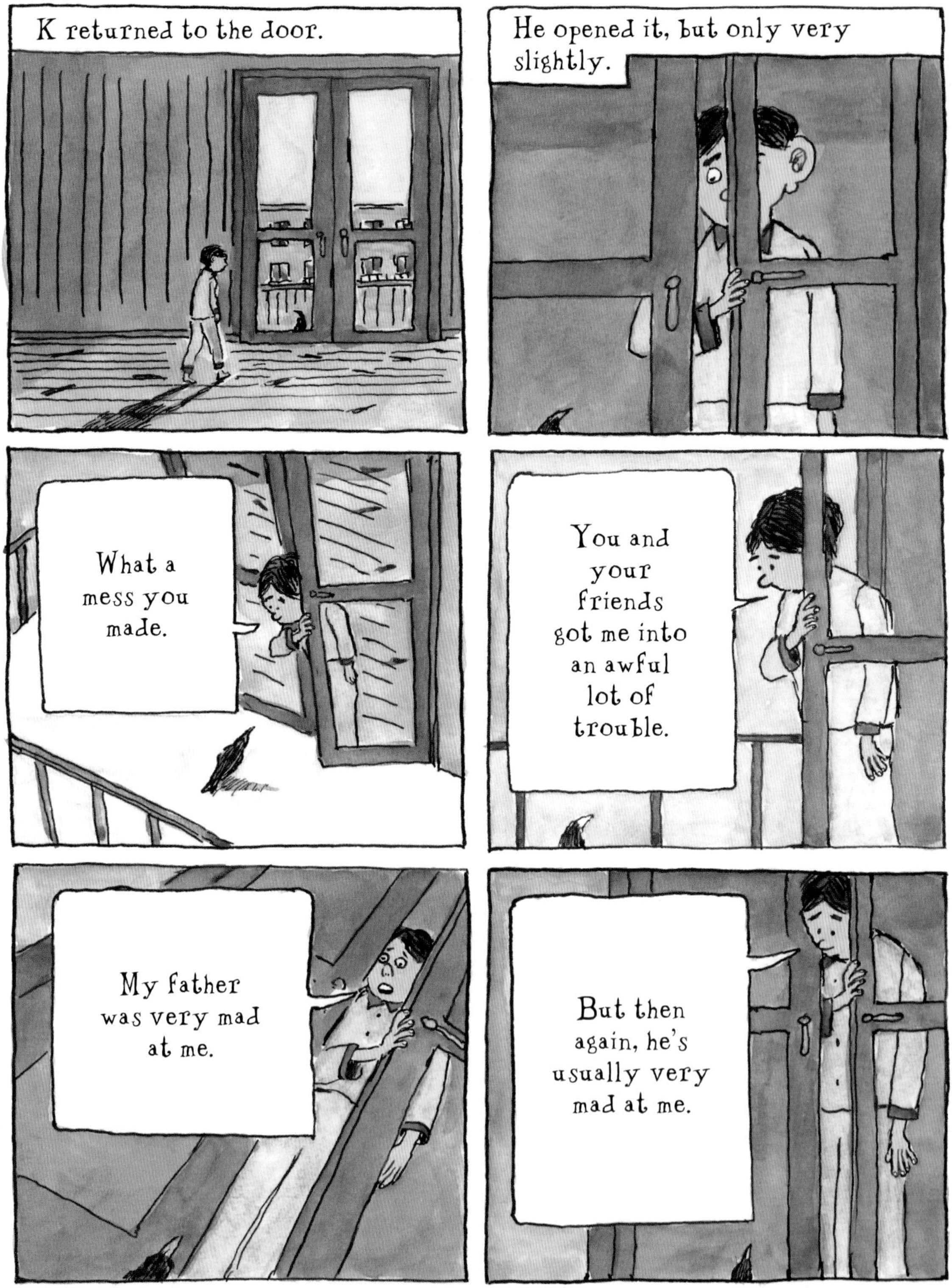
K returned to the door.
He opened it, but only very slightly.
What a mess you made.
You and your friends got me into an awful lot of trouble.
My father was very mad at me.
But then again, he's usually very mad at me.

The crow looked up at K.

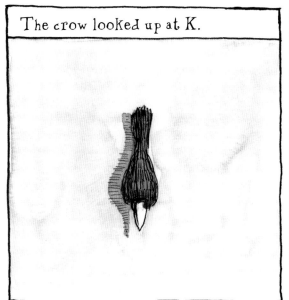

It looked to its right, as if to point at something, then bobbed its head once.

Then it flew off.

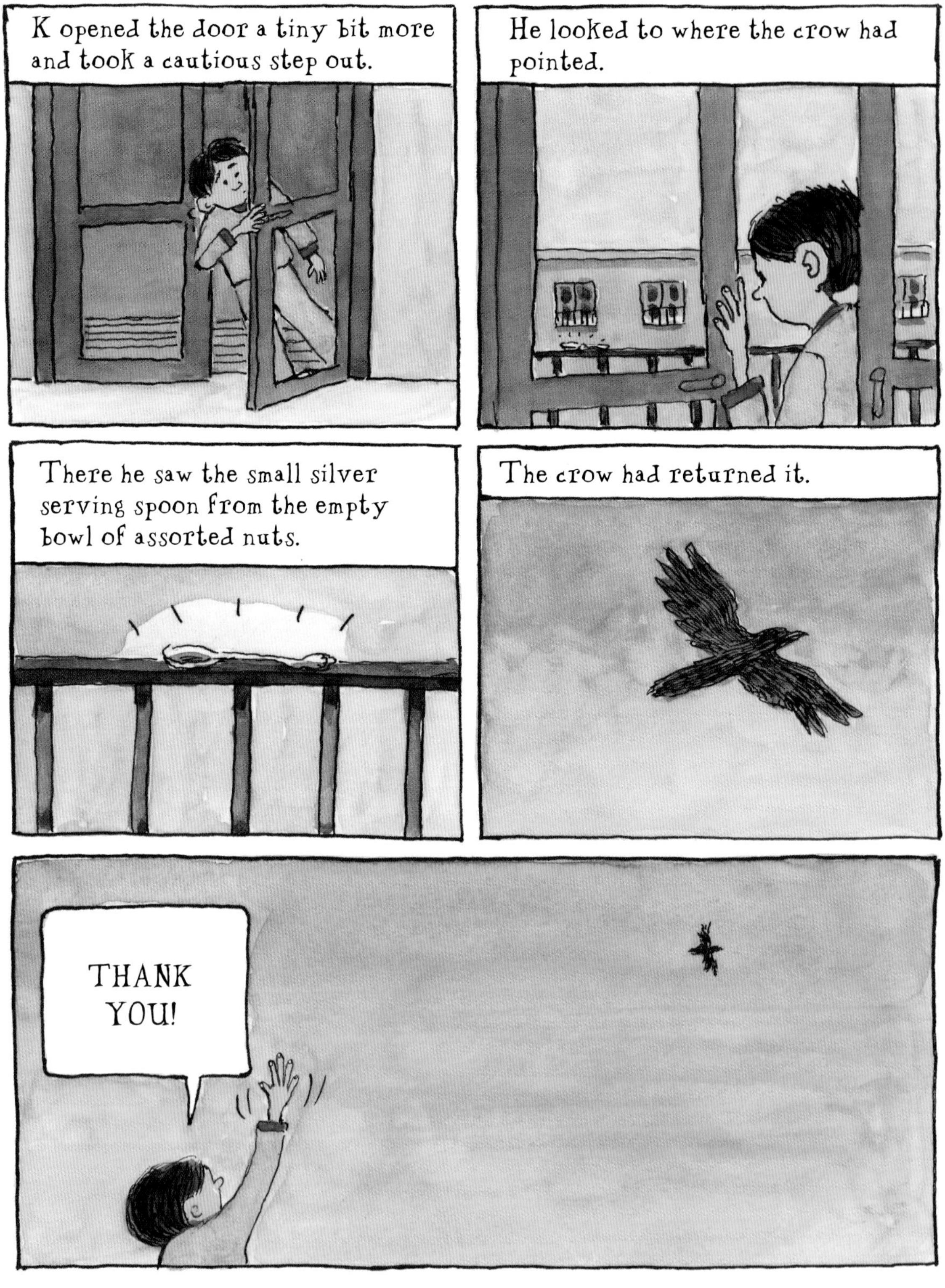

K opened the door a tiny bit more and took a cautious step out.
He looked to where the crow had pointed.
There he saw the small silver serving spoon from the empty bowl of assorted nuts.
The crow had returned it.
THANK YOU!

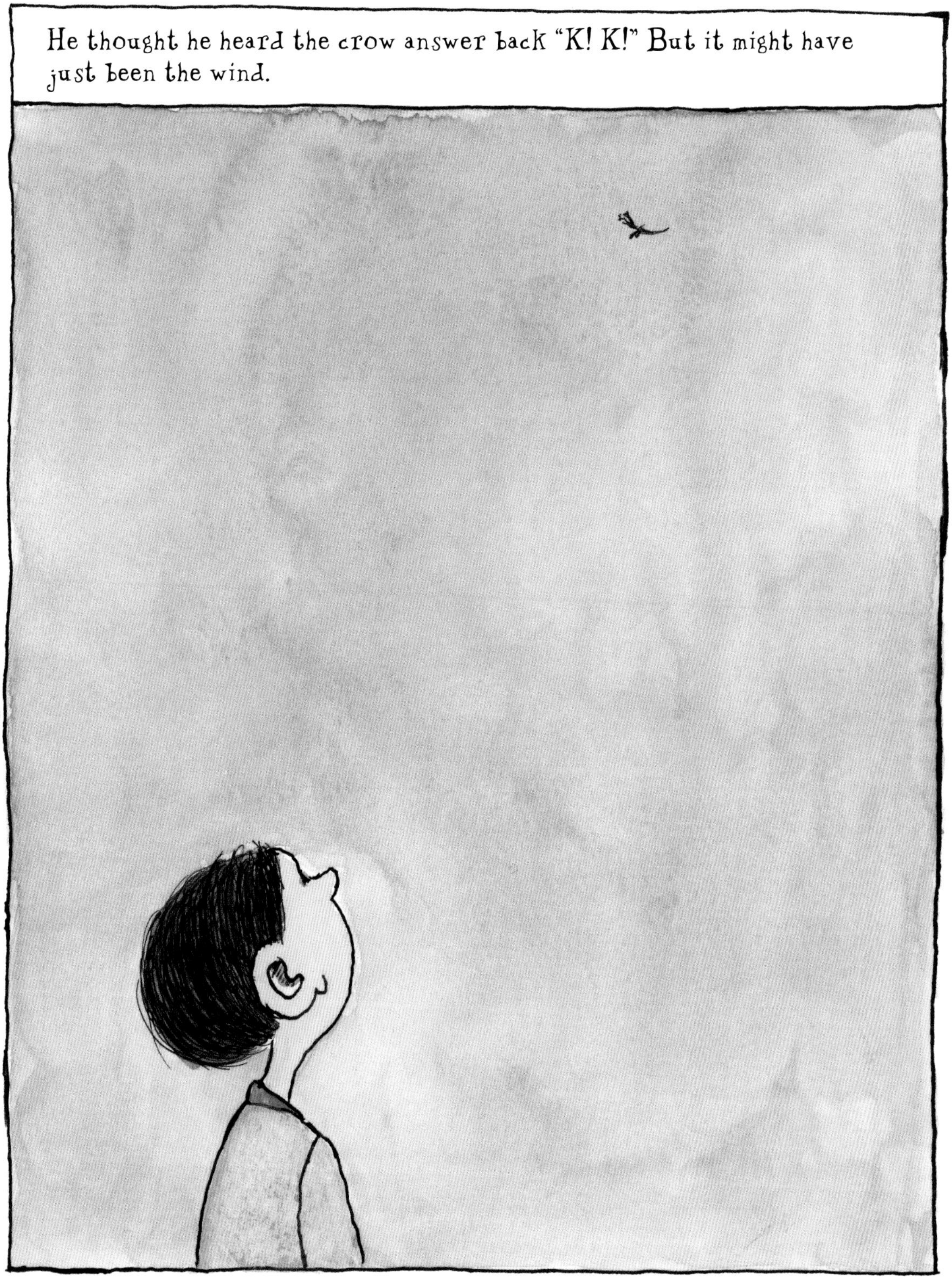
He thought he heard the crow answer back "K! K!" But it might have just been the wind.

K IS
IN
TROUBLE

It was the day of K's field trip.

His class was going to visit the Castle.

Herr Professor X led the class to the tram first thing in the morning.

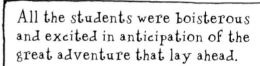

All the students were boisterous and excited in anticipation of the great adventure that lay ahead.

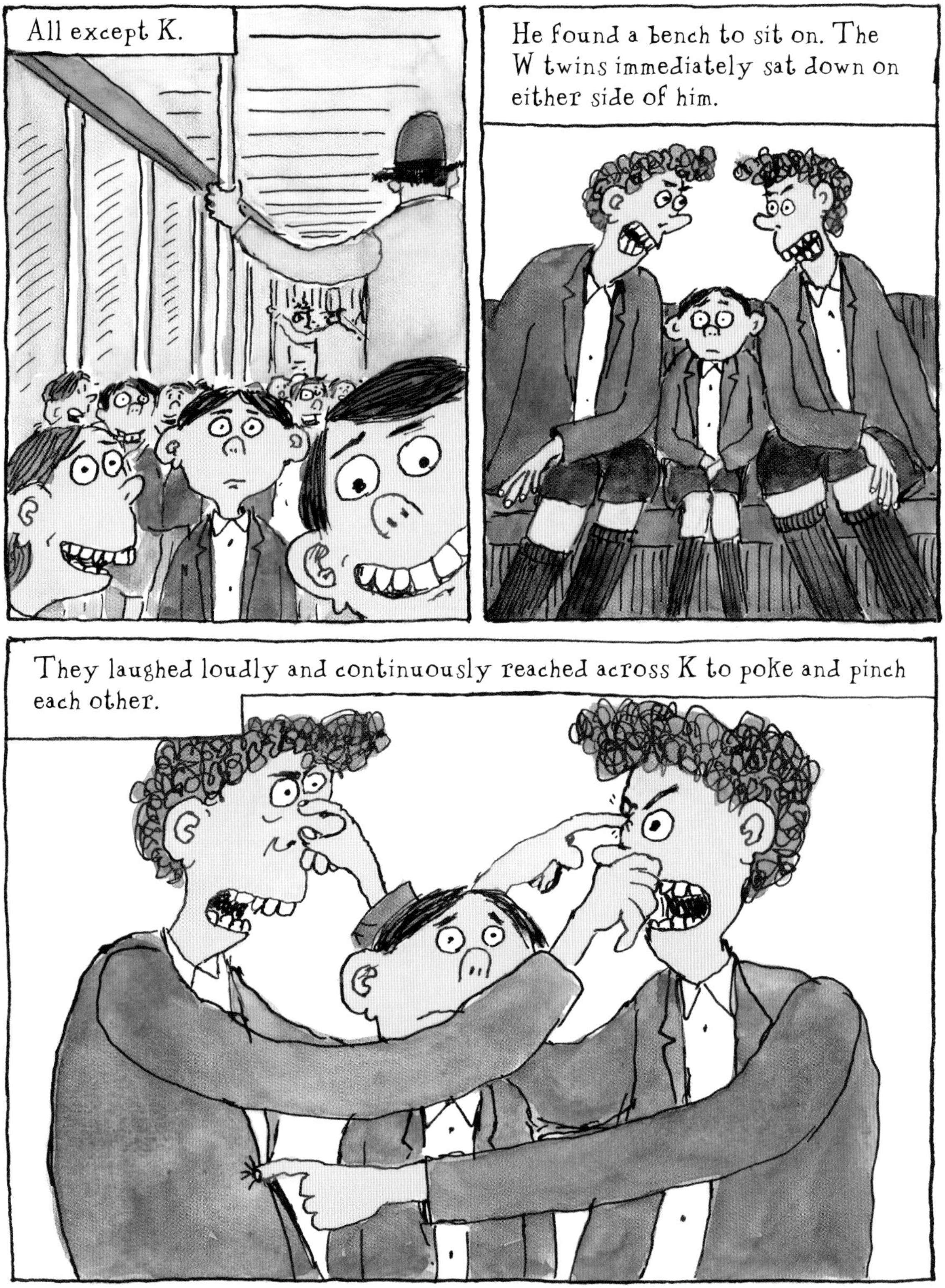
All except K.
He found a bench to sit on. The W twins immediately sat down on either side of him.
They laughed loudly and continuously reached across K to poke and pinch each other.

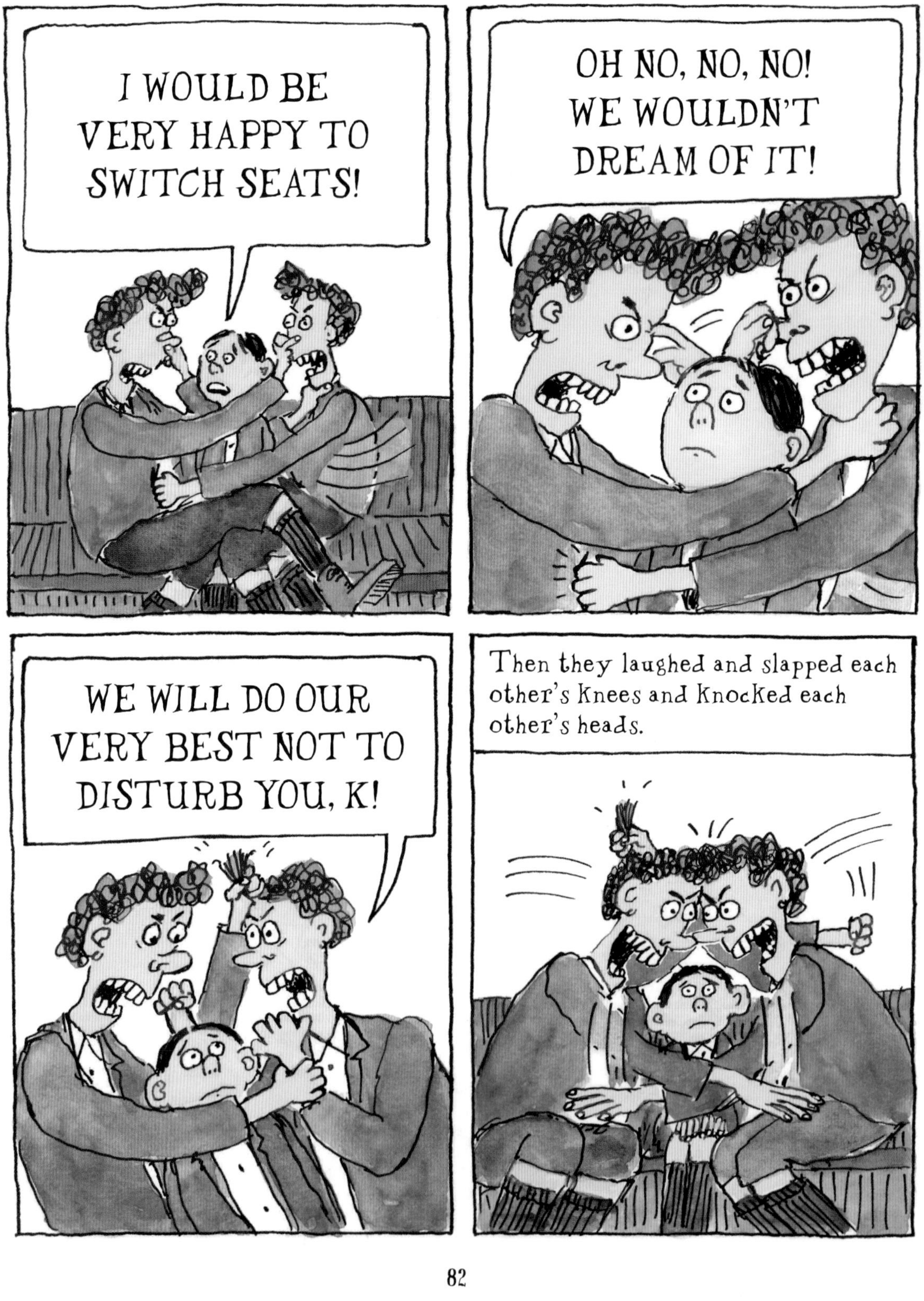
I WOULD BE VERY HAPPY TO SWITCH SEATS!
OH NO, NO, NO! WE WOULDN'T DREAM OF IT!
WE WILL DO OUR VERY BEST NOT TO DISTURB YOU, K!
Then they laughed and slapped each other's knees and knocked each other's heads.

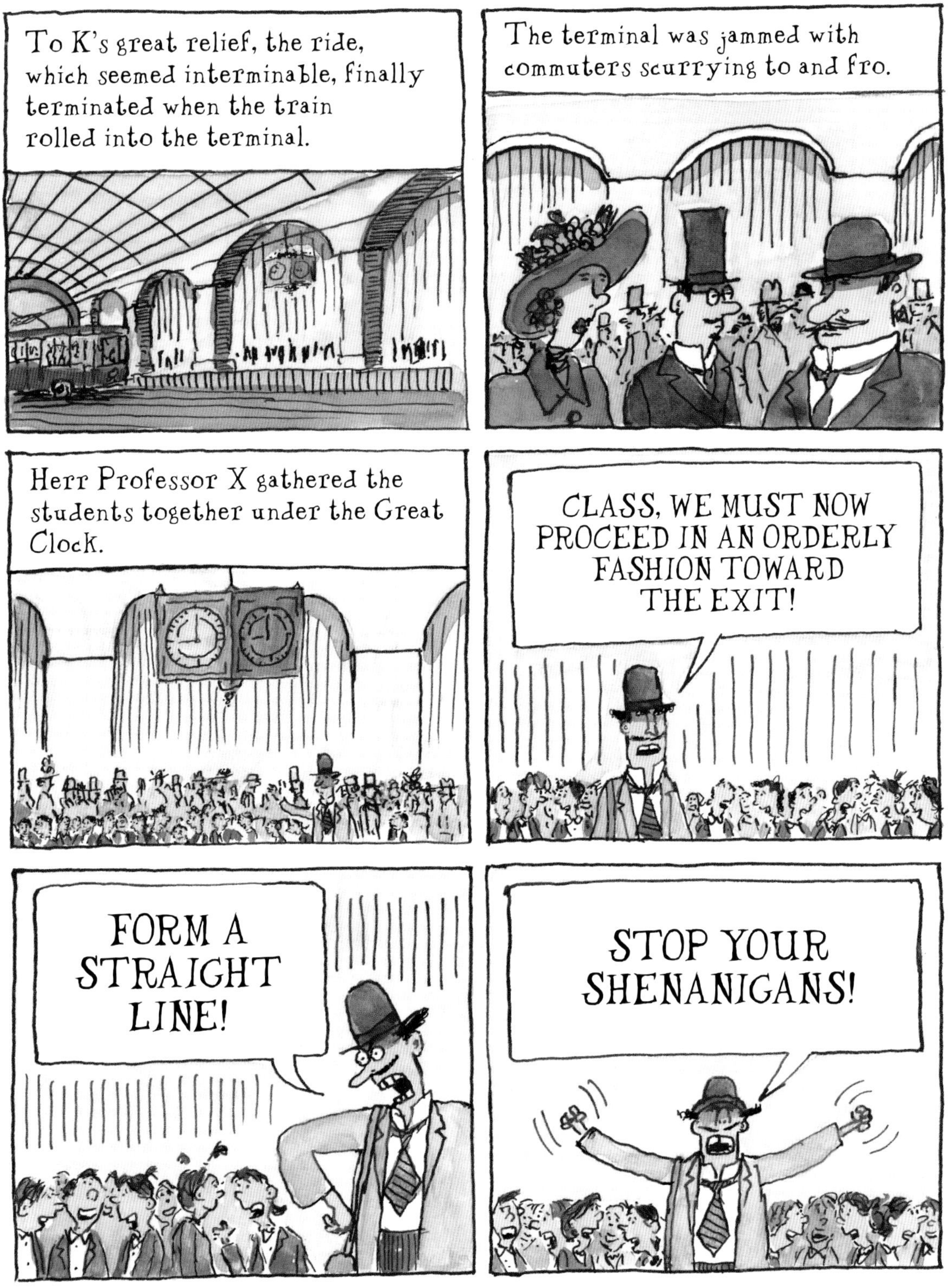

To K's great relief, the ride, which seemed interminable, finally terminated when the train rolled into the terminal.
The terminal was jammed with commuters scurrying to and fro.
Herr Professor X gathered the students together under the Great Clock.
CLASS, WE MUST NOW PROCEED IN AN ORDERLY FASHION TOWARD THE EXIT!
FORM A STRAIGHT LINE!
STOP YOUR SHENANIGANS!

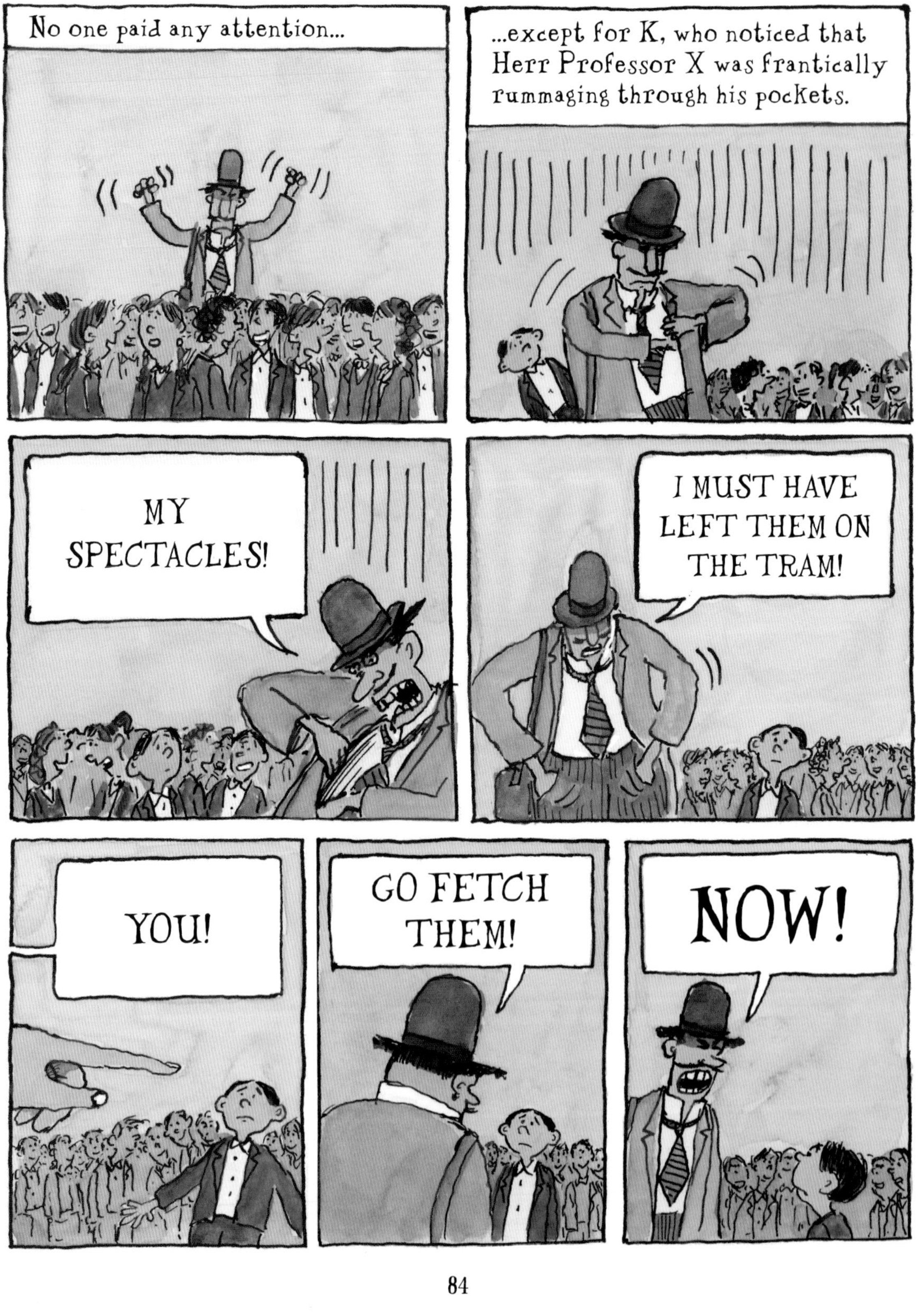
No one paid any attention...
...except for K, who noticed that Herr Professor X was frantically rummaging through his pockets.
MY SPECTACLES!
I MUST HAVE LEFT THEM ON THE TRAM!
YOU!
GO FETCH THEM!
NOW!

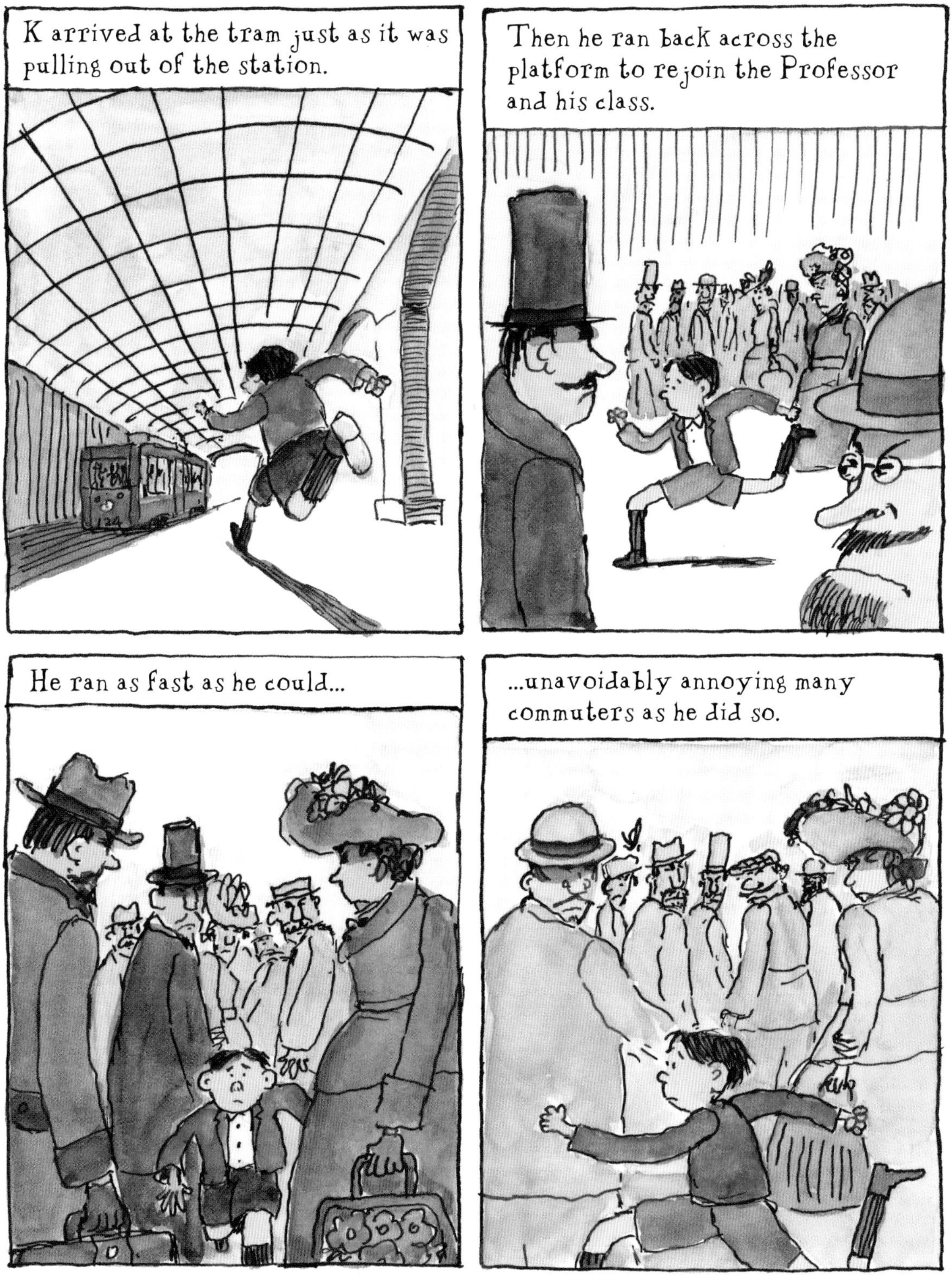
K arrived at the tram just as it was pulling out of the station.
Then he ran back across the platform to rejoin the Professor and his class.
He ran as fast as he could...
...unavoidably annoying many commuters as he did so.

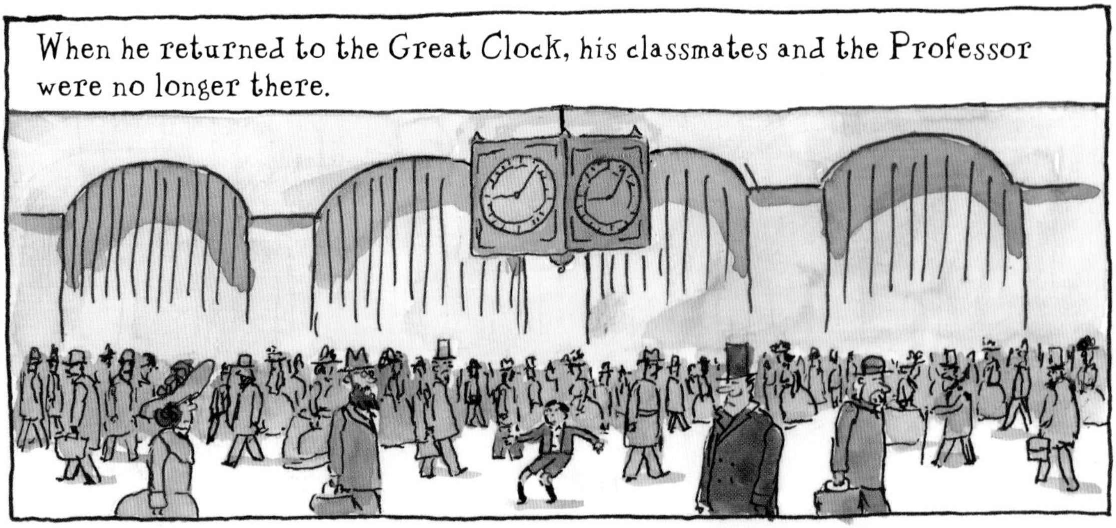
When he returned to the Great Clock, his classmates and the Professor were no longer there.

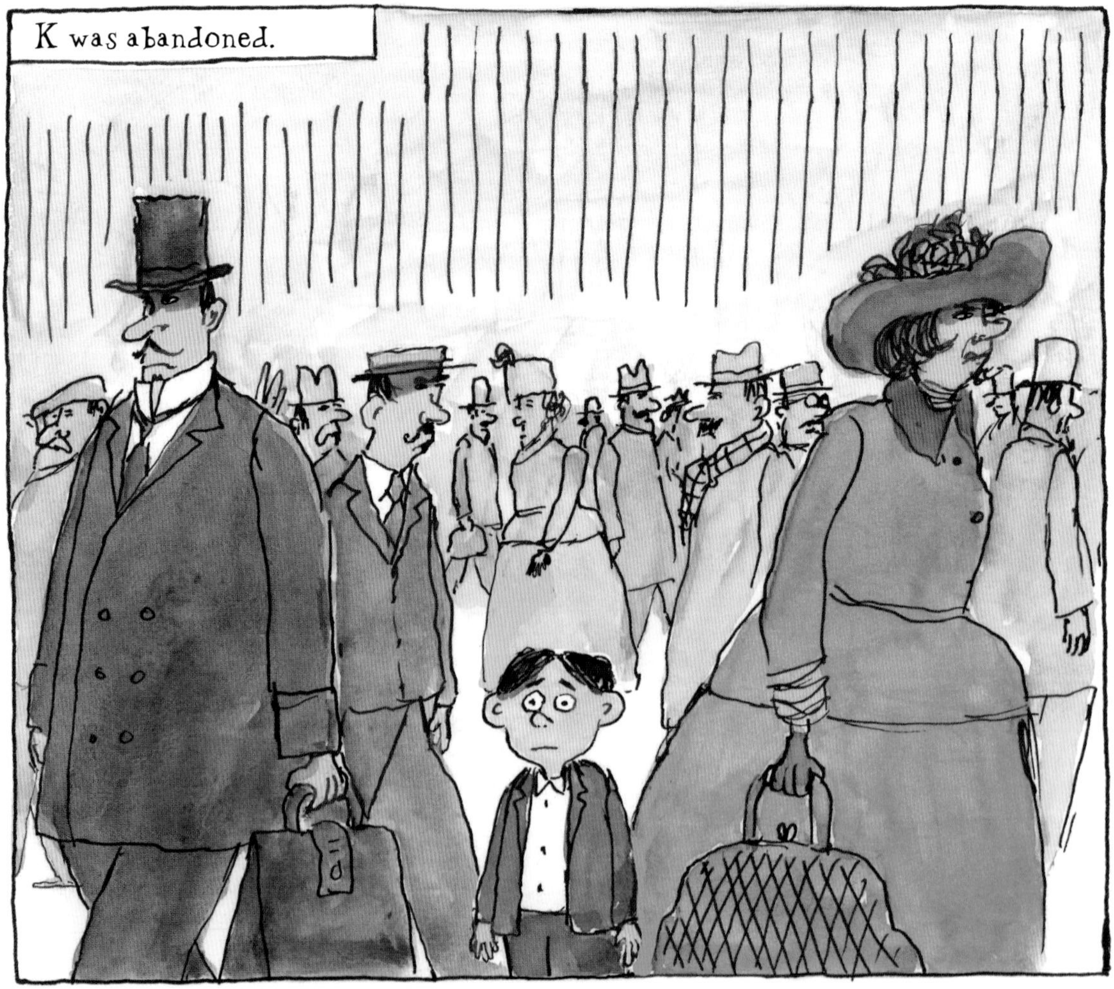
K was abandoned.

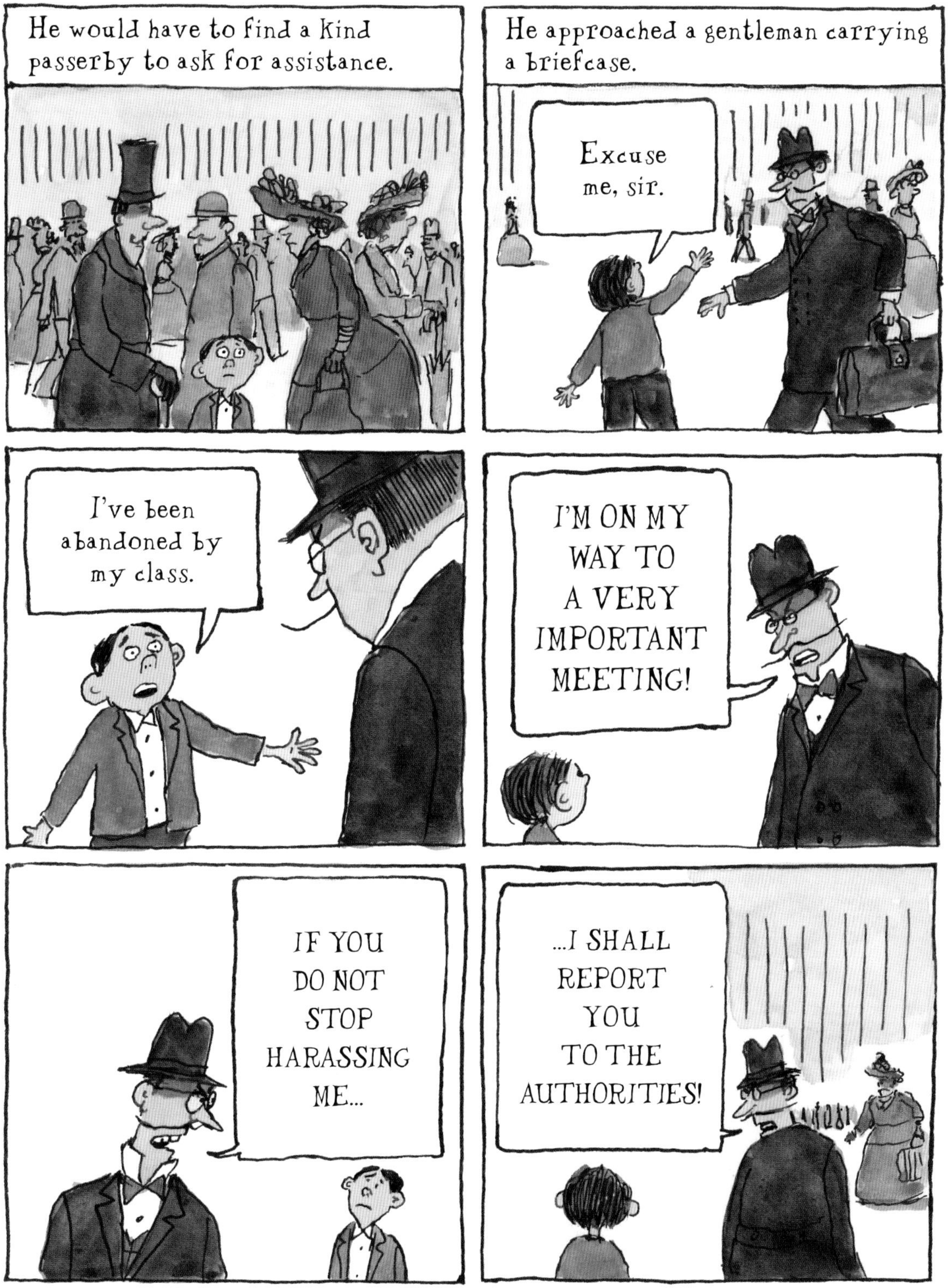
He would have to find a kind passerby to ask for assistance.
He approached a gentleman carrying a briefcase.
Excuse me, sir.
I've been abandoned by my class.
I'M ON MY WAY TO A VERY IMPORTANT MEETING!
IF YOU DO NOT STOP HARASSING ME...
...I SHALL REPORT YOU TO THE AUTHORITIES!

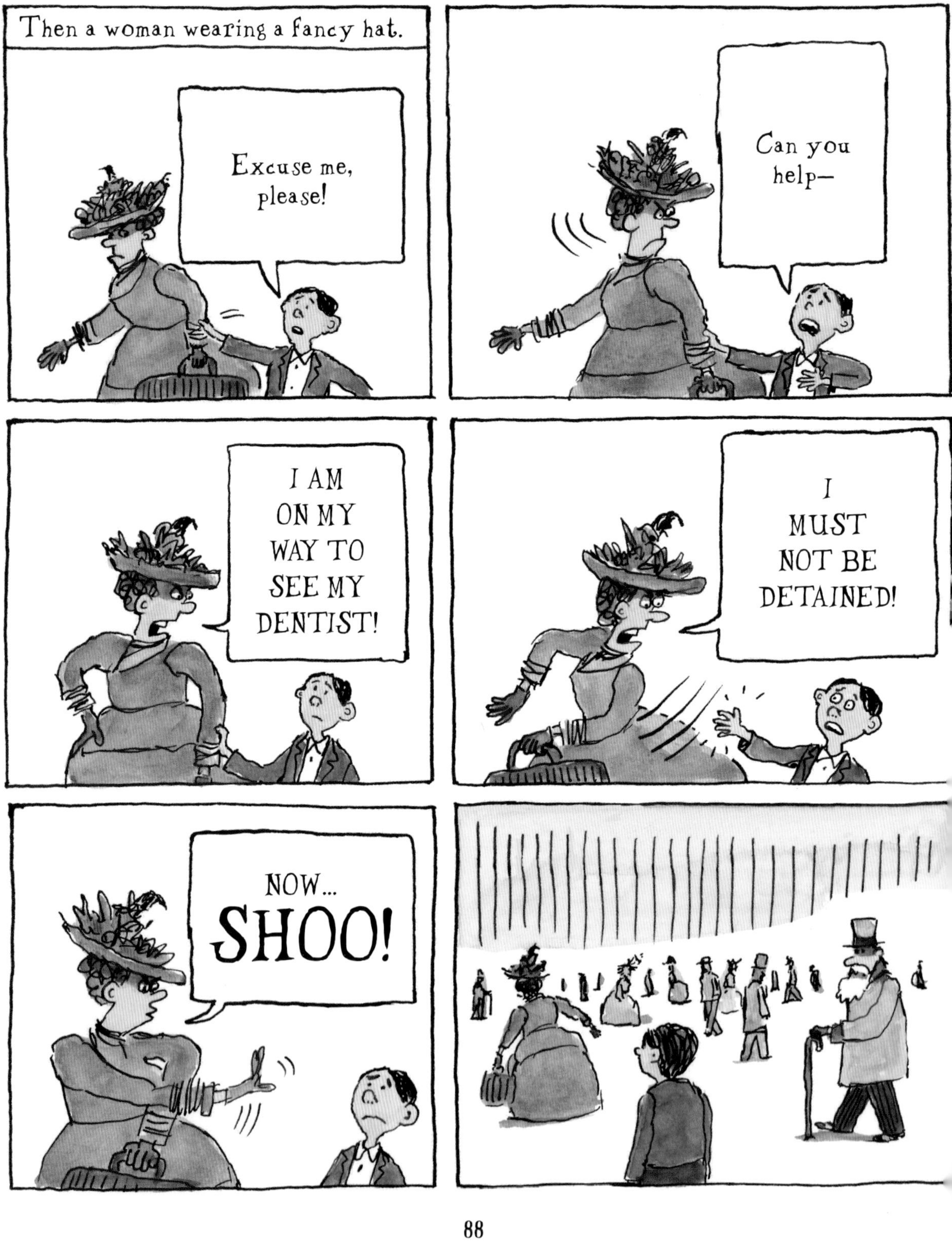
Then a woman wearing a fancy hat.
Excuse me, please!
Can you help—
I AM ON MY WAY TO SEE MY DENTIST!
I MUST NOT BE DETAINED!
NOW... SHOO!

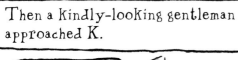
Then a kindly-looking gentleman approached K.

Excuse me, young fellow.

Yes?

Would you happen to know which tram goes to the fish market?

No, but I'm lost, can you...

Excuse me, my good man. Would you happen to know which tram goes to the fish market?

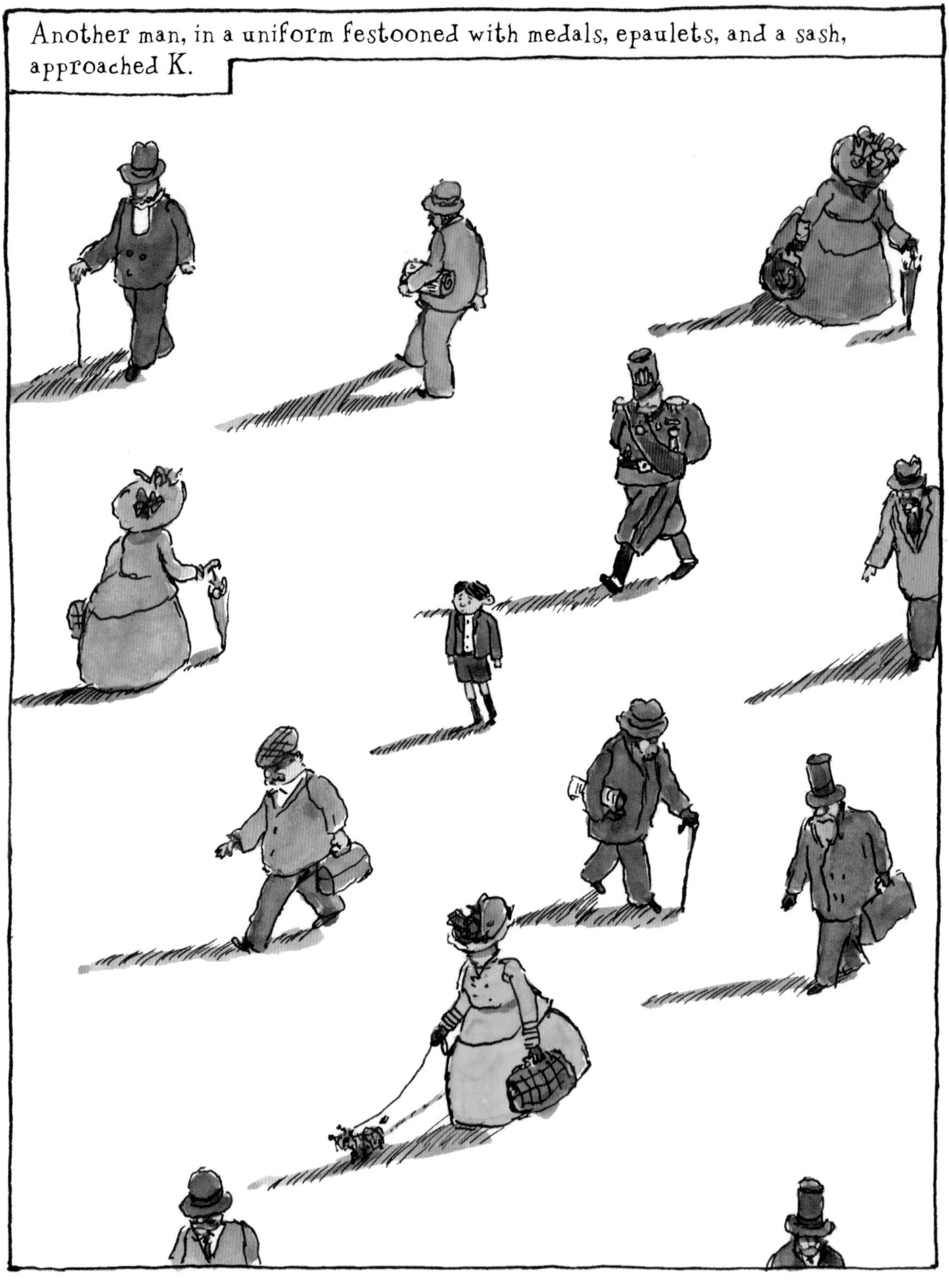
Another man, in a uniform festooned with medals, epaulets, and a sash, approached K.

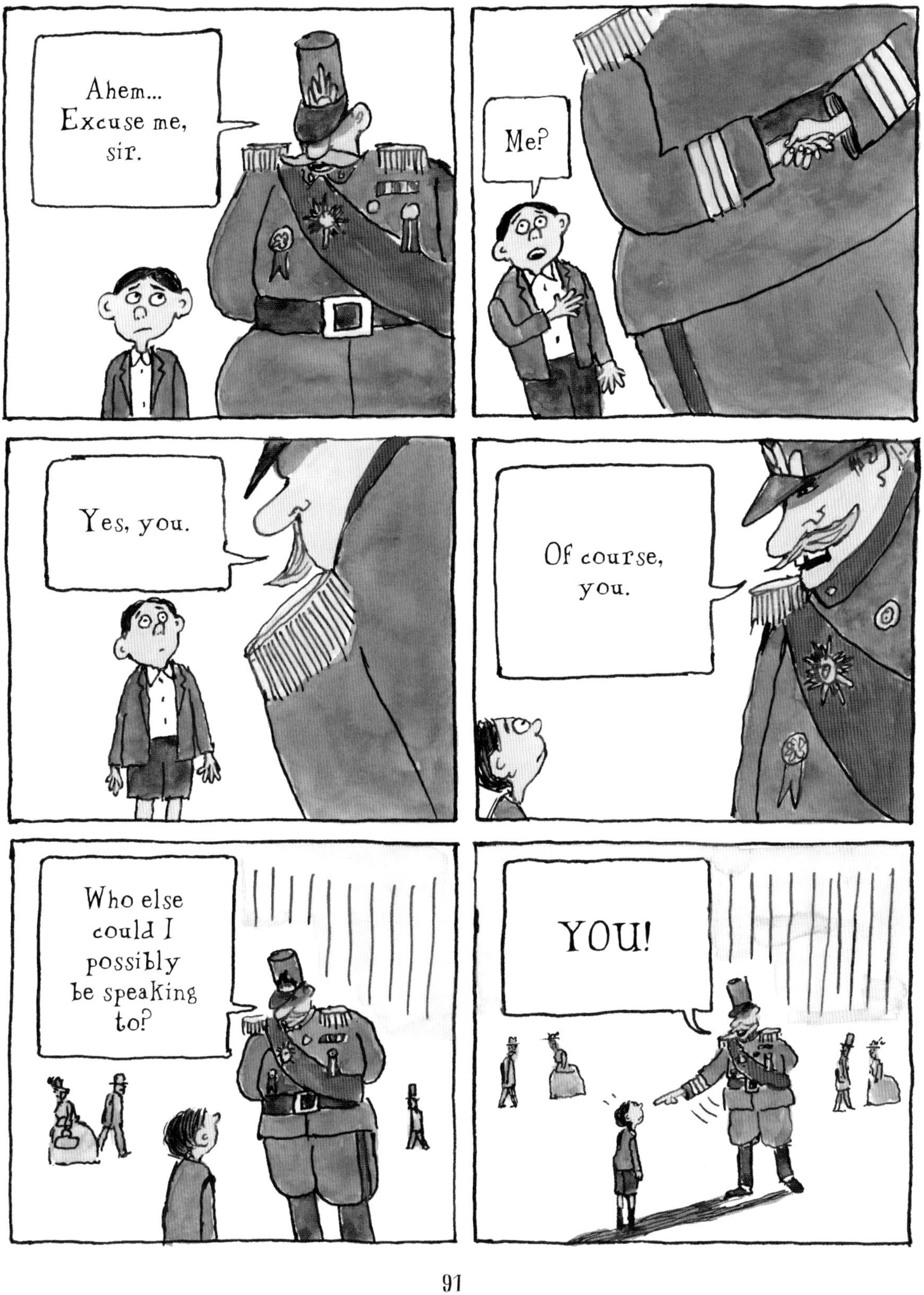
Ahem... Excuse me, sir.
Me?
Yes, you.
Of course, you.
Who else could I possibly be speaking to?
YOU!

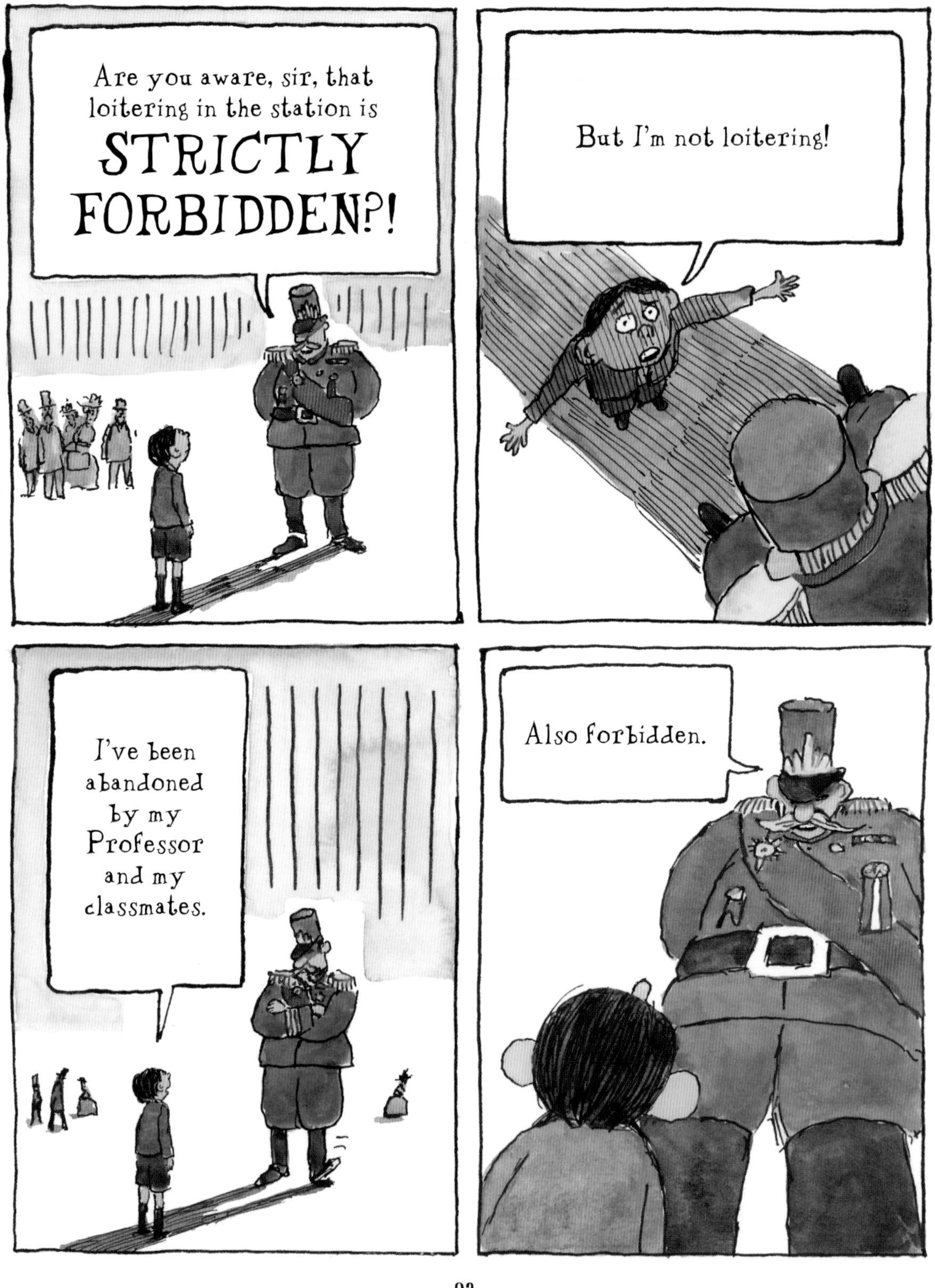
Are you aware, sir, that loitering in the station is STRICTLY FORBIDDEN?!
But I'm not loitering!
I've been abandoned by my Professor and my classmates.
Also forbidden.

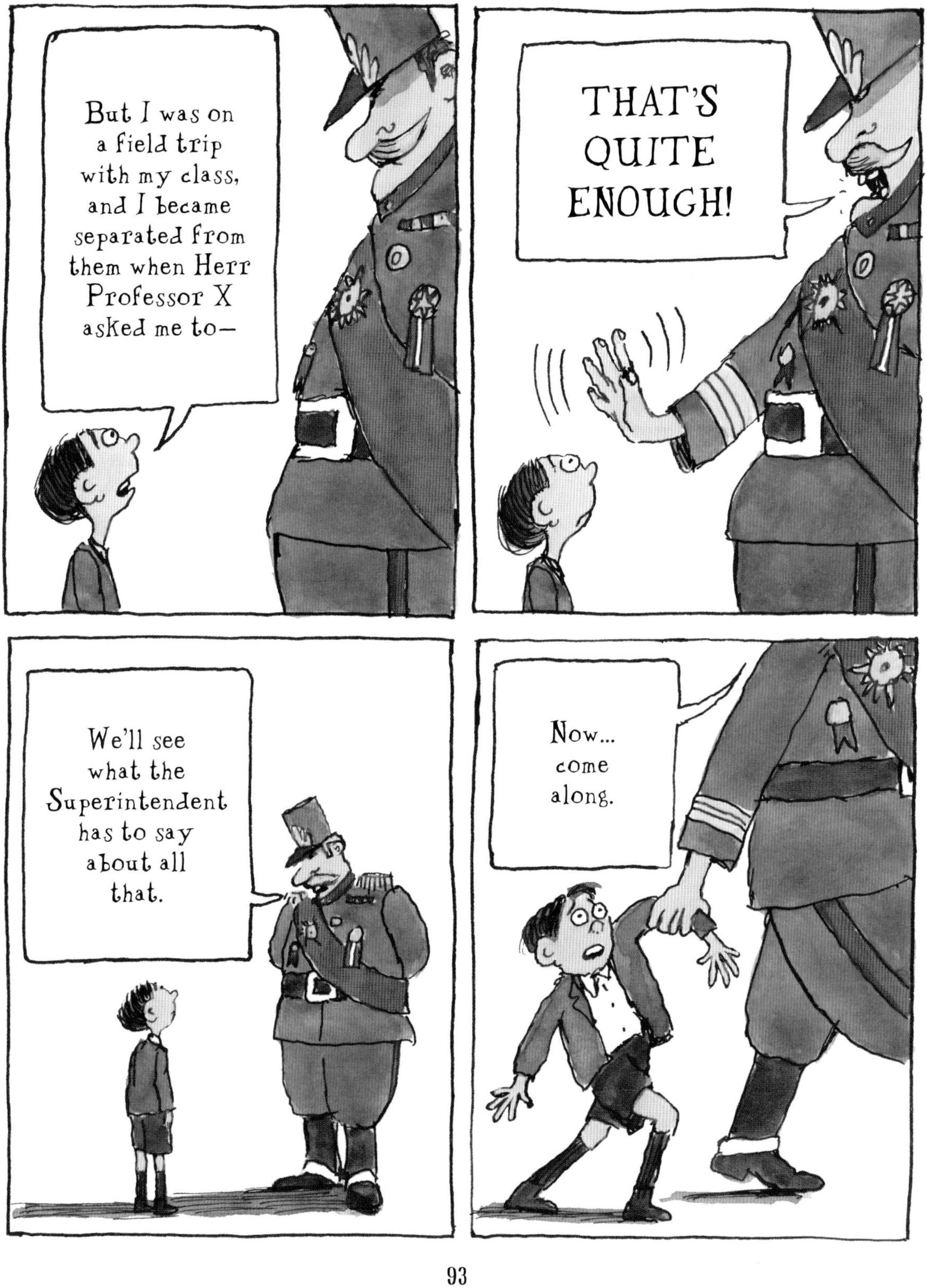
But I was on a field trip with my class, and I became separated from them when Herr Professor X asked me to—
THAT'S QUITE ENOUGH!
We'll see what the Superintendent has to say about all that.
Now... come along.

The Officer marched K through the station...

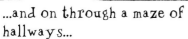

...and on through a maze of hallways...

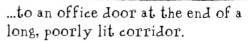

...to an office door at the end of a long, poorly lit corridor.

OFFICE OF THE SUPERINTENDENT

SUPERINTENDENT

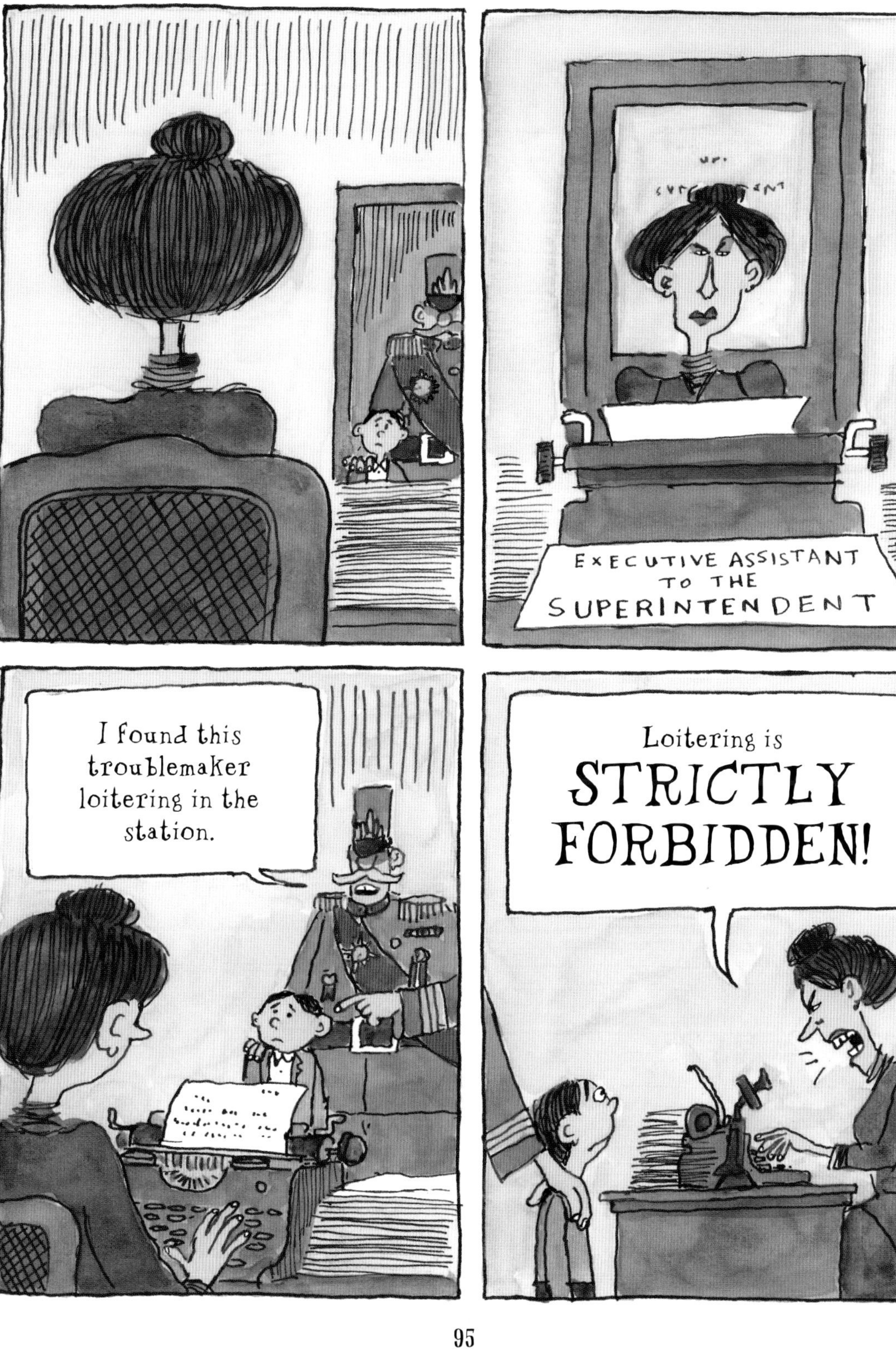
EXECUTIVE ASSISTANT TO THE SUPERINTENDENT
I found this troublemaker loitering in the station.
Loitering is STRICTLY FORBIDDEN!

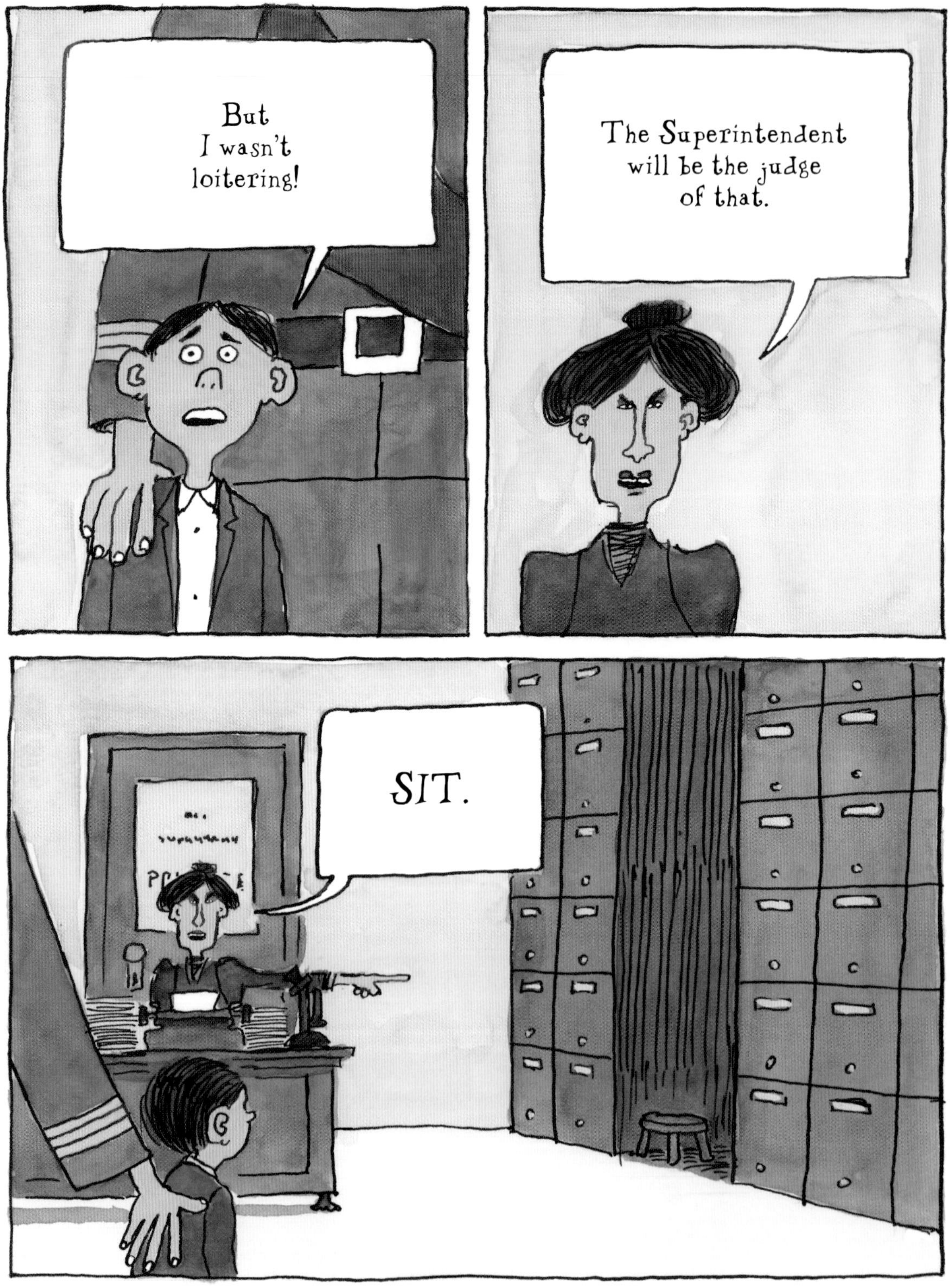
But I wasn't loitering!
The Superintendent will be the judge of that.
SIT.

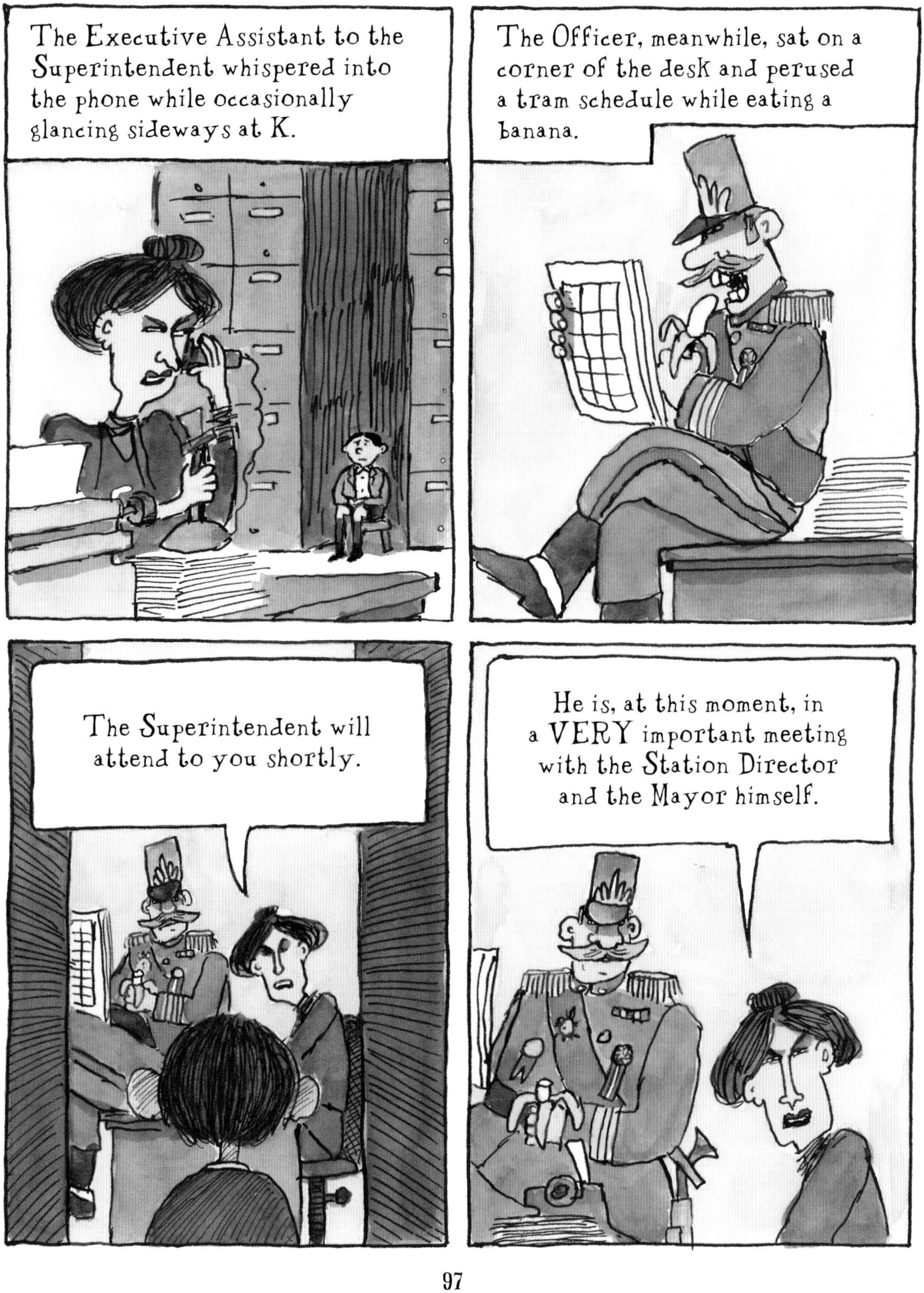
The Executive Assistant to the Superintendent whispered into the phone while occasionally glancing sideways at K.
The Officer, meanwhile, sat on a corner of the desk and perused a tram schedule while eating a banana.
The Superintendent will attend to you shortly.
He is, at this moment, in a VERY important meeting with the Station Director and the Mayor himself.

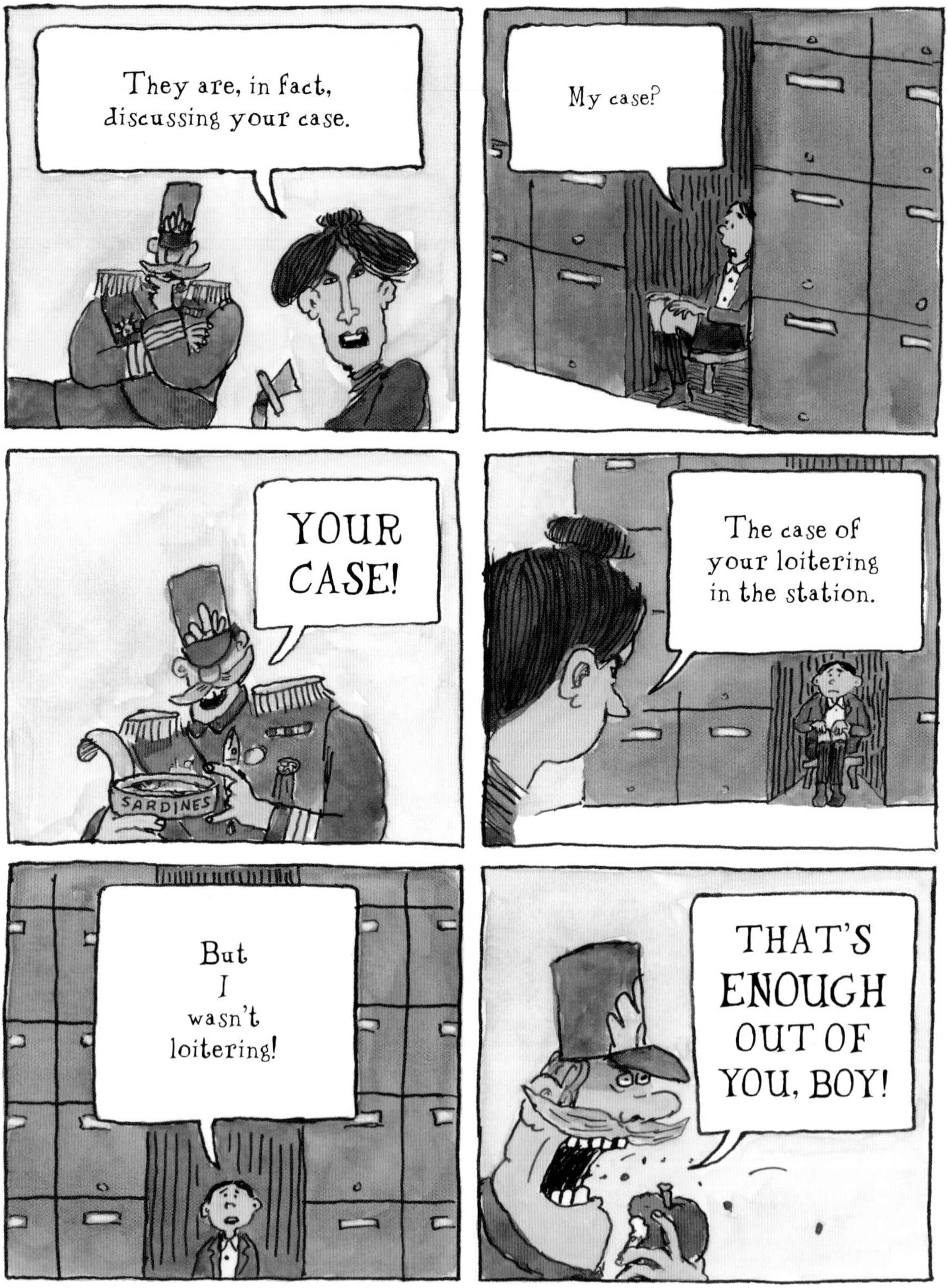
They are, in fact, discussing your case.
My case?
YOUR CASE!
SARDINES
The case of your loitering in the station.
But I wasn't loitering!
THAT'S ENOUGH OUT OF YOU, BOY!

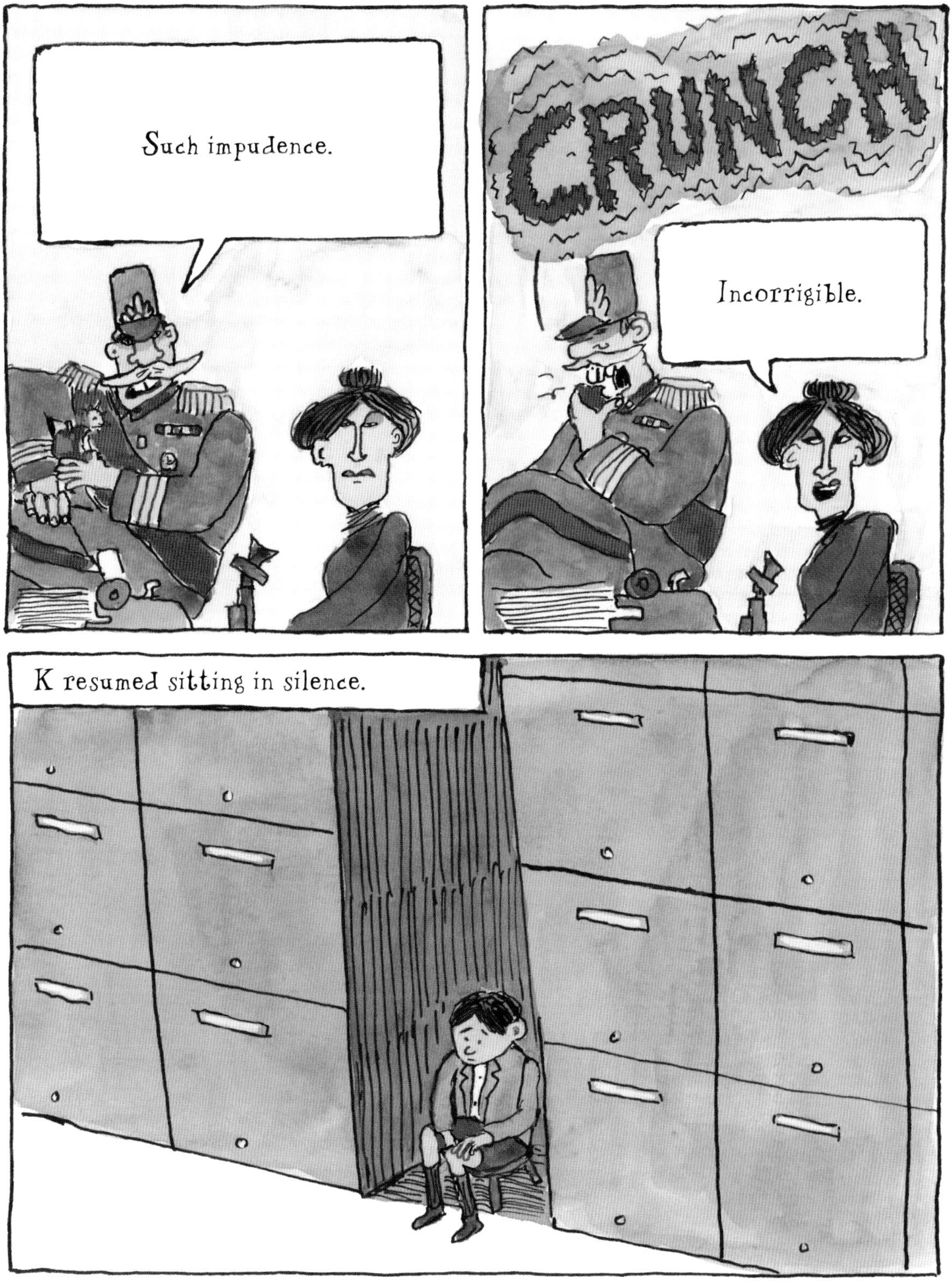
Such impudence.
CRUNCH
Incorrigible.
K resumed sitting in silence.

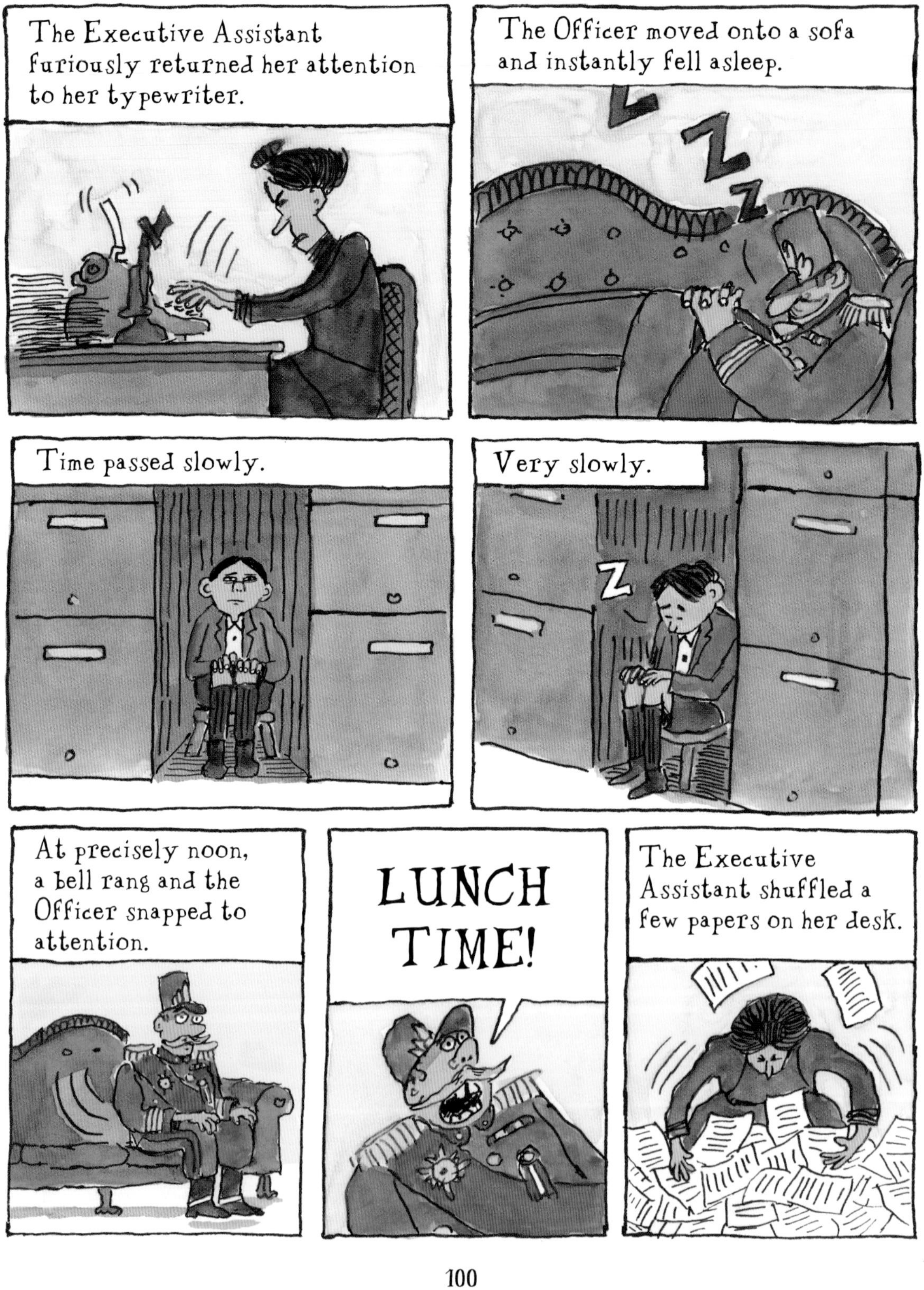
The Executive Assistant furiously returned her attention to her typewriter.
The Officer moved onto a sofa and instantly fell asleep.
Z
Z
Z
Time passed slowly.
Very slowly.
Z
At precisely noon, a bell rang and the Officer snapped to attention.
LUNCH TIME!
The Executive Assistant shuffled a few papers on her desk.

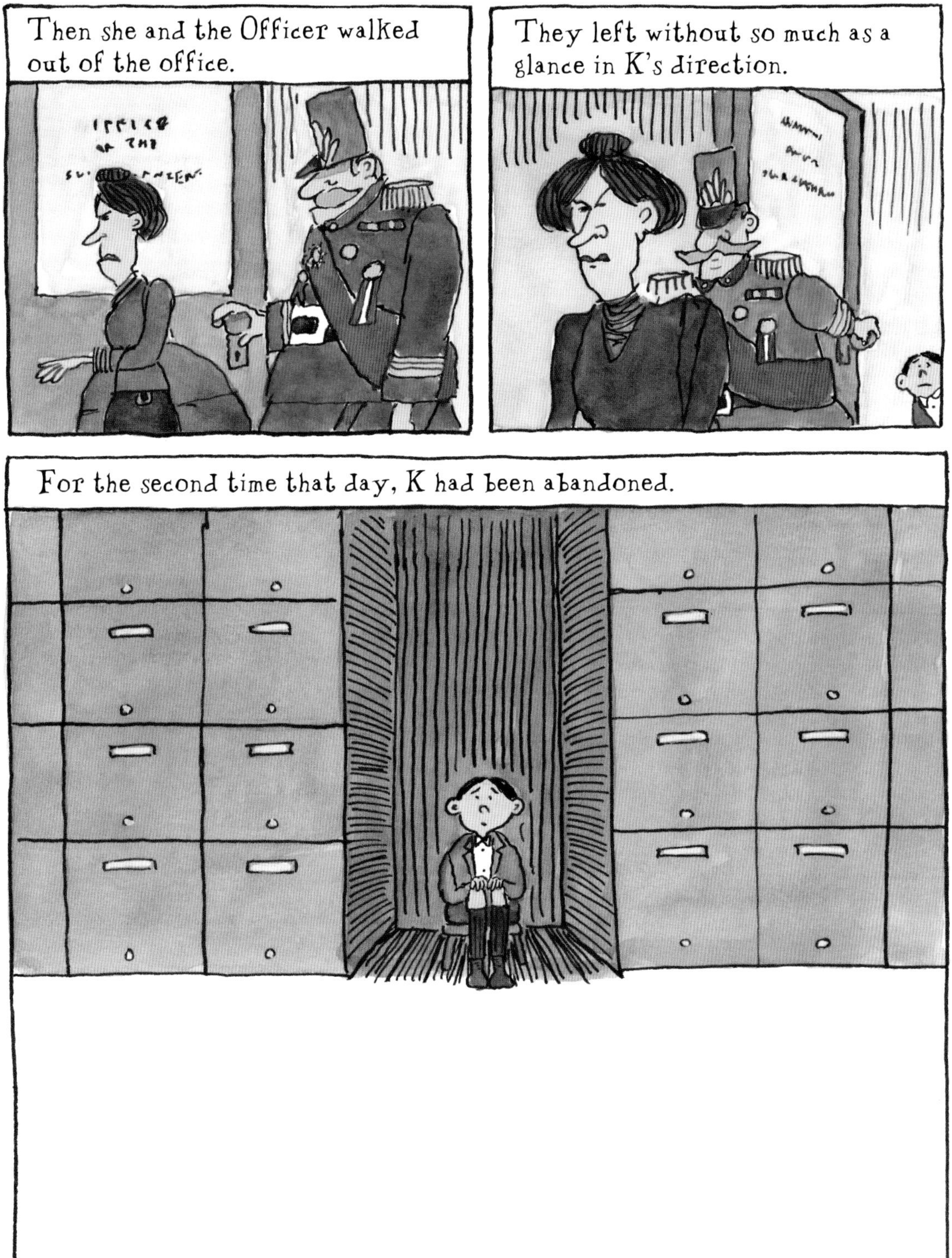
Then she and the Officer walked out of the office.
They left without so much as a glance in K's direction.
For the second time that day, K had been abandoned.

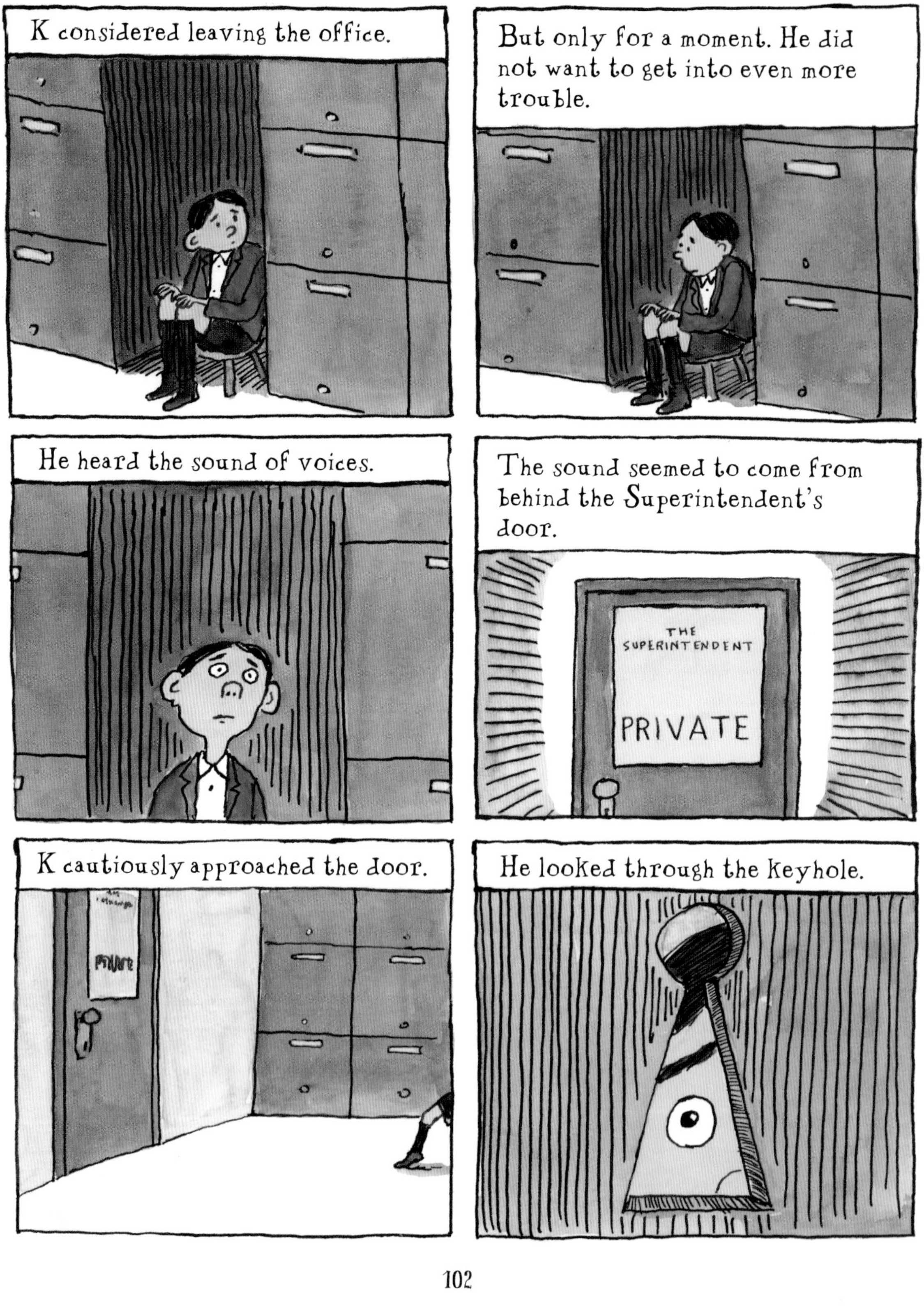
K considered leaving the office.
But only for a moment. He did not want to get into even more trouble.
He heard the sound of voices.
The sound seemed to come from behind the Superintendent's door.
THE SUPERINTENDENT
PRIVATE
K cautiously approached the door.
He looked through the keyhole.

K saw three men sitting at a large desk.

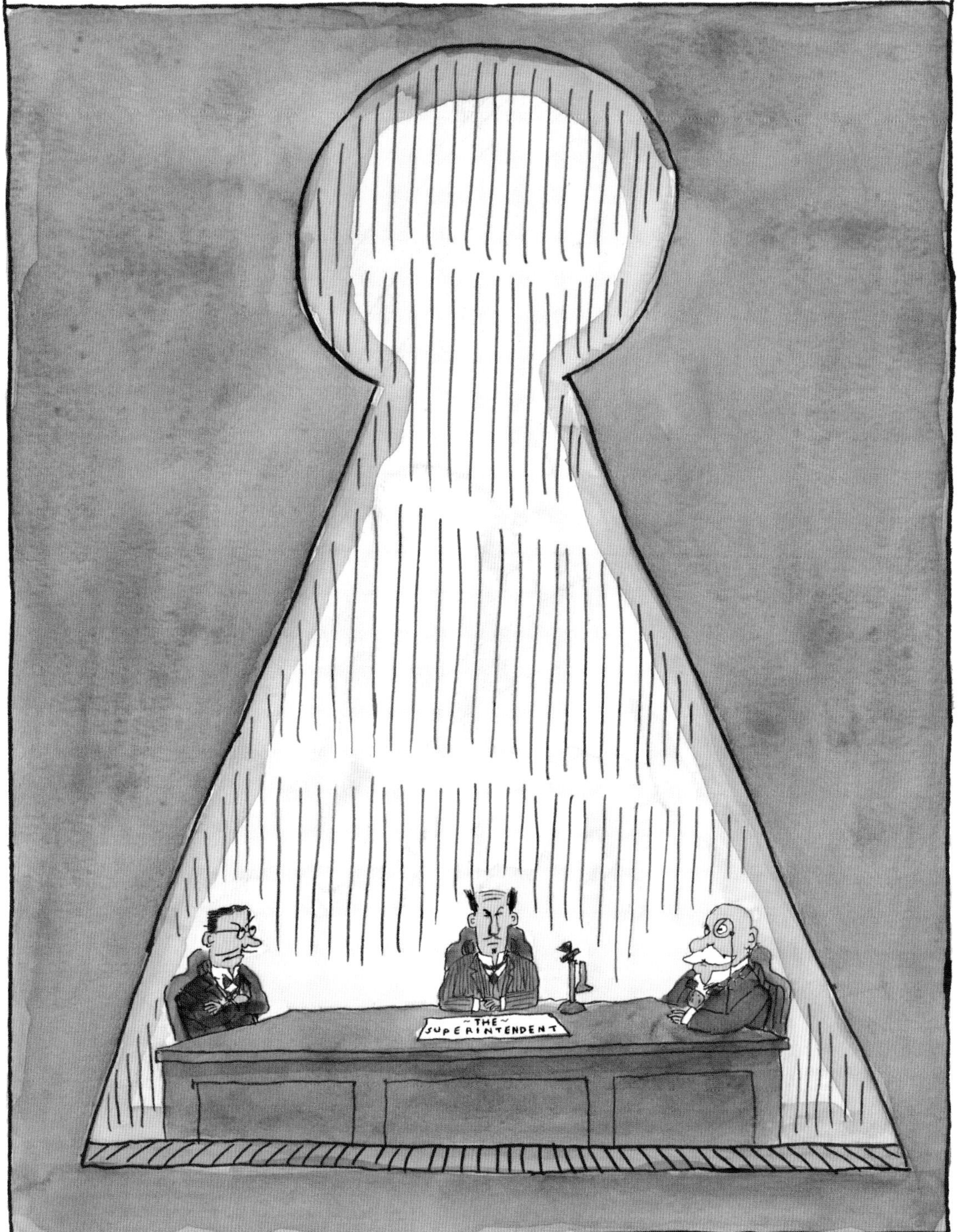
~THE~
SUPERINTENDENT

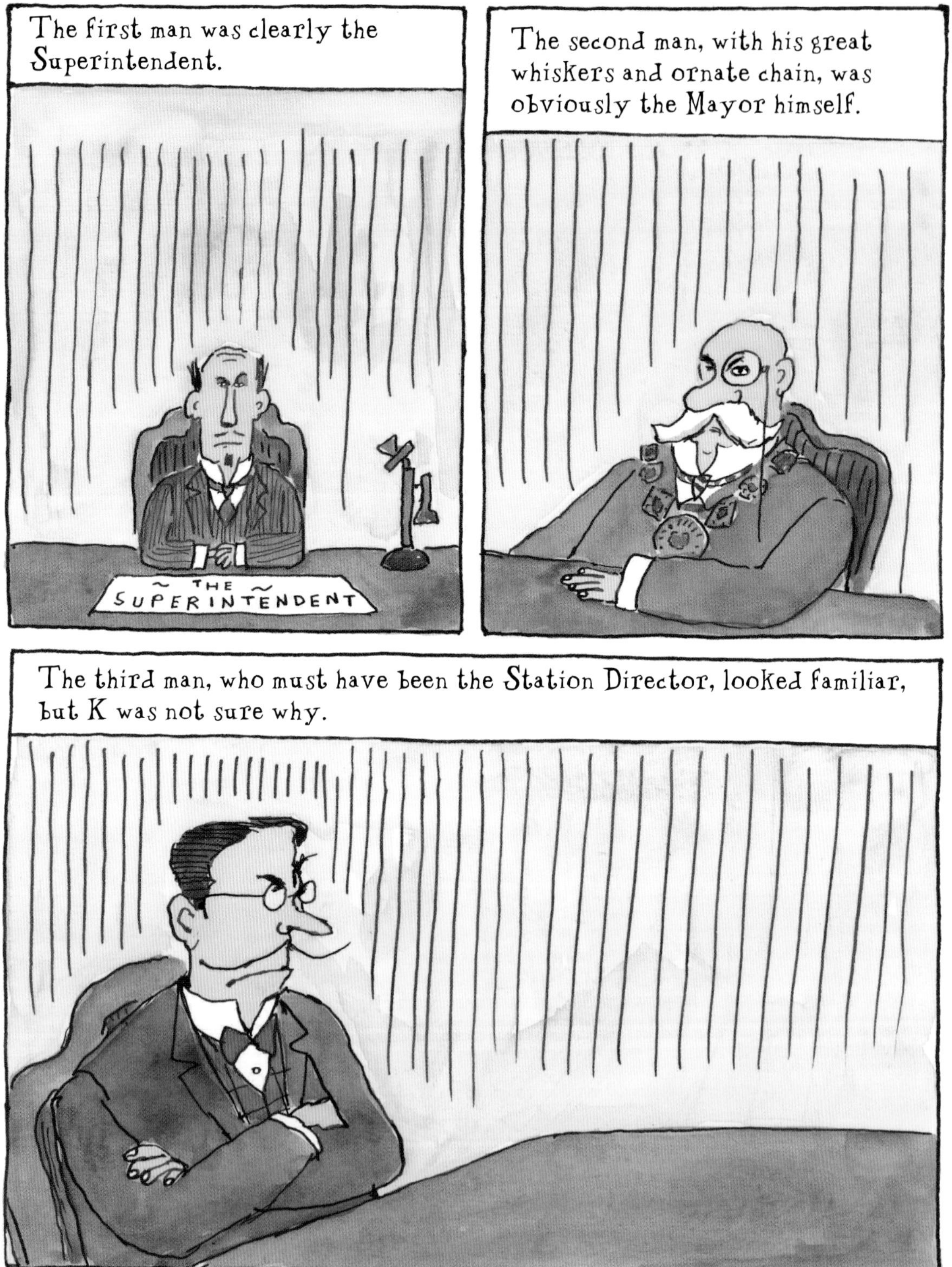
The first man was clearly the Superintendent.
~ THE ~ SUPERINTENDENT
The second man, with his great whiskers and ornate chain, was obviously the Mayor himself.
The third man, who must have been the Station Director, looked familiar, but K was not sure why.

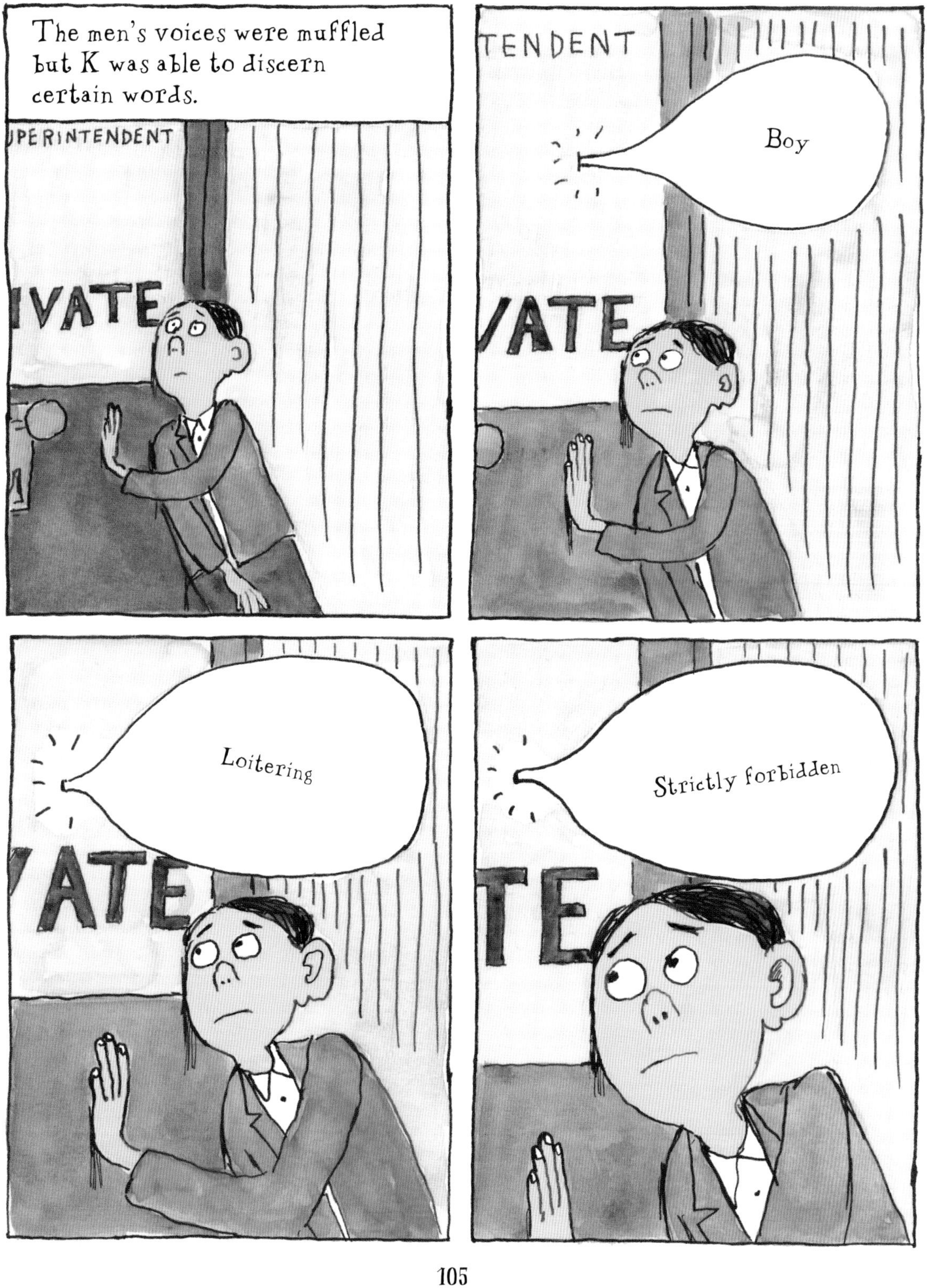
The men's voices were muffled but K was able to discern certain words.
UPERINTENDENT
IVATE
TENDENT
Boy
VATE
Loitering
VATE
Strictly forbidden
TE

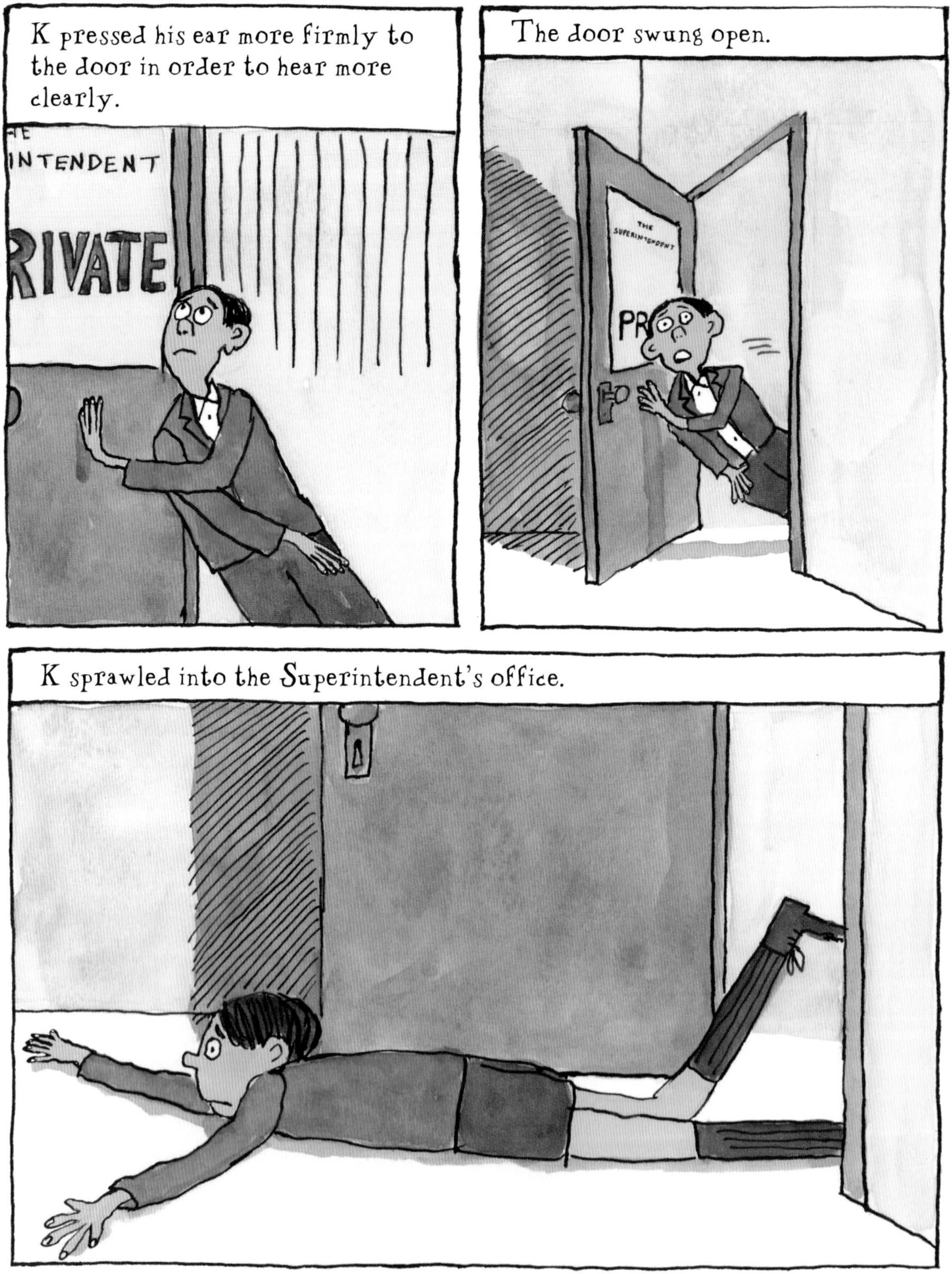
K pressed his ear more firmly to the door in order to hear more clearly.
INTENDENT
RIVATE
The door swung open.
PR
K sprawled into the Superintendent's office.

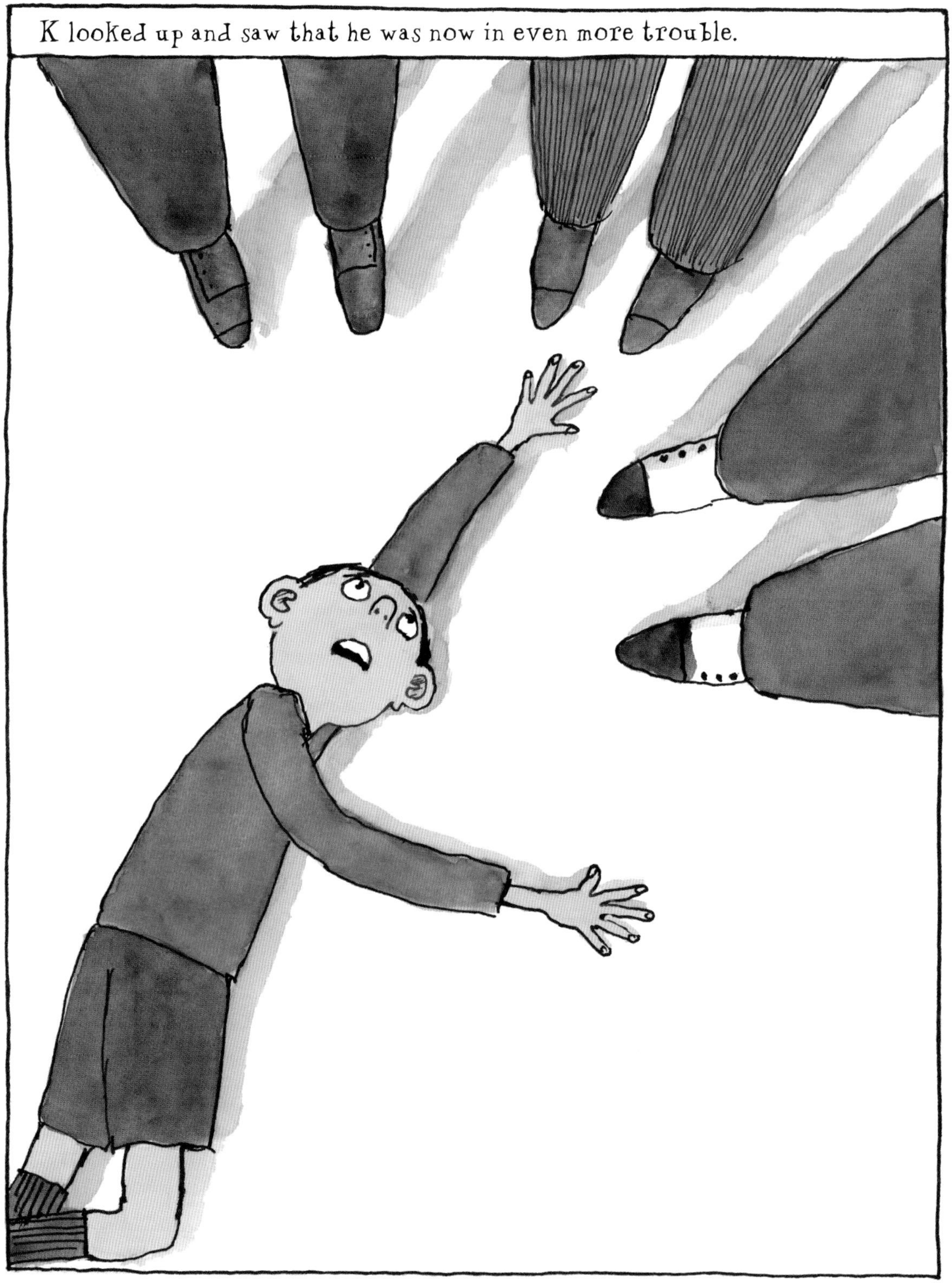
K looked up and saw that he was now in even more trouble.

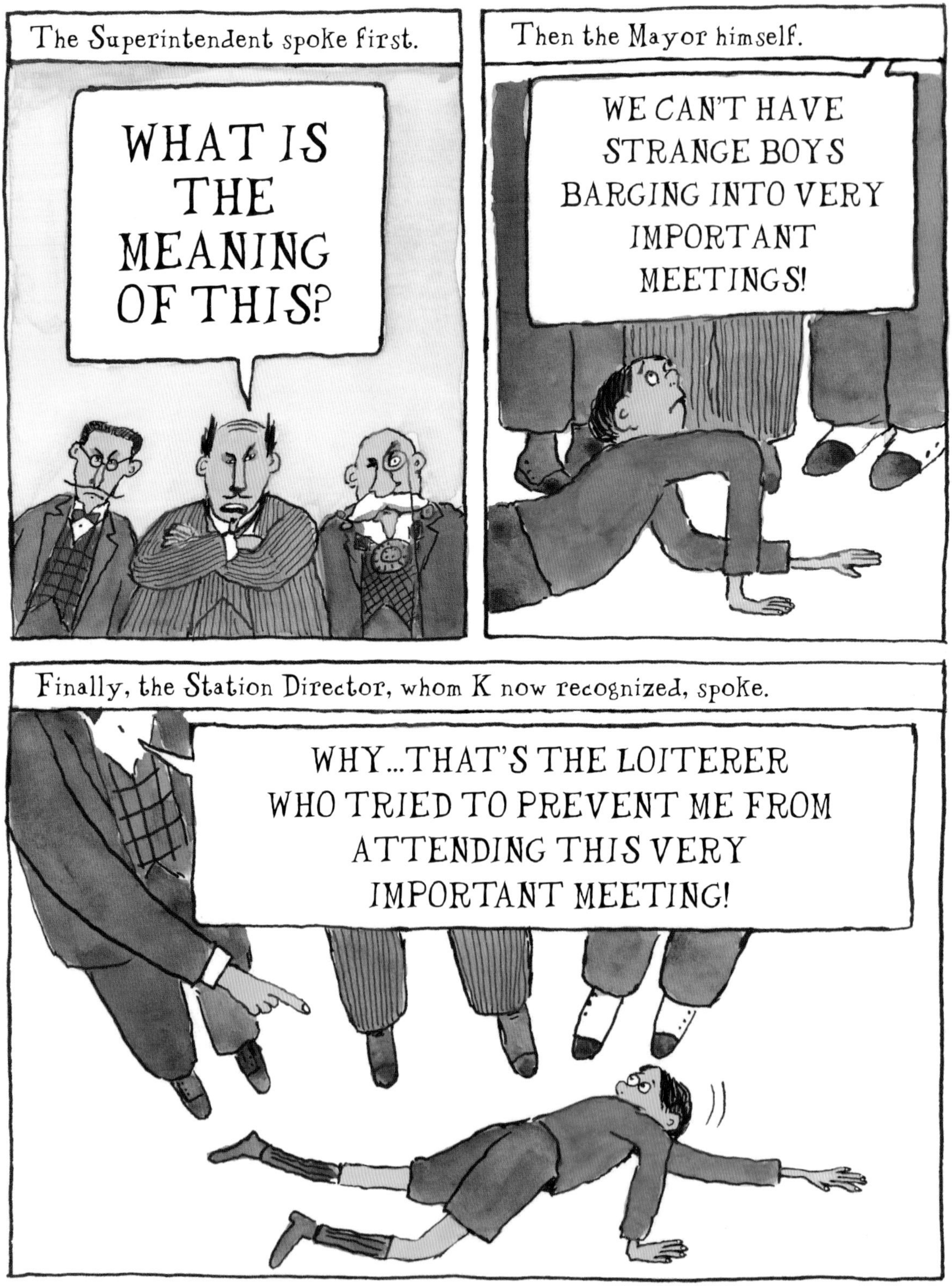
The Superintendent spoke first.
WHAT IS THE MEANING OF THIS?
Then the Mayor himself.
WE CAN'T HAVE STRANGE BOYS BARGING INTO VERY IMPORTANT MEETINGS!
Finally, the Station Director, whom K now recognized, spoke.
WHY...THAT'S THE LOITERER WHO TRIED TO PREVENT ME FROM ATTENDING THIS VERY IMPORTANT MEETING!

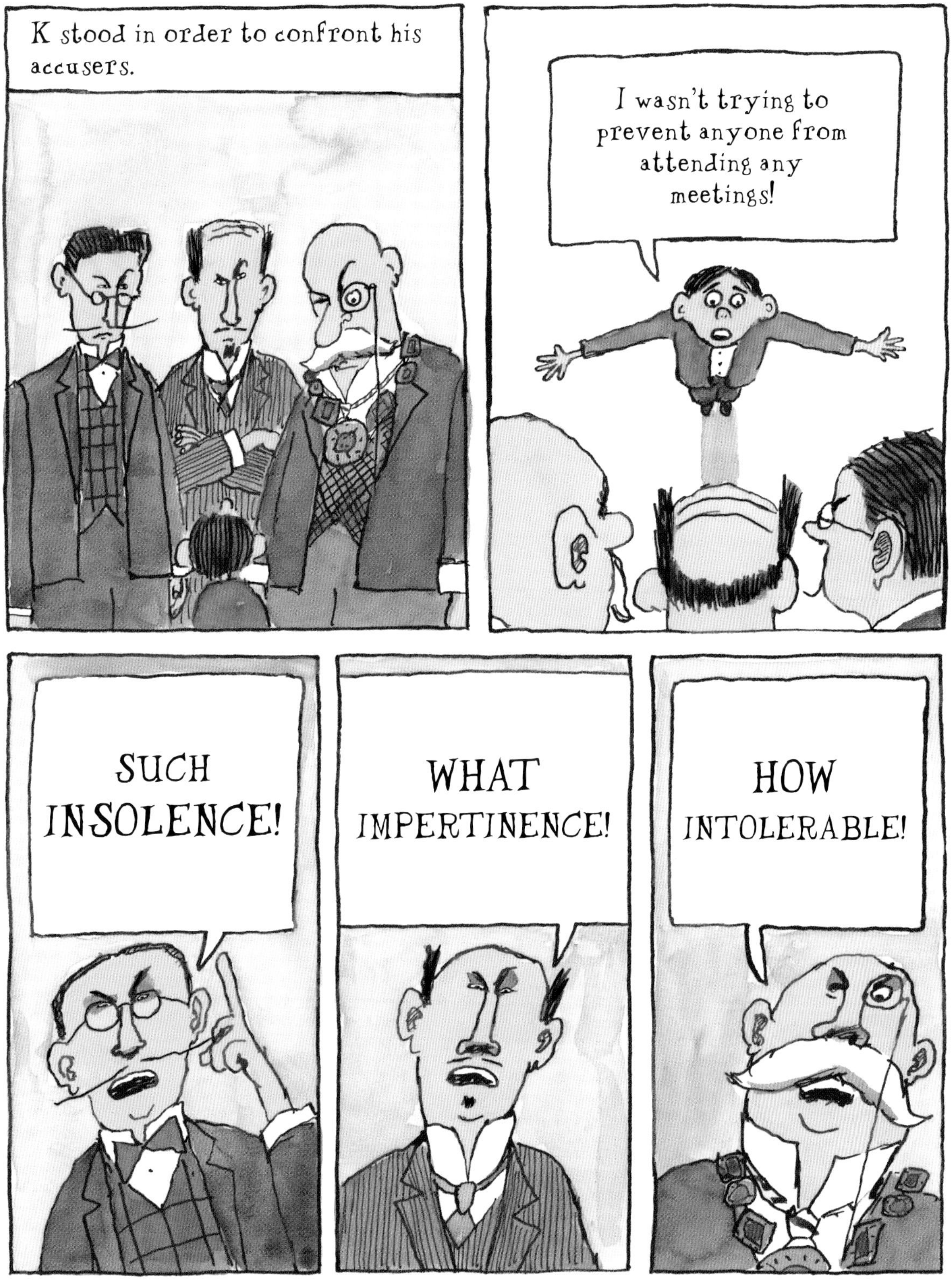
K stood in order to confront his accusers.
I wasn't trying to prevent anyone from attending any meetings!
SUCH INSOLENCE!
WHAT IMPERTINENCE!
HOW INTOLERABLE!

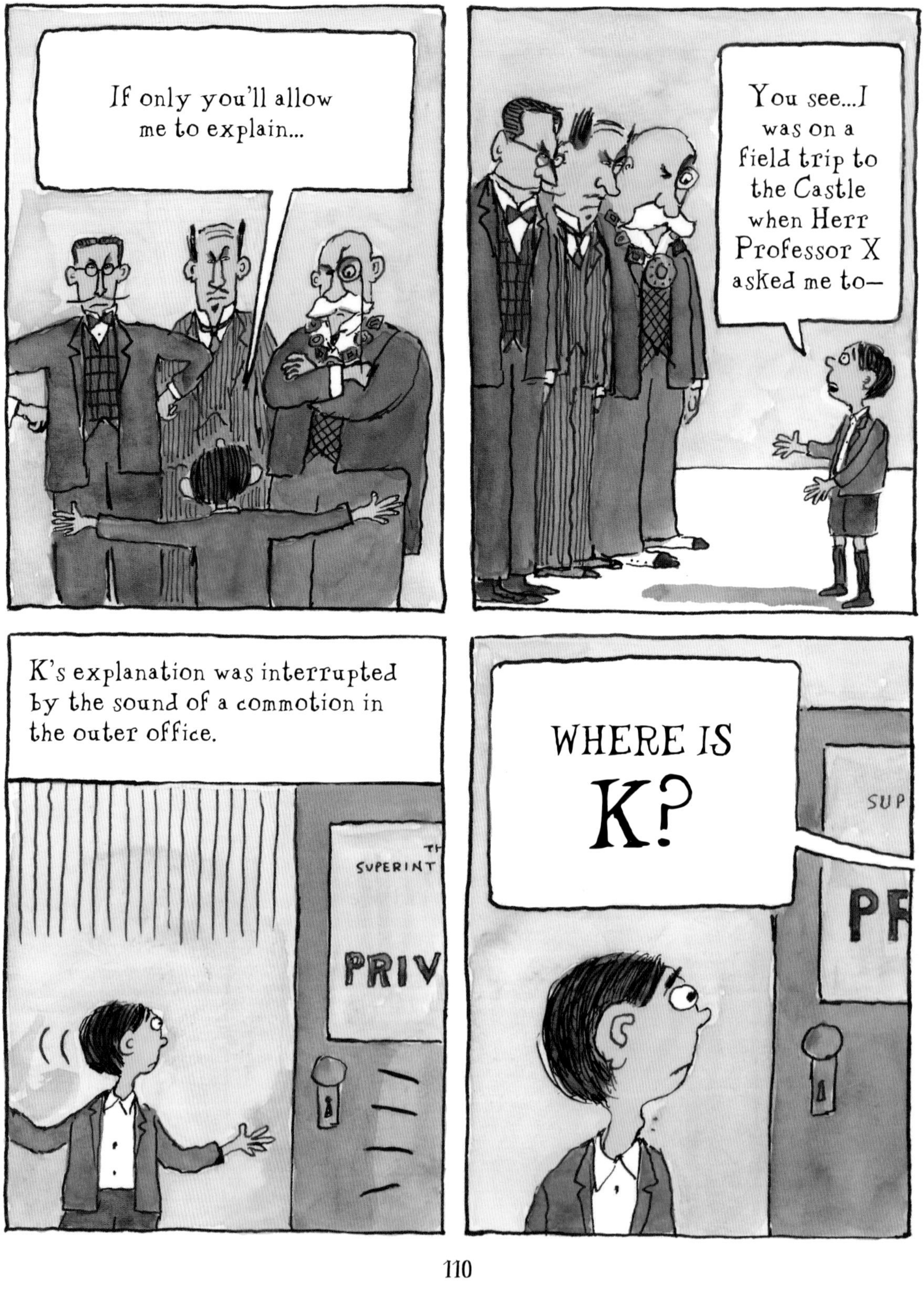
If only you'll allow me to explain...
You see...I was on a field trip to the Castle when Herr Professor X asked me to—
K's explanation was interrupted by the sound of a commotion in the outer office.
SUPERINT
PRIV
WHERE IS K?
SUP
PR

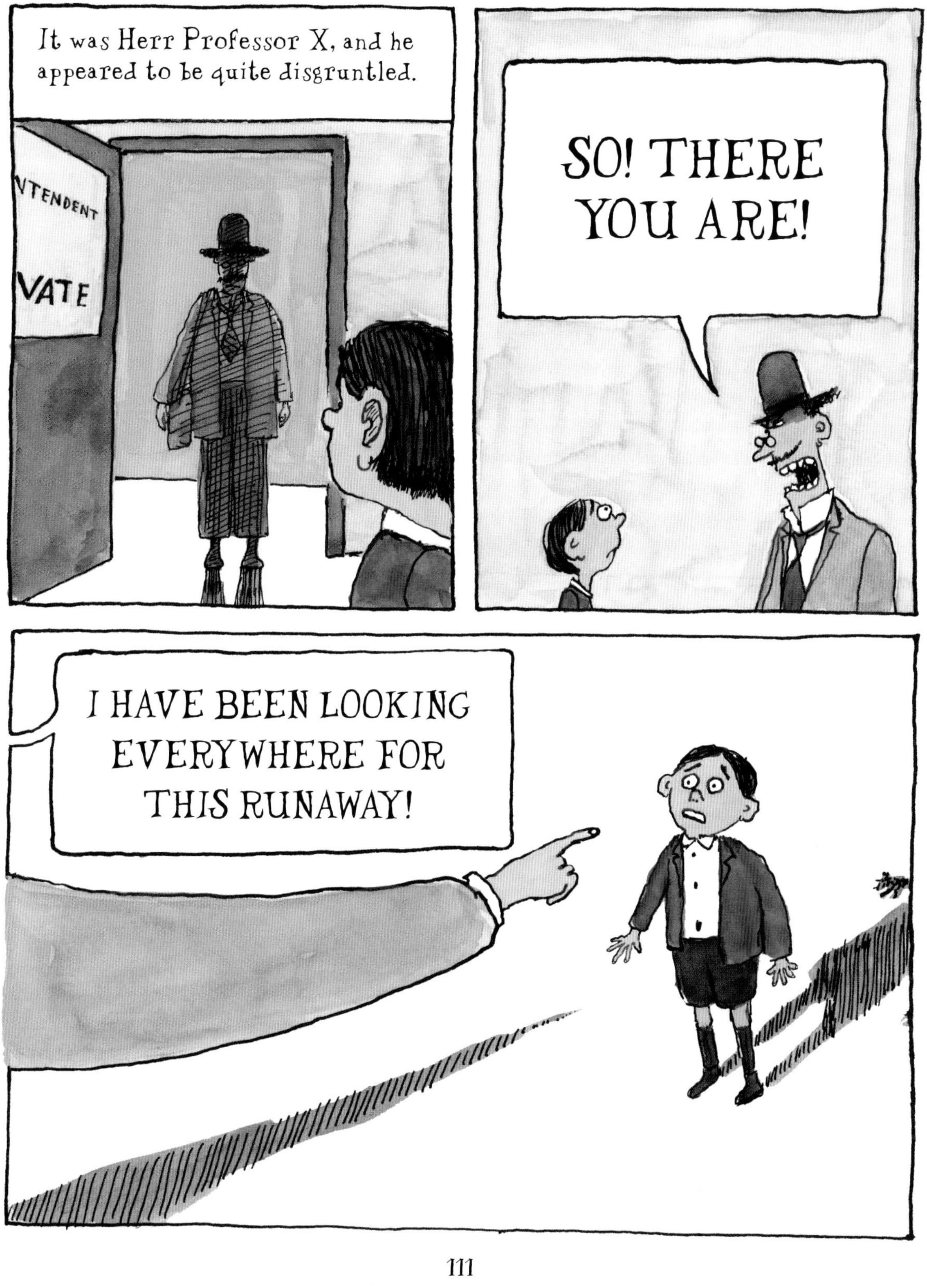
It was Herr Professor X, and he appeared to be quite disgruntled.
NTENDENT
VATE
SO! THERE YOU ARE!
I HAVE BEEN LOOKING EVERYWHERE FOR THIS RUNAWAY!

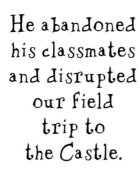

He abandoned his classmates and disrupted our field trip to the Castle.

Well...he was found loitering in the tram station.

Then he barged into our VERY IMPORTANT MEETING.

He is clearly up to no good, this one.

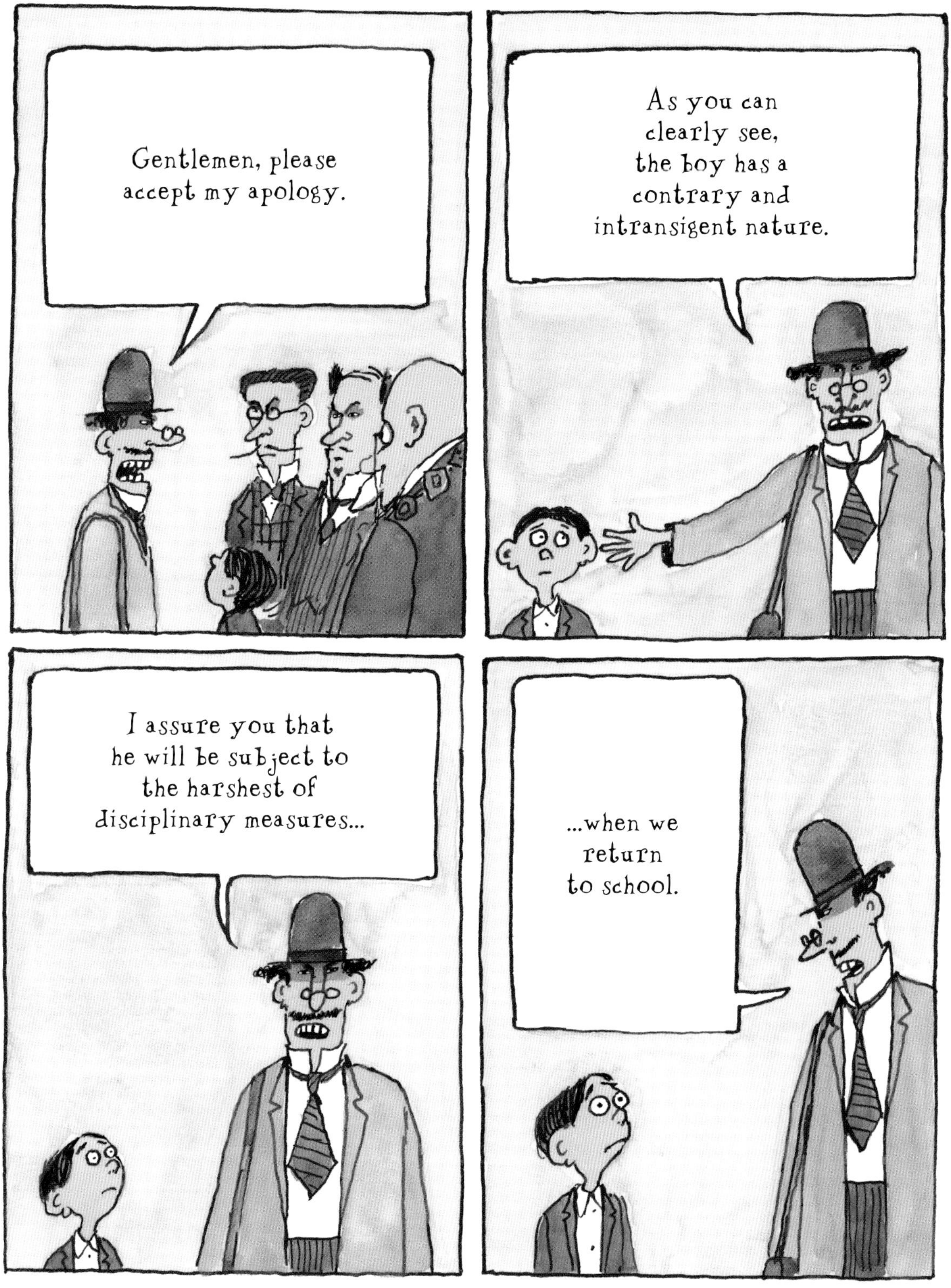
Gentlemen, please accept my apology.
As you can clearly see, the boy has a contrary and intransigent nature.
I assure you that he will be subject to the harshest of disciplinary measures...
...when we return to school.

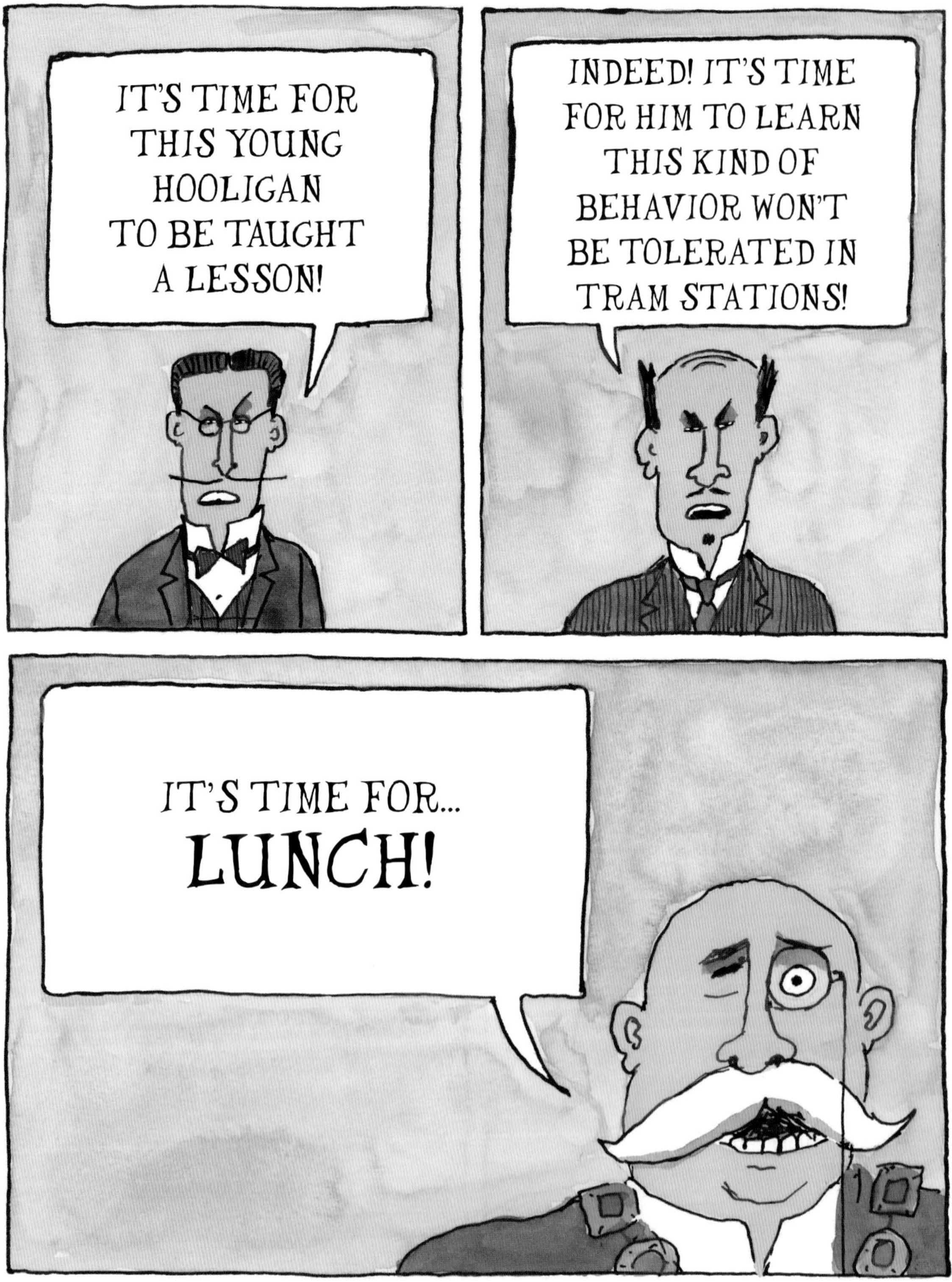
IT'S TIME FOR THIS YOUNG HOOLIGAN TO BE TAUGHT A LESSON!
INDEED! IT'S TIME FOR HIM TO LEARN THIS KIND OF BEHAVIOR WON'T BE TOLERATED IN TRAM STATIONS!
IT'S TIME FOR... LUNCH!

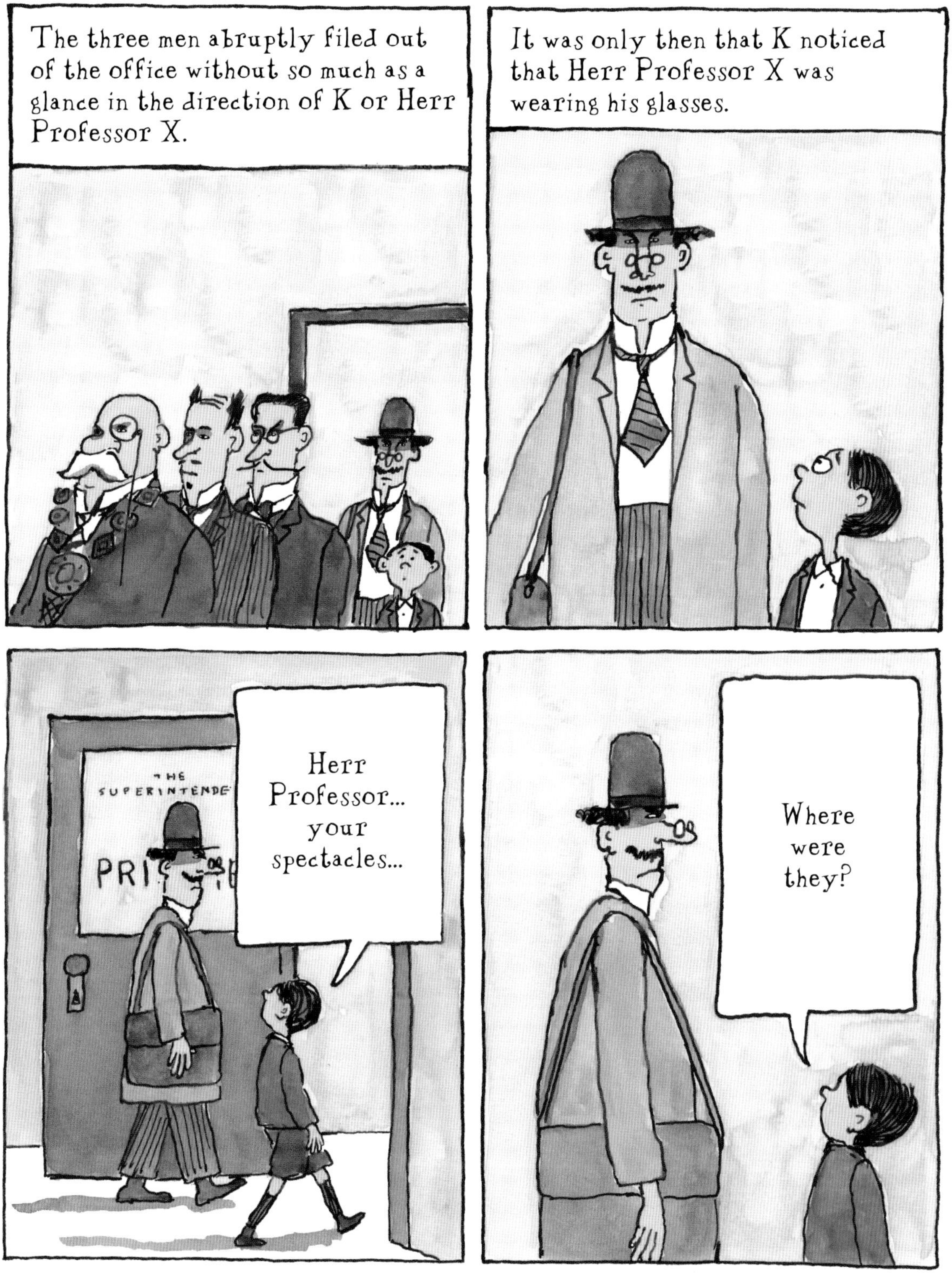
The three men abruptly filed out of the office without so much as a glance in the direction of K or Herr Professor X.
It was only then that K noticed that Herr Professor X was wearing his glasses.
Herr Professor... your spectacles...
Where were they?

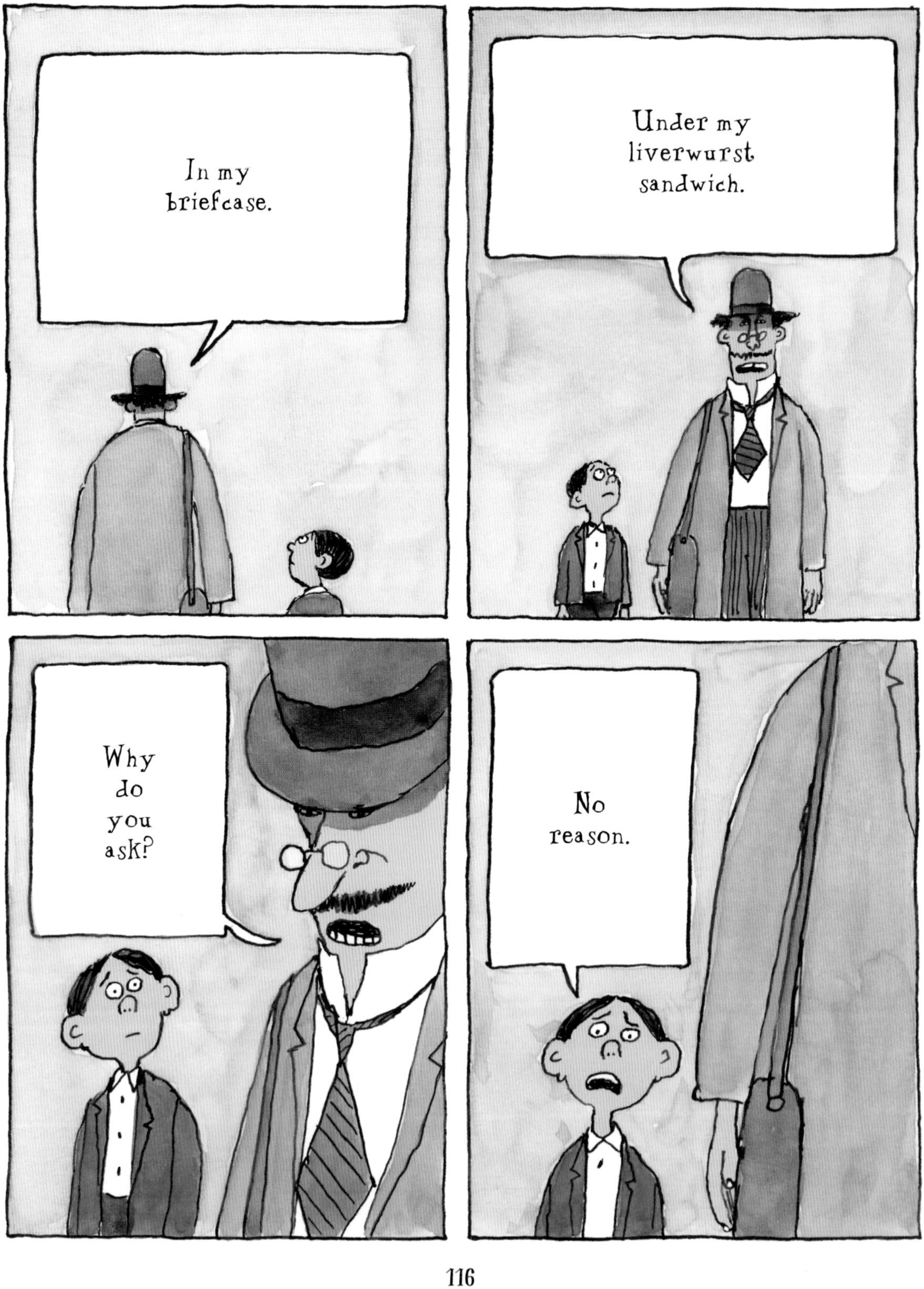
In my briefcase.
Under my liverwurst sandwich.
Why do you ask?
No reason.

K IS SENT ON AN ERRAND

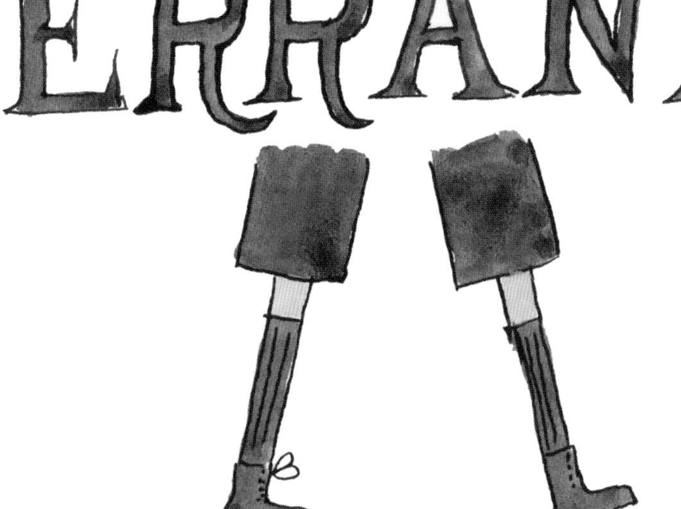

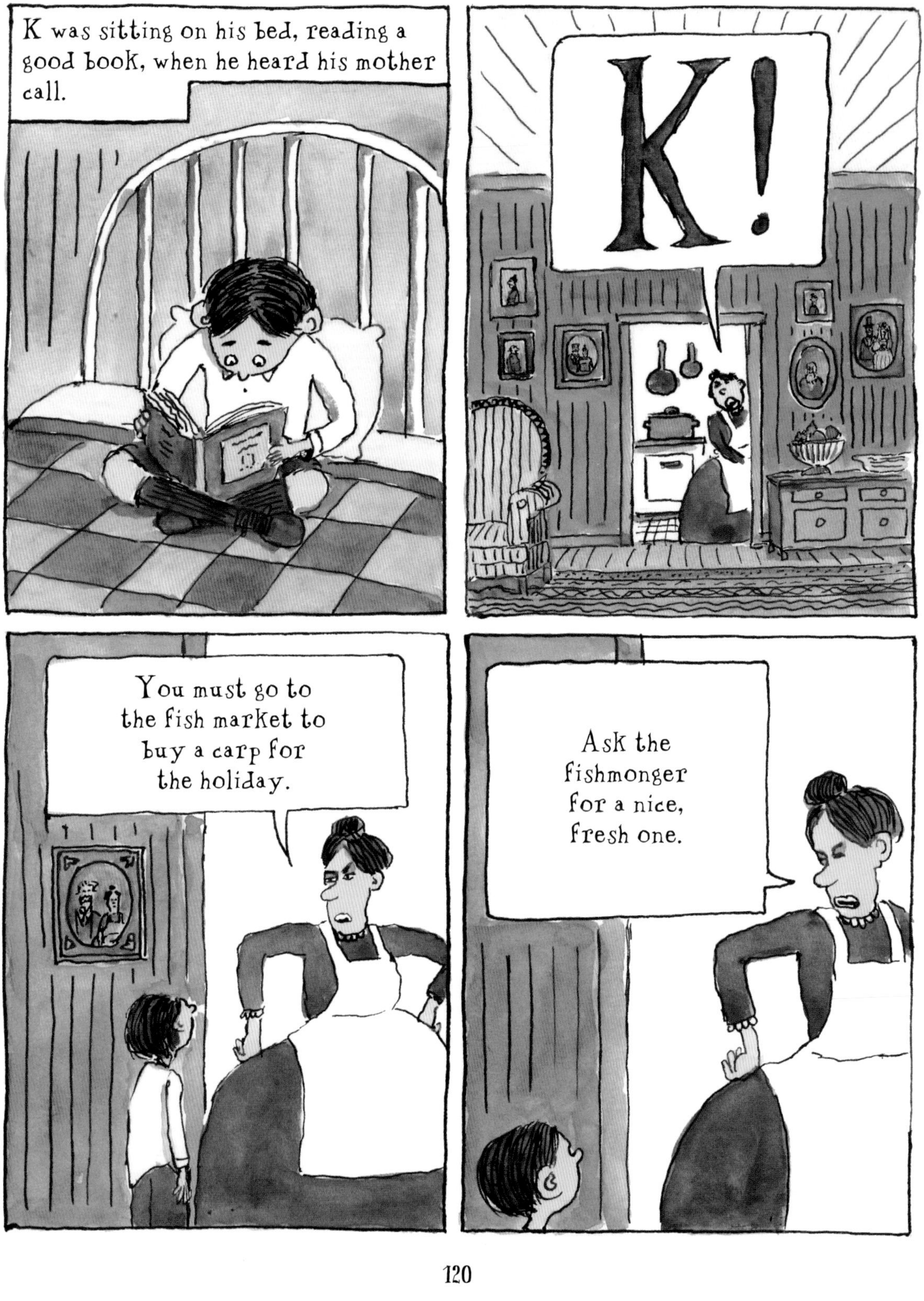
K was sitting on his bed, reading a good book, when he heard his mother call.
K!
You must go to the fish market to buy a carp for the holiday.
Ask the fishmonger for a nice, fresh one.

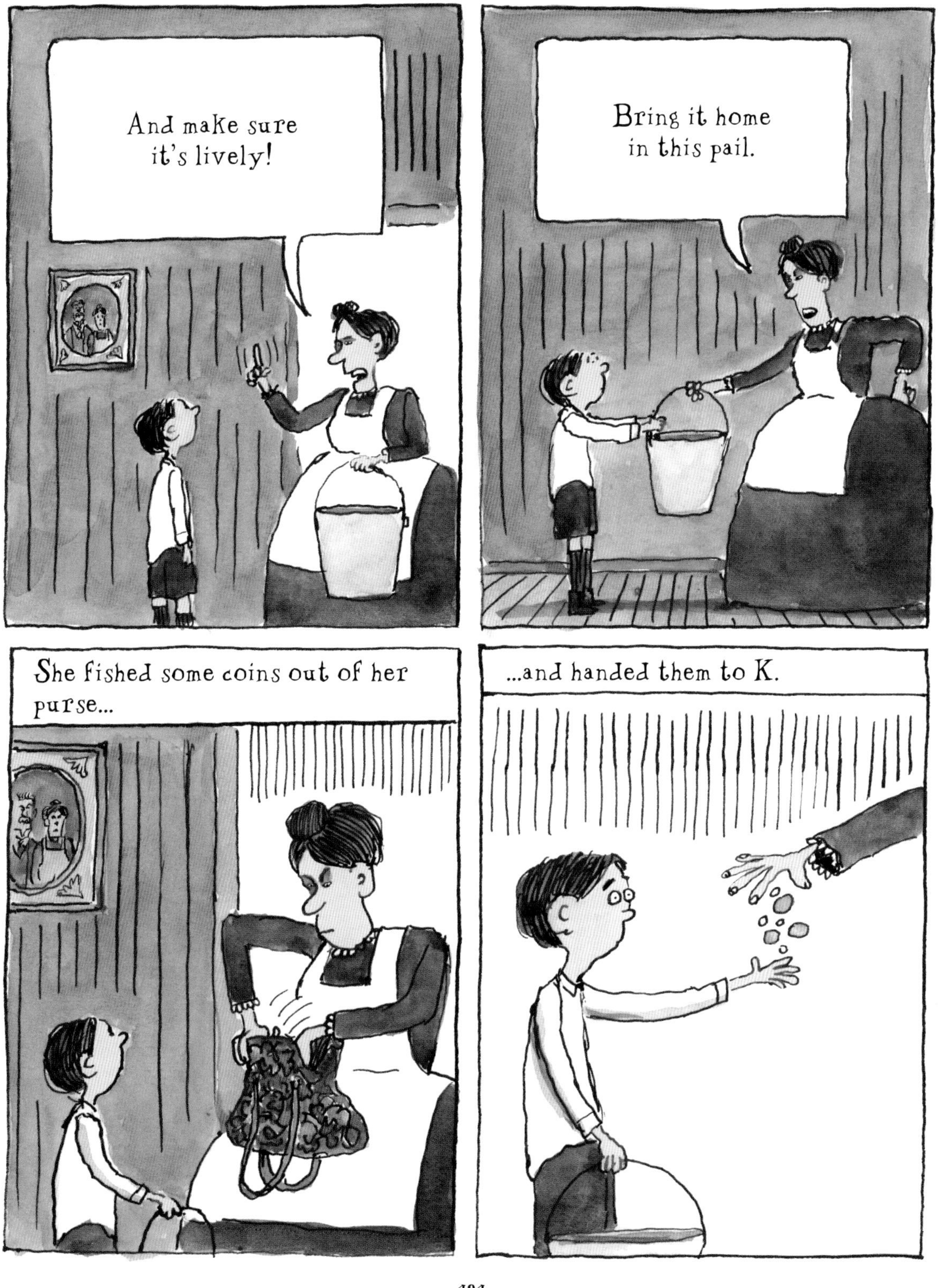
And make sure it's lively!
Bring it home in this pail.
She fished some coins out of her purse...
...and handed them to K.

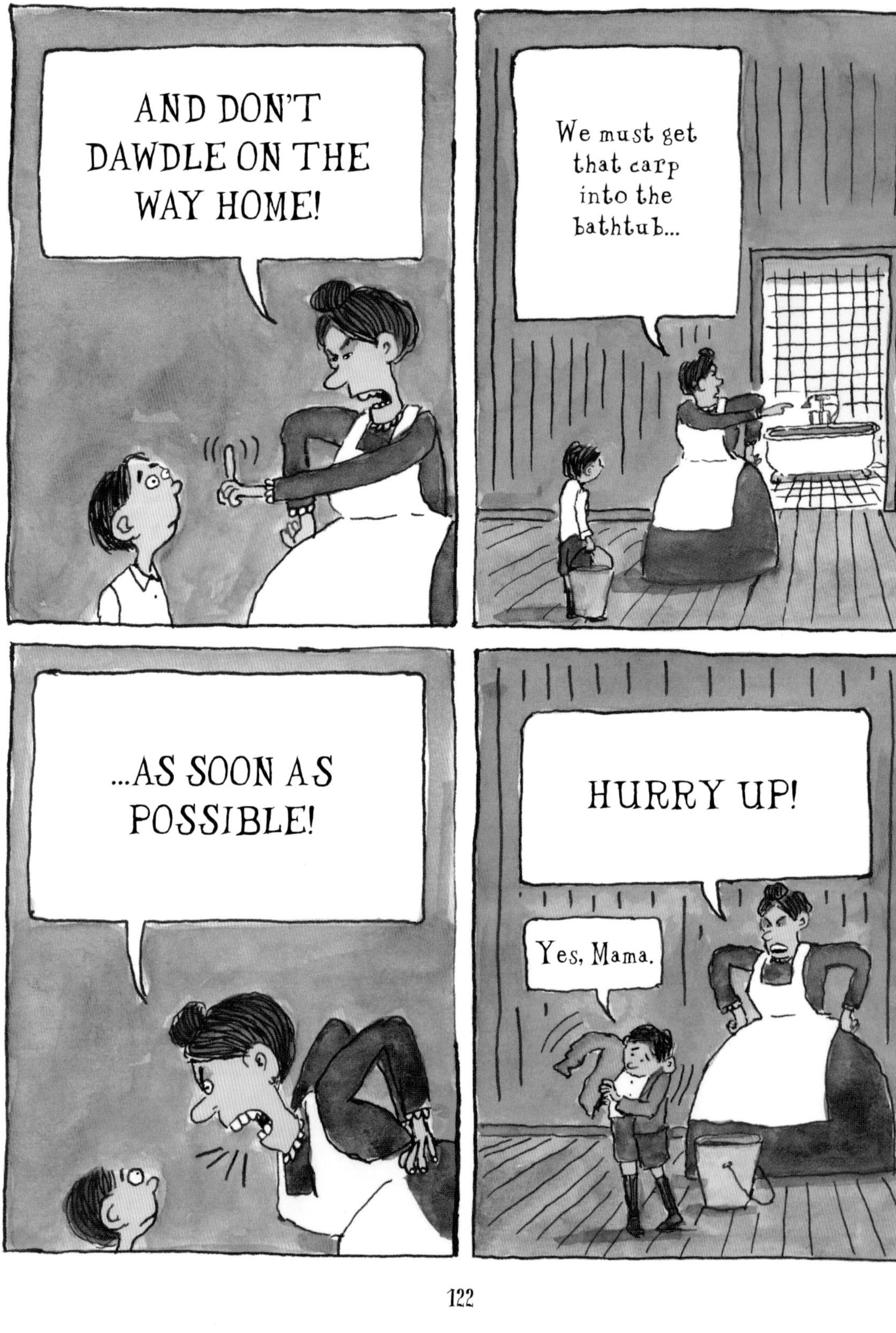
AND DON'T DAWDLE ON THE WAY HOME!
We must get that carp into the bathtub...
...AS SOON AS POSSIBLE!
HURRY UP!
Yes, Mama.

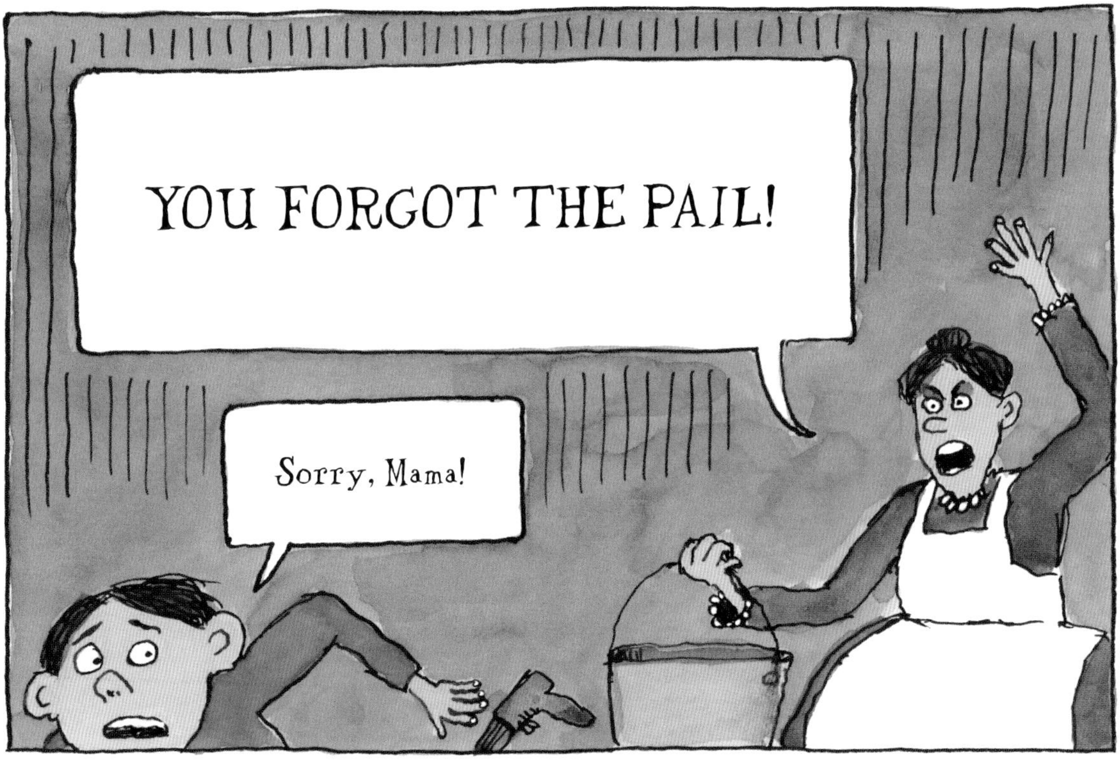
YOU FORGOT THE PAIL!
Sorry, Mama!

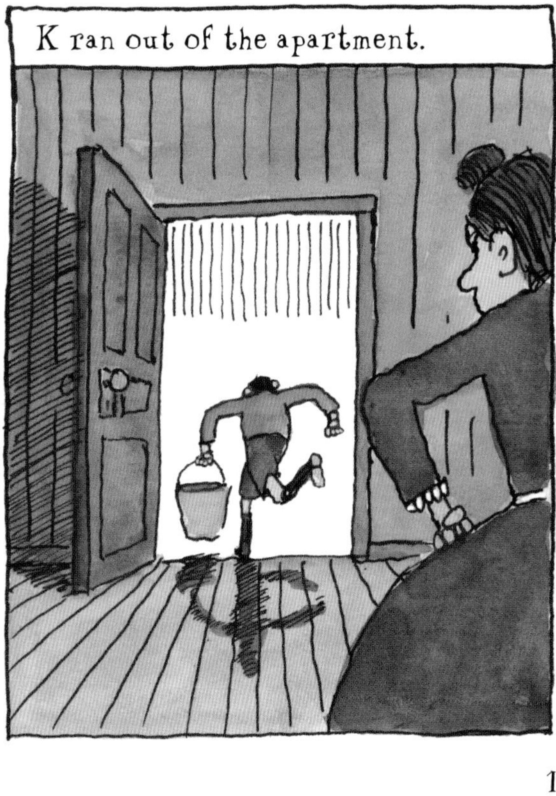
K ran out of the apartment.

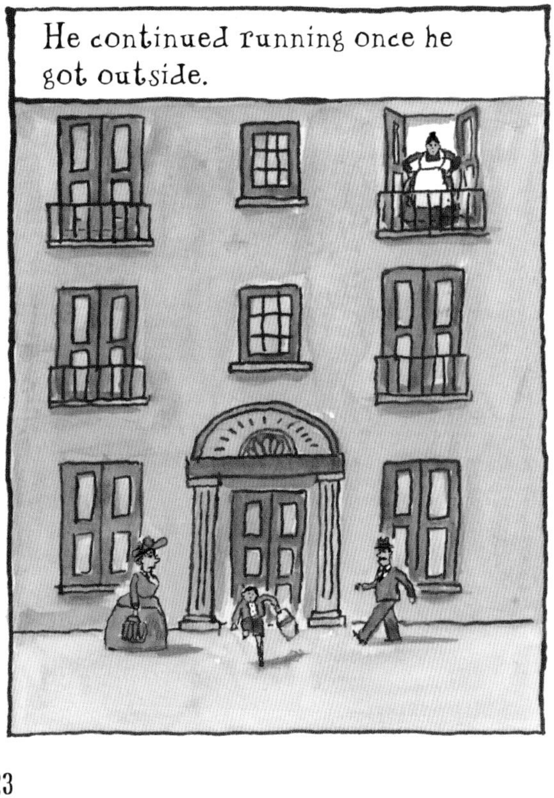
He continued running once he got outside.

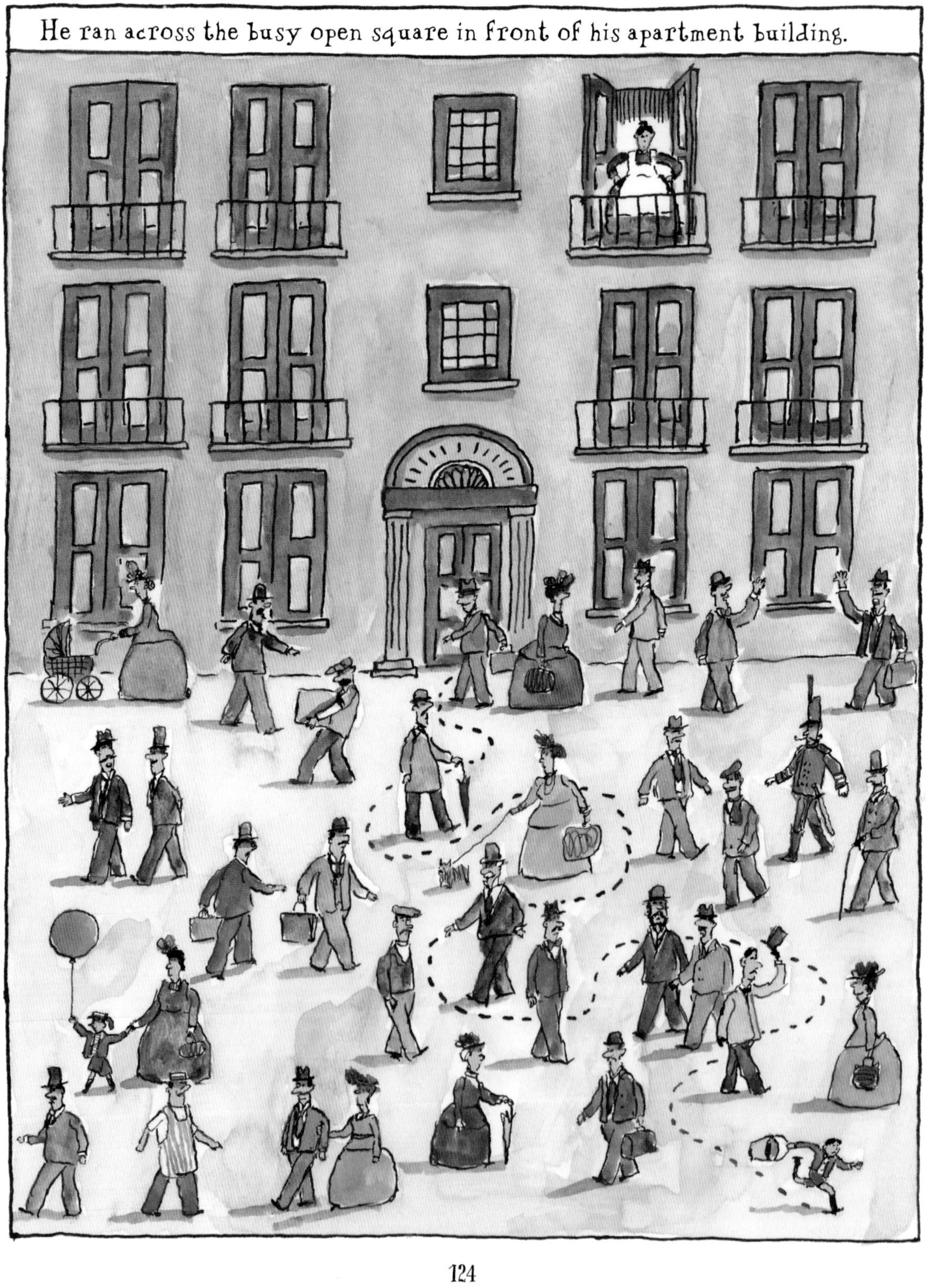
He ran across the busy open square in front of his apartment building.

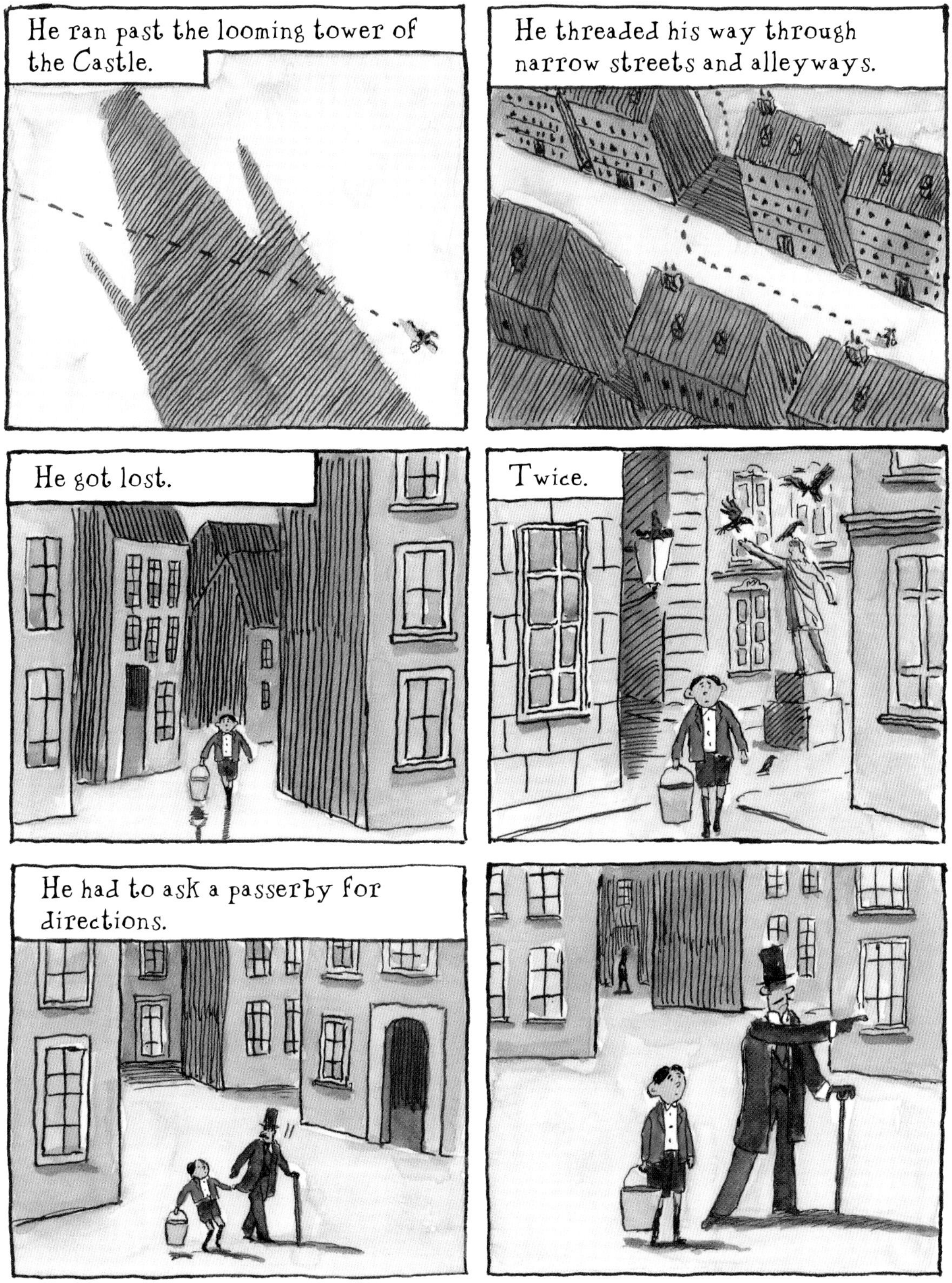
He ran past the looming tower of the Castle.
He threaded his way through narrow streets and alleyways.
He got lost.
Twice.
He had to ask a passerby for directions.

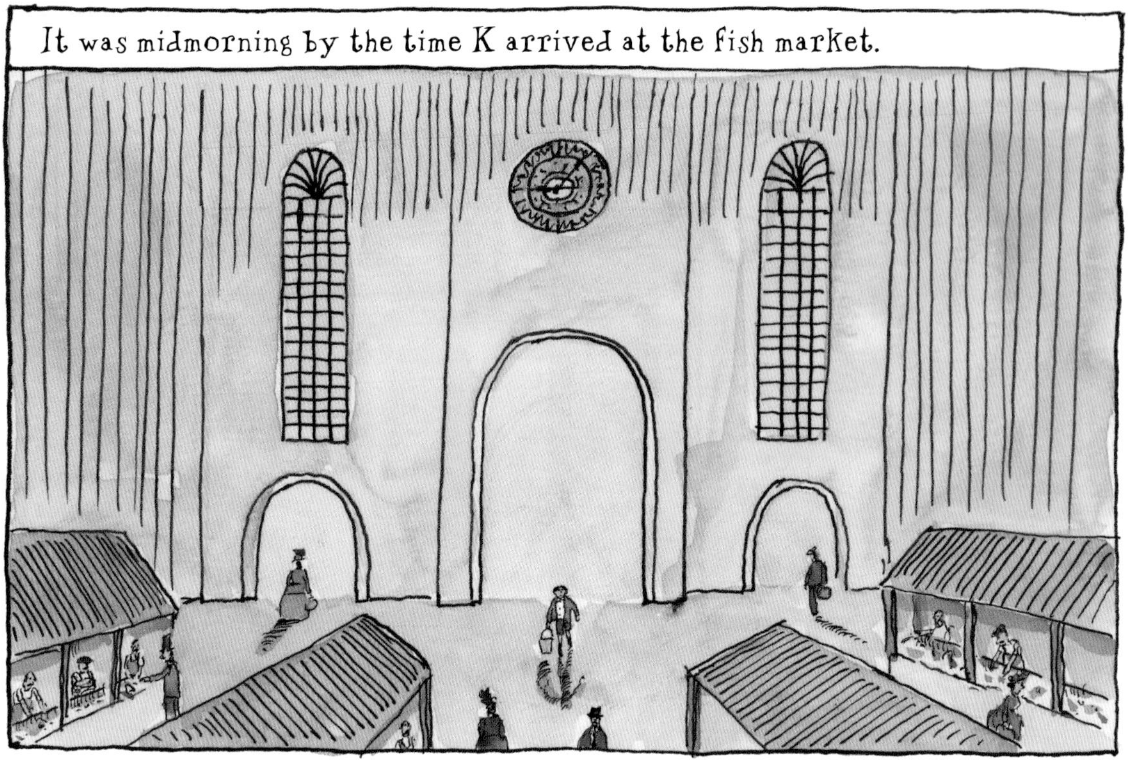
It was midmorning by the time K arrived at the fish market.

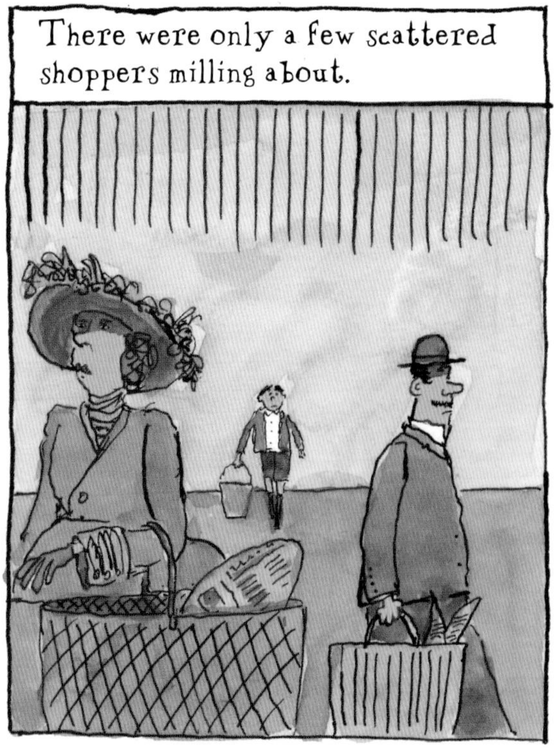
There were only a few scattered shoppers milling about.

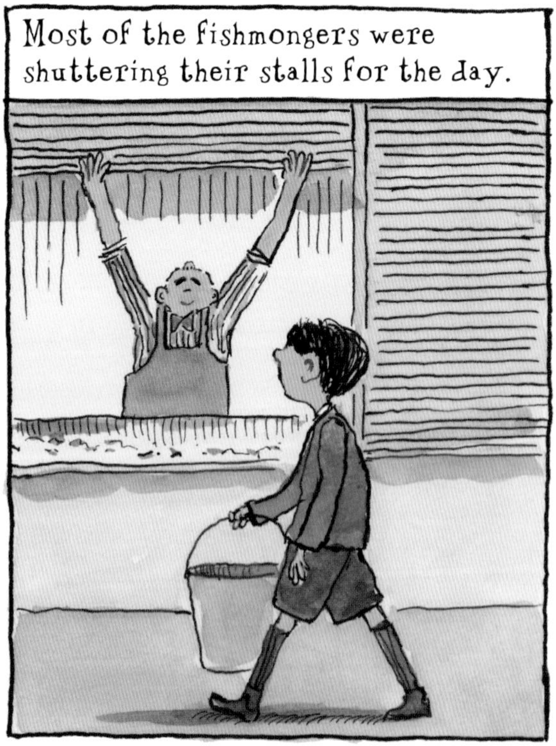
Most of the fishmongers were shuttering their stalls for the day.

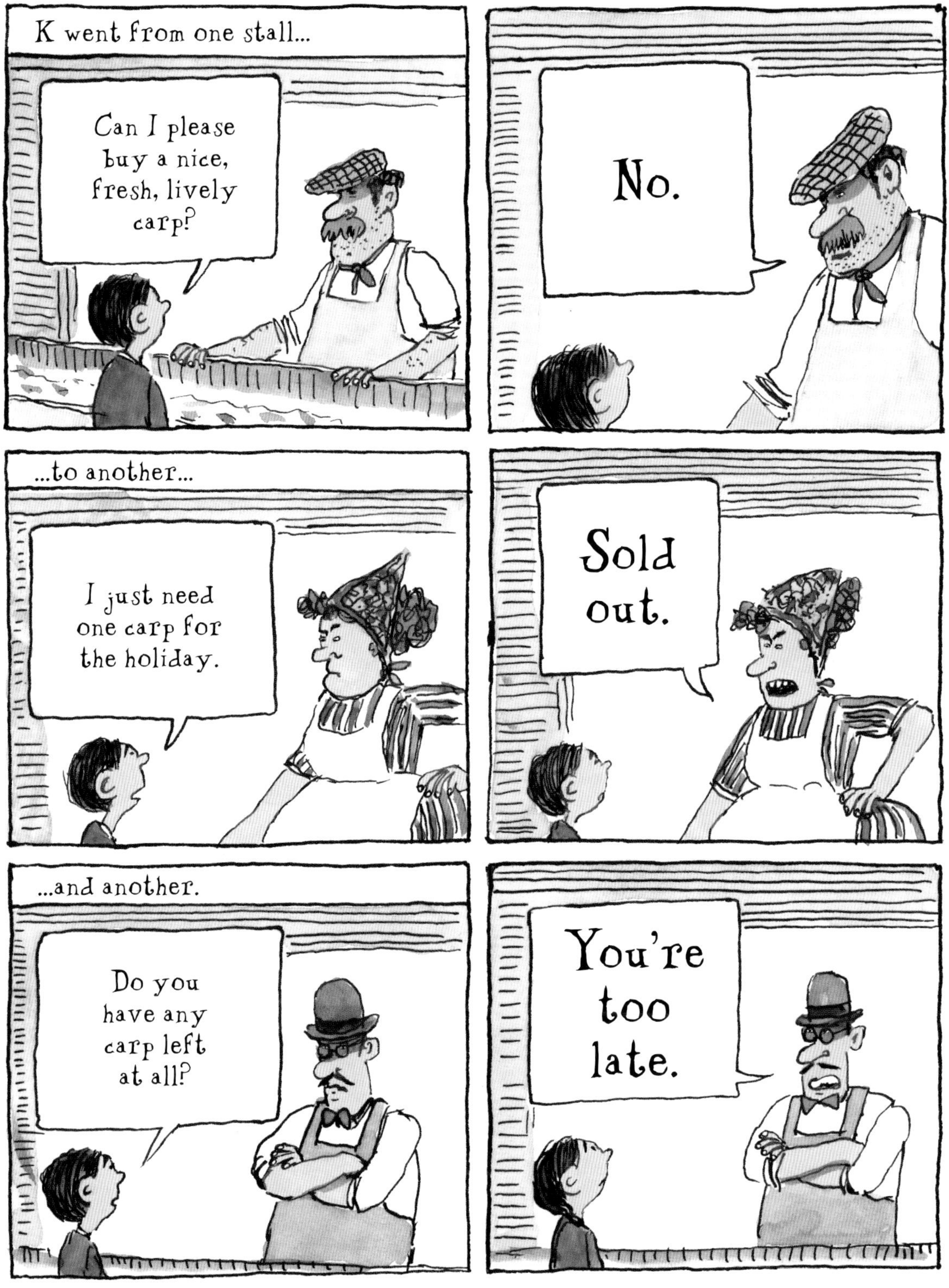
K went from one stall...
Can I please buy a nice, fresh, lively carp?
No.
...to another...
I just need one carp for the holiday.
Sold out.
...and another.
Do you have any carp left at all?
You're too late.

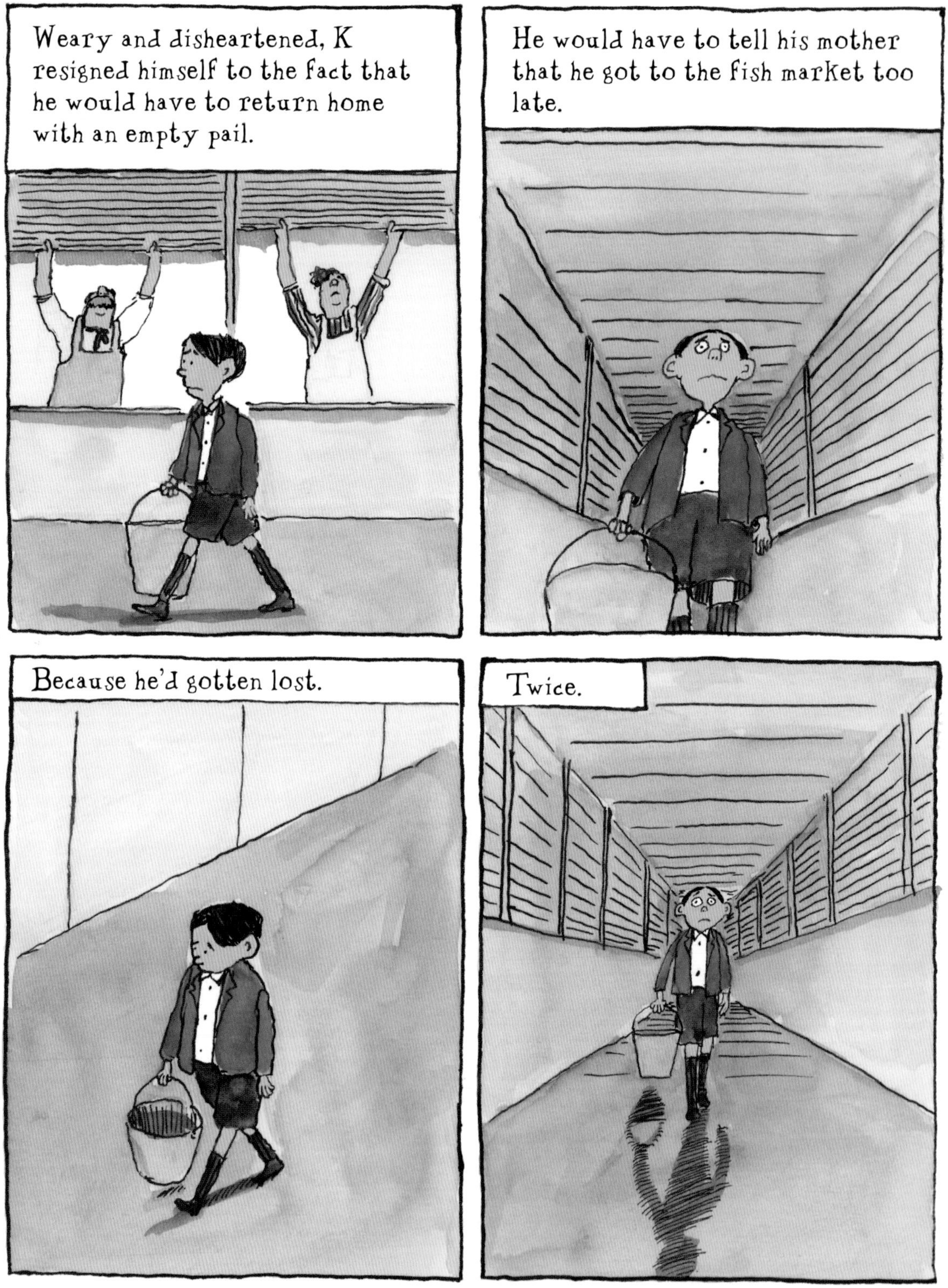
Weary and disheartened, K resigned himself to the fact that he would have to return home with an empty pail.
He would have to tell his mother that he got to the fish market too late.
Because he'd gotten lost.
Twice.

That...

...it...

...was...

...ALL...

...HIS...

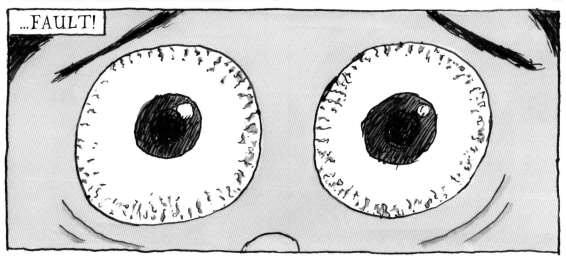

...FAULT!

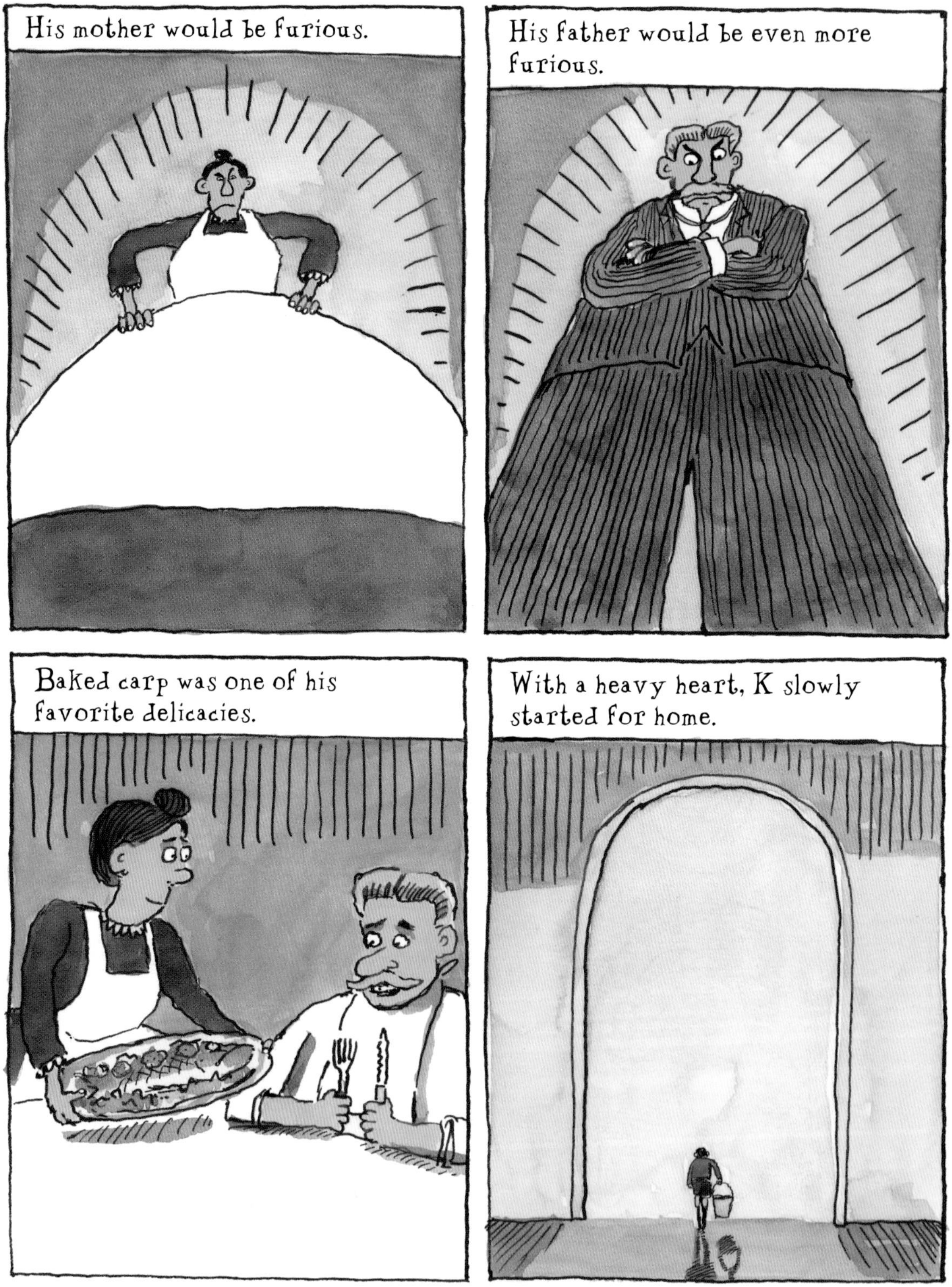
His mother would be furious.
His father would be even more furious.
Baked carp was one of his favorite delicacies.
With a heavy heart, K slowly started for home.

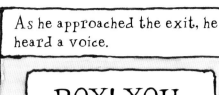

As he approached the exit, he heard a voice.

BOY! YOU, BOY! WAIT A MOMENT!

Who? Me?

Yes, you. Of course, you. Who else could I be speaking to?

I heard you were looking for a carp.

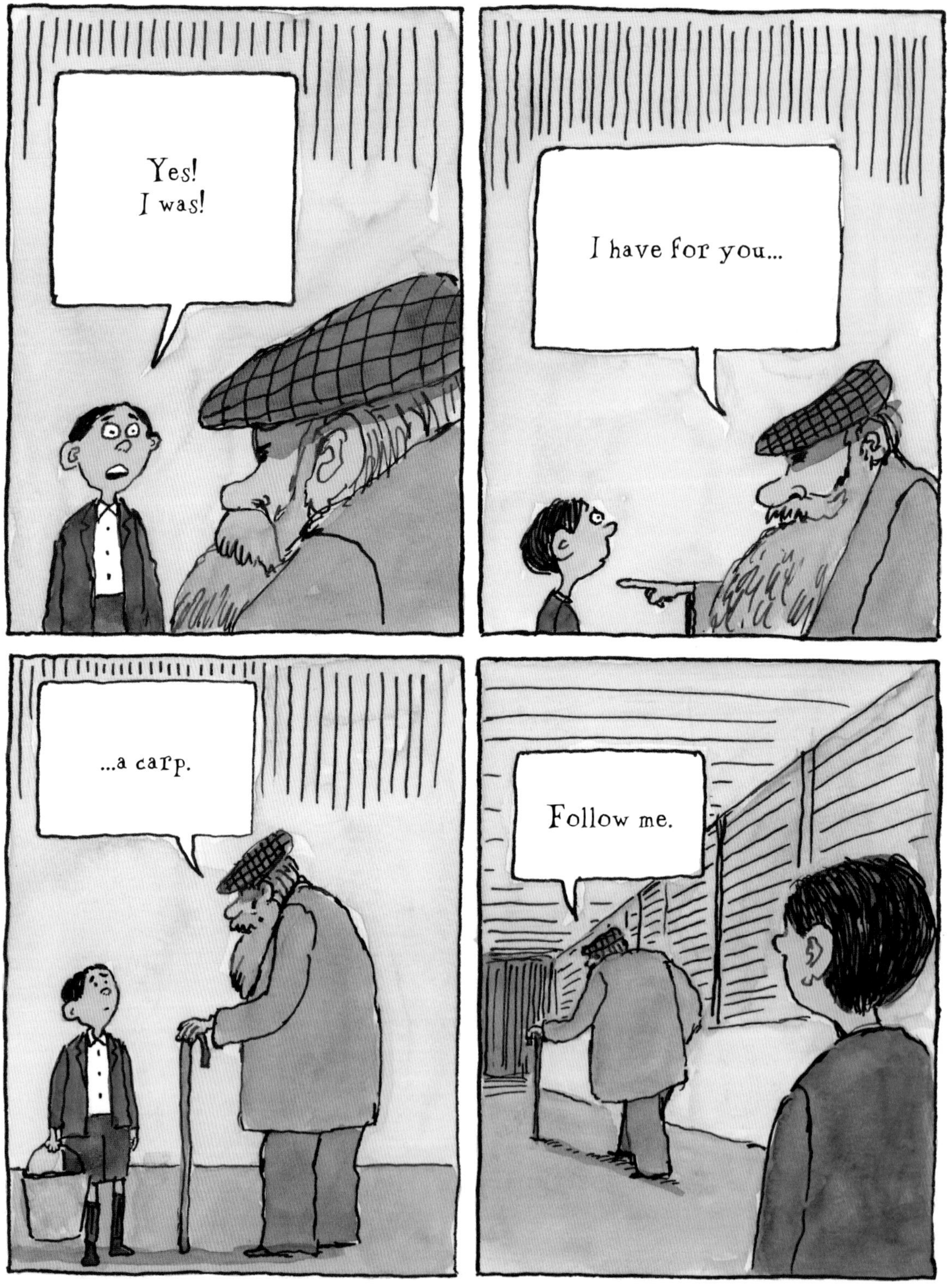
Yes!
I was!
I have for you...
...a carp.
Follow me.

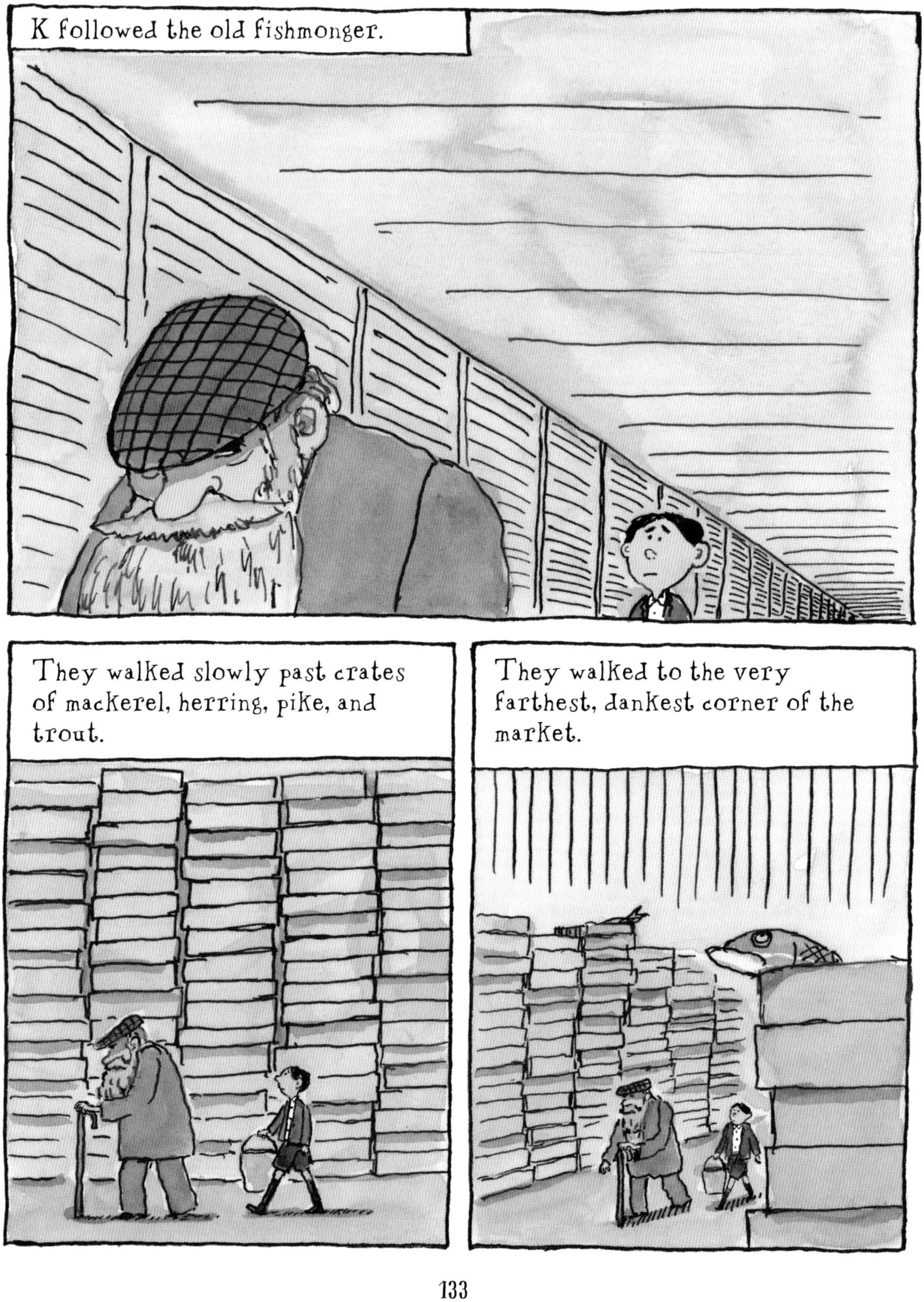
K followed the old fishmonger.
They walked slowly past crates of mackerel, herring, pike, and trout.
They walked to the very farthest, dankest corner of the market.

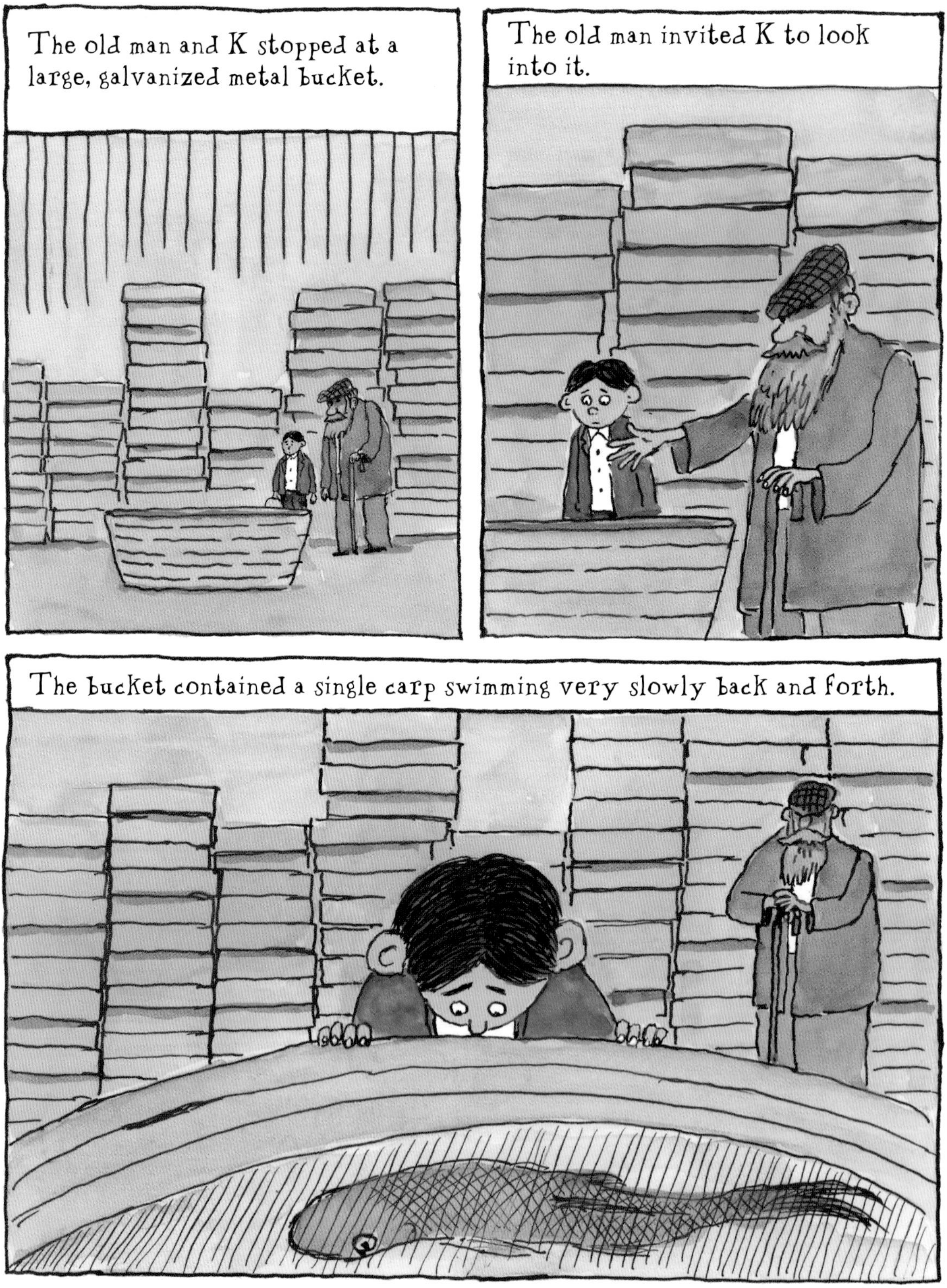
The old man and K stopped at a large, galvanized metal bucket.
The old man invited K to look into it.
The bucket contained a single carp swimming very slowly back and forth.

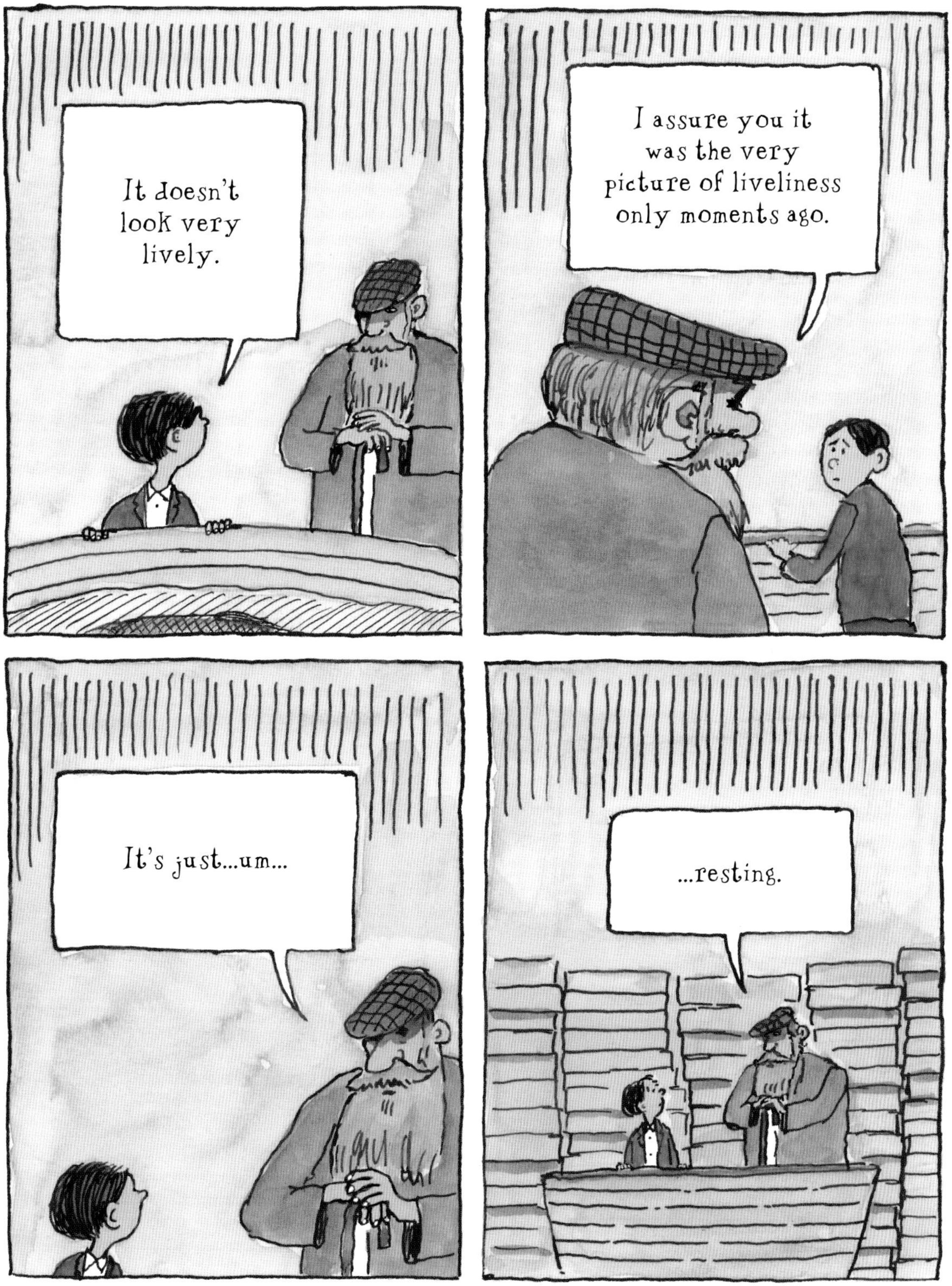
It doesn't look very lively.
I assure you it was the very picture of liveliness only moments ago.
It's just...um...
...resting.

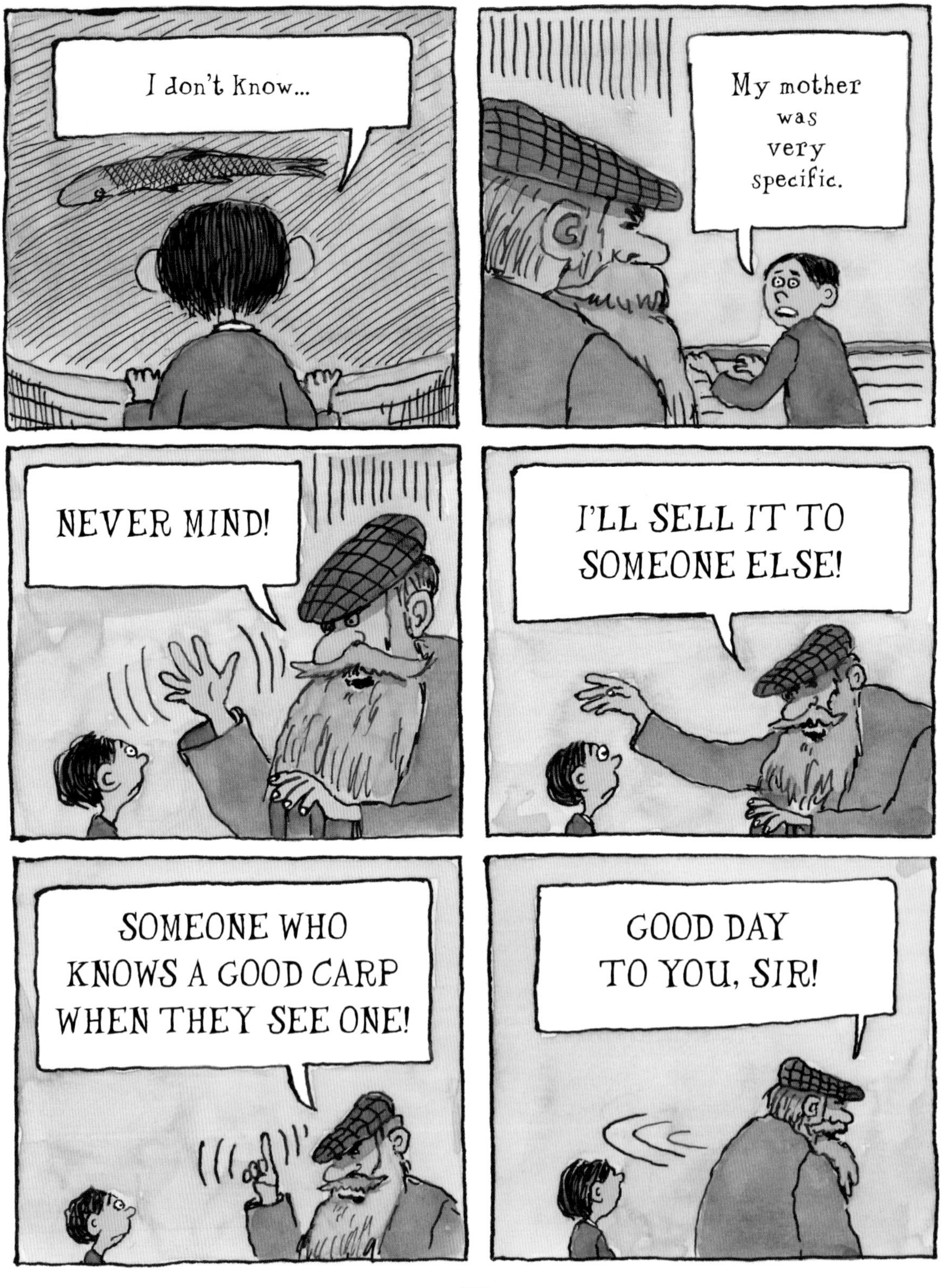
I don't know...
My mother was very specific.
NEVER MIND!
I'LL SELL IT TO SOMEONE ELSE!
SOMEONE WHO KNOWS A GOOD CARP WHEN THEY SEE ONE!
GOOD DAY TO YOU, SIR!

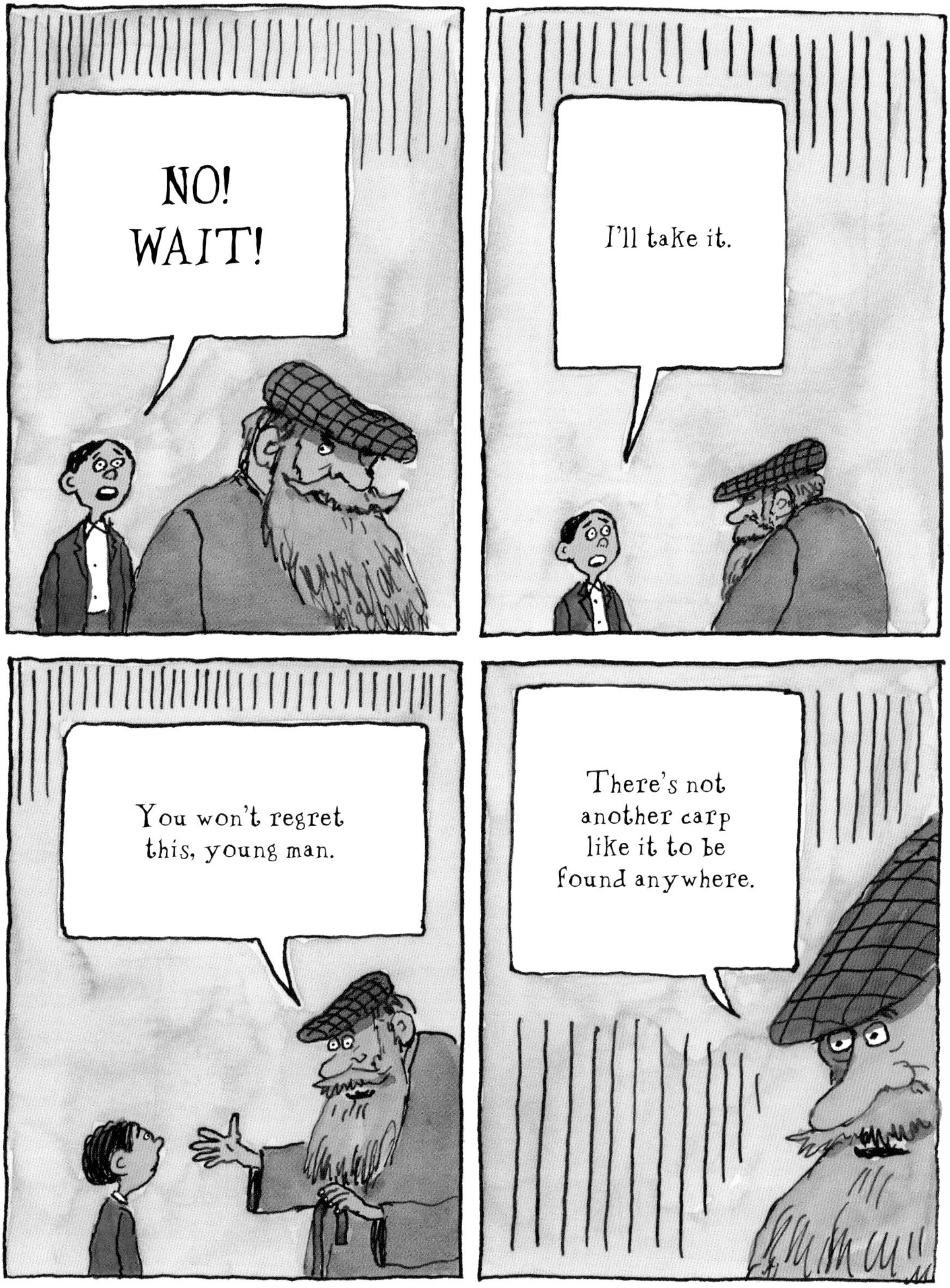
NO! WAIT!
I'll take it.
You won't regret this, young man.
There's not another carp like it to be found anywhere.

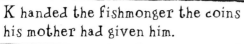
K handed the fishmonger the coins his mother had given him.

And the pail.

The fishmonger filled the pail with water.

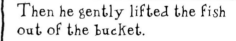

Then he gently lifted the fish out of the bucket.

138

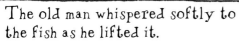
The old man whispered softly to the fish as he lifted it.

There you go, old friend.

Easy does it.

Time to say goodbye.

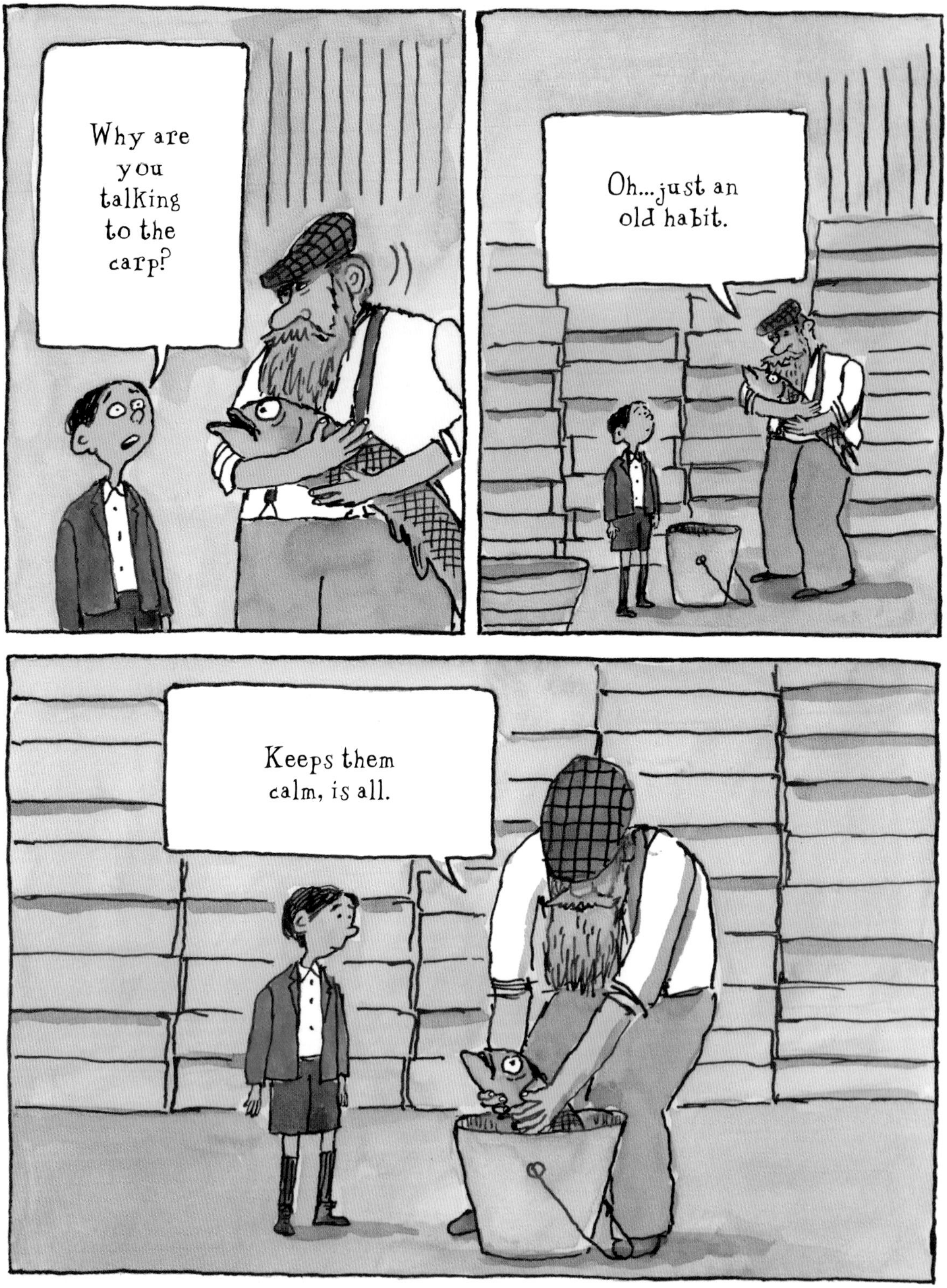
Why are you talking to the carp?
Oh...just an old habit.
Keeps them calm, is all.

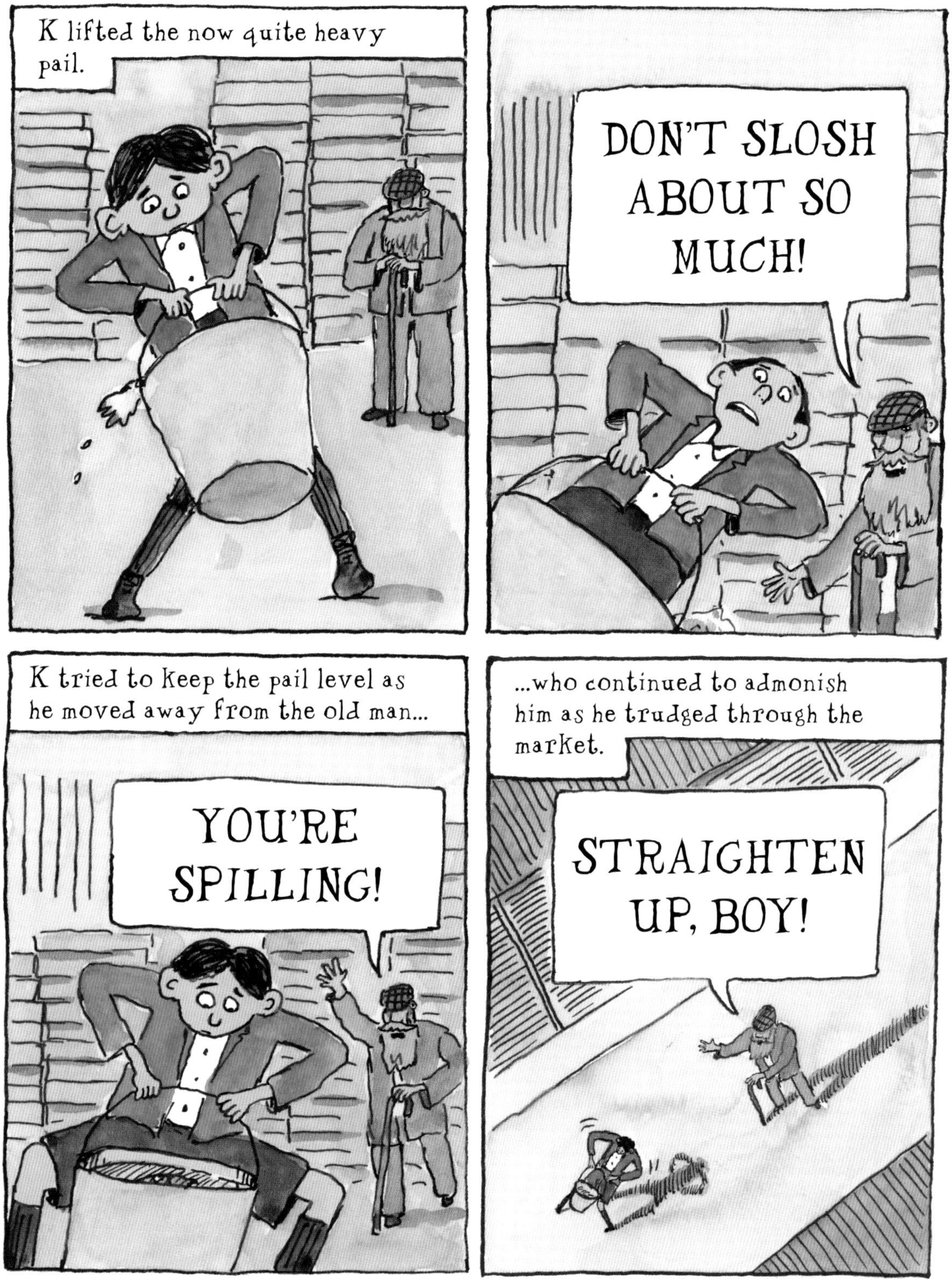
K lifted the now quite heavy pail.
DON'T SLOSH ABOUT SO MUCH!
K tried to keep the pail level as he moved away from the old man...
YOU'RE SPILLING!
...who continued to admonish him as he trudged through the market.
STRAIGHTEN UP, BOY!

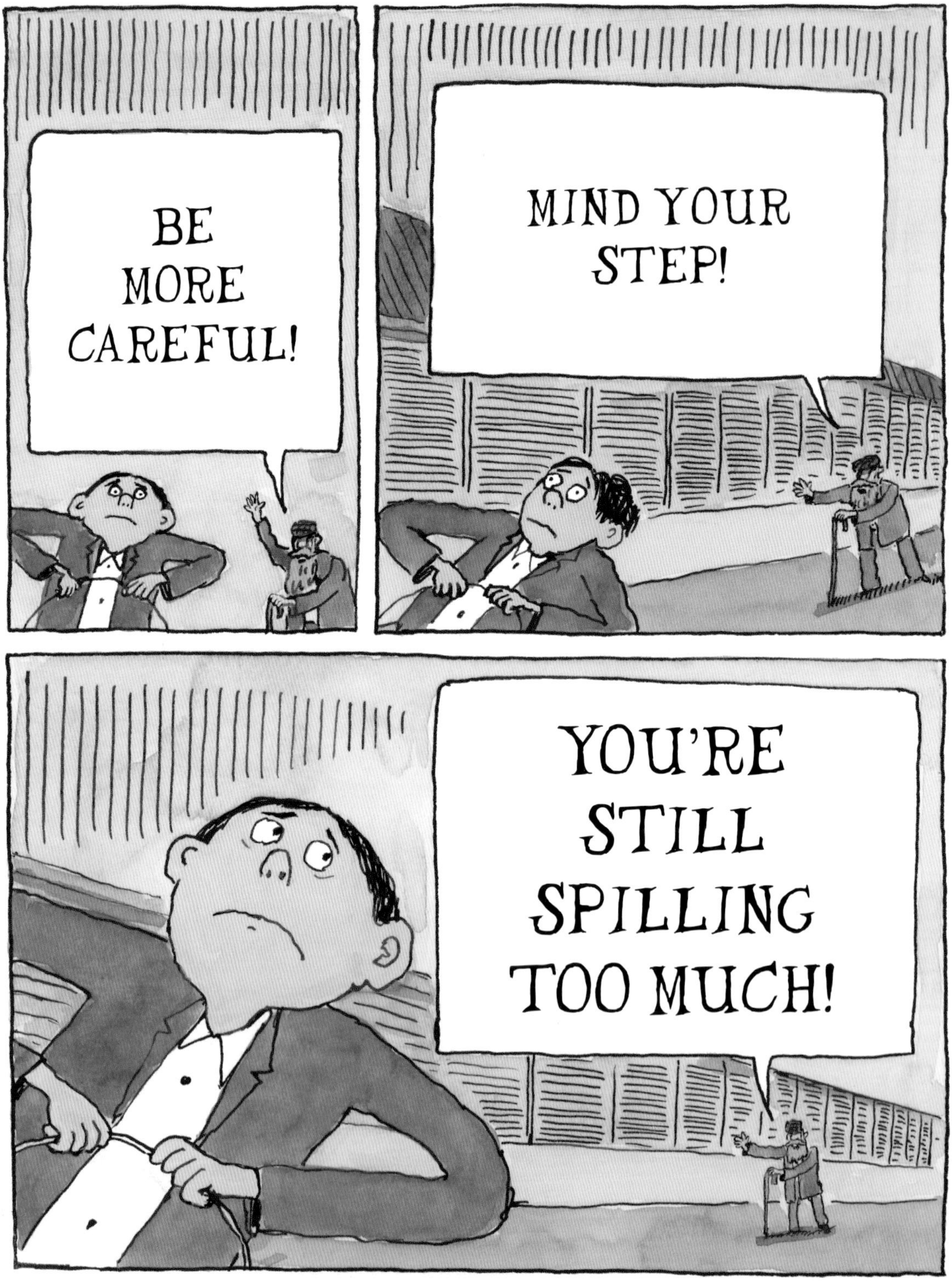
BE MORE CAREFUL!
MIND YOUR STEP!
YOU'RE STILL SPILLING TOO MUCH!

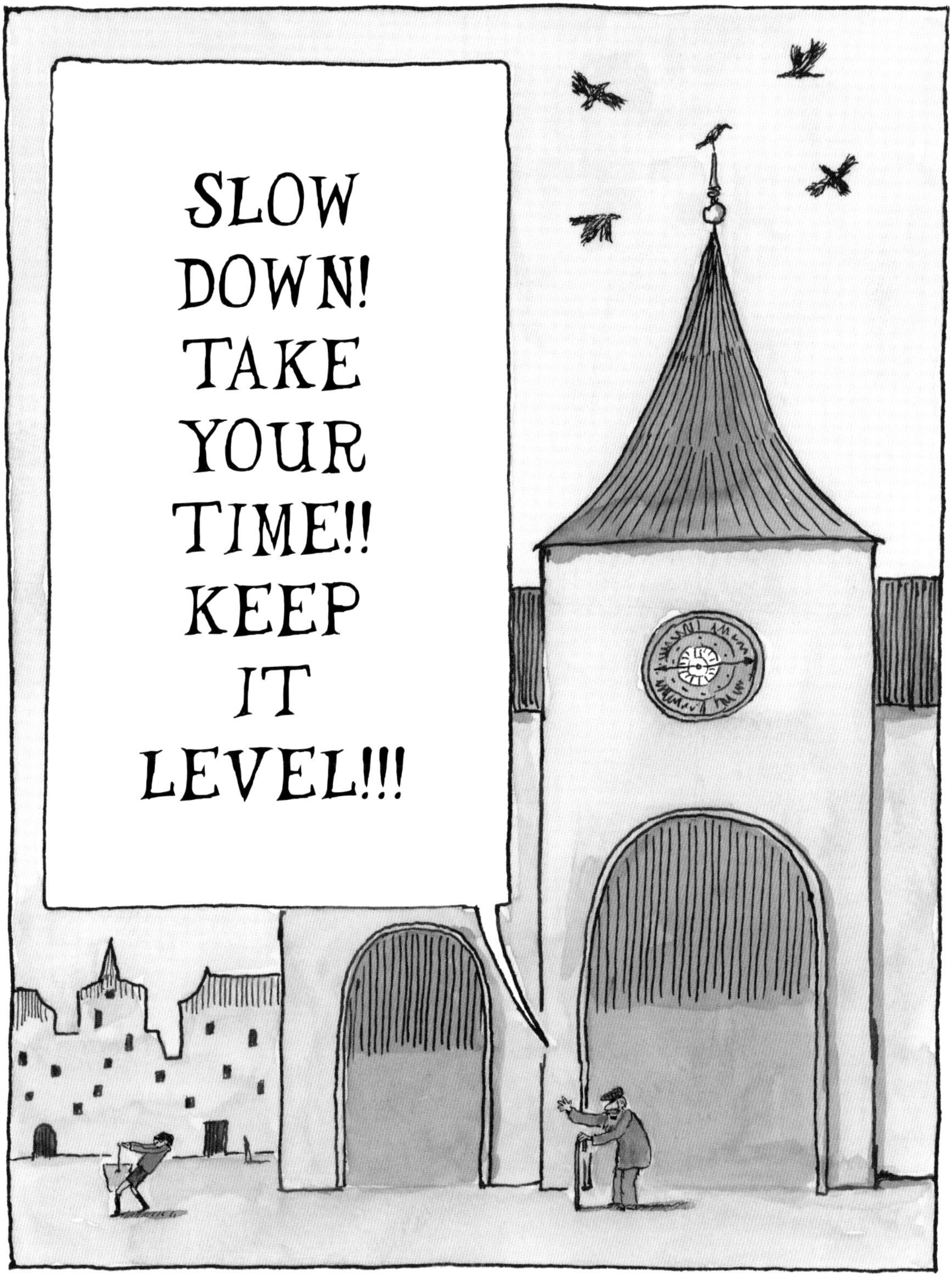
SLOW DOWN! TAKE YOUR TIME!! KEEP IT LEVEL!!!

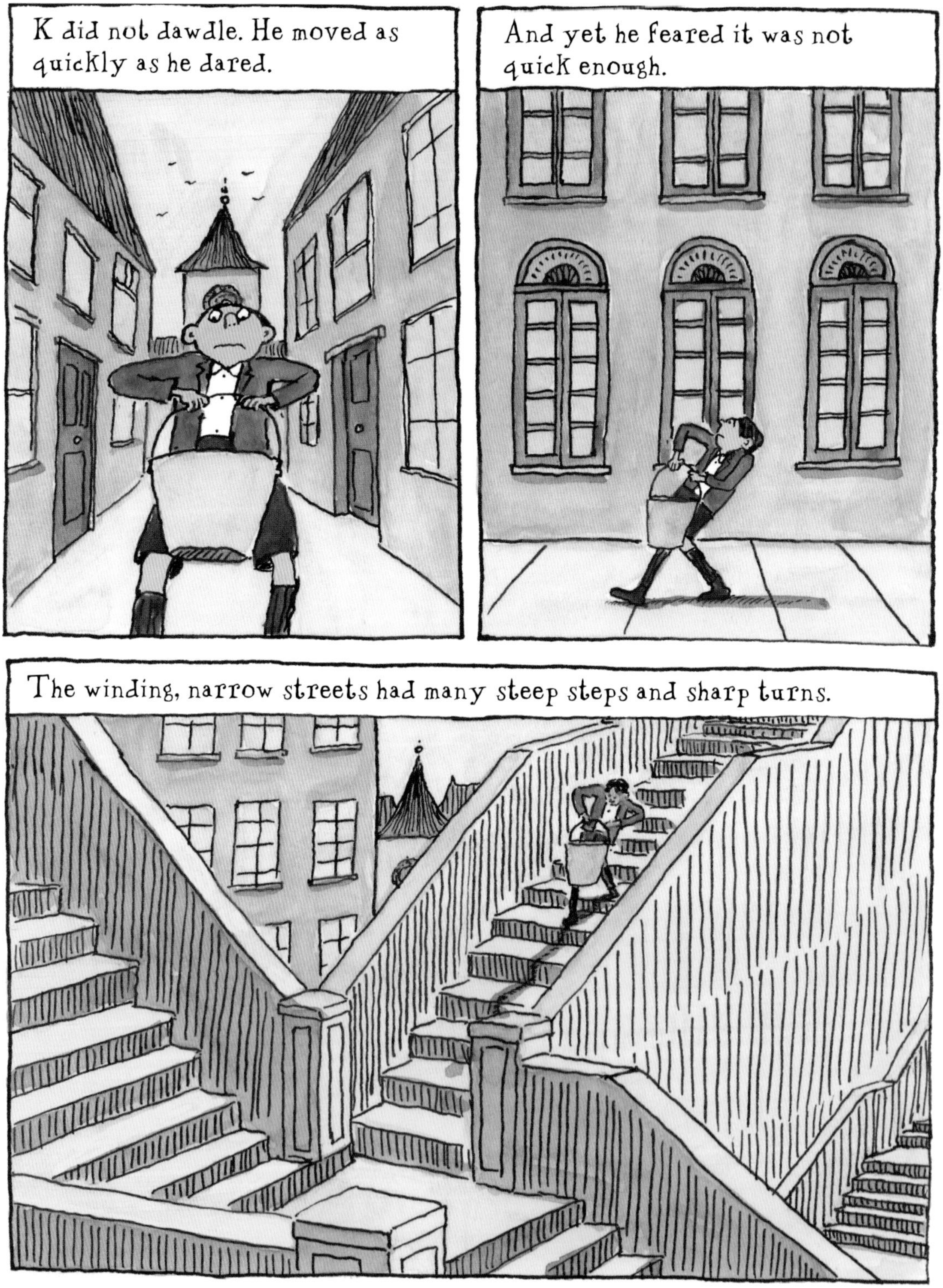
K did not dawdle. He moved as quickly as he dared.
And yet he feared it was not quick enough.
The winding, narrow streets had many steep steps and sharp turns.

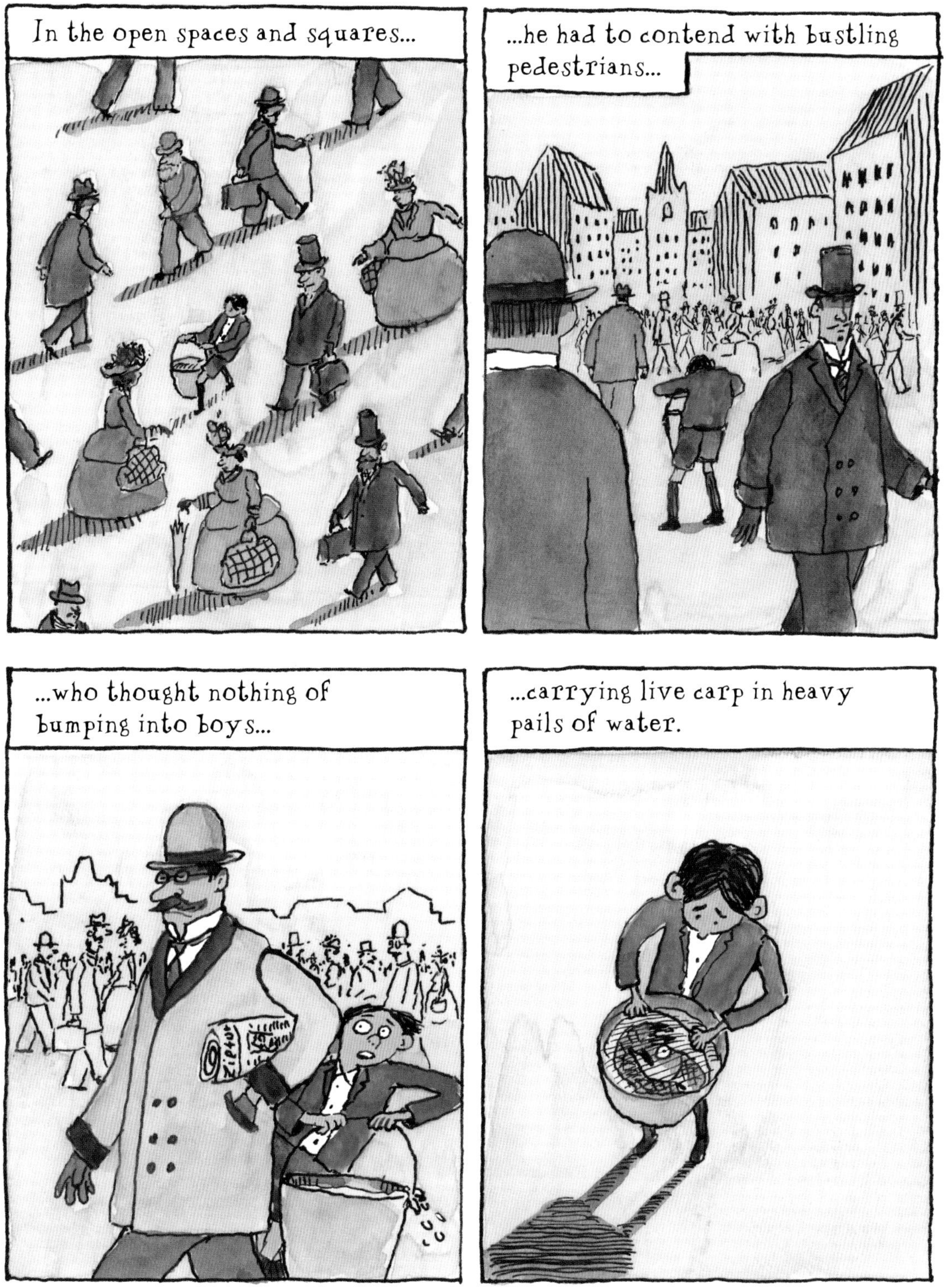
In the open spaces and squares...
...he had to contend with bustling pedestrians...
...who thought nothing of bumping into boys...
...carrying live carp in heavy pails of water.

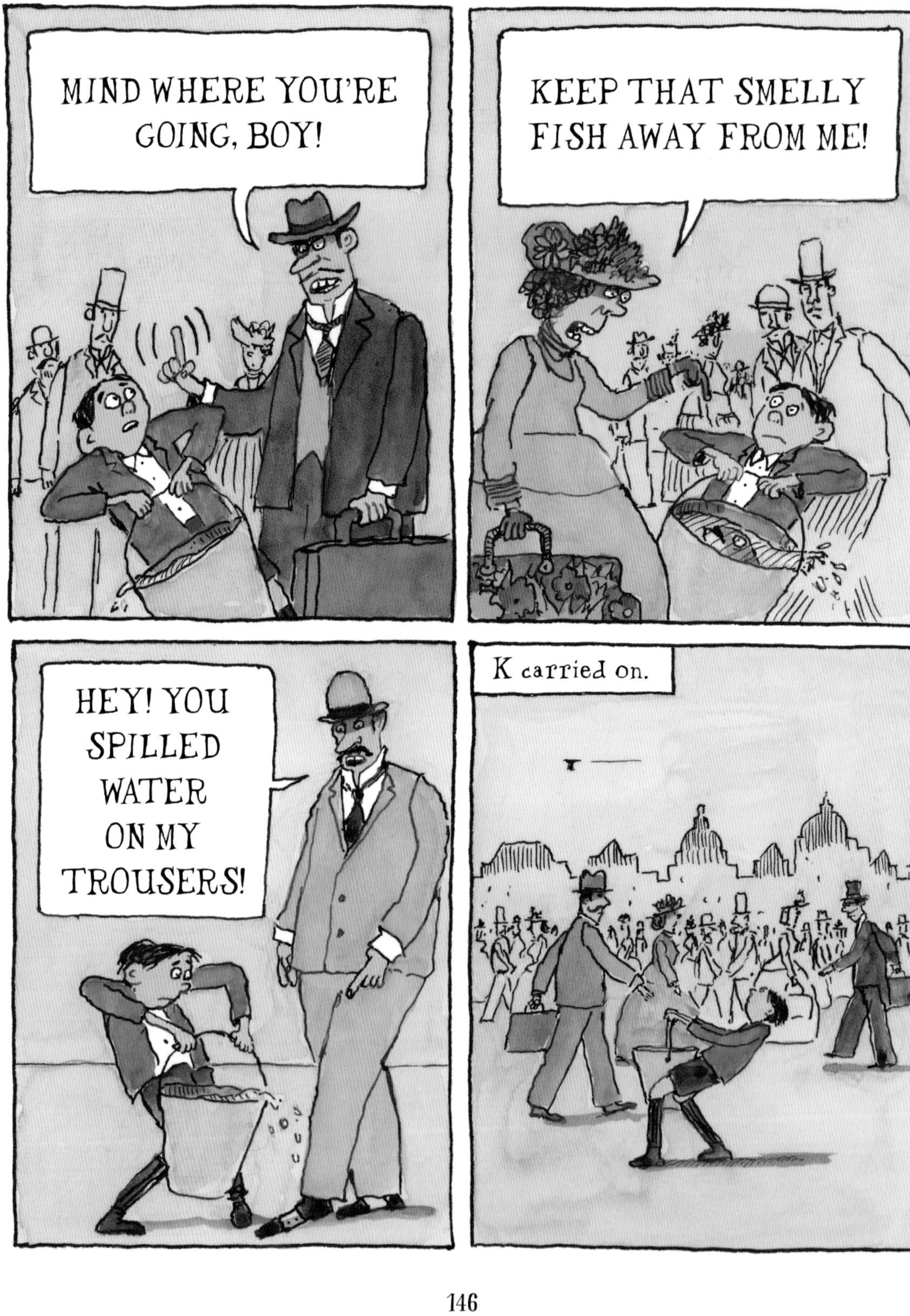
MIND WHERE YOU'RE GOING, BOY!
KEEP THAT SMELLY FISH AWAY FROM ME!
HEY! YOU SPILLED WATER ON MY TROUSERS!
K carried on.

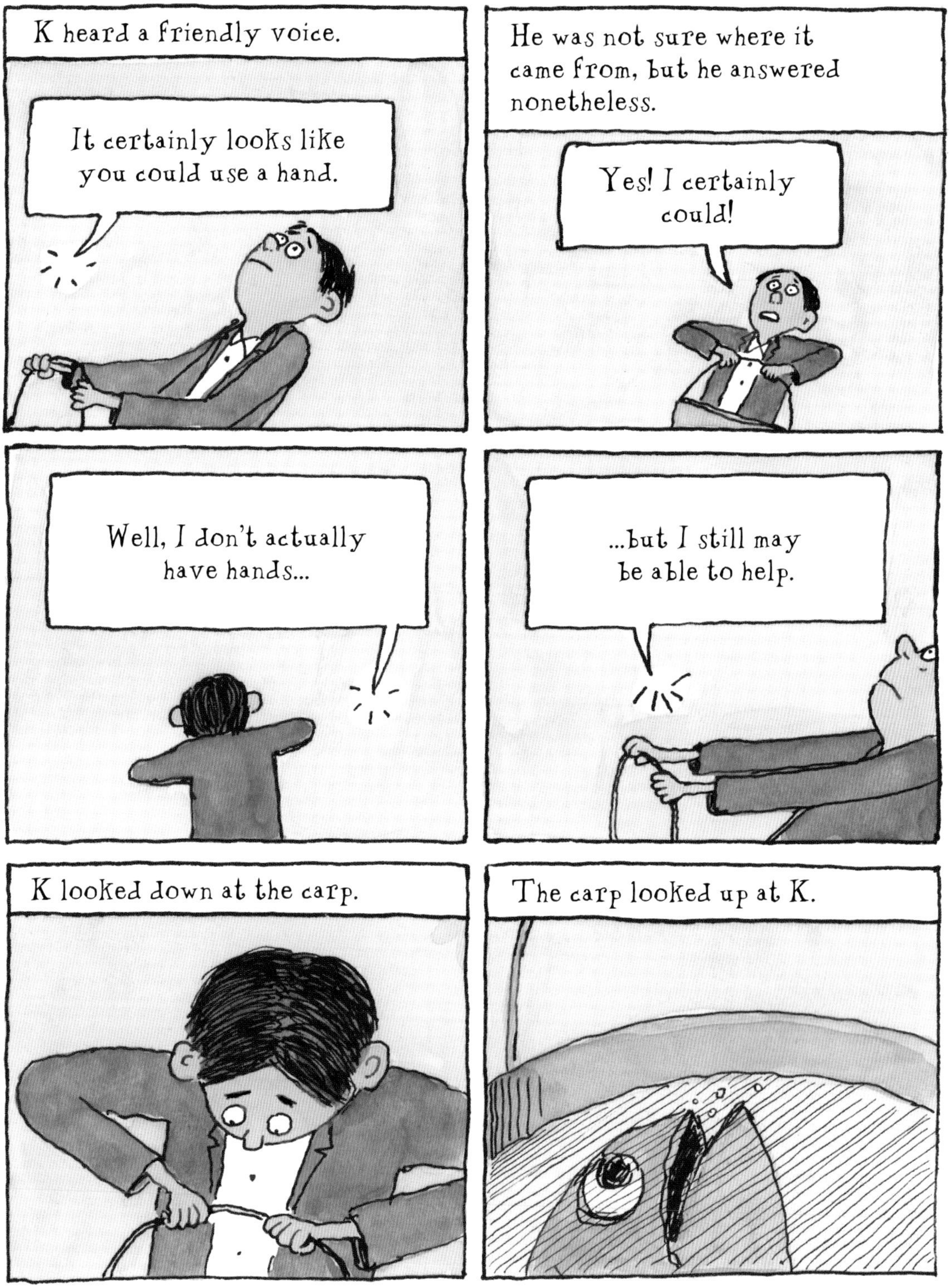
K heard a friendly voice.
It certainly looks like you could use a hand.
He was not sure where it came from, but he answered nonetheless.
Yes! I certainly could!
Well, I don't actually have hands...
...but I still may be able to help.
K looked down at the carp.
The carp looked up at K.

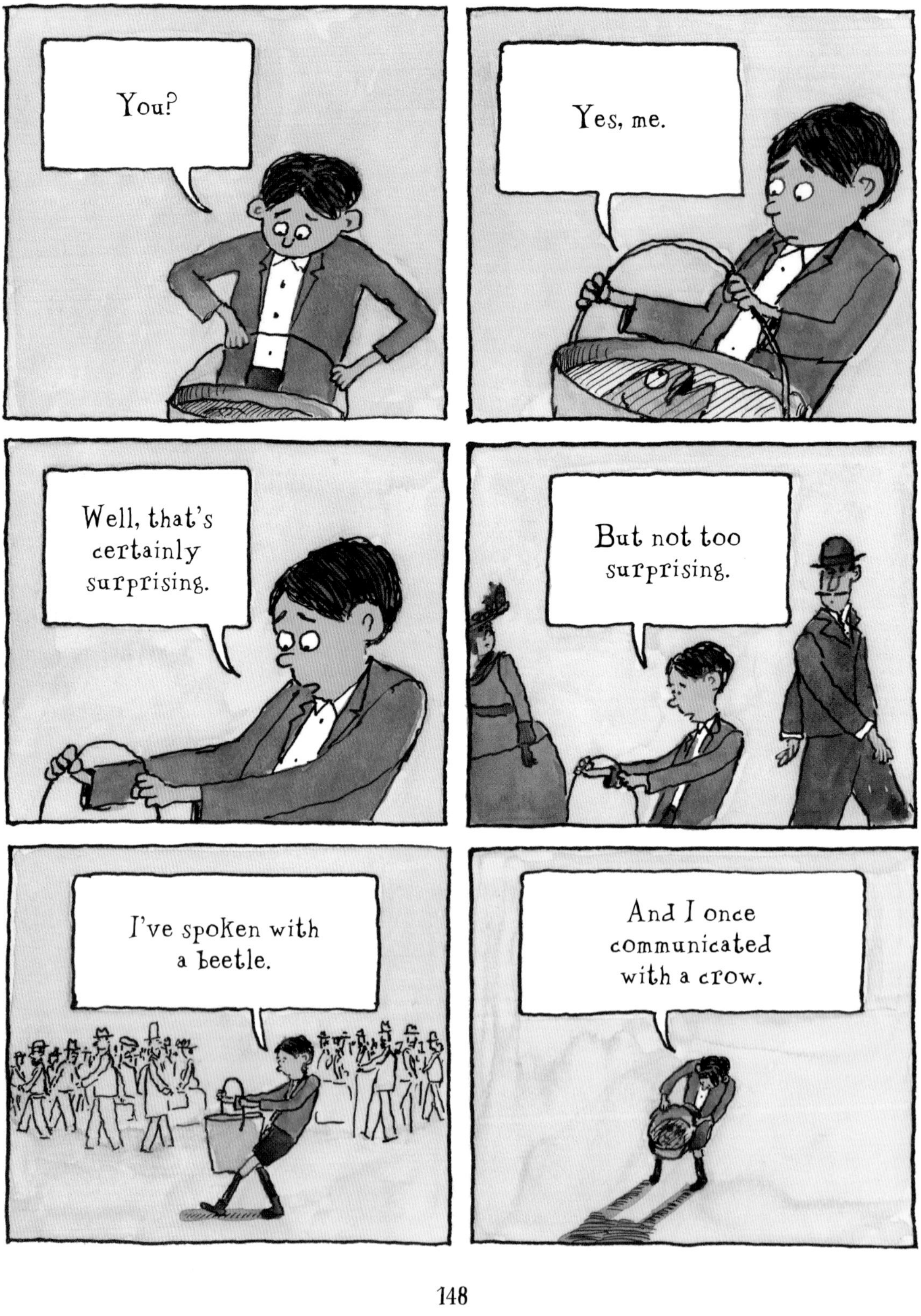
You?
Yes, me.
Well, that's certainly surprising.
But not too surprising.
I've spoken with a beetle.
And I once communicated with a crow.

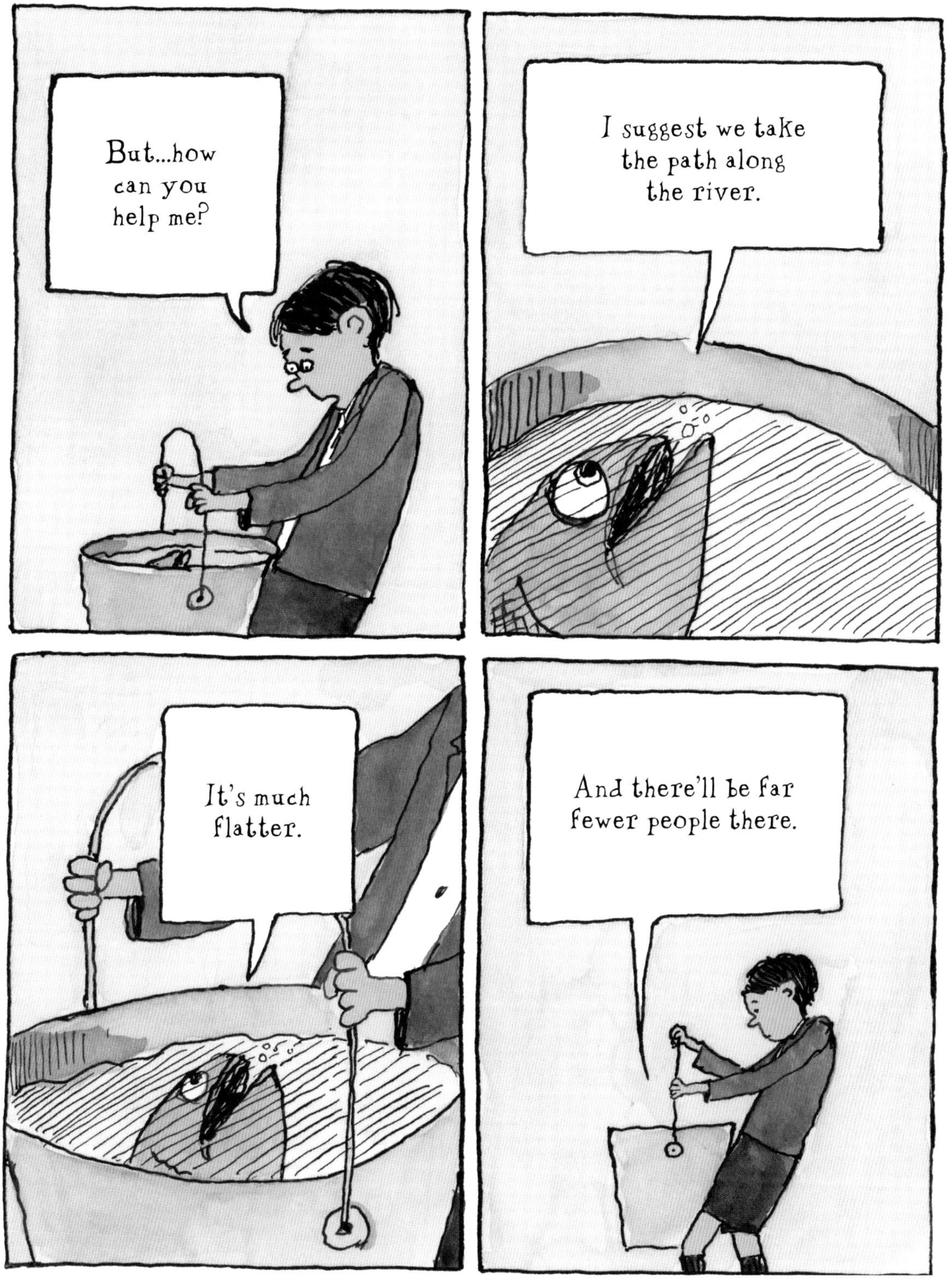
But...how can you help me?
I suggest we take the path along the river.
It's much flatter.
And there'll be far fewer people there.

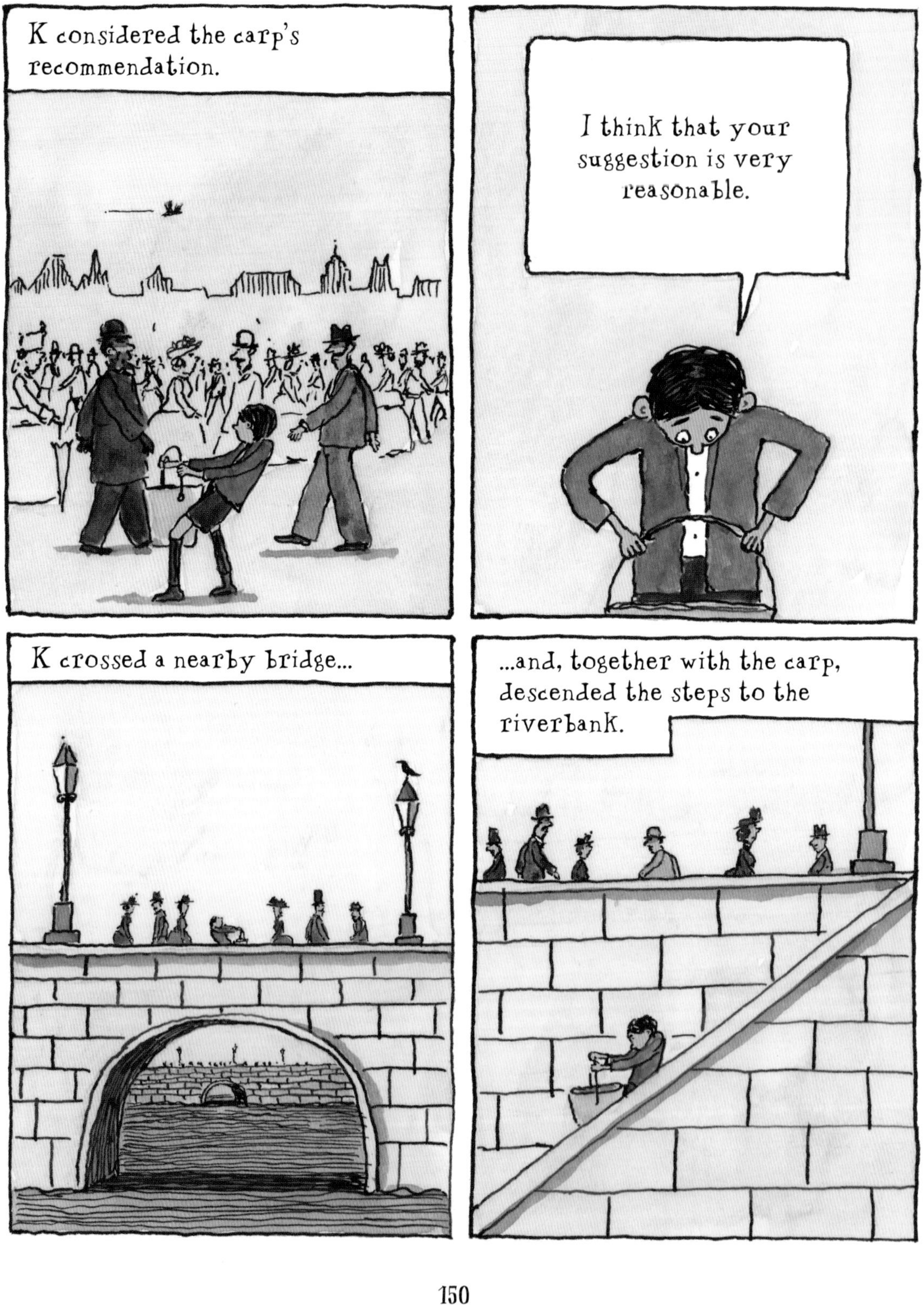
K considered the carp's recommendation.
I think that your suggestion is very reasonable.
K crossed a nearby bridge...
...and, together with the carp, descended the steps to the riverbank.

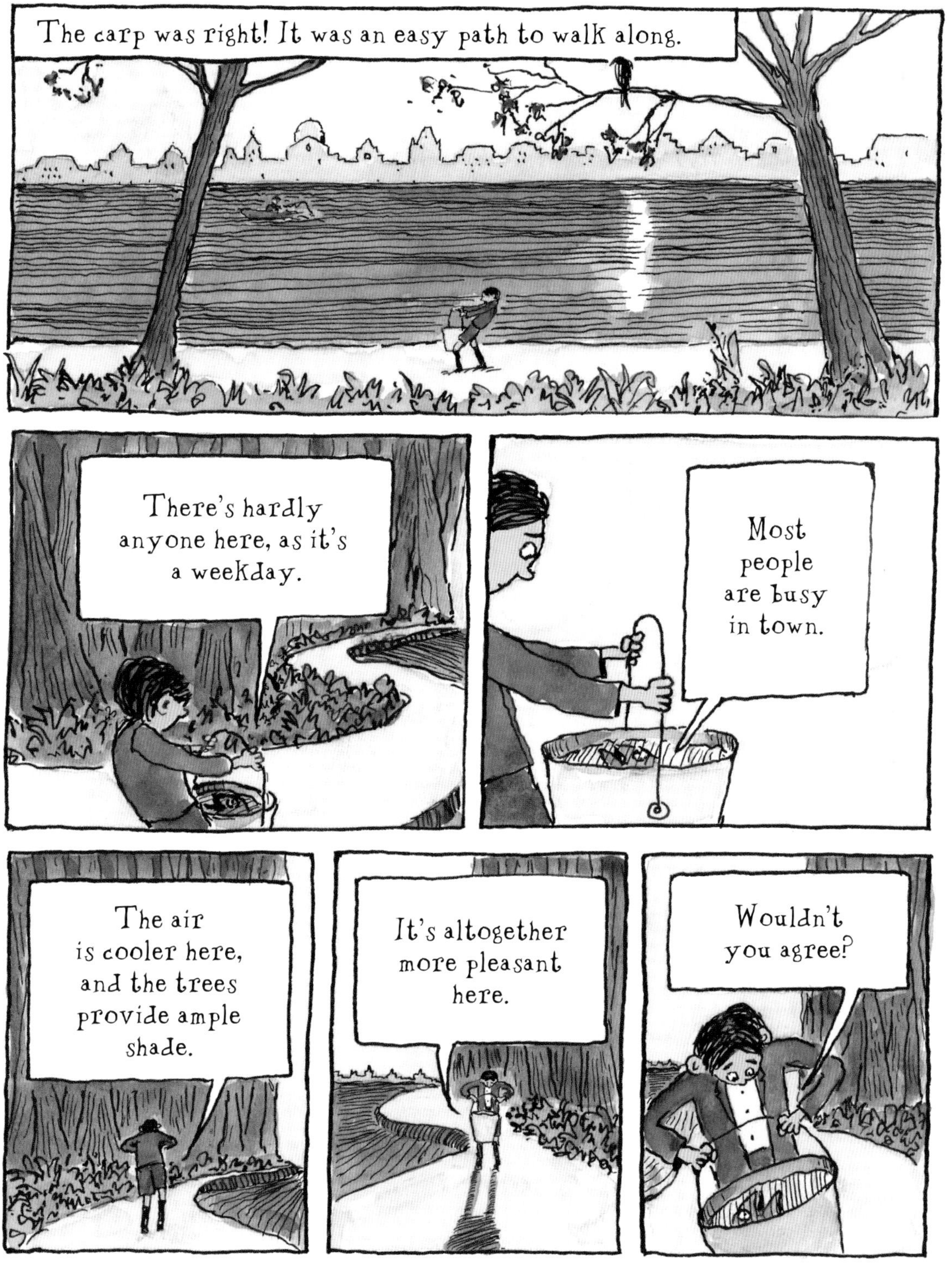
The carp was right! It was an easy path to walk along.
There's hardly anyone here, as it's a weekday.
Most people are busy in town.
The air is cooler here, and the trees provide ample shade.
It's altogether more pleasant here.
Wouldn't you agree?

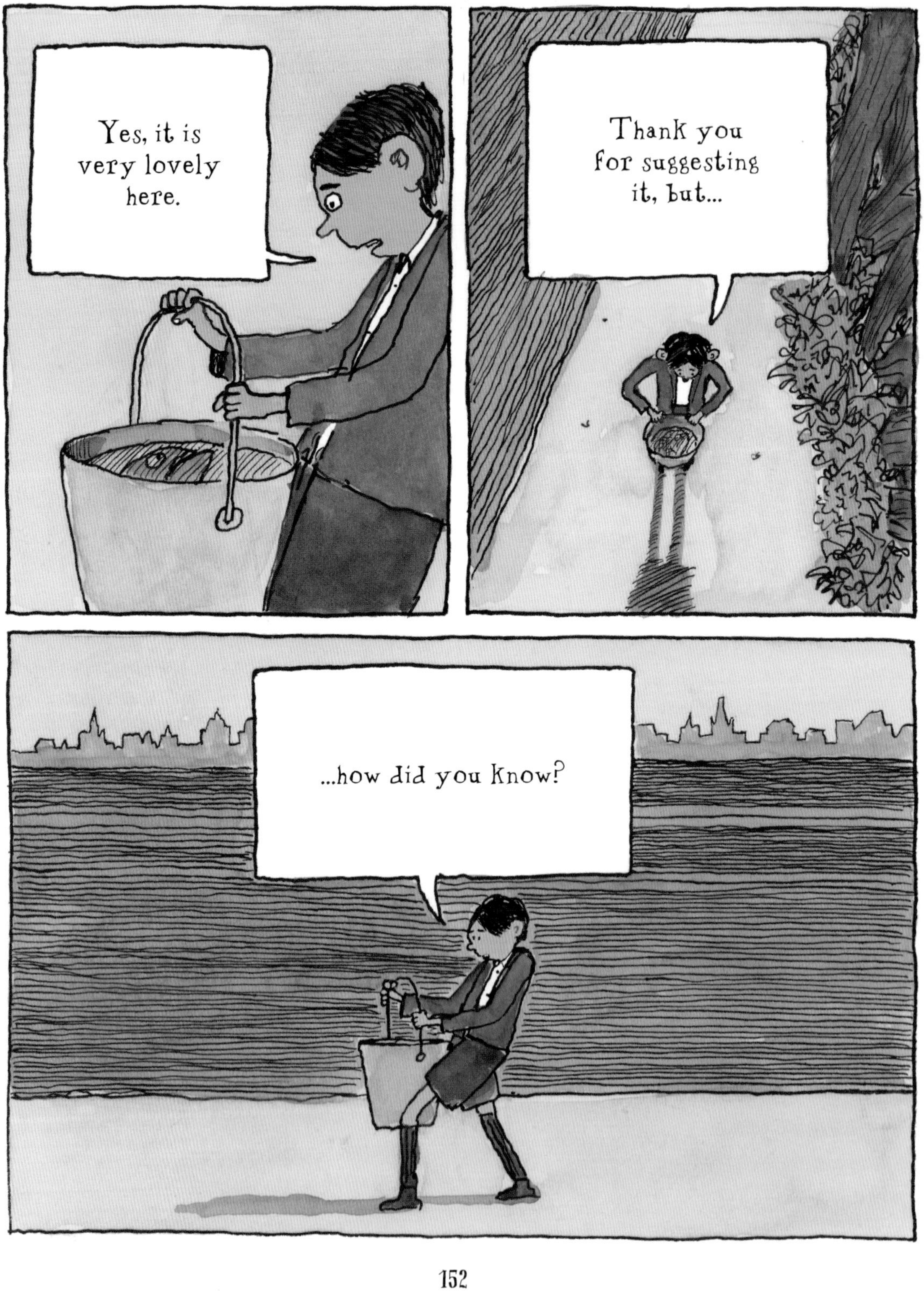
Yes, it is very lovely here.
Thank you for suggesting it, but...
...how did you know?

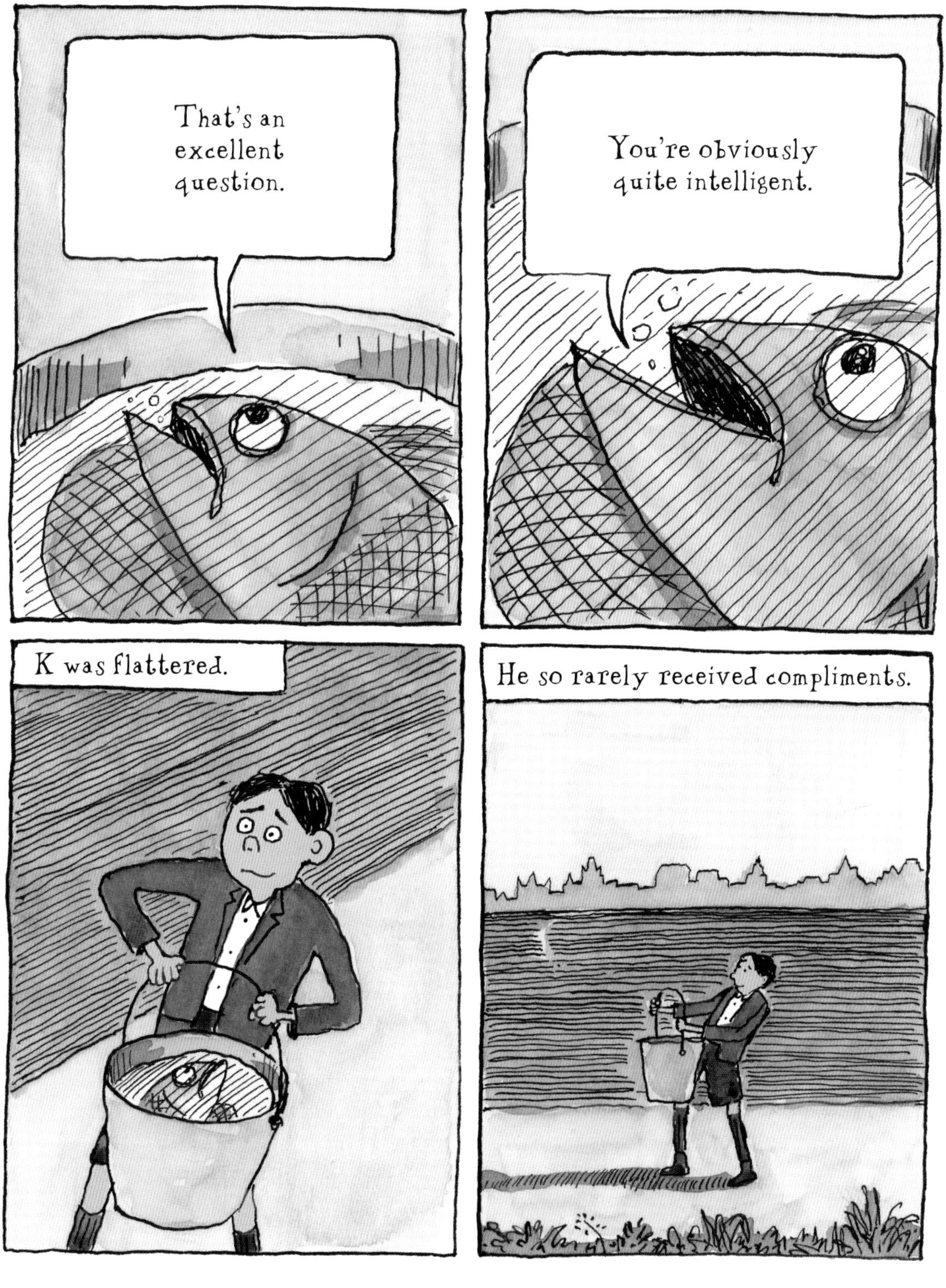
That's an excellent question.
You're obviously quite intelligent.
K was flattered.
He so rarely received compliments.

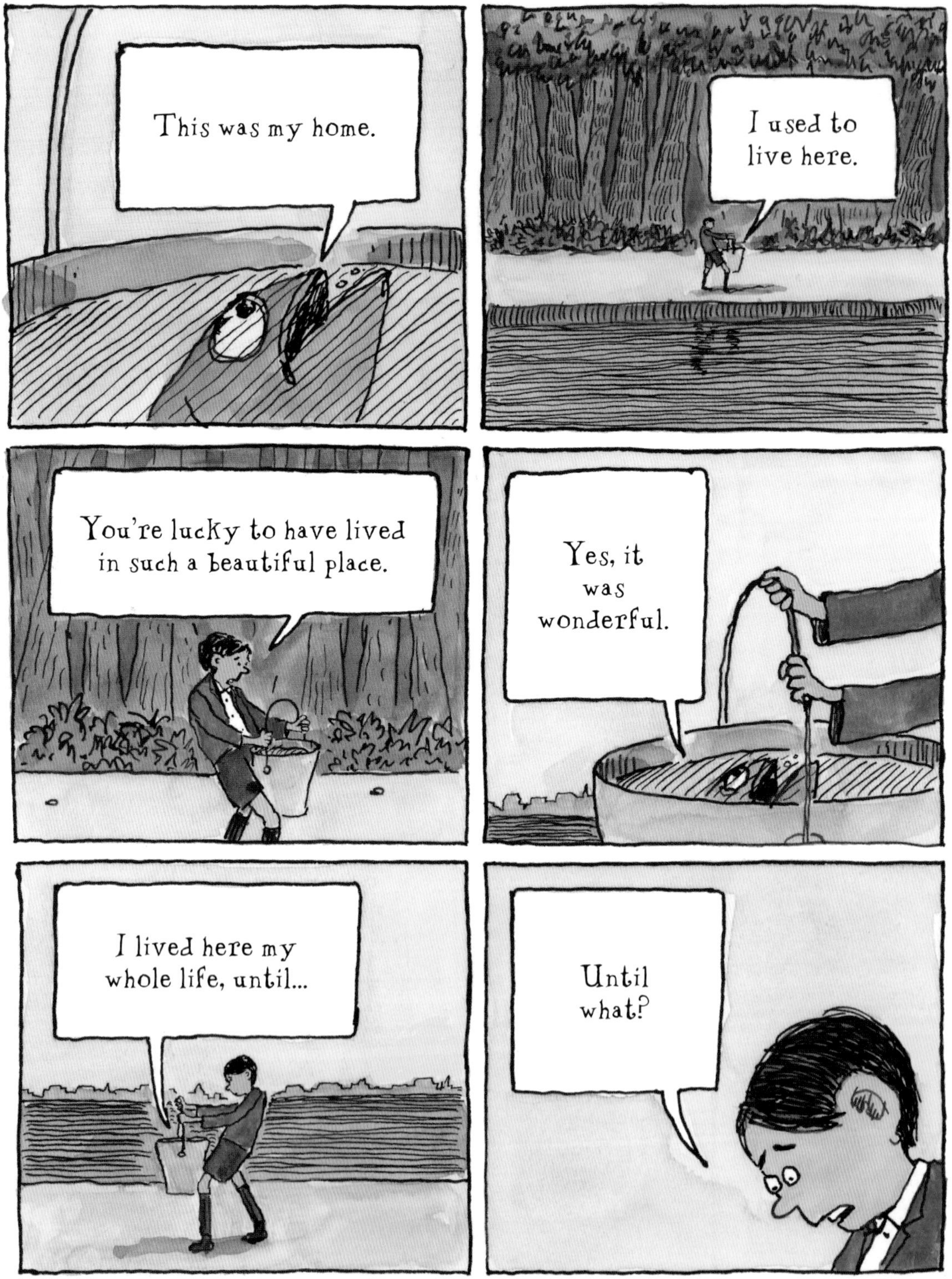
This was my home.
I used to live here.
You're lucky to have lived in such a beautiful place.
Yes, it was wonderful.
I lived here my whole life, until...
Until what?

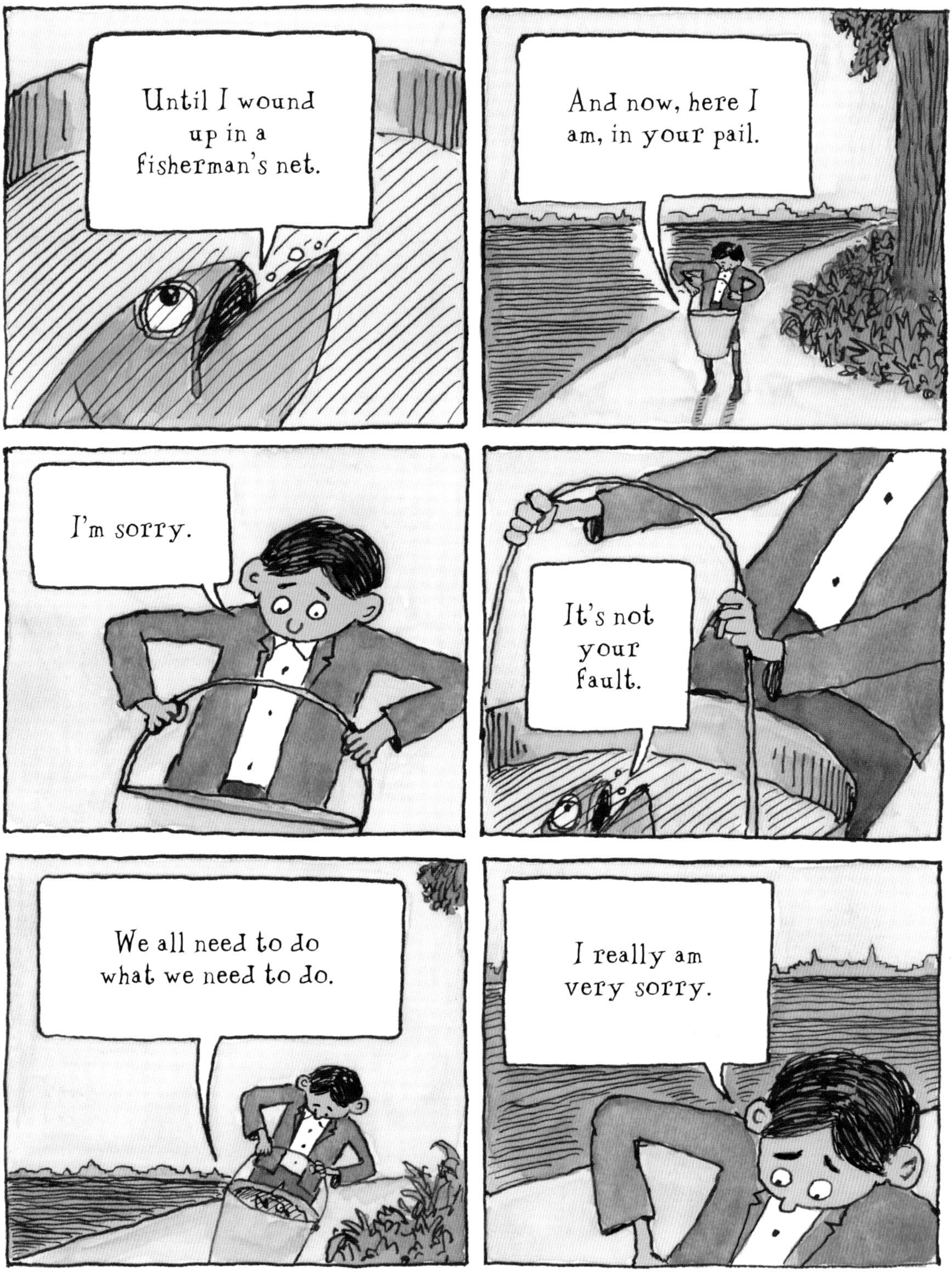
Until I wound up in a fisherman's net.
And now, here I am, in your pail.
I'm sorry.
It's not your fault.
We all need to do what we need to do.
I really am very sorry.

K and the carp continued walking along the riverbank in silence, each thinking their own thoughts.

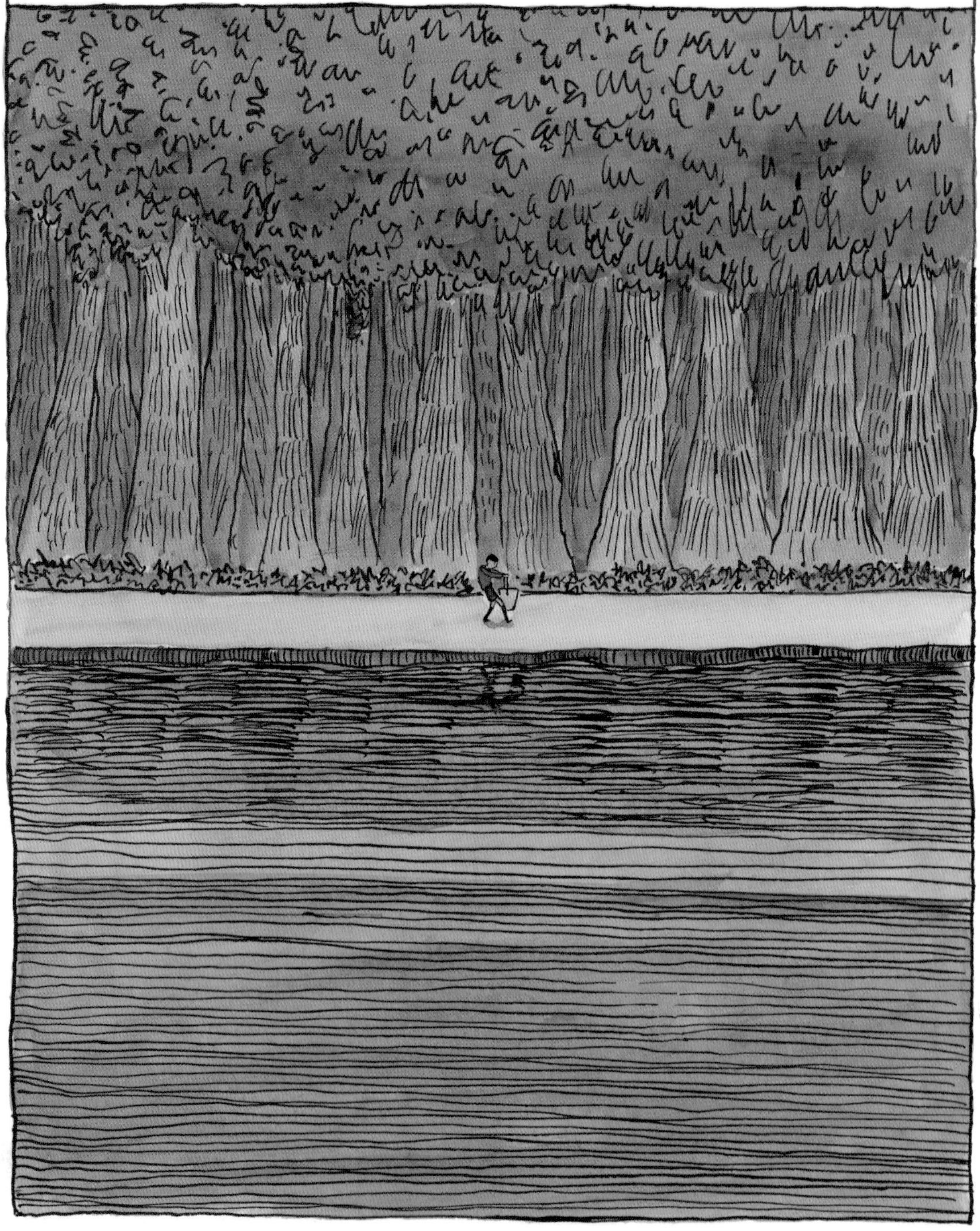

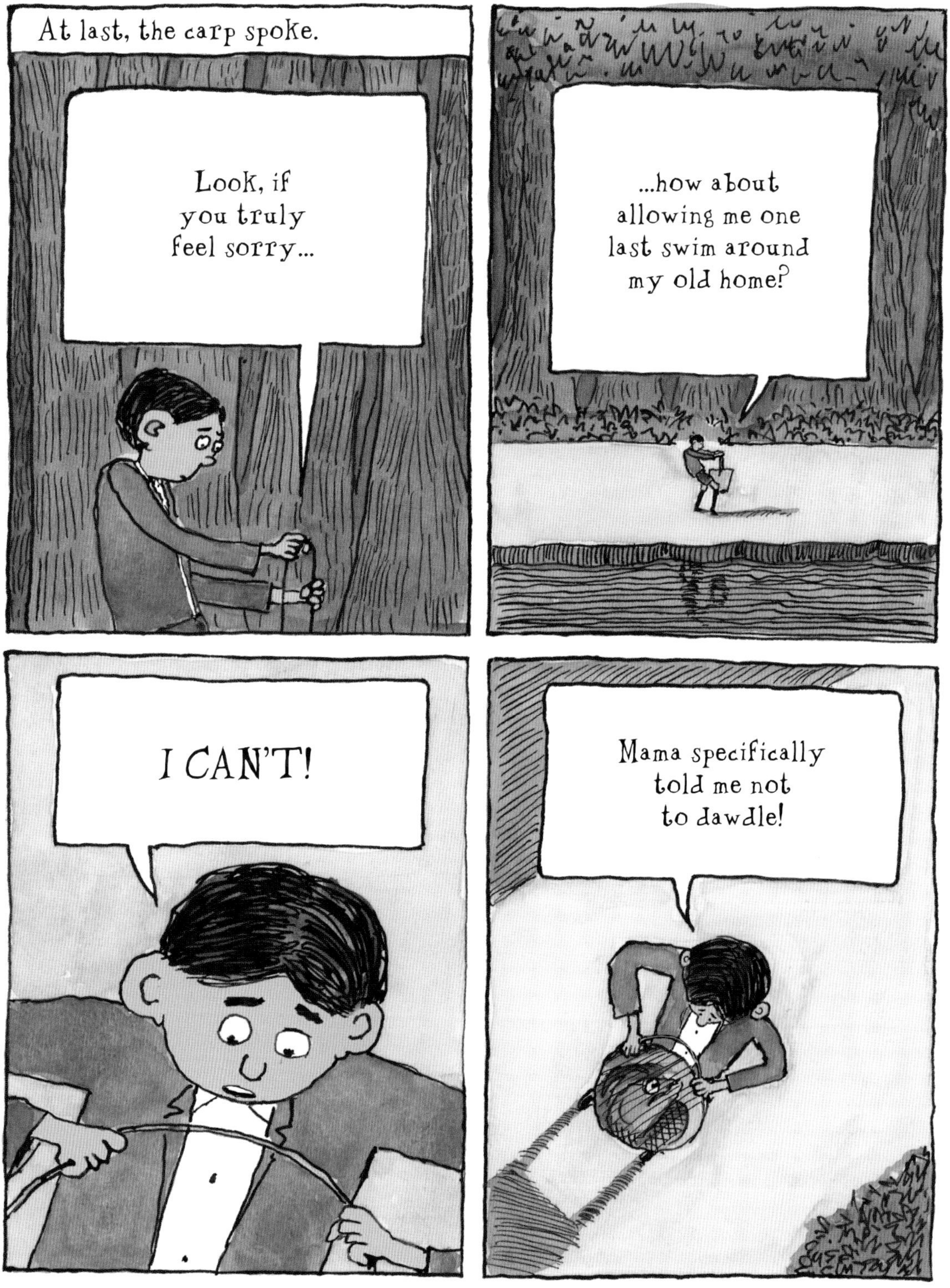
At last, the carp spoke.
Look, if you truly feel sorry...
...how about allowing me one last swim around my old home?
I CAN'T!
Mama specifically told me not to dawdle!

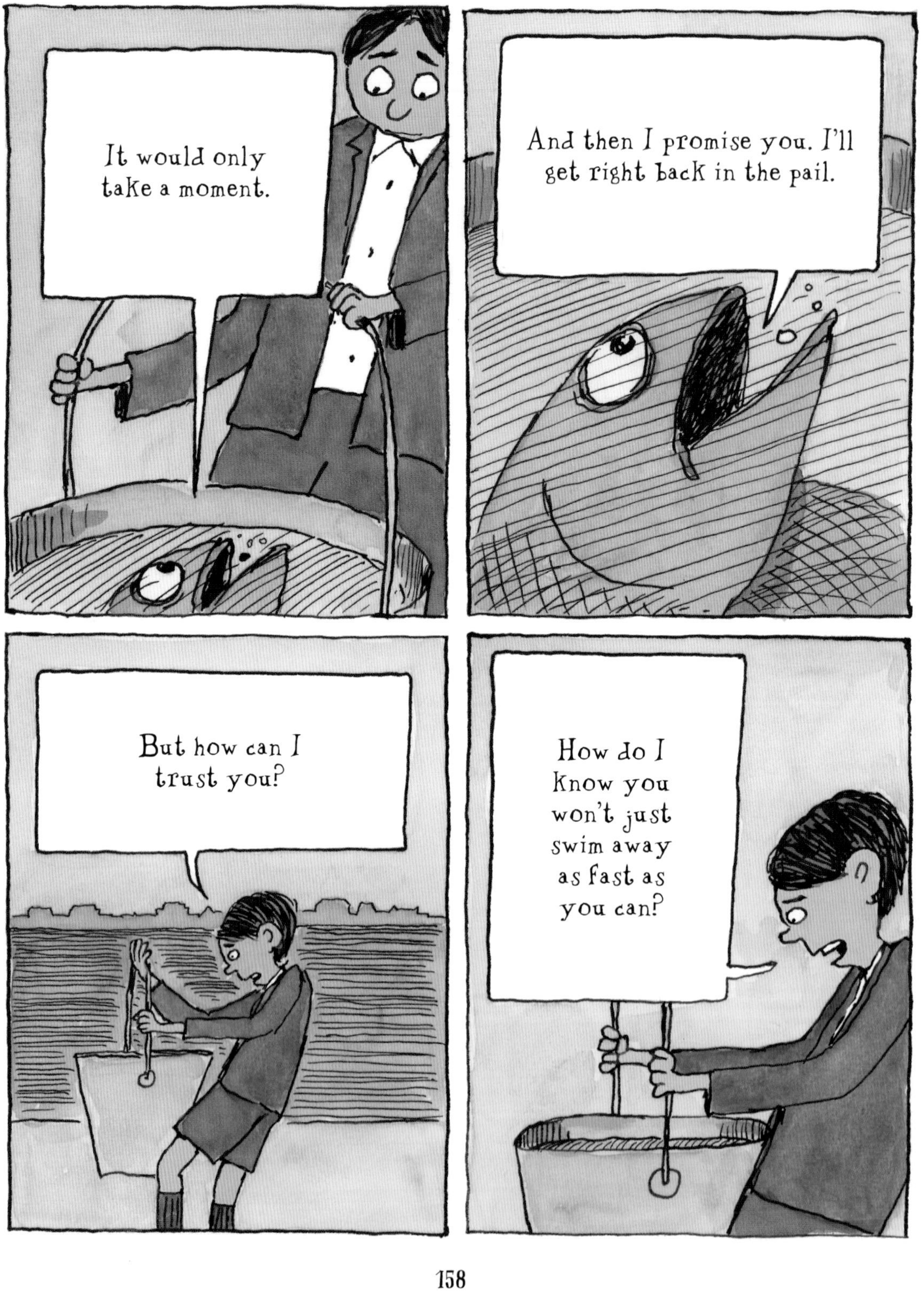
It would only take a moment.
And then I promise you. I'll get right back in the pail.
But how can I trust you?
How do I know you won't just swim away as fast as you can?

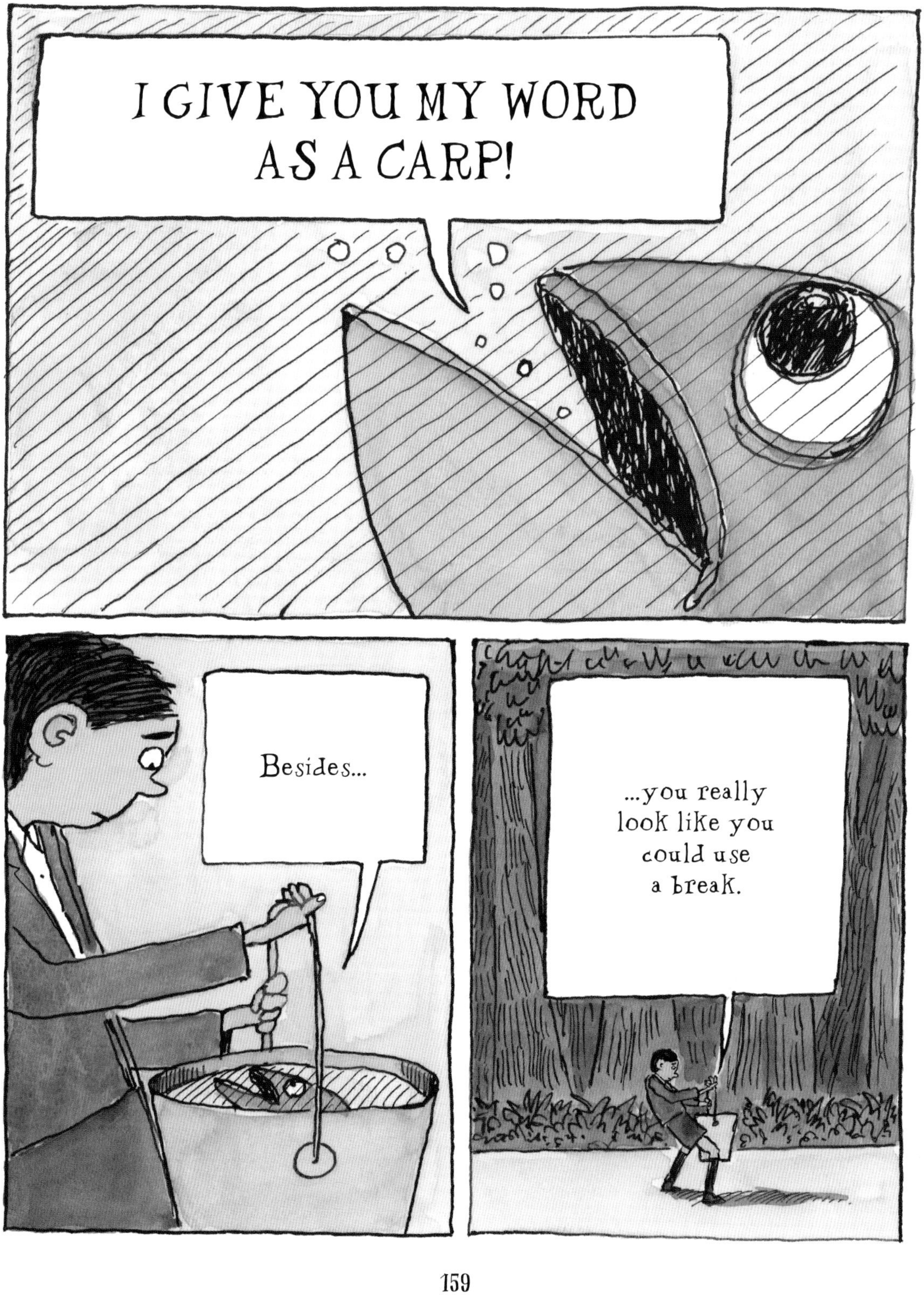
I GIVE YOU MY WORD AS A CARP!
Besides...
...you really look like you could use a break.

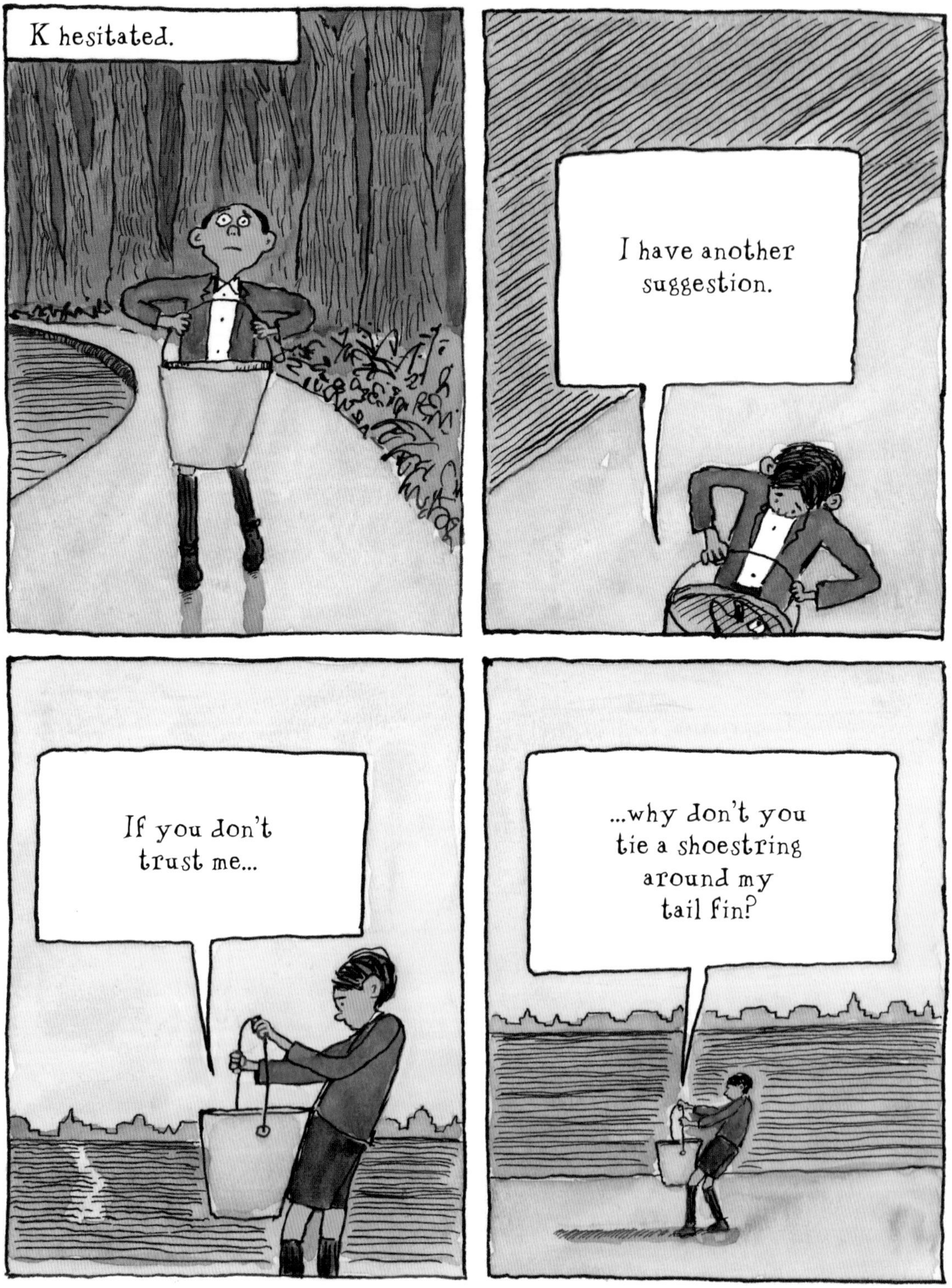
K hesitated.
I have another suggestion.
If you don't trust me...
...why don't you tie a shoestring around my tail fin?

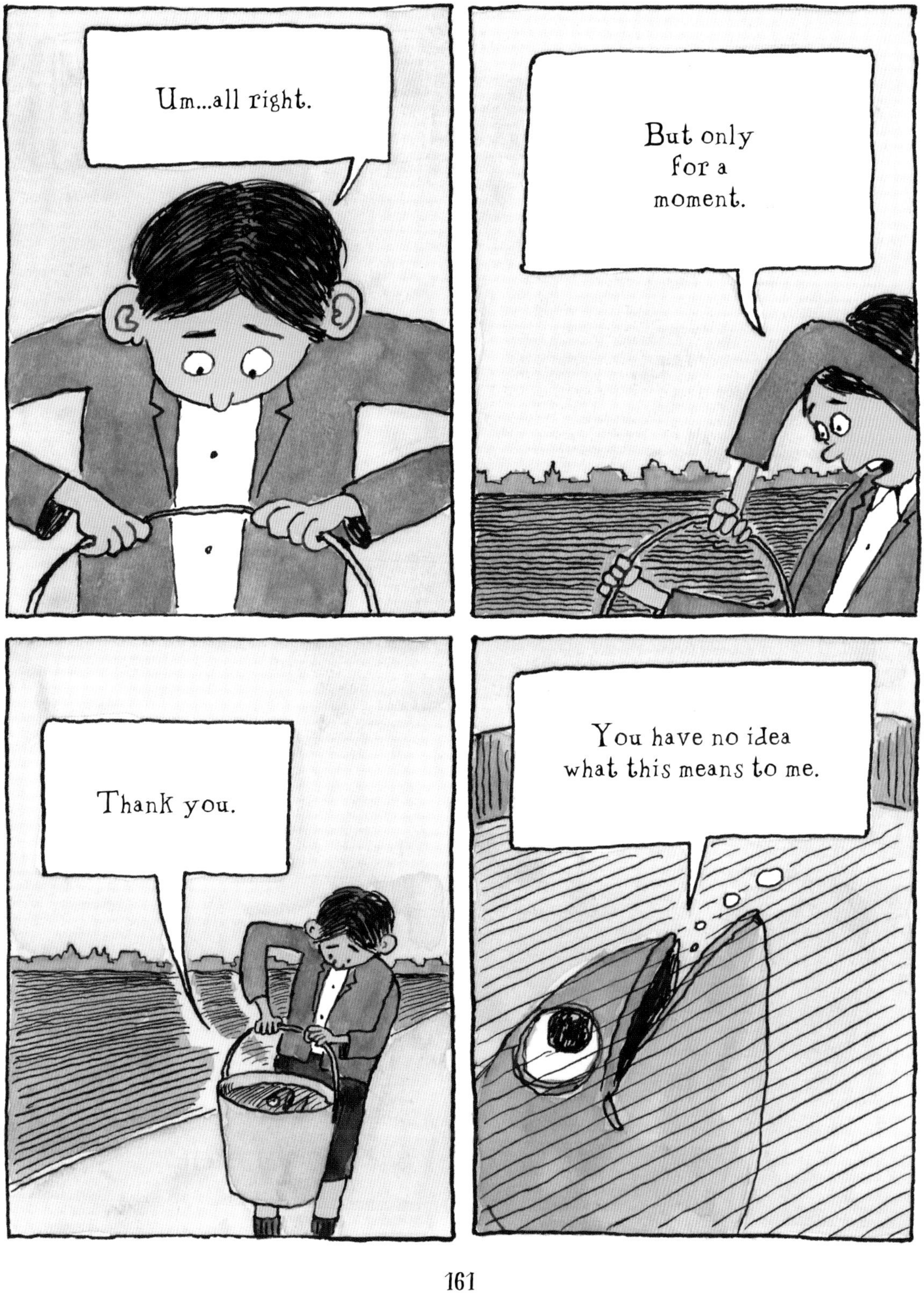
Um...all right.
But only for a moment.
Thank you.
You have no idea what this means to me.

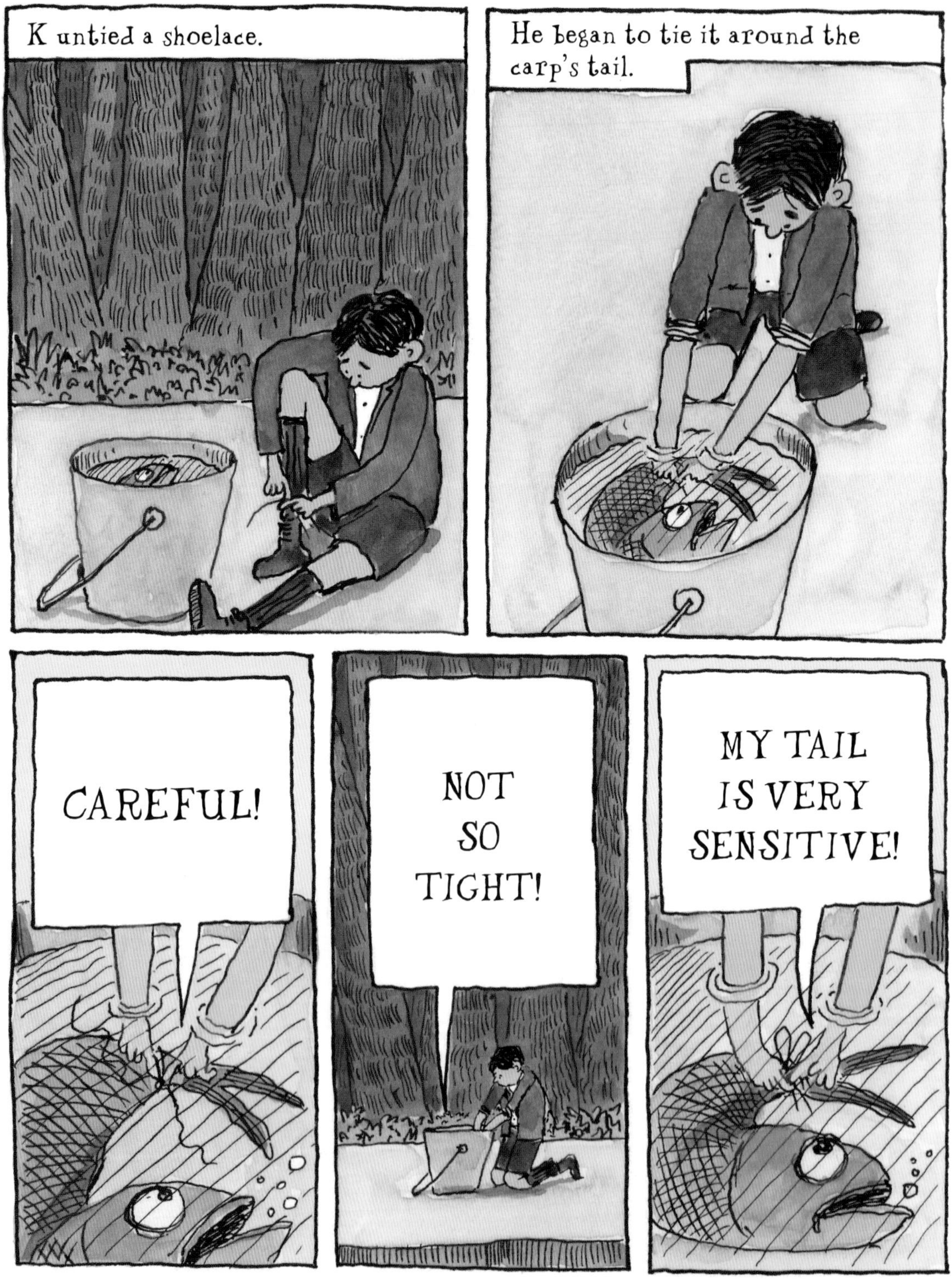
K untied a shoelace.
He began to tie it around the carp's tail.
CAREFUL!
NOT SO TIGHT!
MY TAIL IS VERY SENSITIVE!

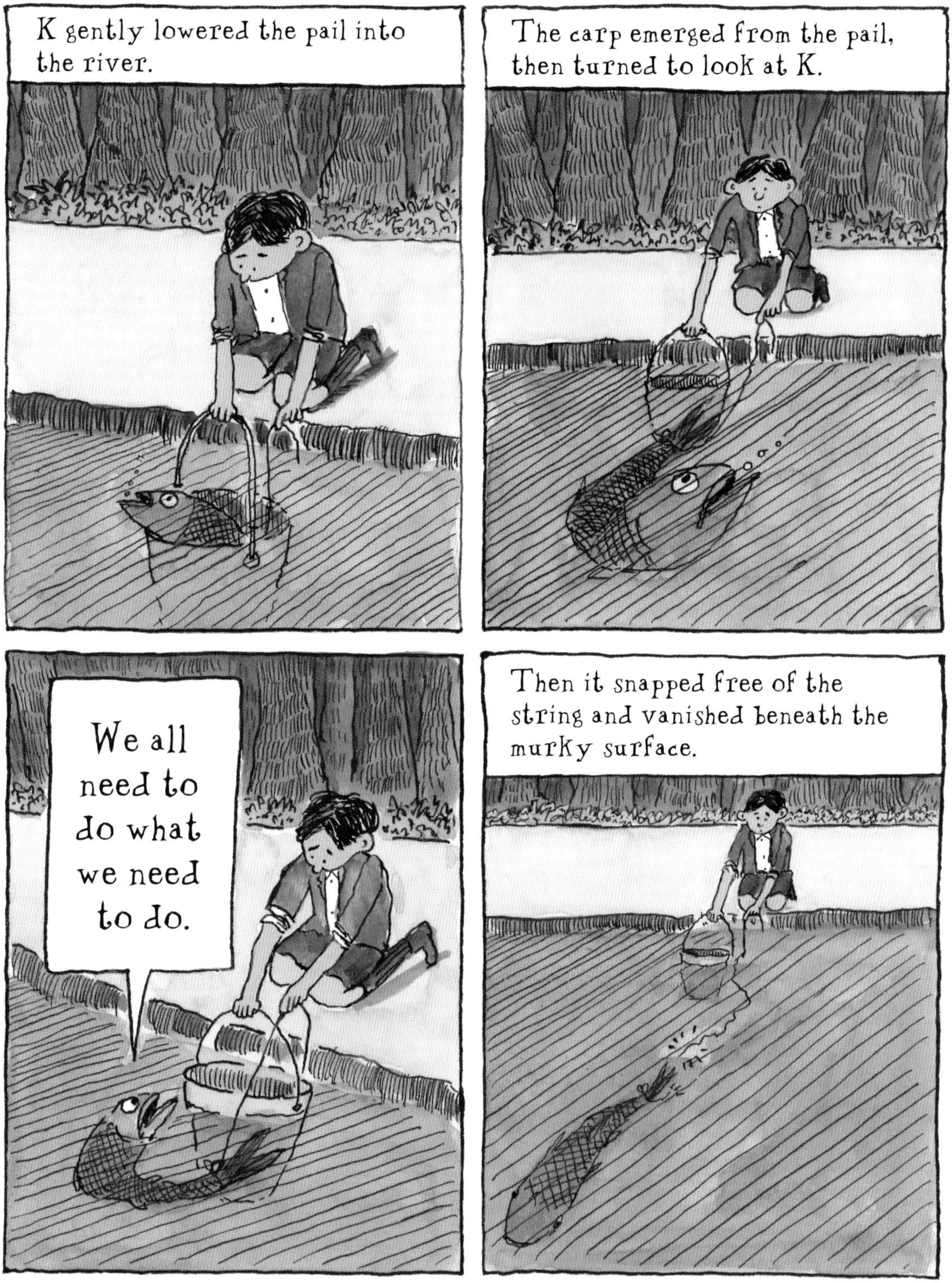
K gently lowered the pail into the river.
The carp emerged from the pail, then turned to look at K.
We all need to do what we need to do.
Then it snapped free of the string and vanished beneath the murky surface.

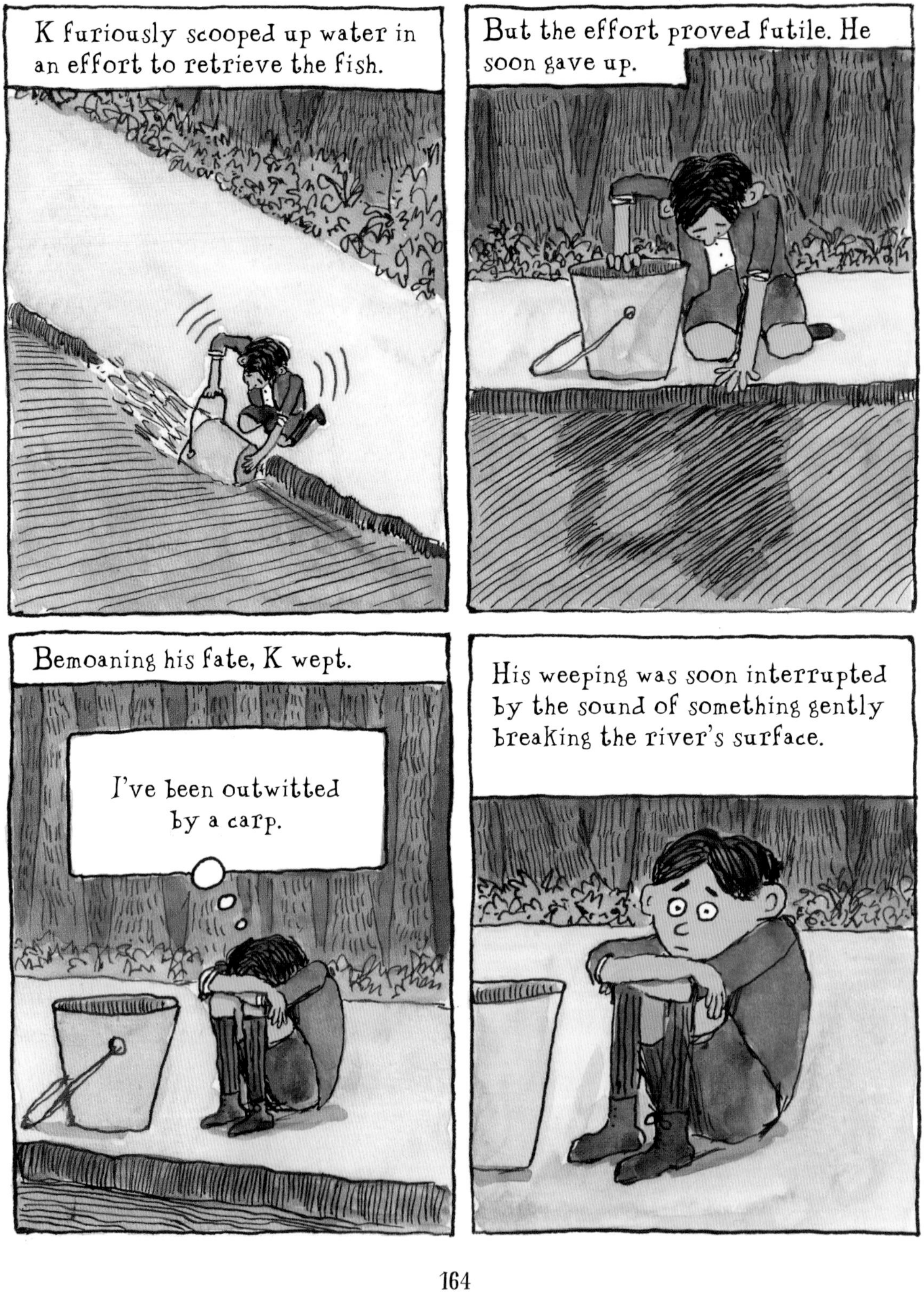
K furiously scooped up water in an effort to retrieve the fish.
But the effort proved futile. He soon gave up.
Bemoaning his fate, K wept.
I've been outwitted by a carp.
His weeping was soon interrupted by the sound of something gently breaking the river's surface.

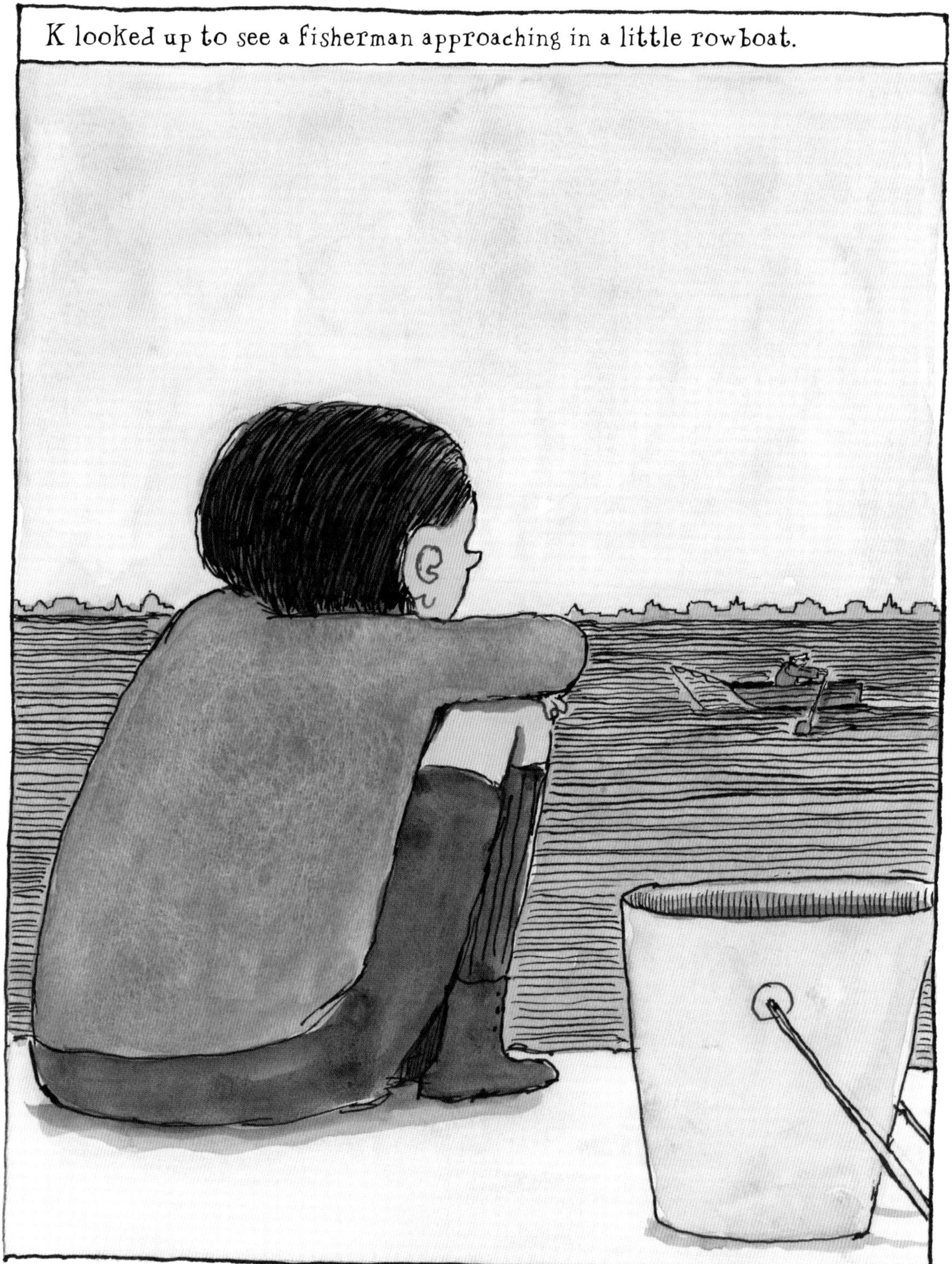
K looked up to see a fisherman approaching in a little rowboat.

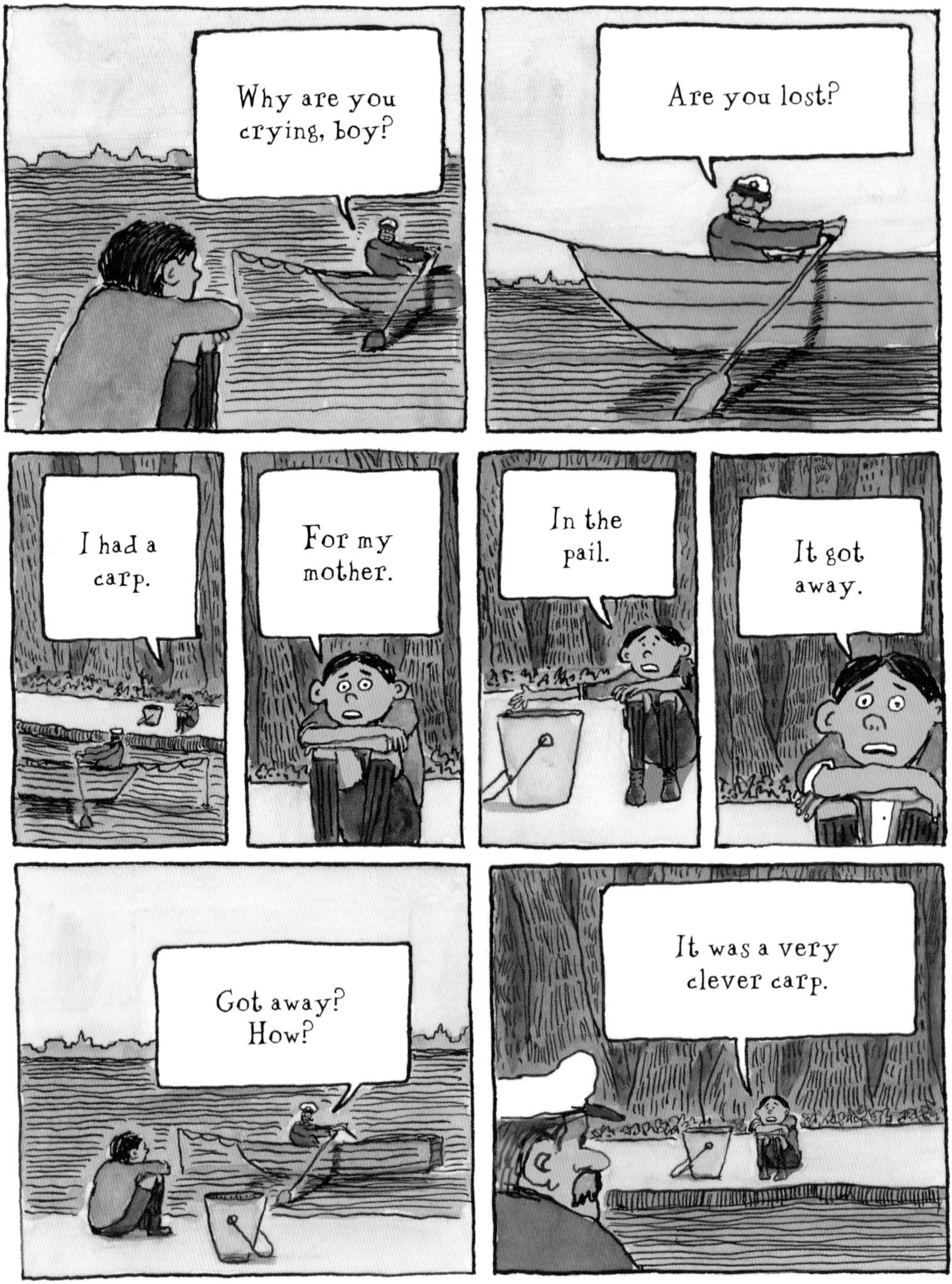
Why are you crying, boy?
Are you lost?
I had a carp.
For my mother.
In the pail.
It got away.
Got away? How?
It was a very clever carp.

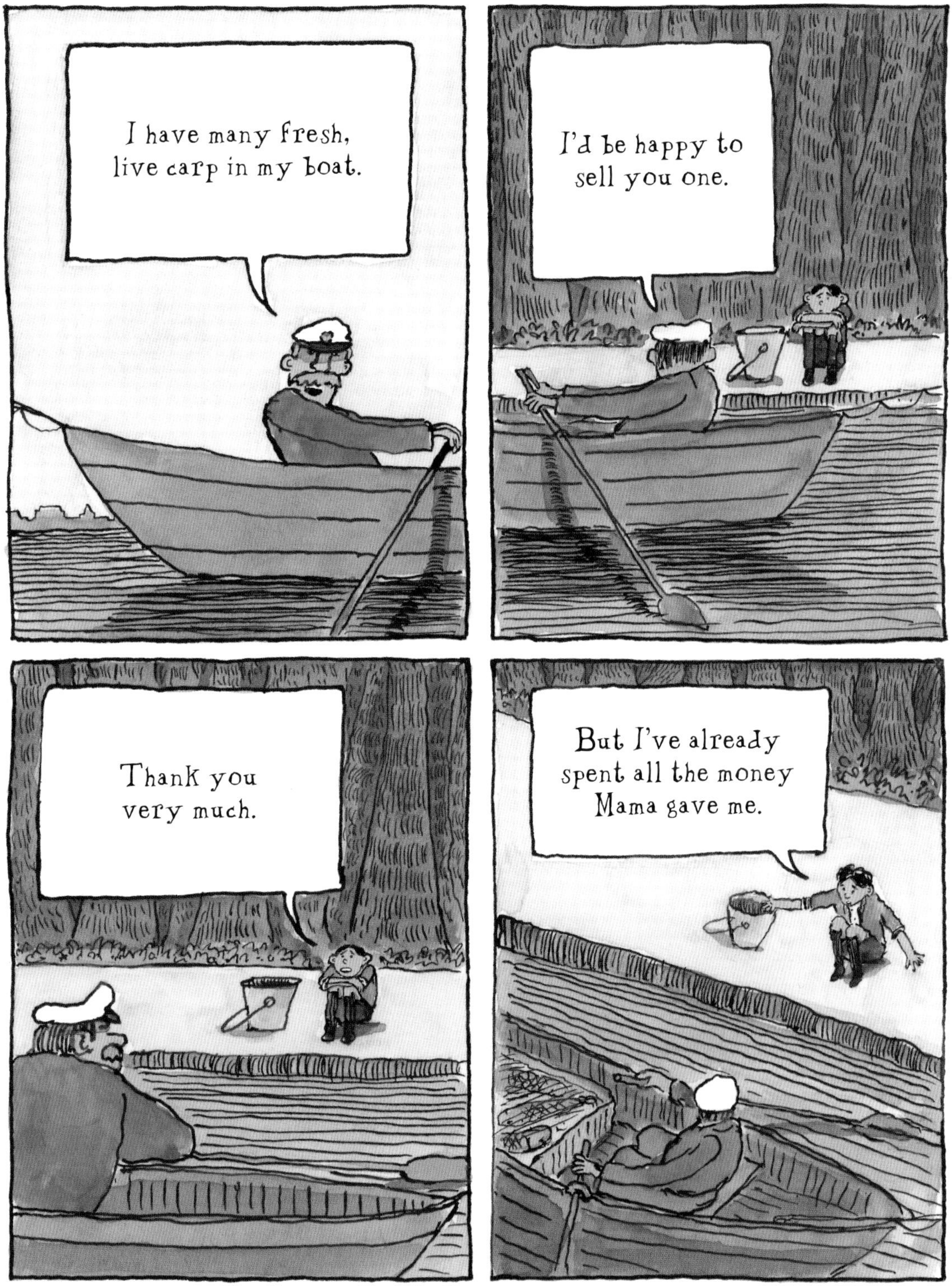
I have many fresh, live carp in my boat.
I'd be happy to sell you one.
Thank you very much.
But I've already spent all the money Mama gave me.

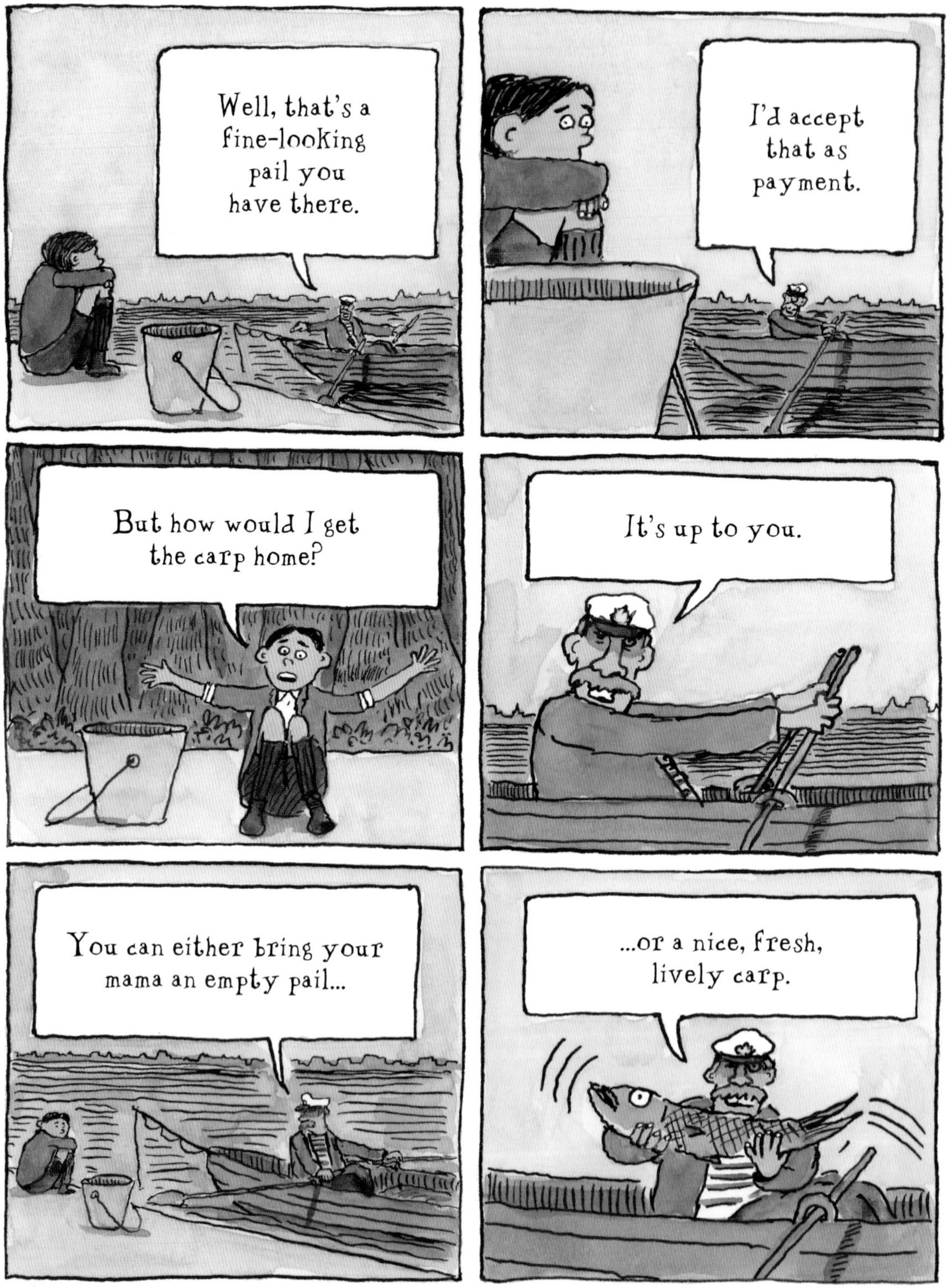
Well, that's a fine-looking pail you have there.
I'd accept that as payment.
But how would I get the carp home?
It's up to you.
You can either bring your mama an empty pail...
...or a nice, fresh, lively carp.

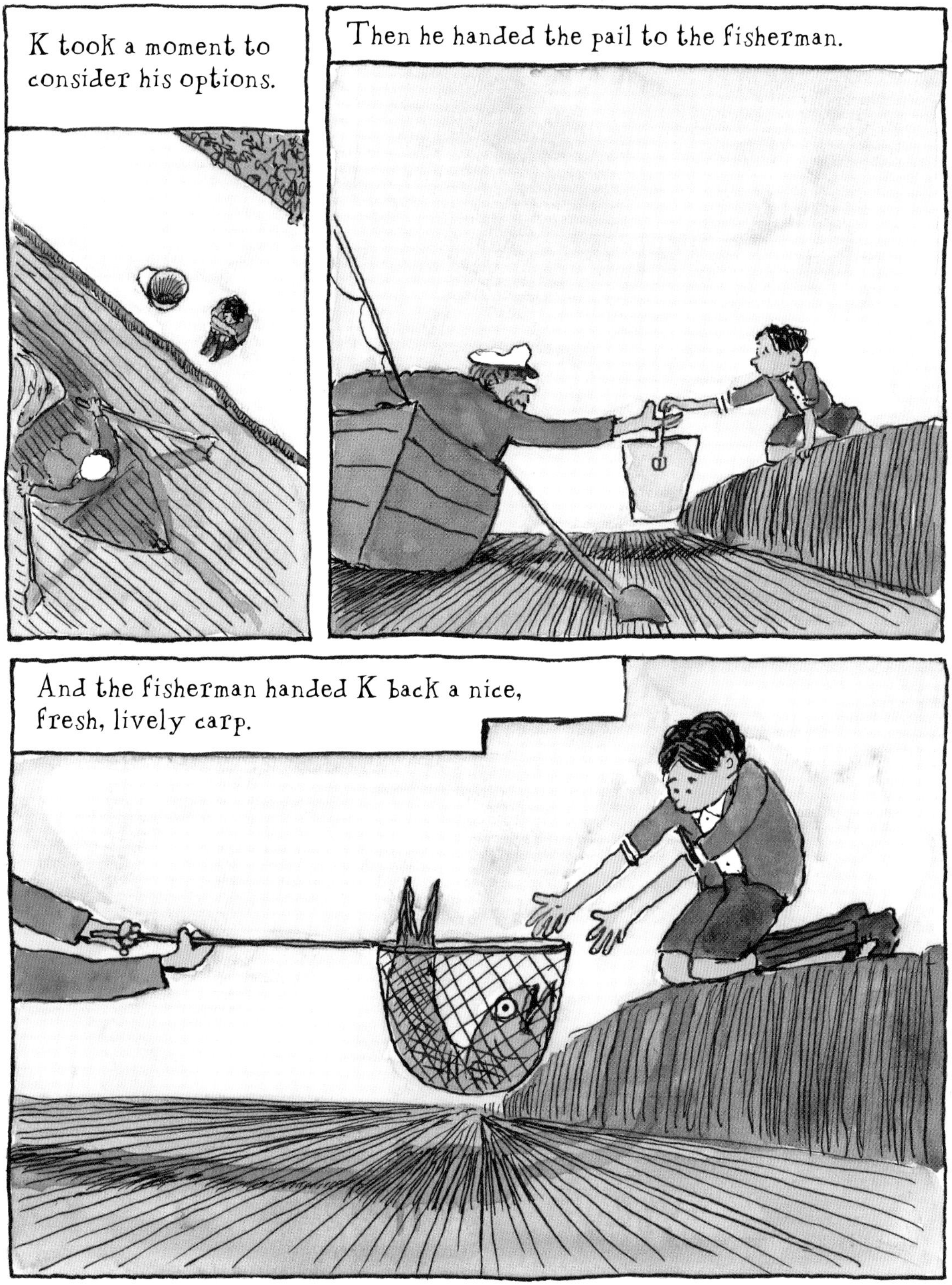
K took a moment to consider his options.
Then he handed the pail to the fisherman.
And the fisherman handed K back a nice, fresh, lively carp.

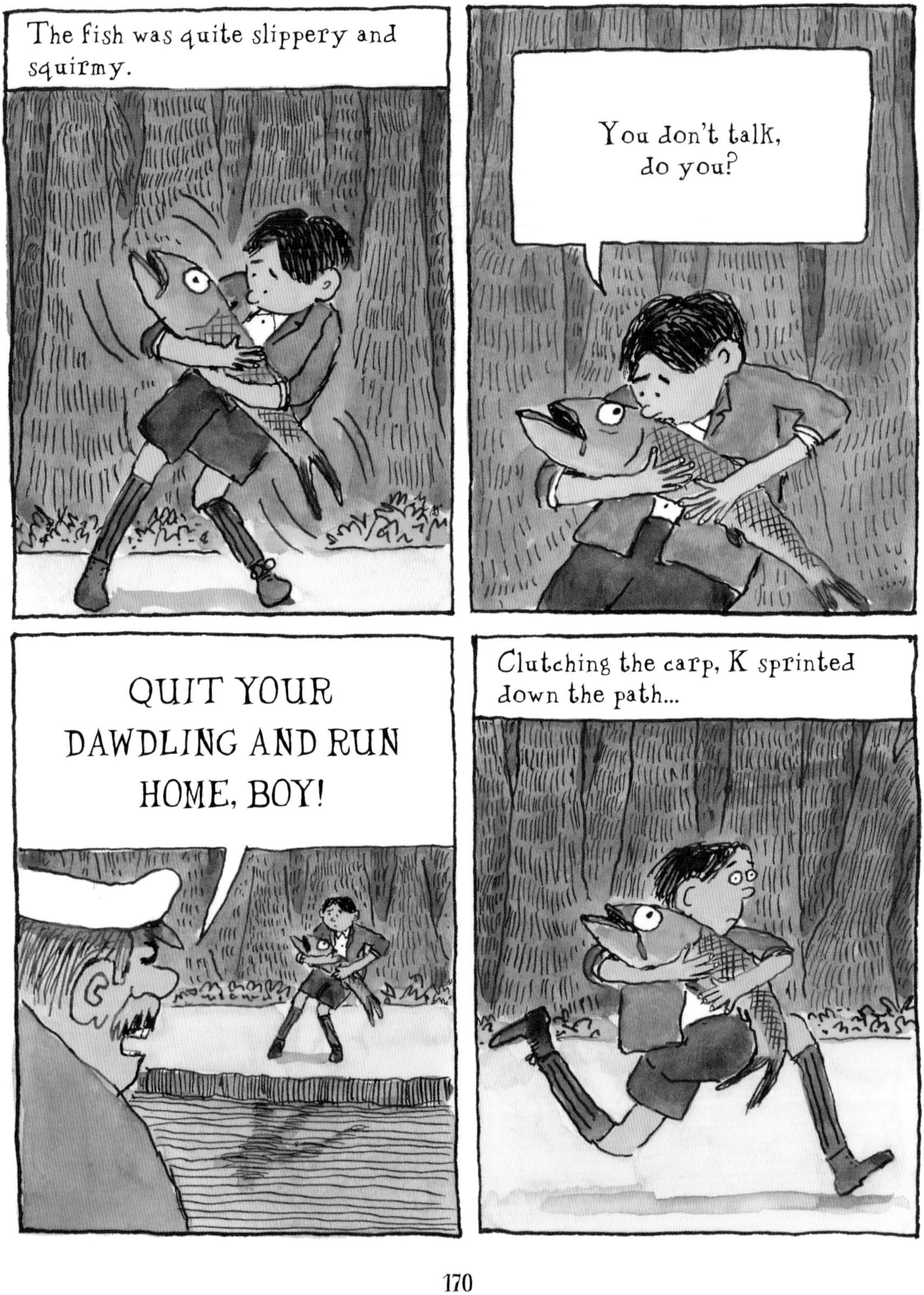
The fish was quite slippery and squirmy.
You don't talk, do you?
QUIT YOUR DAWDLING AND RUN HOME, BOY!
Clutching the carp, K sprinted down the path...

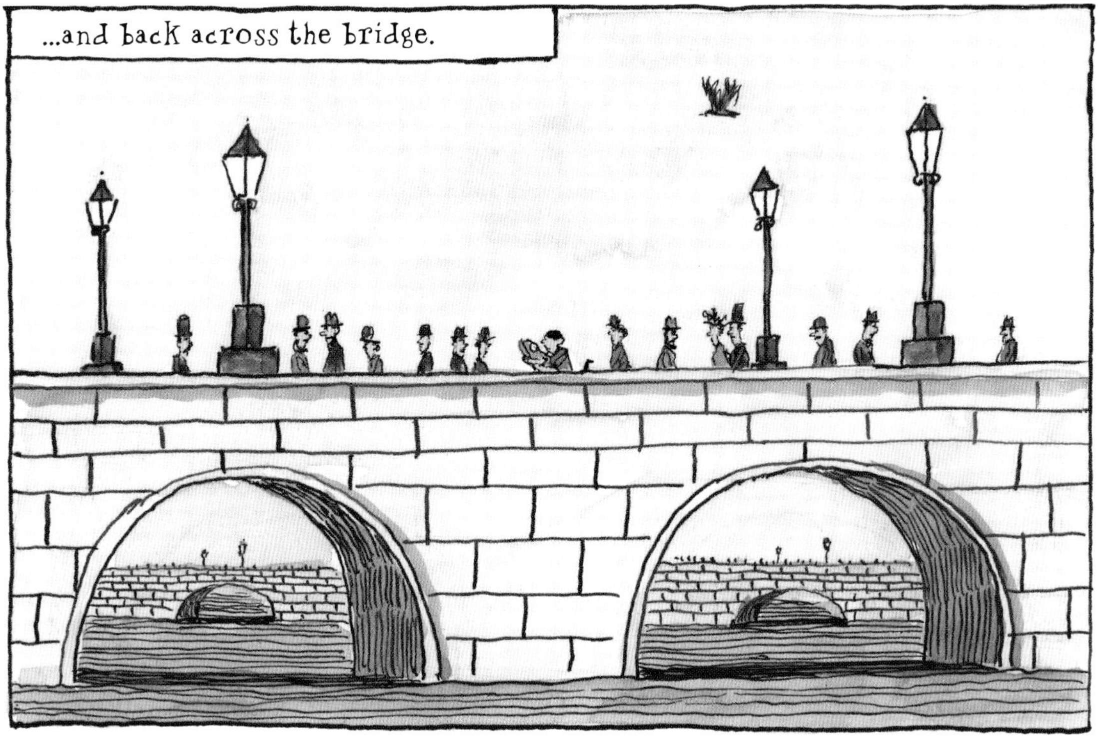
...and back across the bridge.

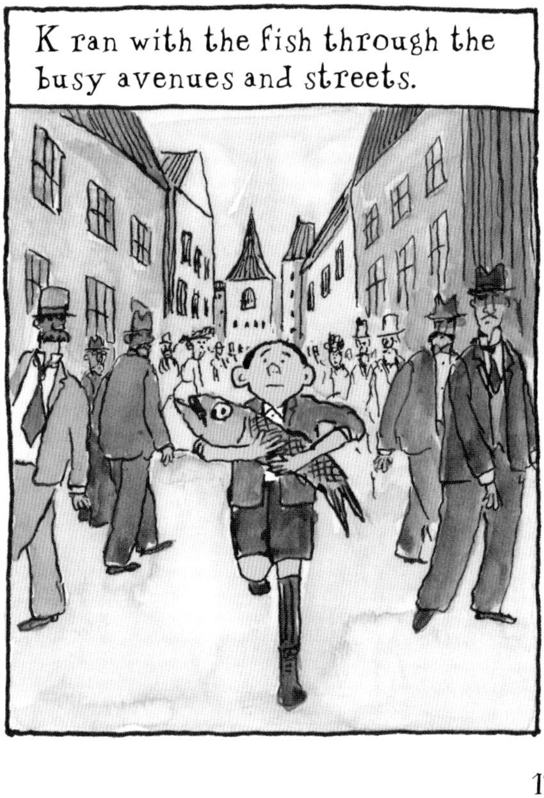
K ran with the fish through the busy avenues and streets.

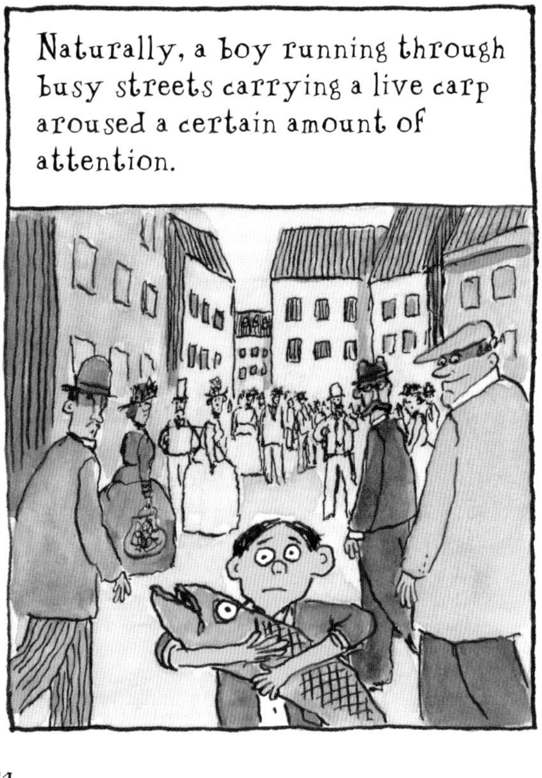
Naturally, a boy running through busy streets carrying a live carp aroused a certain amount of attention.

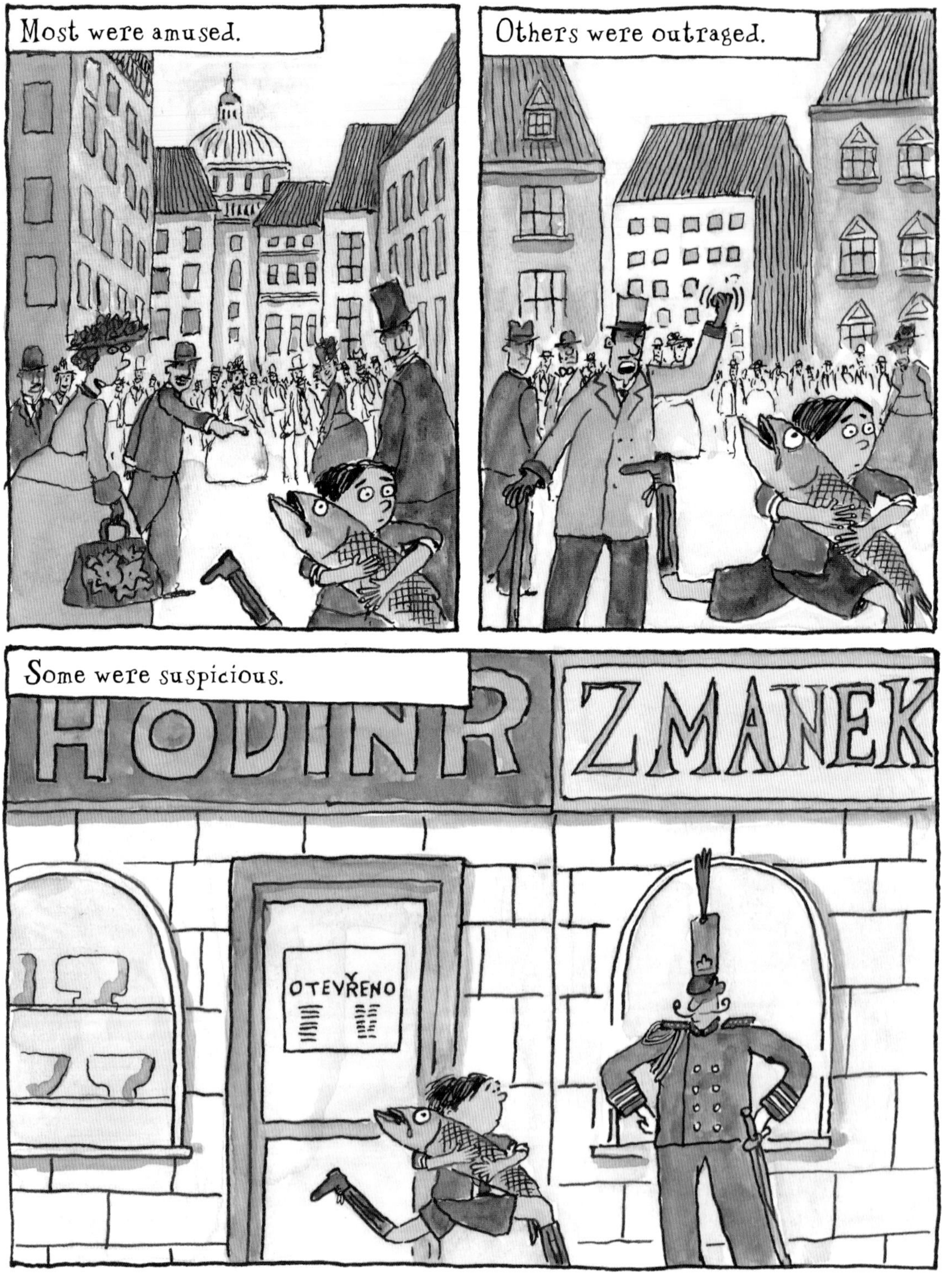
Most were amused.
Others were outraged.
Some were suspicious.
HODINR
ZMANEK
OTEVŘENO

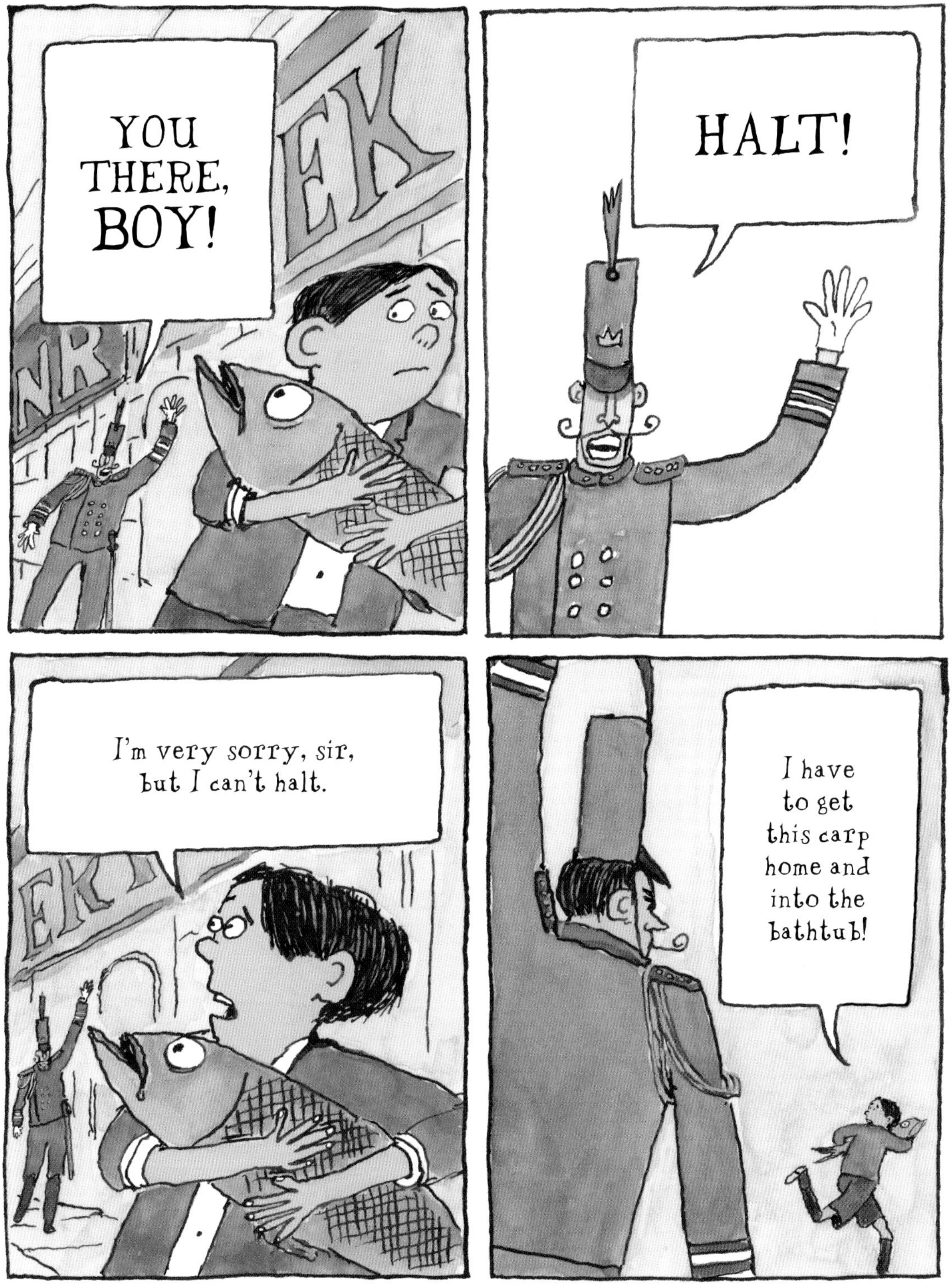
YOU THERE, BOY!
HALT!
I'm very sorry, sir, but I can't halt.
I have to get this carp home and into the bathtub!

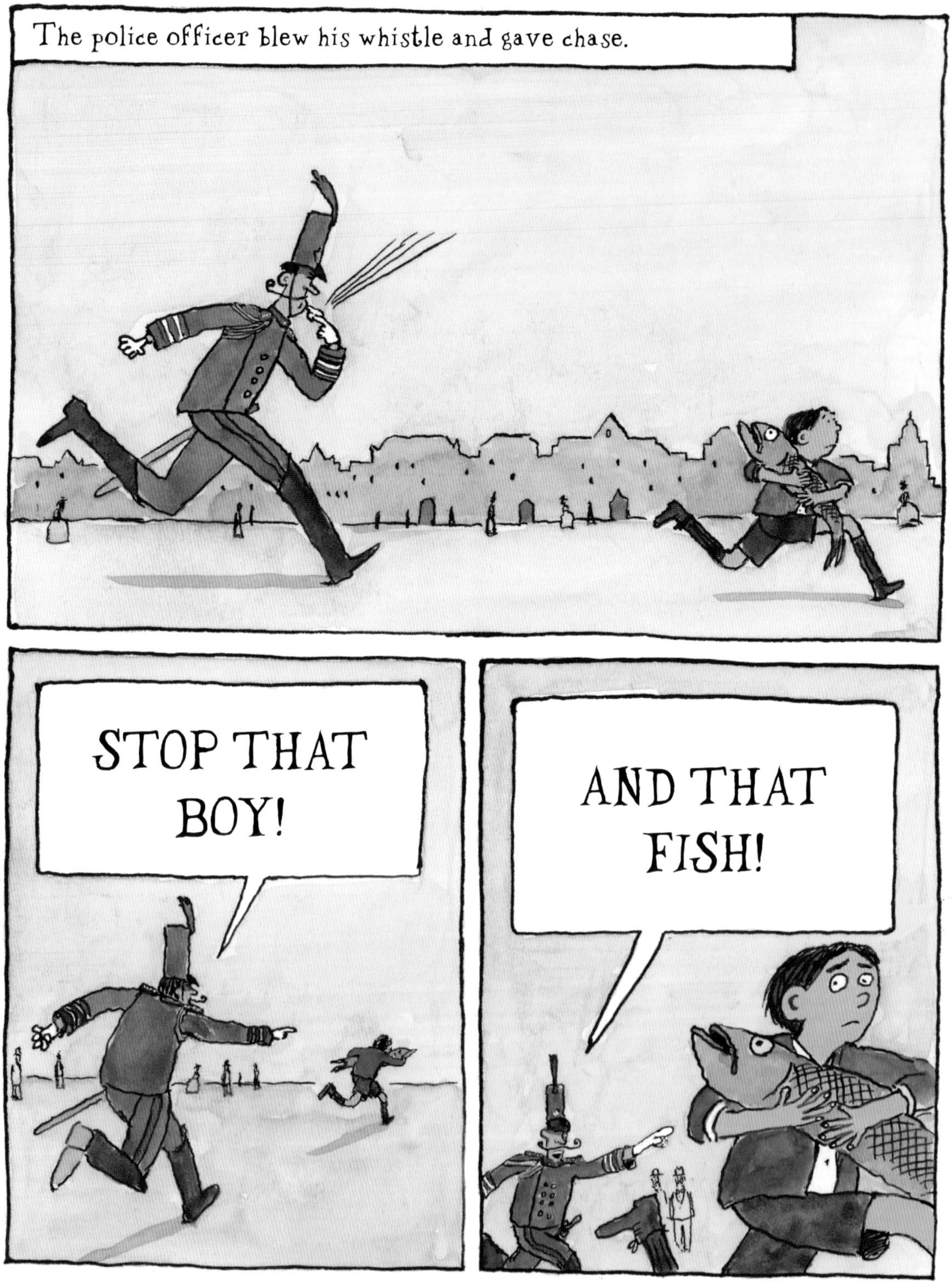
The police officer blew his whistle and gave chase.
STOP THAT BOY!
AND THAT FISH!

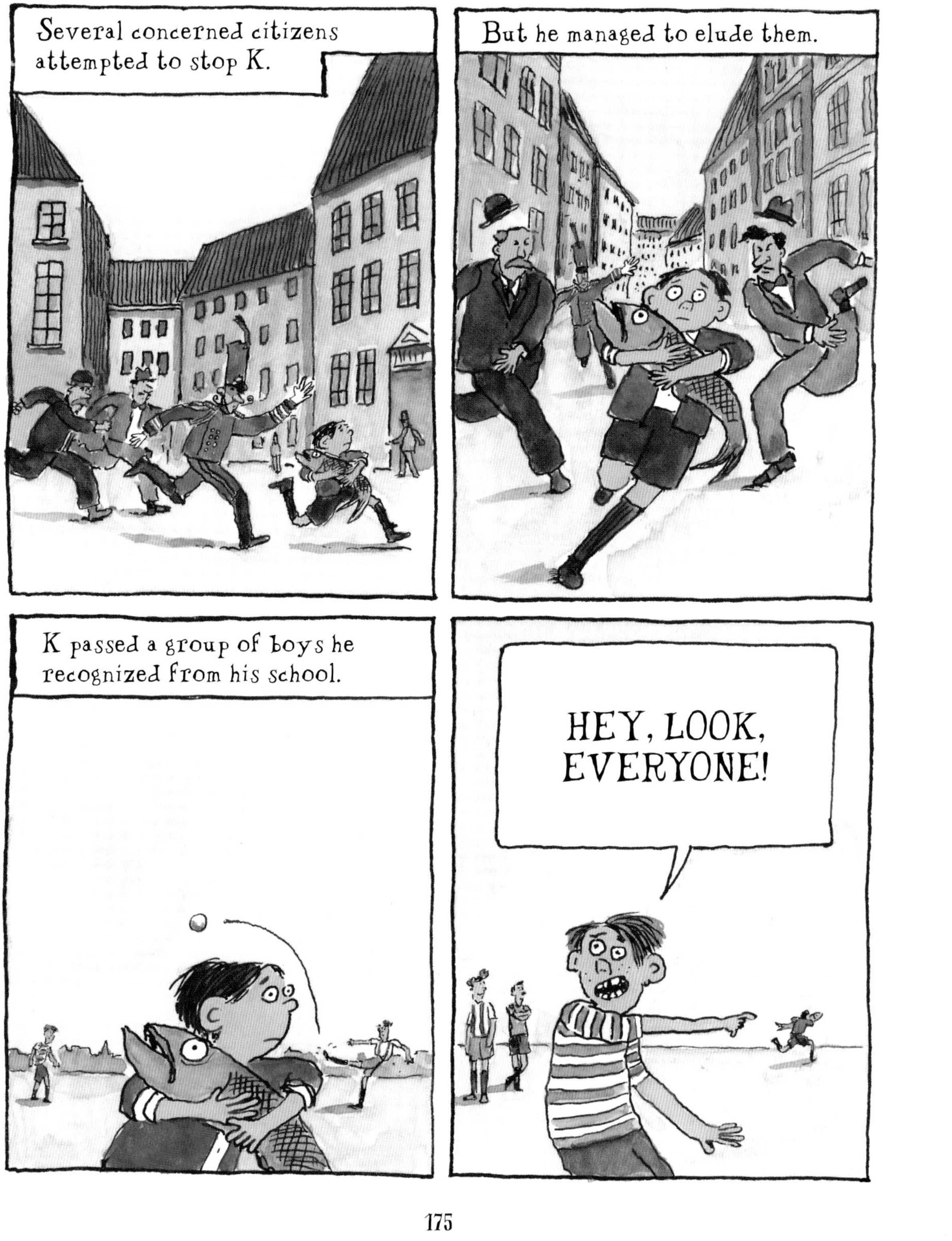
Several concerned citizens attempted to stop K.
But he managed to elude them.
K passed a group of boys he recognized from his school.
HEY, LOOK, EVERYONE!

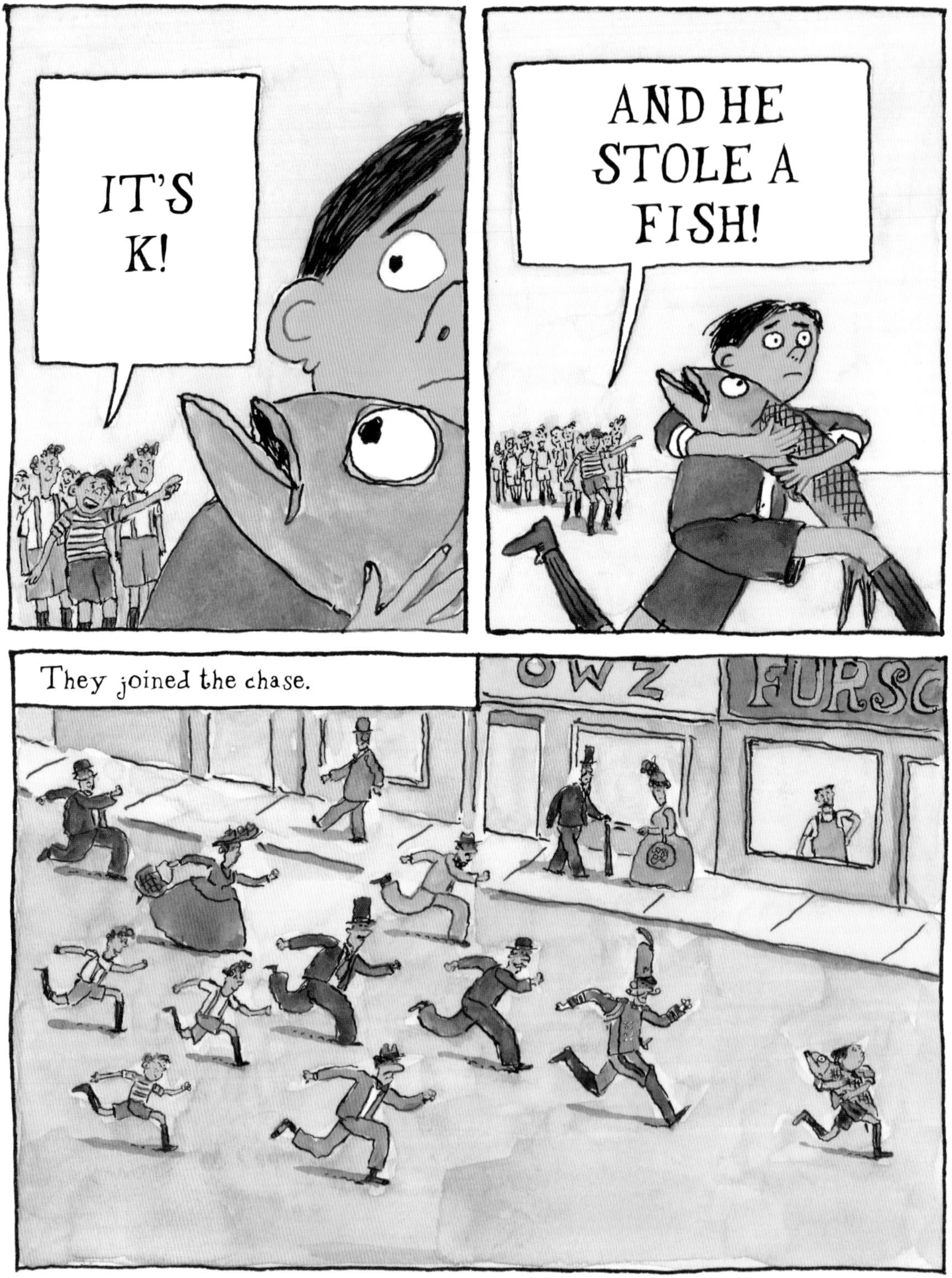
IT'S K!
AND HE STOLE A FISH!
They joined the chase.
OWZ
FURSC

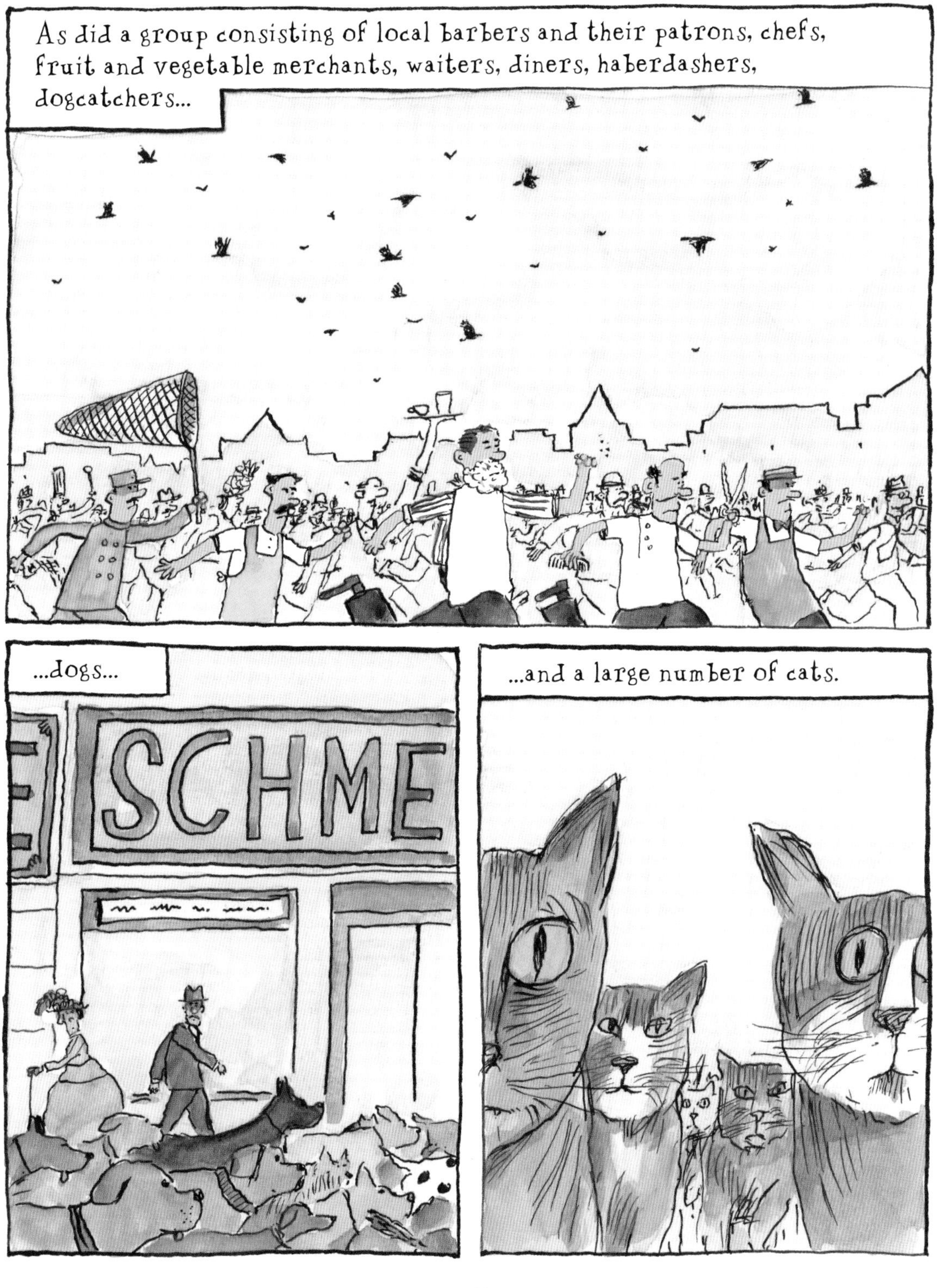
As did a group consisting of local barbers and their patrons, chefs, fruit and vegetable merchants, waiters, diners, haberdashers, dogcatchers...
...dogs...
SCHME
...and a large number of cats.

They pursued K down narrow streets and alleys...

...past the looming tower of the Castle...

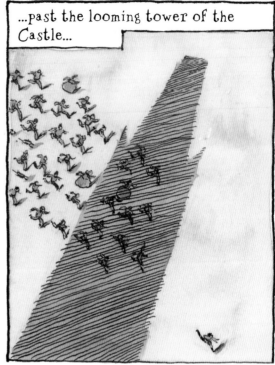

...across the open square in front of his building...

...up the stairs to his apartment...

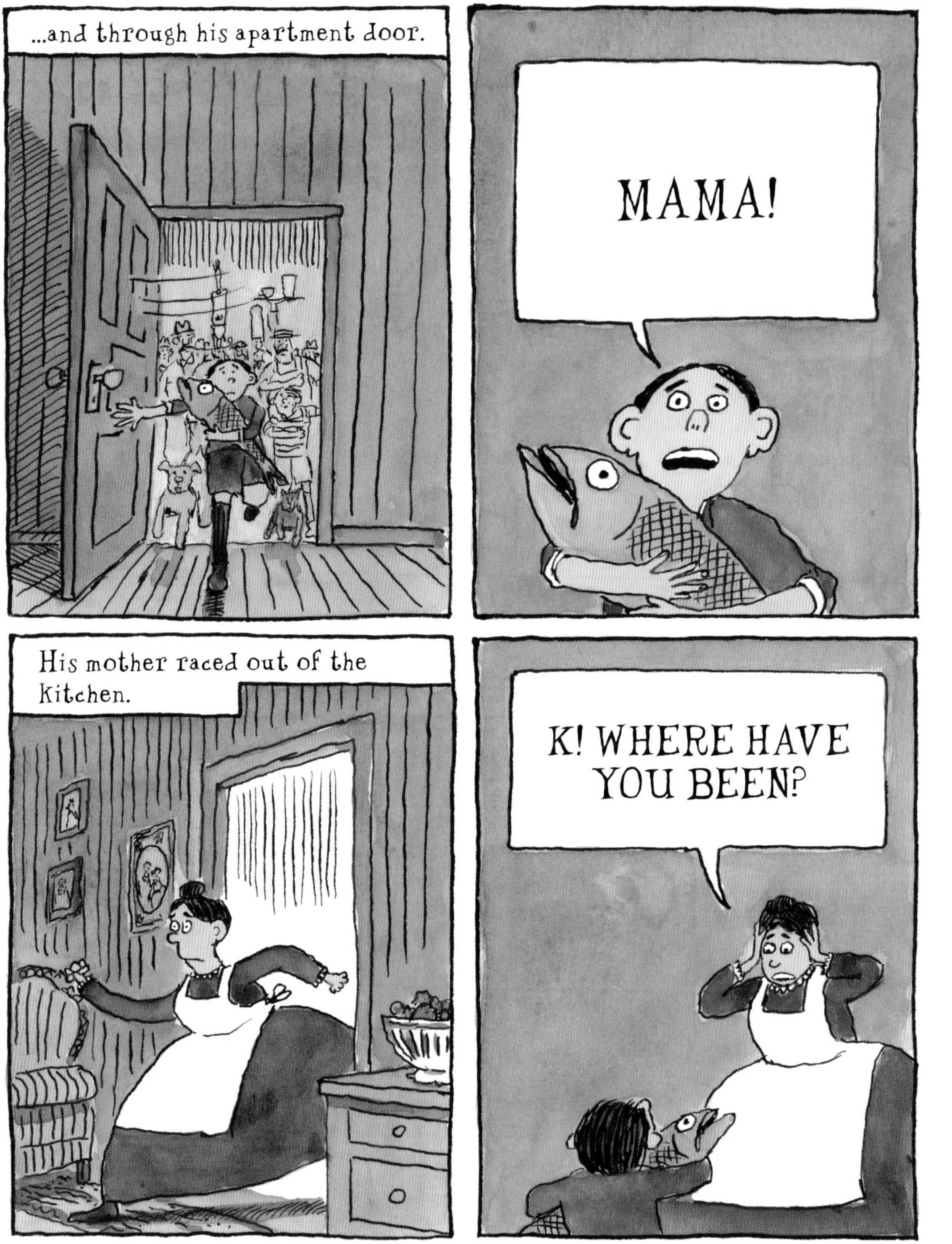
...and through his apartment door.
MAMA!
His mother raced out of the kitchen.
K! WHERE HAVE YOU BEEN?

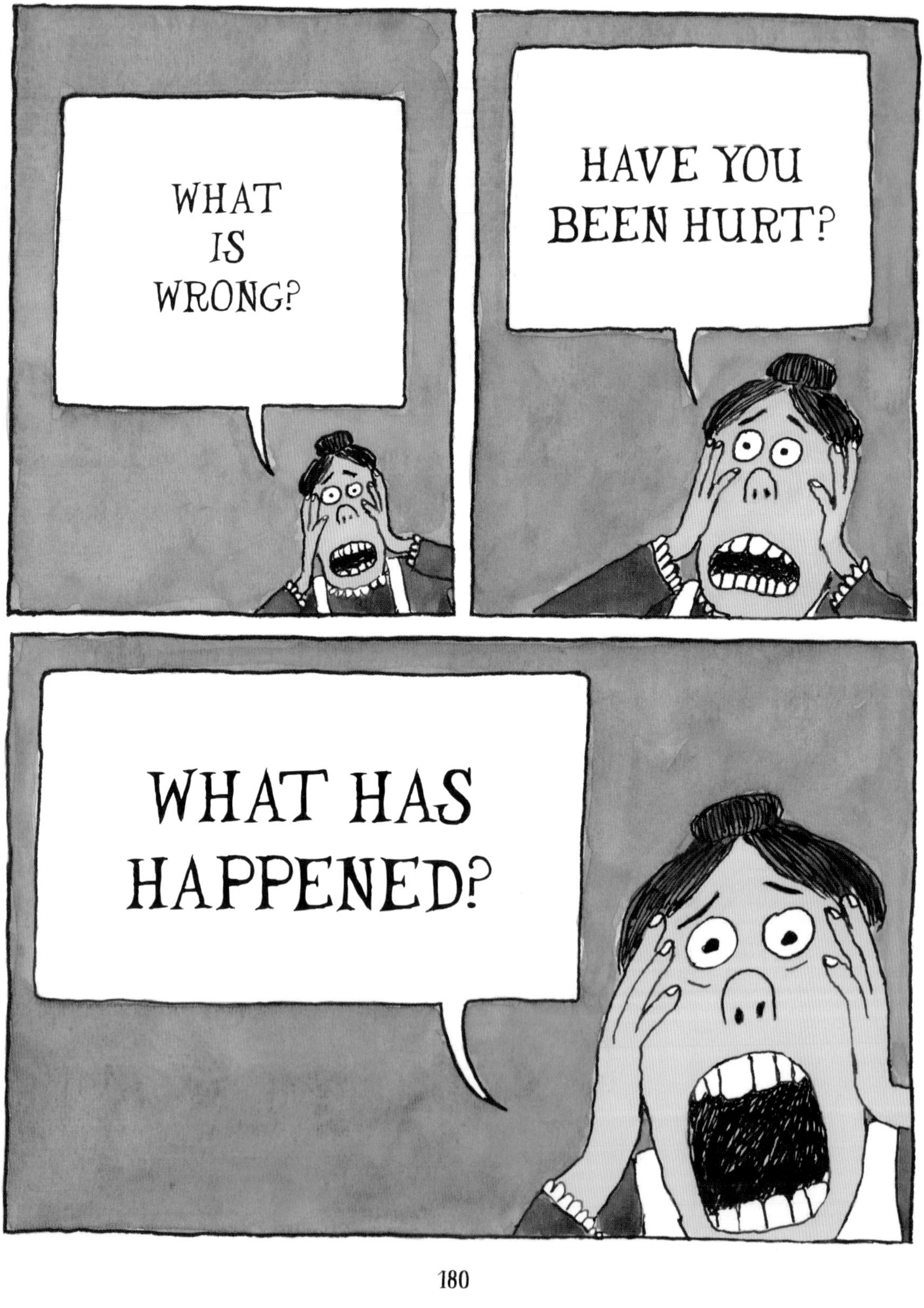
WHAT IS WRONG?
HAVE YOU BEEN HURT?
WHAT HAS HAPPENED?

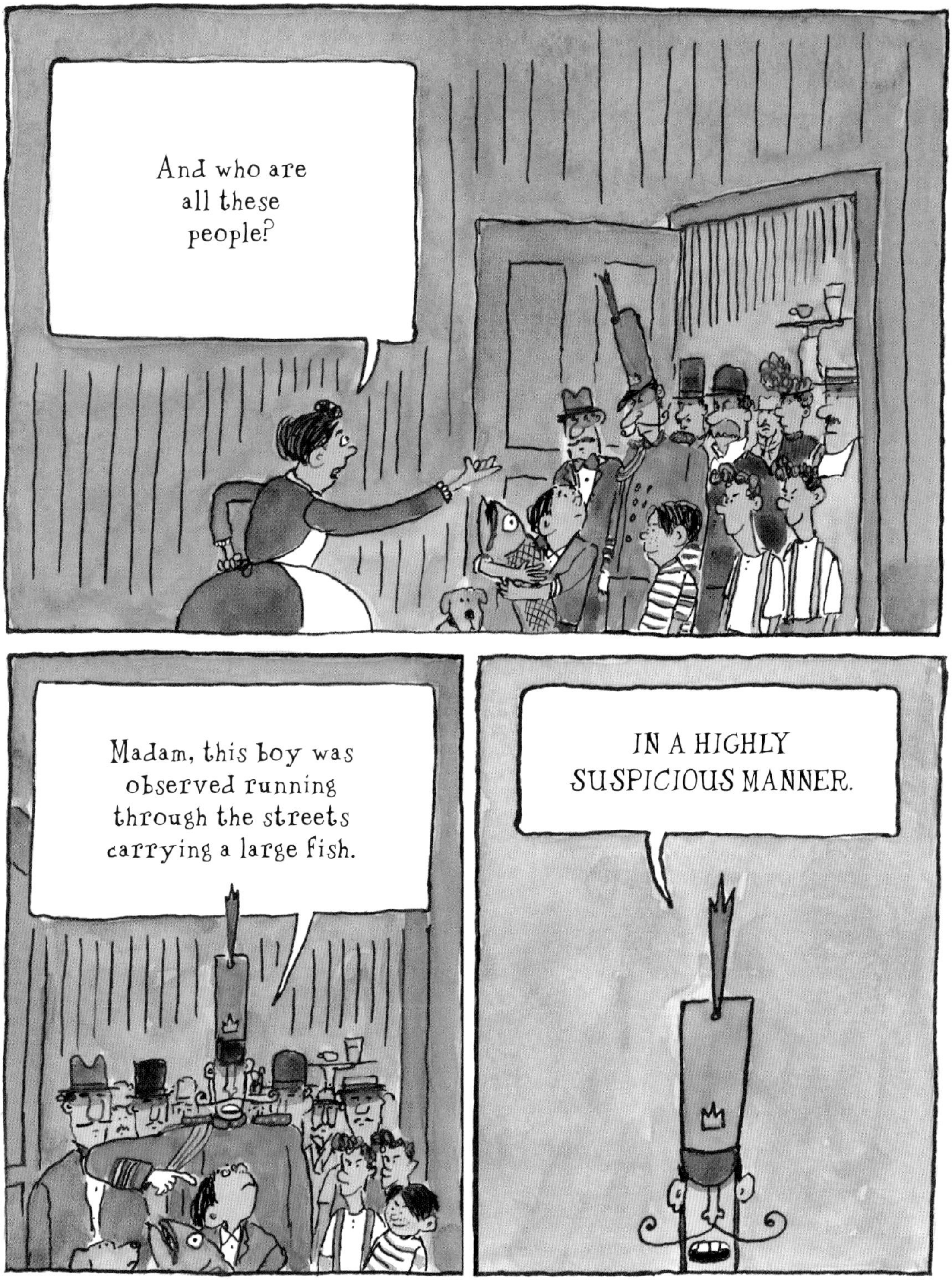
And who are all these people?
Madam, this boy was observed running through the streets carrying a large fish.
IN A HIGHLY SUSPICIOUS MANNER.

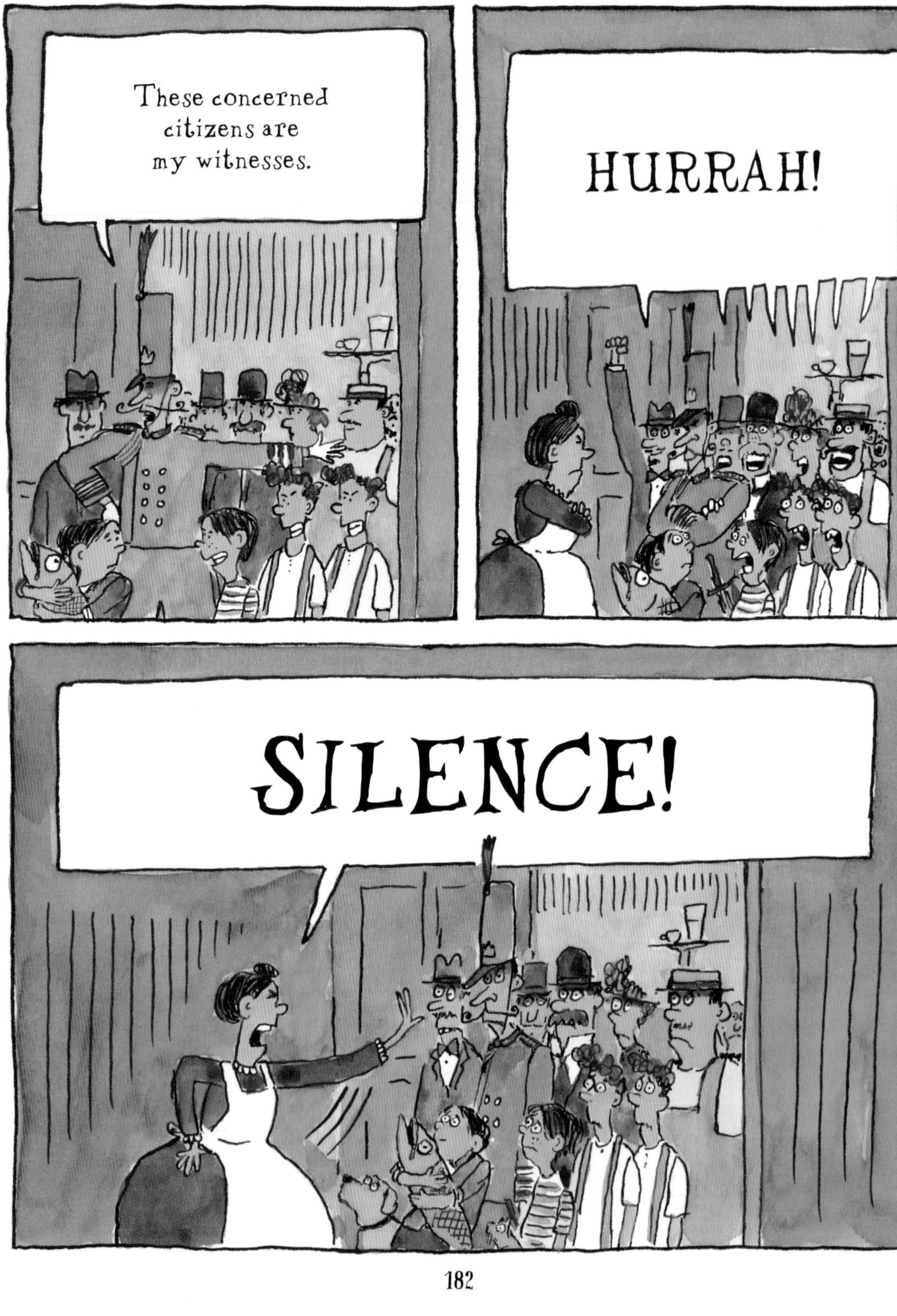
These concerned citizens are my witnesses.
HURRAH!
SILENCE!

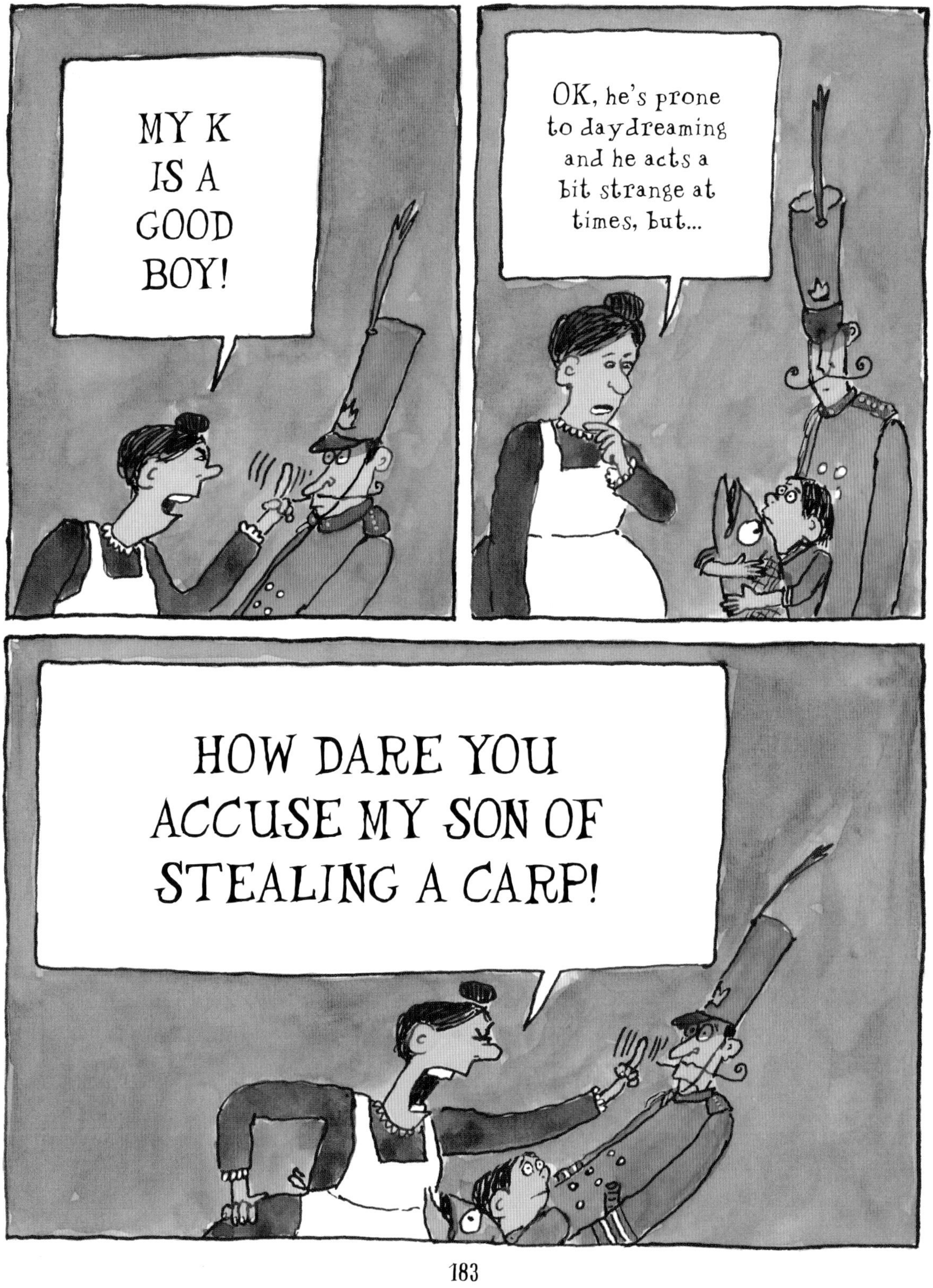
MY K IS A GOOD BOY!
OK, he's prone to daydreaming and he acts a bit strange at times, but...
HOW DARE YOU ACCUSE MY SON OF STEALING A CARP!

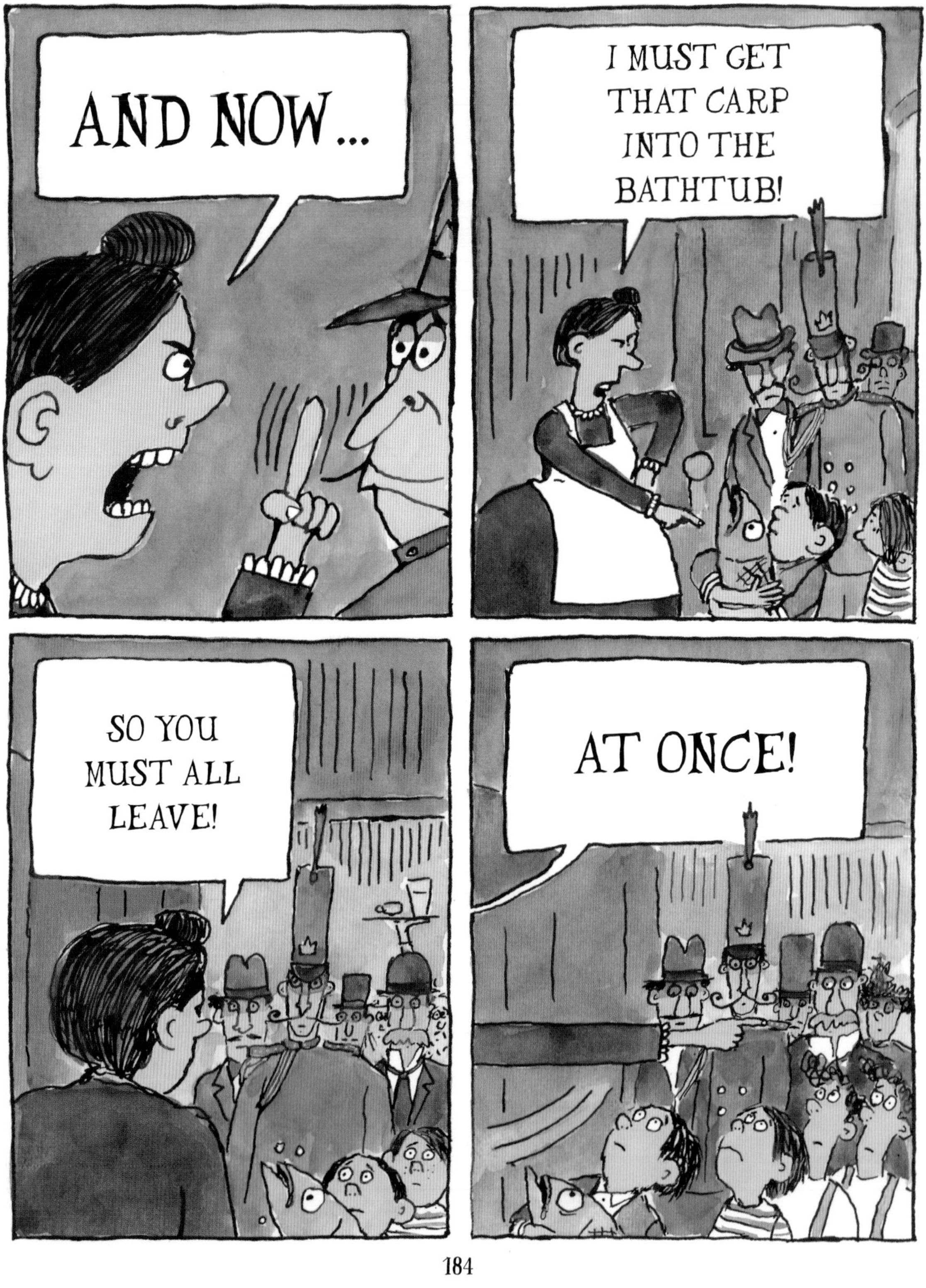
AND NOW...
I MUST GET THAT CARP INTO THE BATHTUB!
SO YOU MUST ALL LEAVE!
AT ONCE!

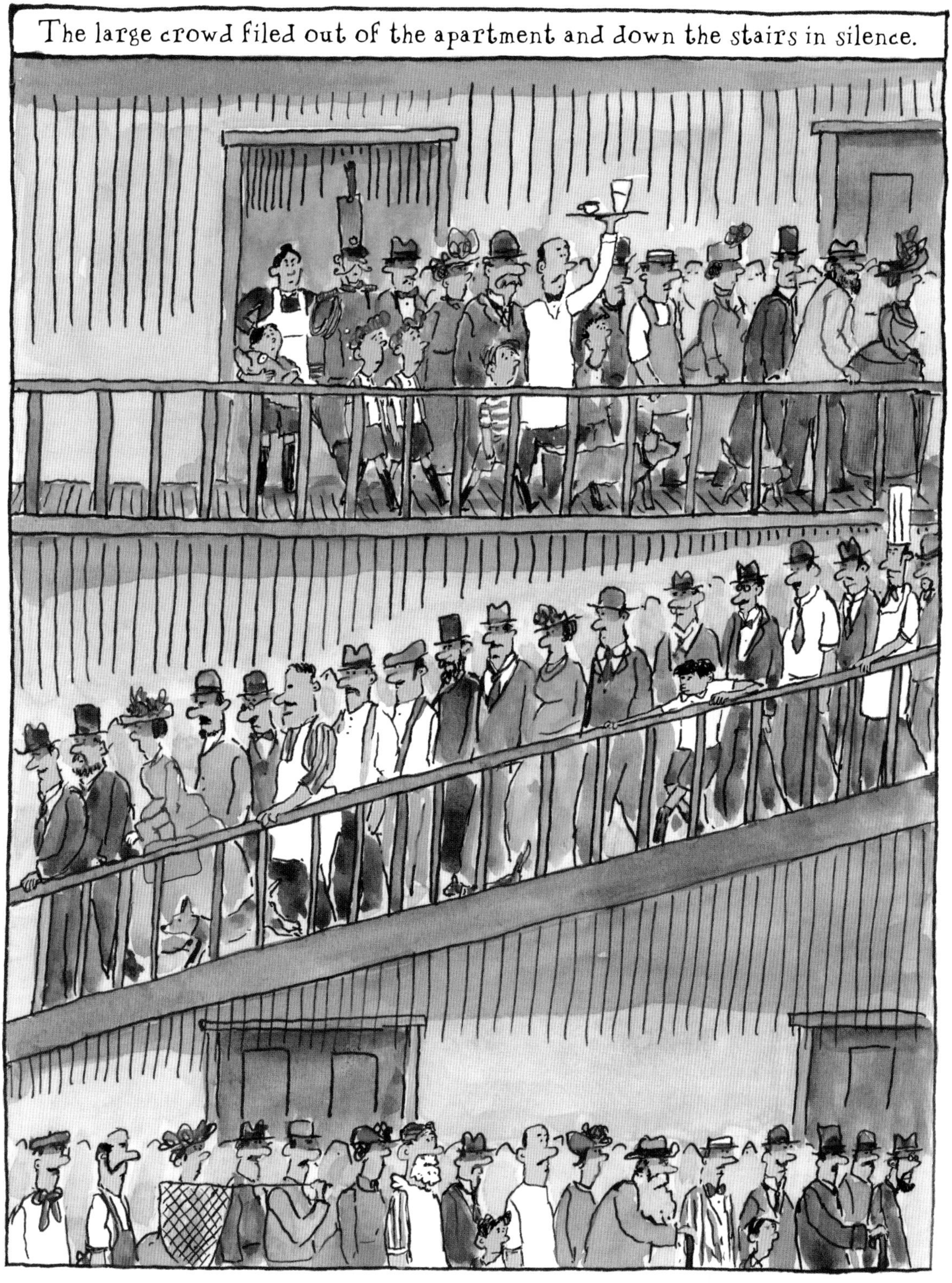
The large crowd filed out of the apartment and down the stairs in silence.

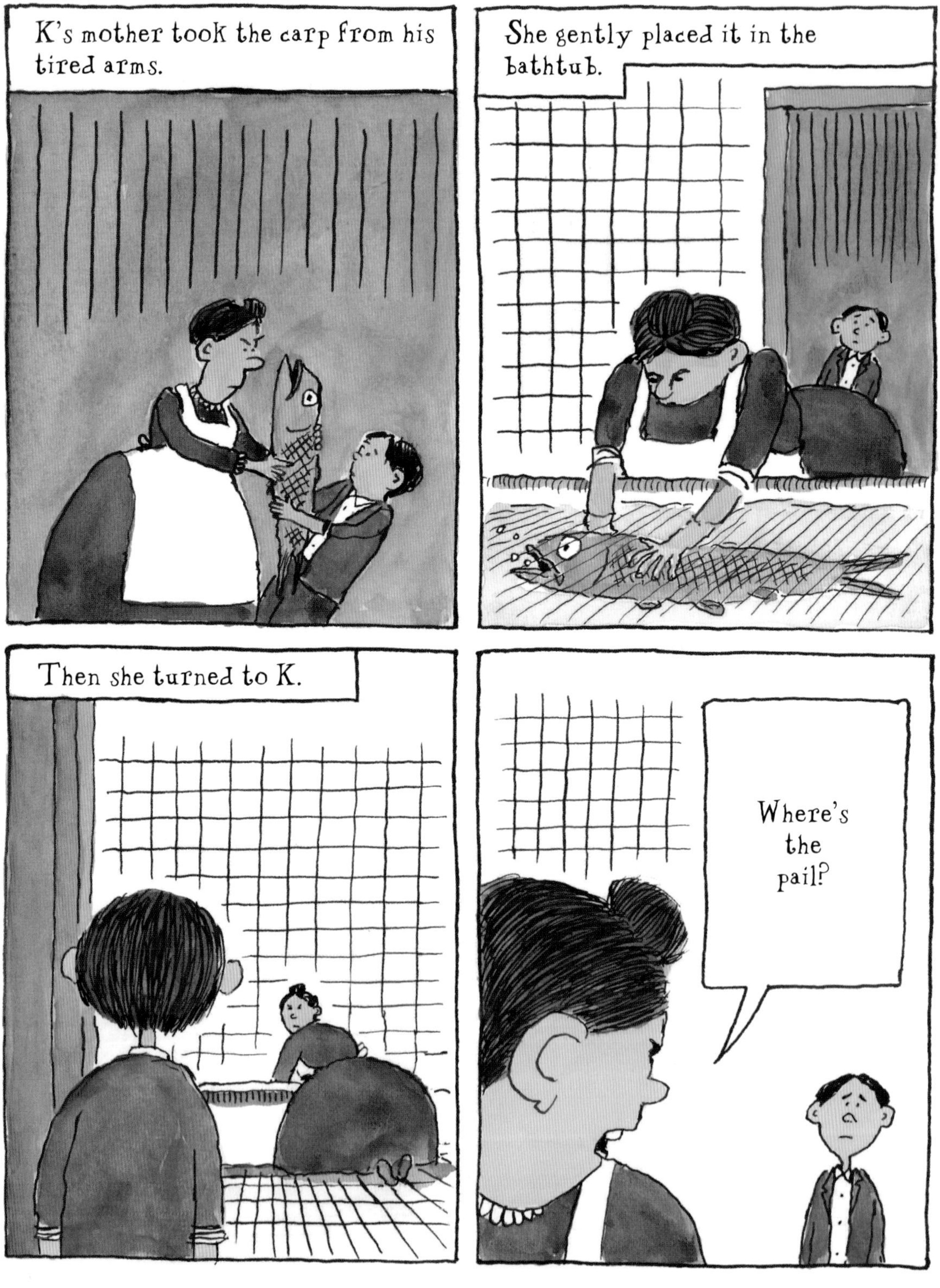
K's mother took the carp from his tired arms.
She gently placed it in the bathtub.
Then she turned to K.
Where's the pail?

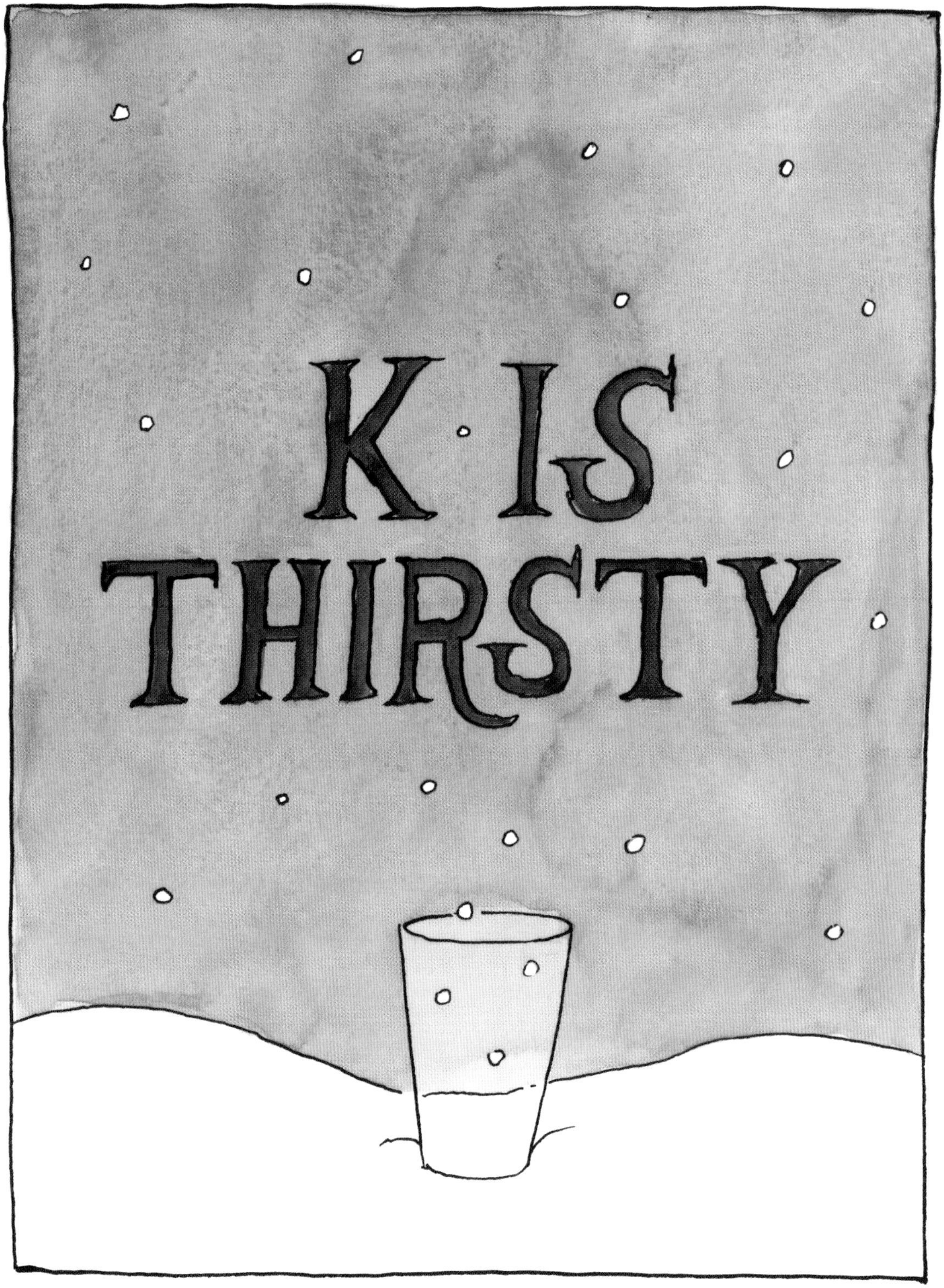
K IS
THIRSTY

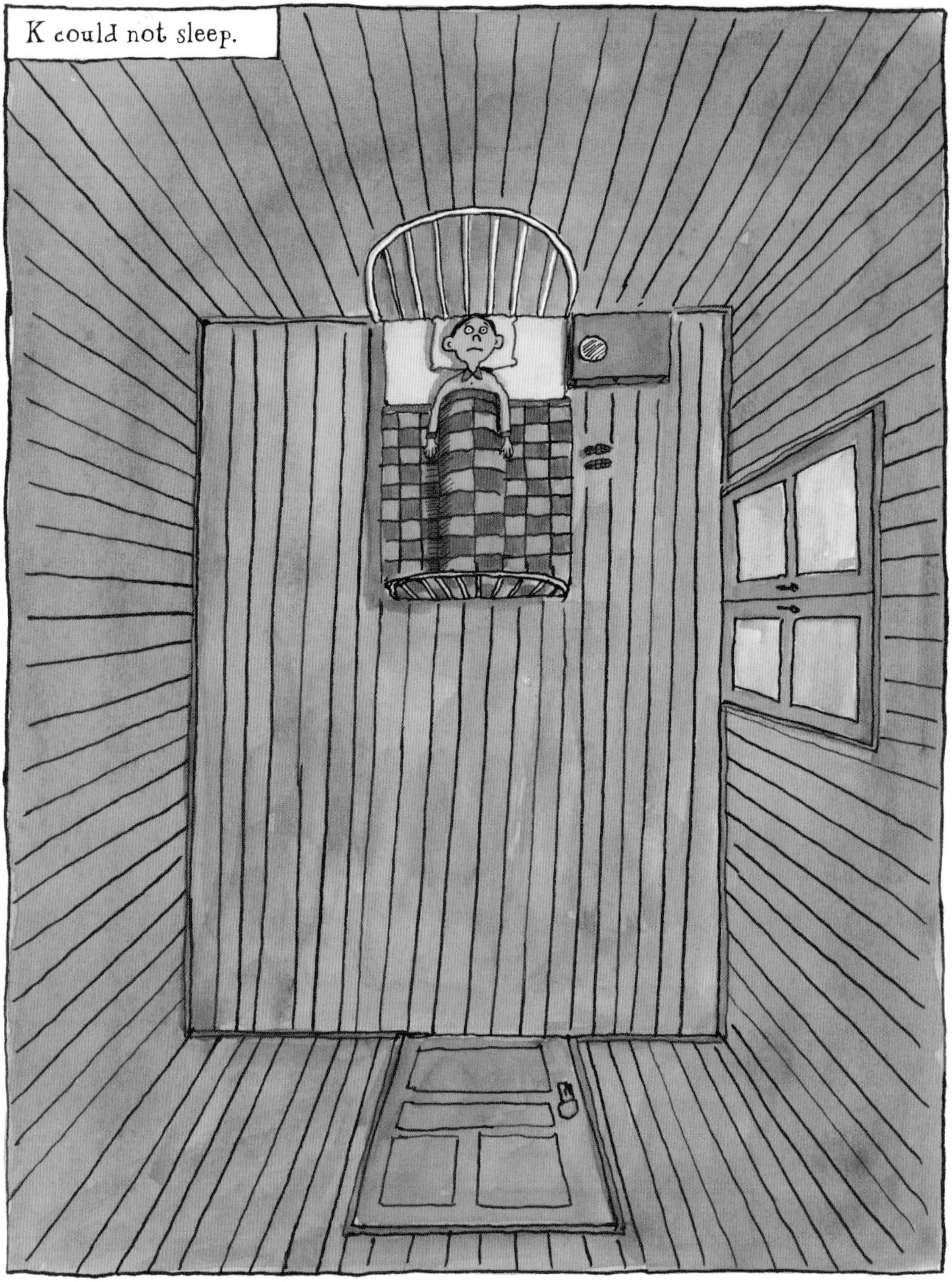
K could not sleep.

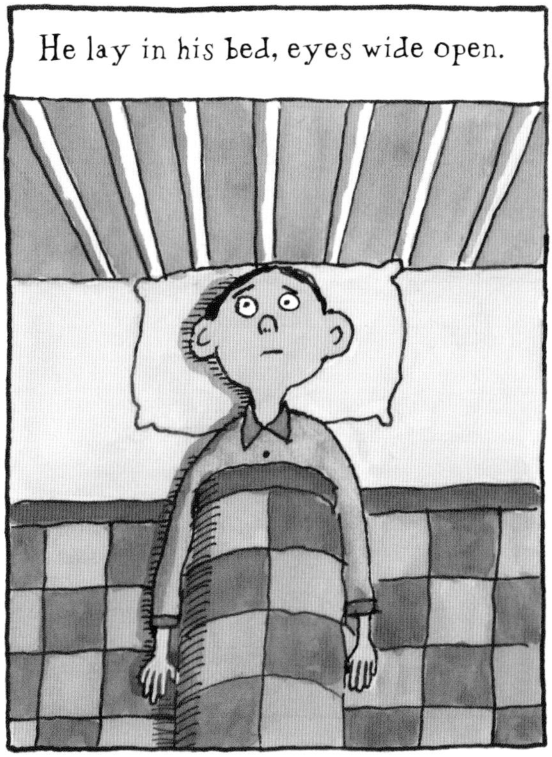
He lay in his bed, eyes wide open.

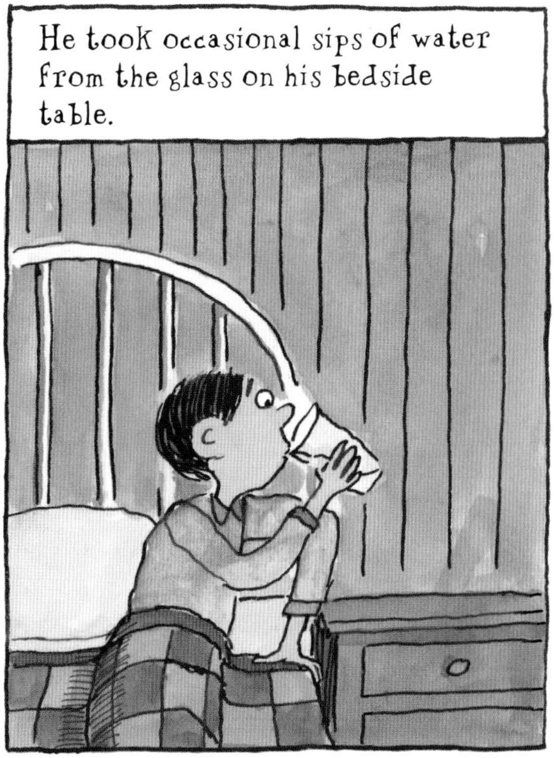
He took occasional sips of water from the glass on his bedside table.

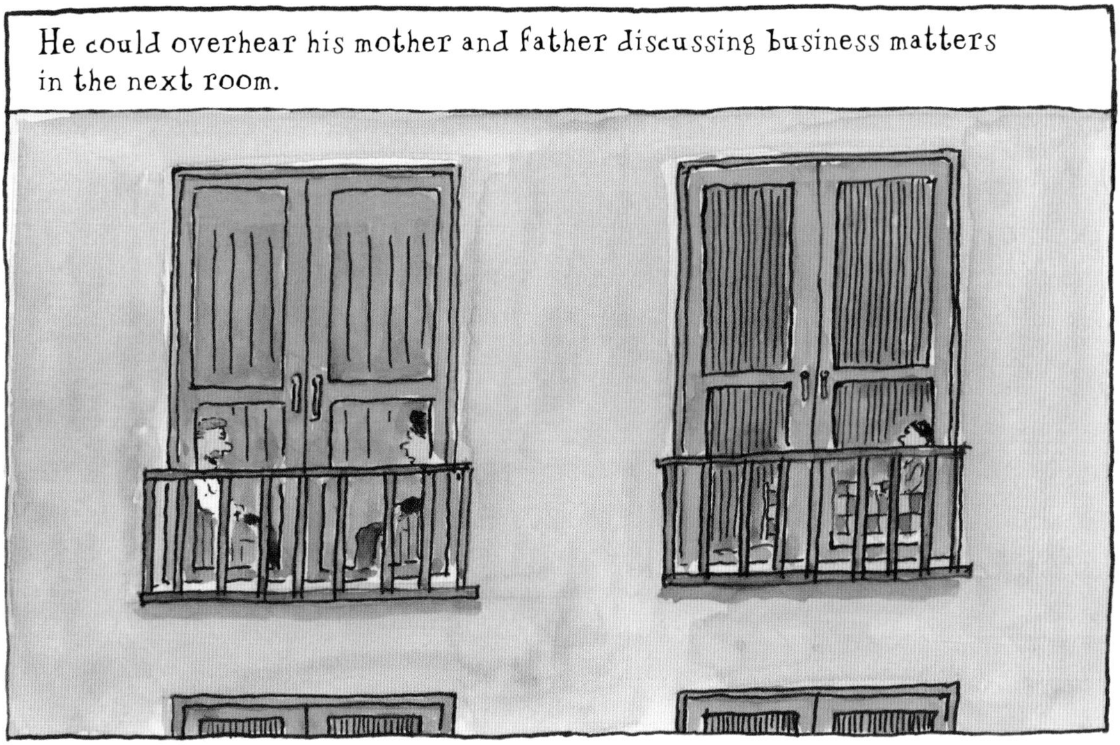
He could overhear his mother and father discussing business matters in the next room.

Someone in the apartment above was thumping around in heavy boots.

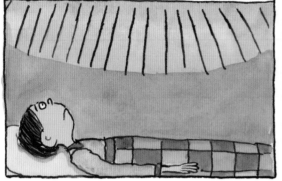

A howling wind rattled his balcony doors.

K sipped the last sip of water from his glass.

Then he got out of bed...

...picked up his glass...

...and approached the bedroom door.

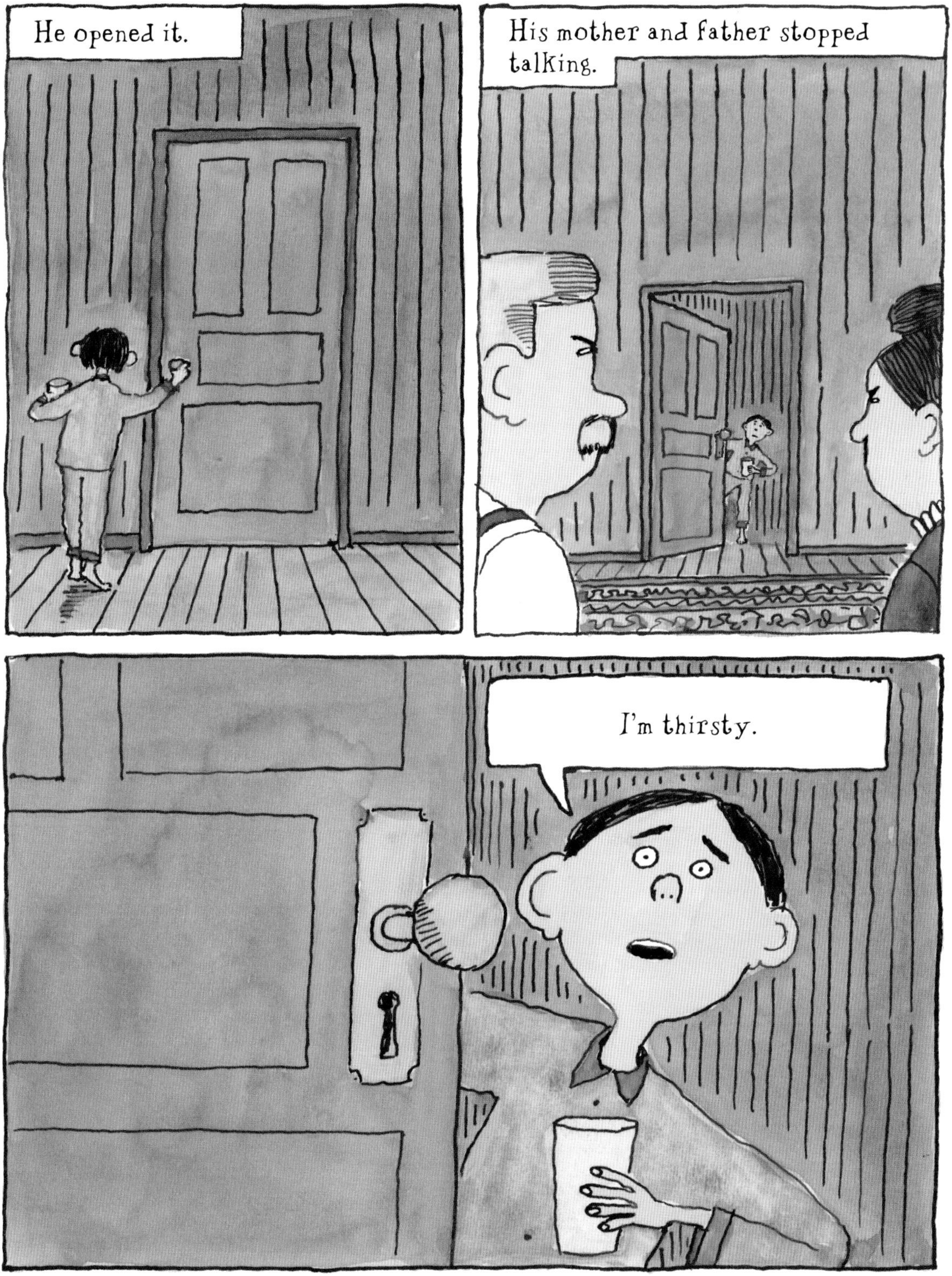
He opened it.
His mother and father stopped talking.
I'm thirsty.

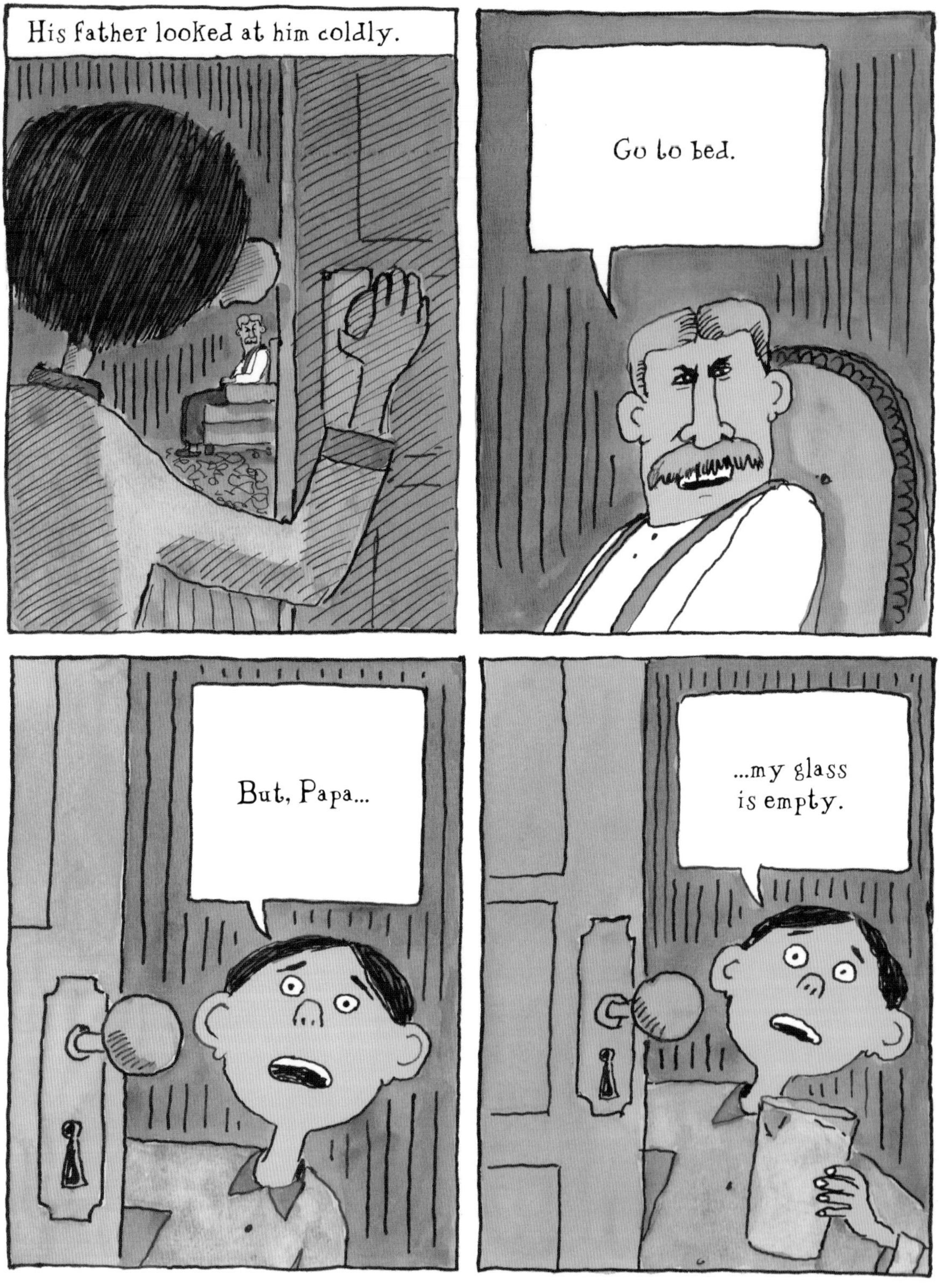
His father looked at him coldly.
Go to bed.
But, Papa...
...my glass is empty.

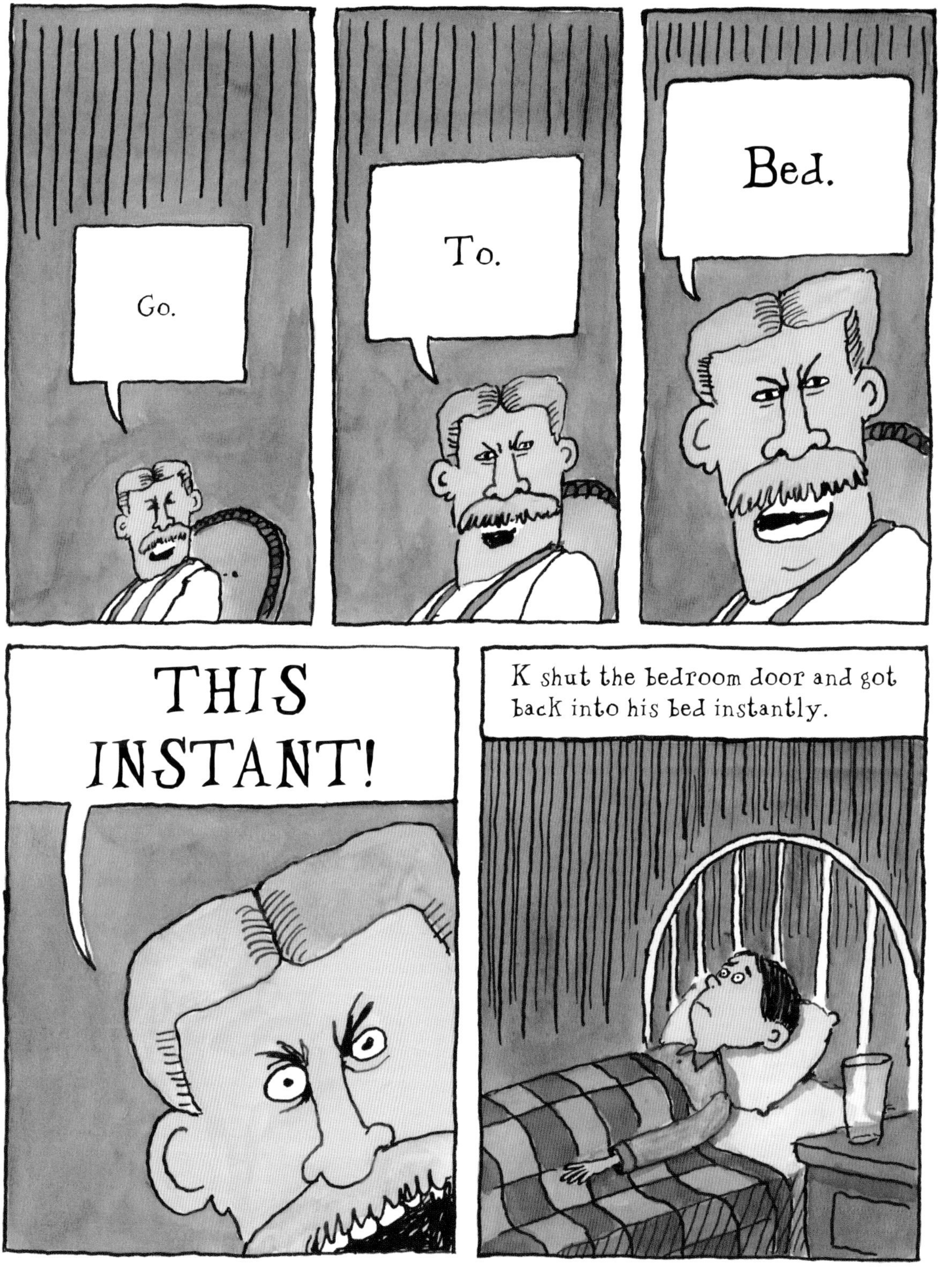
Go.
To.
Bed.
THIS INSTANT!
K shut the bedroom door and got back into his bed instantly.

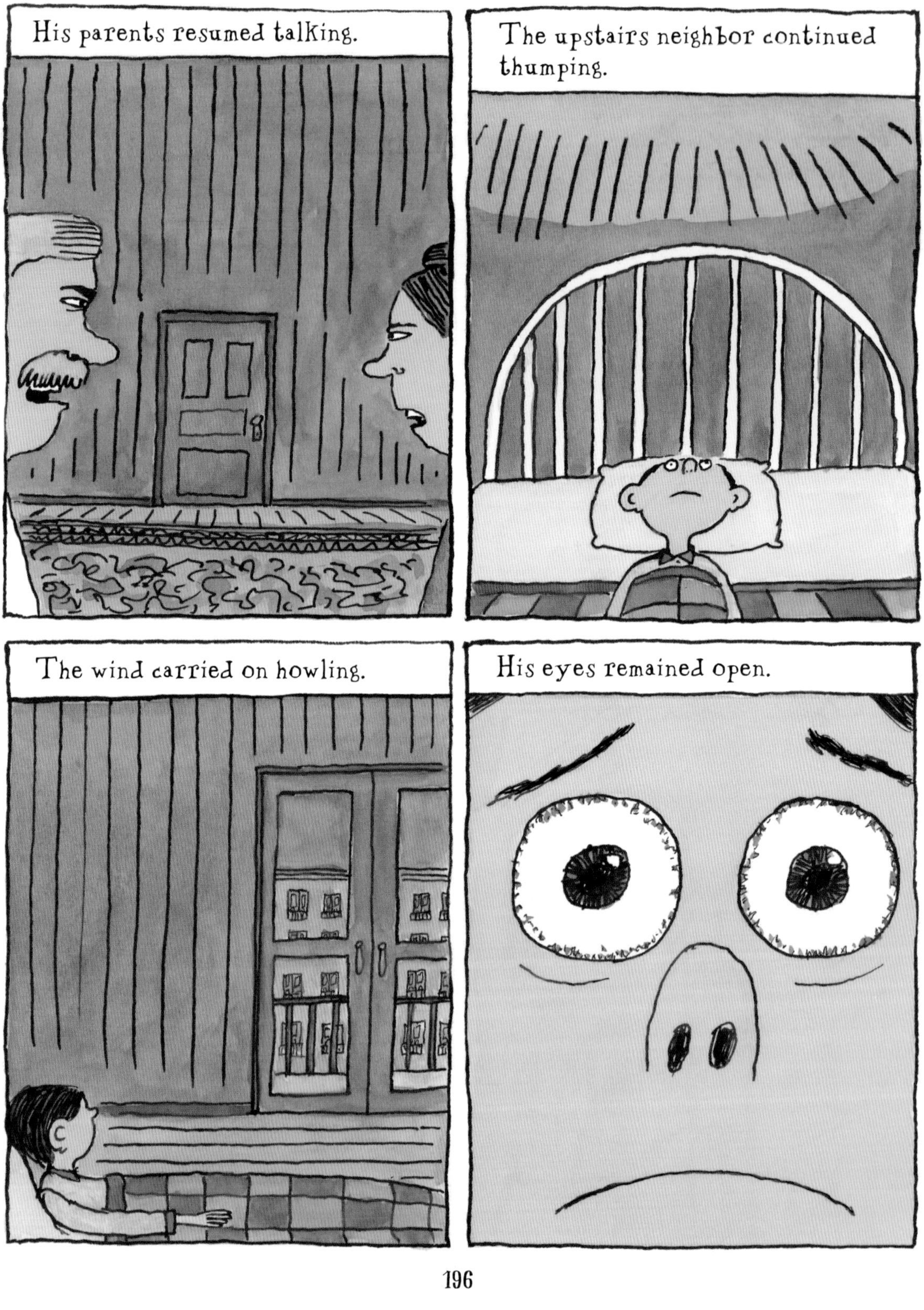
His parents resumed talking.
The upstairs neighbor continued thumping.
The wind carried on howling.
His eyes remained open.

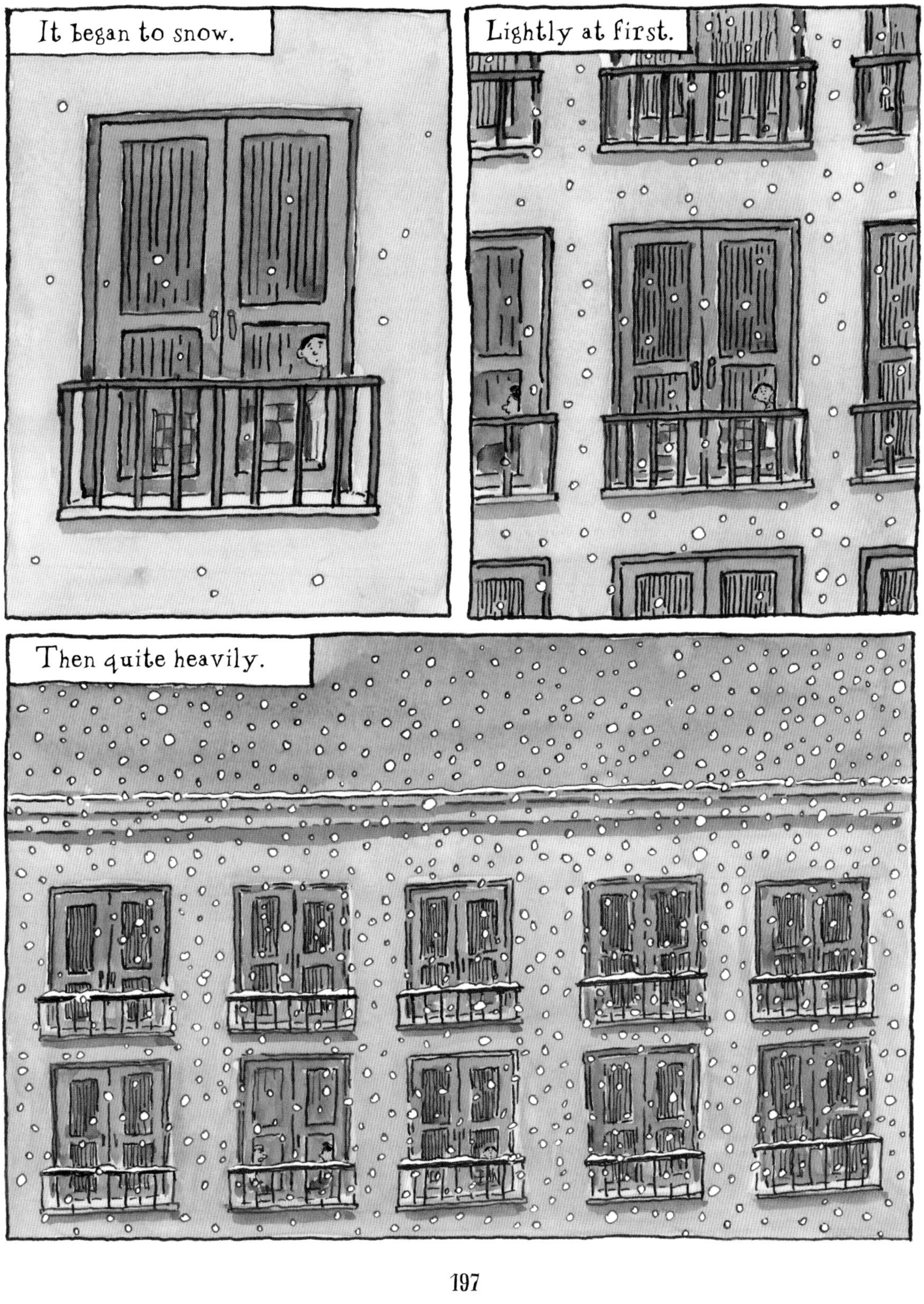
It began to snow.
Lightly at first.
Then quite heavily.

He watched the snow accumulate.

He arose once more and slipped on his slippers.

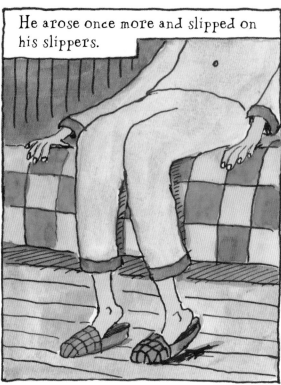

He took the empty glass from his bedside table...

...and approached his little balcony.

K stepped outside.

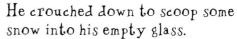

He crouched down to scoop some snow into his empty glass.

As he did so, a strong wind suddenly gusted...

...and swung the balcony door shut.

It was locked.

K tapped lightly on the glass.

There was no response.

So he tapped a bit harder.

Then harder still.

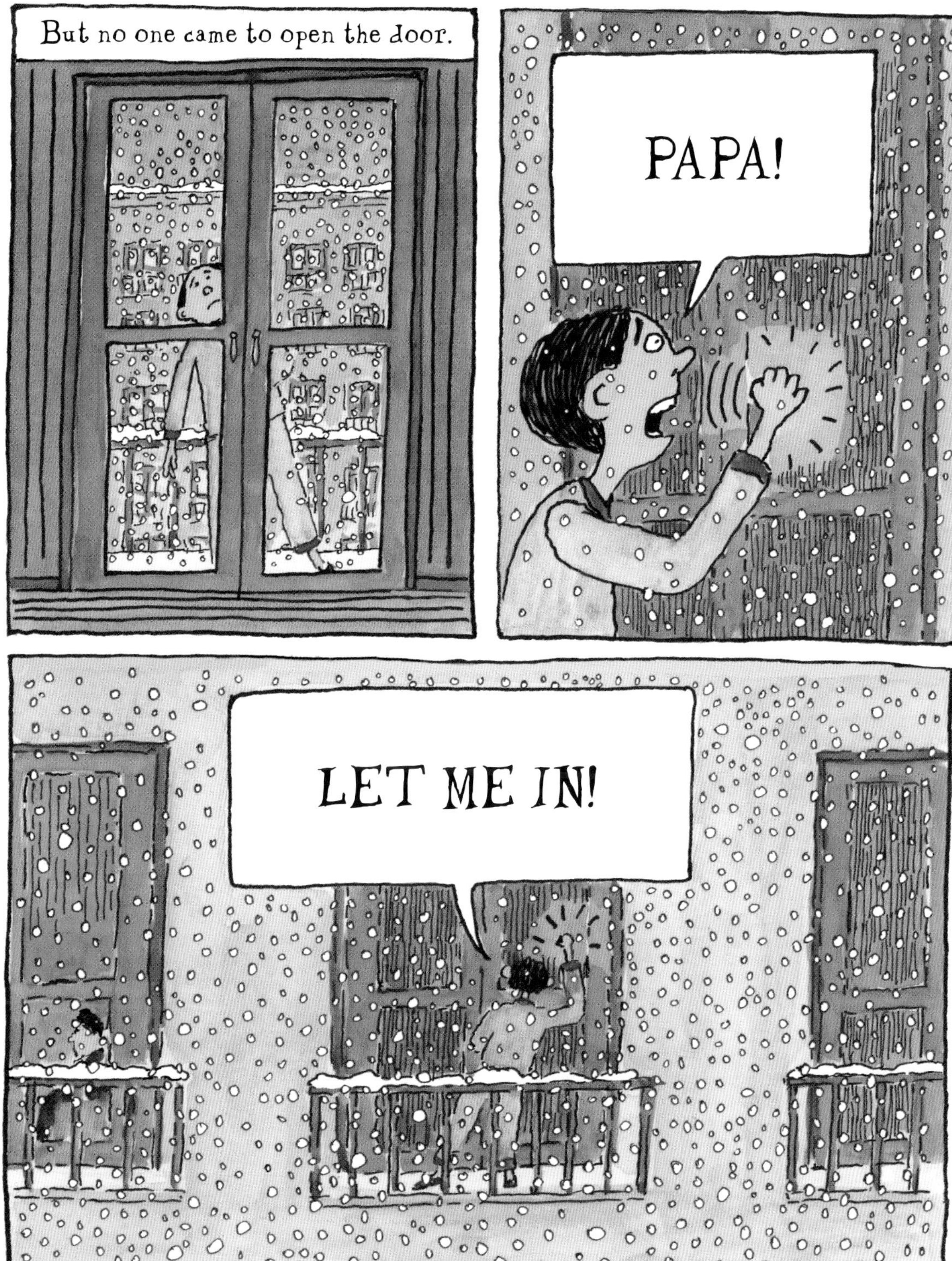

But no one came to open the door.
PAPA!
LET ME IN!

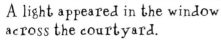
A light appeared in the window across the courtyard.

A man wearing pajamas emerged onto the balcony.

YOU THERE! BOY!

WHAT'S ALL THAT RACKET?

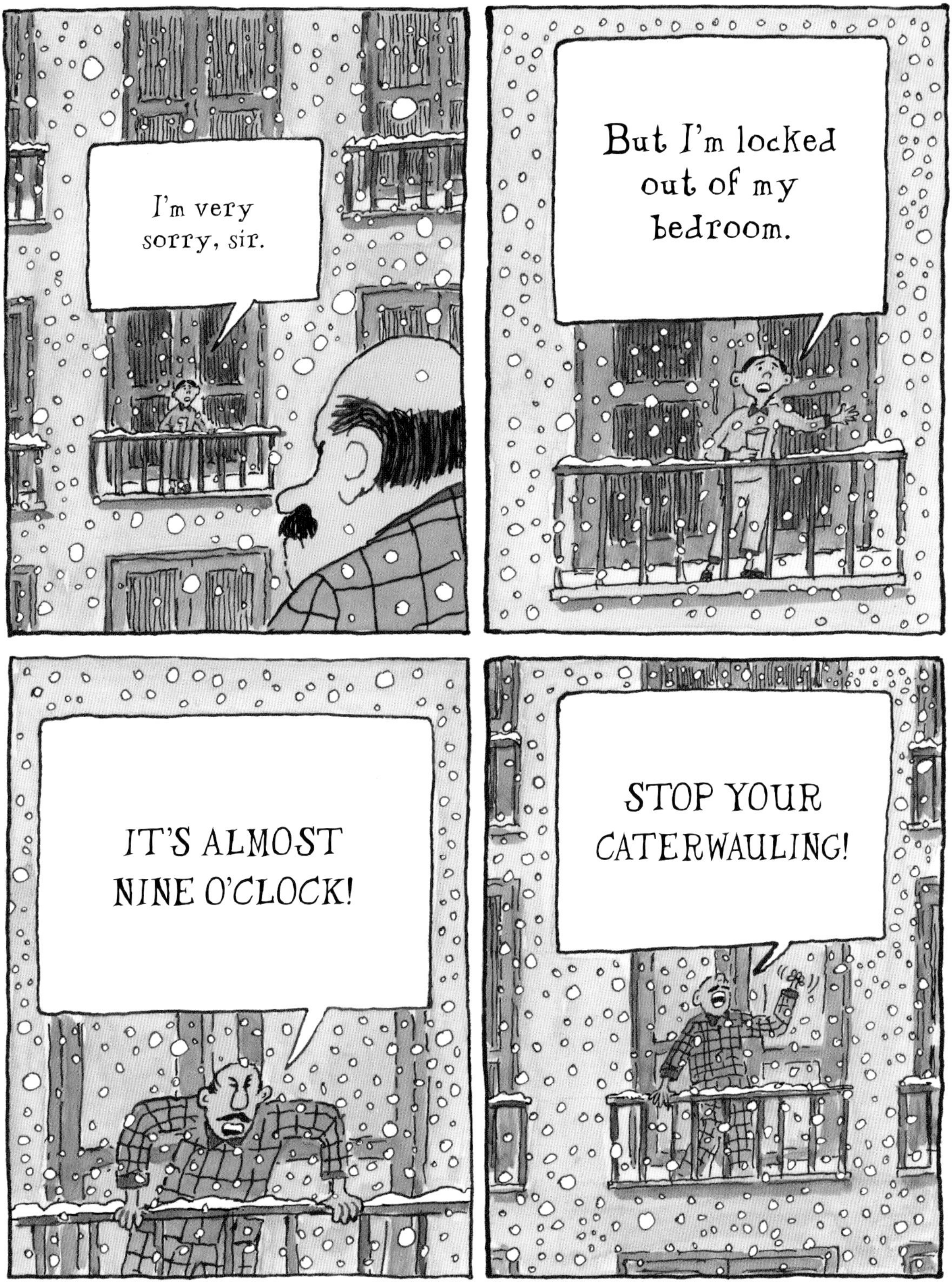
I'm very sorry, sir.
But I'm locked out of my bedroom.
IT'S ALMOST NINE O'CLOCK!
STOP YOUR CATERWAULING!

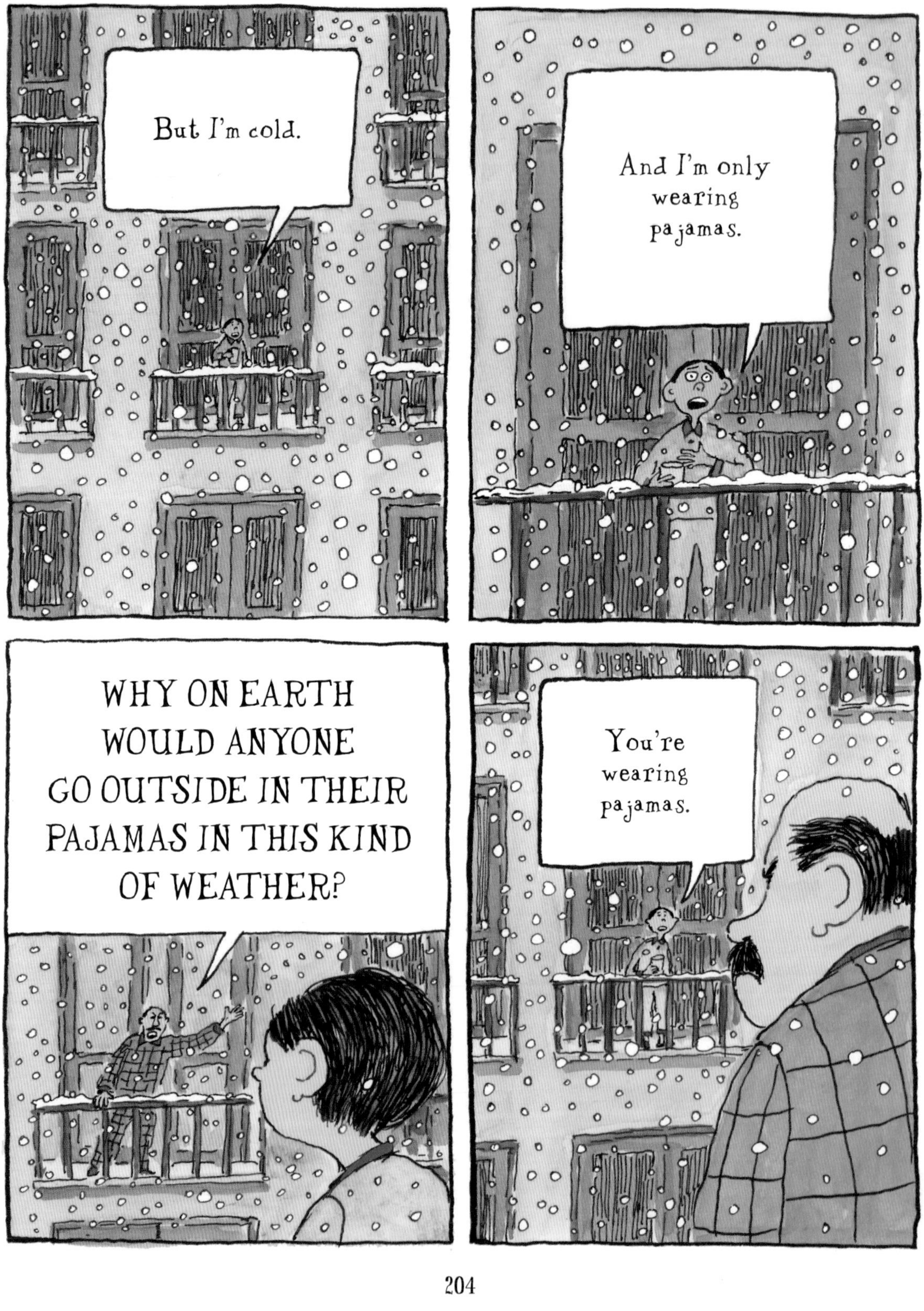
But I'm cold.
And I'm only wearing pajamas.
WHY ON EARTH WOULD ANYONE GO OUTSIDE IN THEIR PAJAMAS IN THIS KIND OF WEATHER?
You're wearing pajamas.

A second balcony light came on...

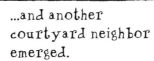

...and another courtyard neighbor emerged.

WHAT'S GOING ON HERE?

AND WHY IS EVERYONE YELLING?

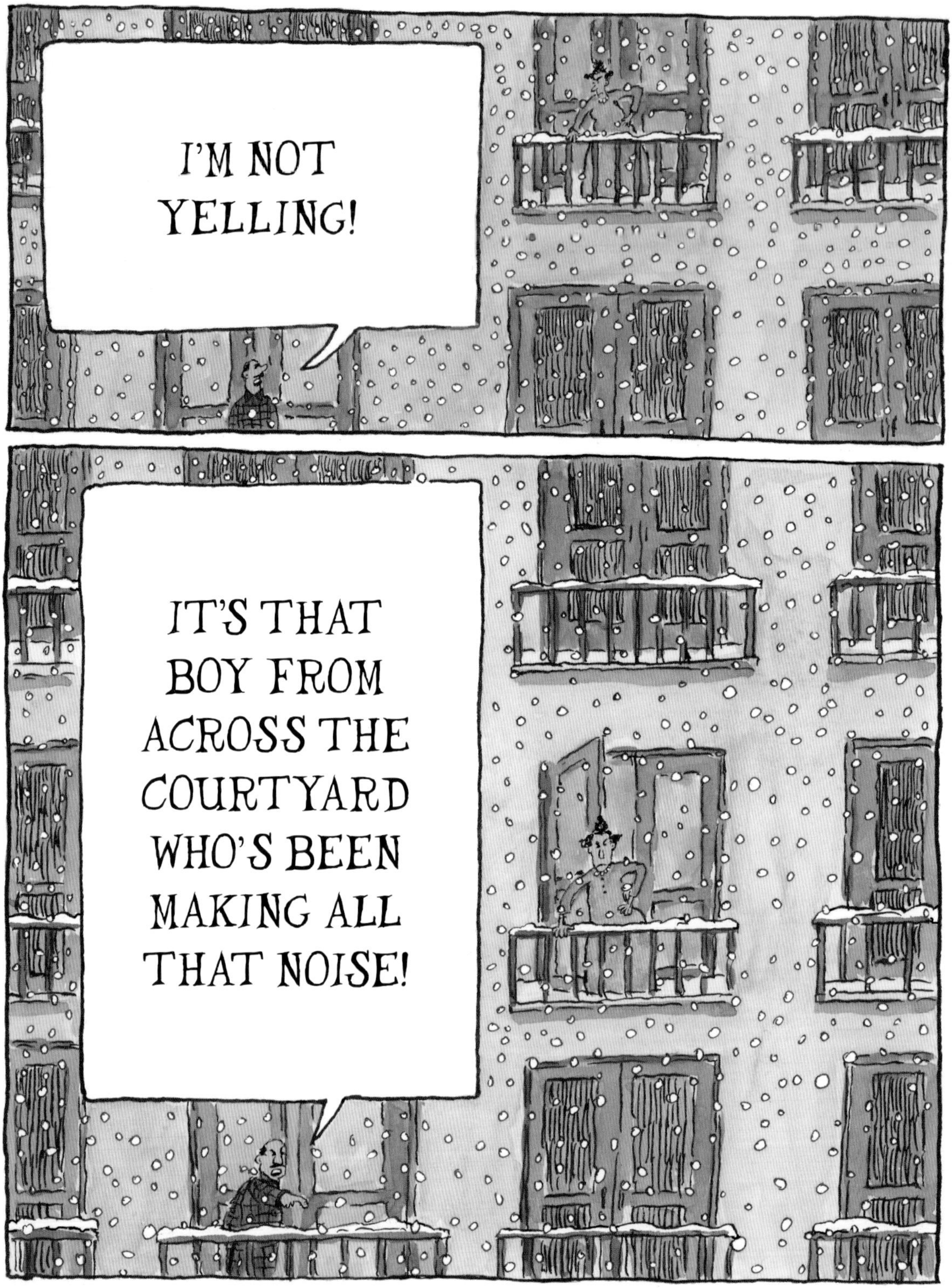
I'M NOT YELLING!
IT'S THAT BOY FROM ACROSS THE COURTYARD WHO'S BEEN MAKING ALL THAT NOISE!

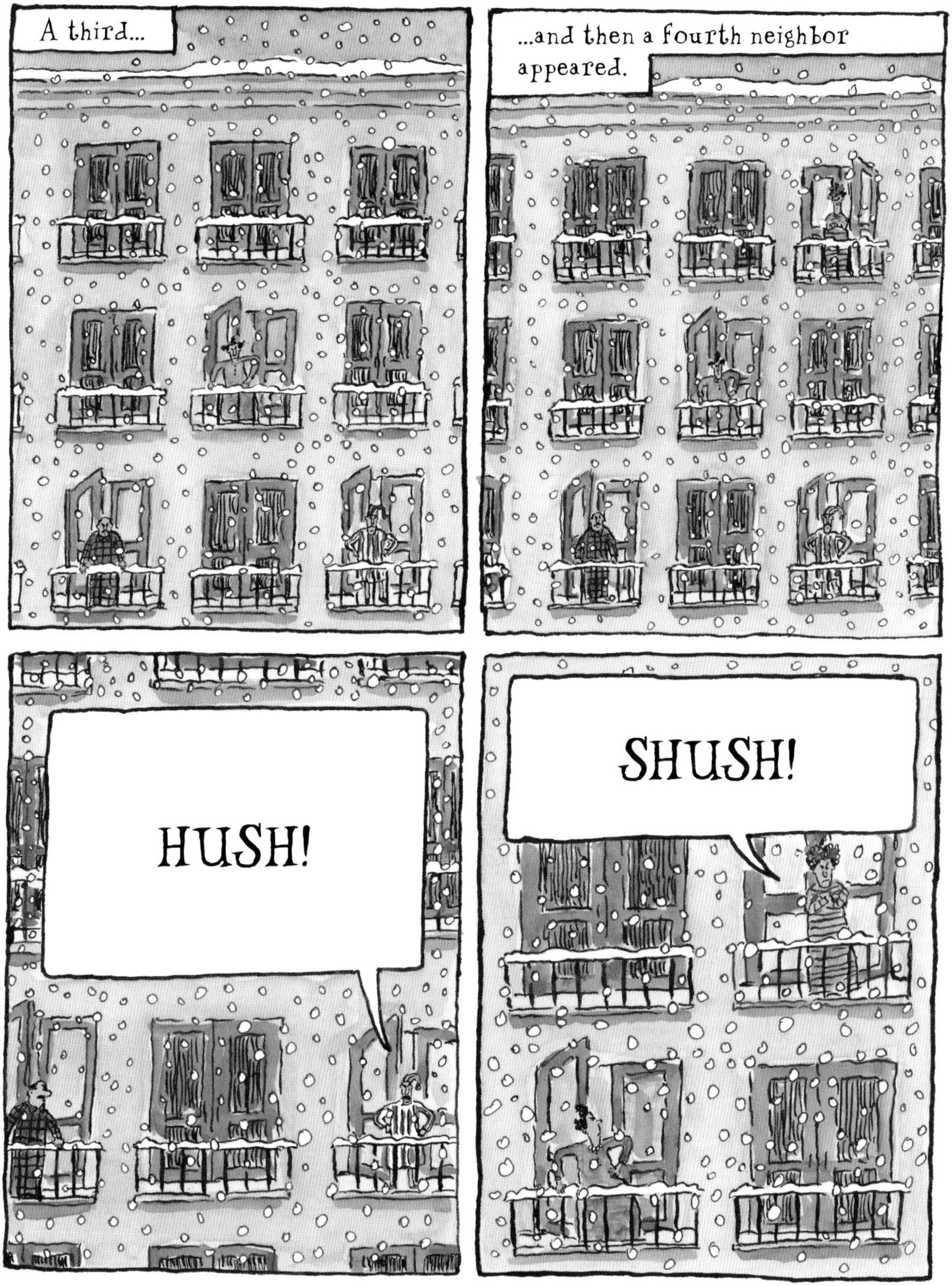
A third...
...and then a fourth neighbor appeared.
HUSH!
SHUSH!

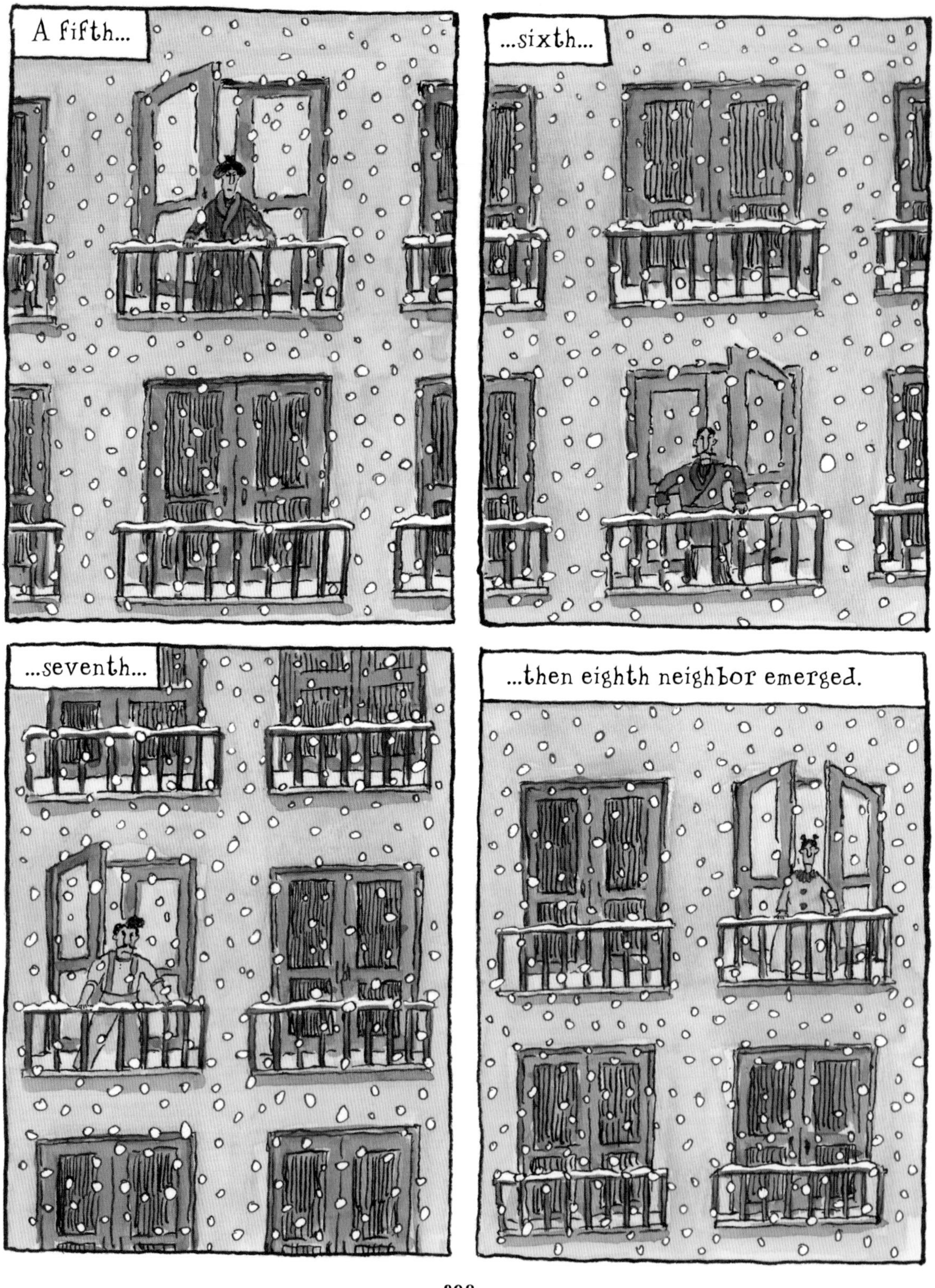
A fifth...
...sixth...
...seventh...
...then eighth neighbor emerged.

Moments later, the entire courtyard was filled with voices demanding to know where all the noise was coming from.

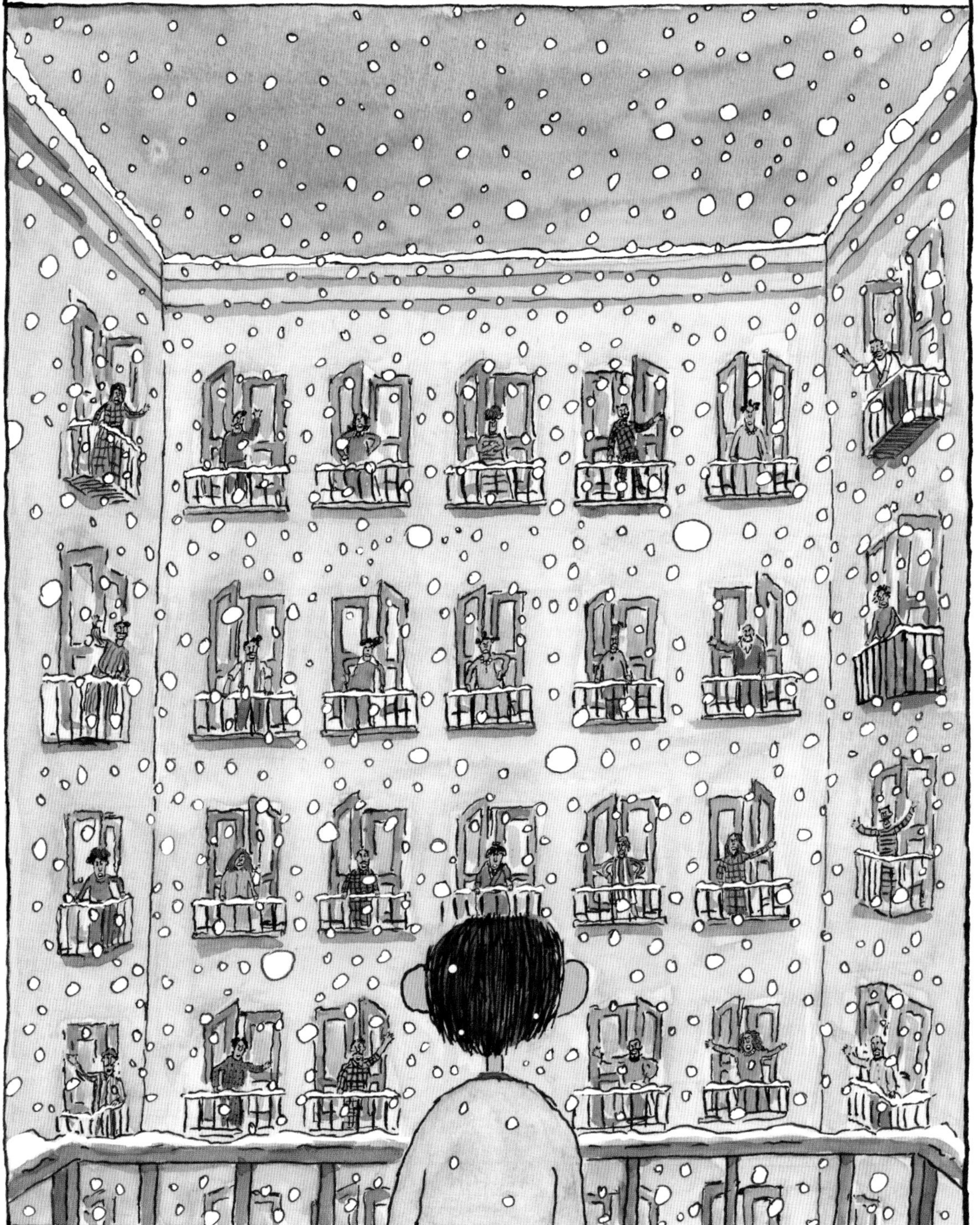

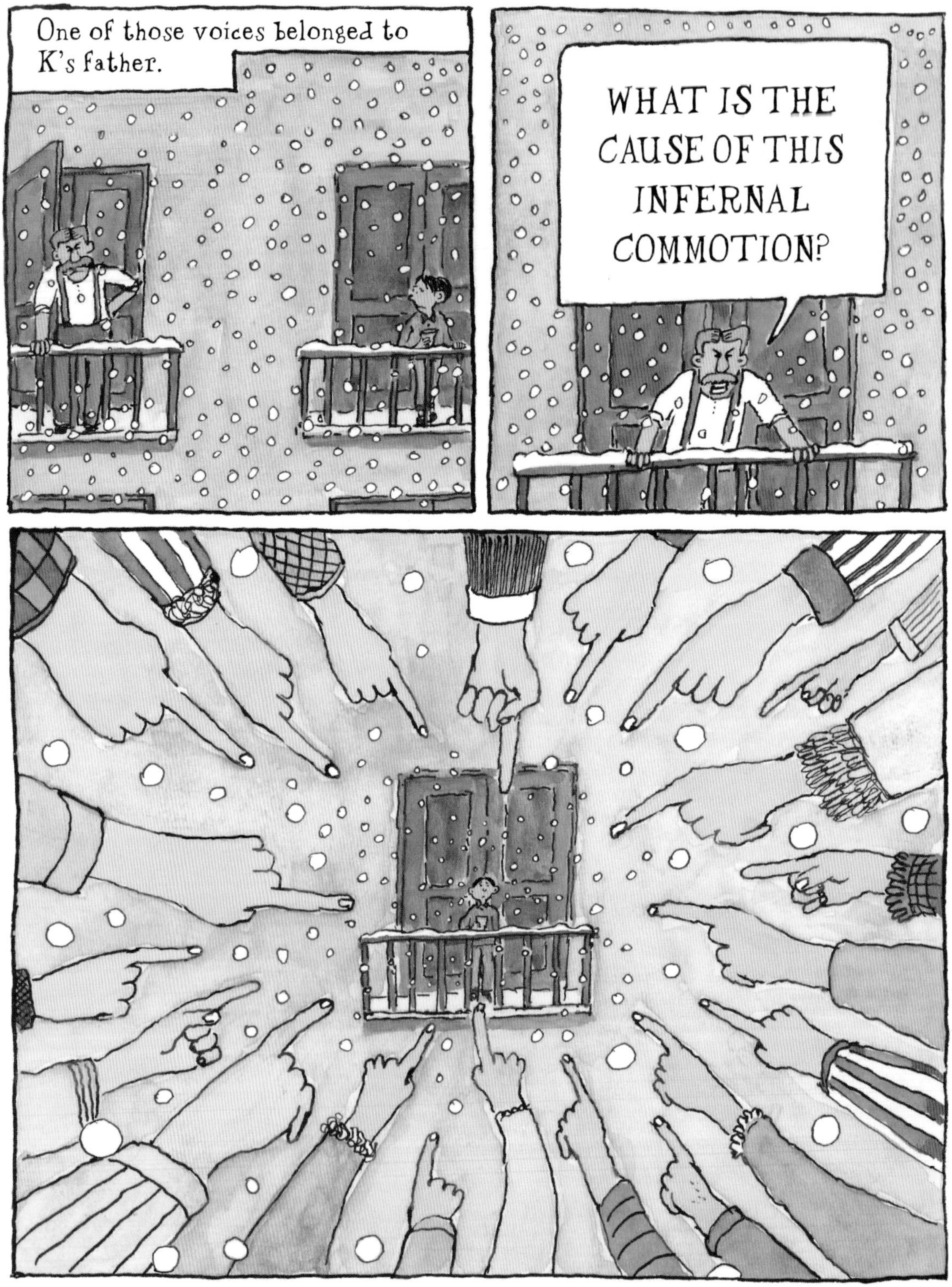
One of those voices belonged to K's father.
WHAT IS THE CAUSE OF THIS INFERNAL COMMOTION?

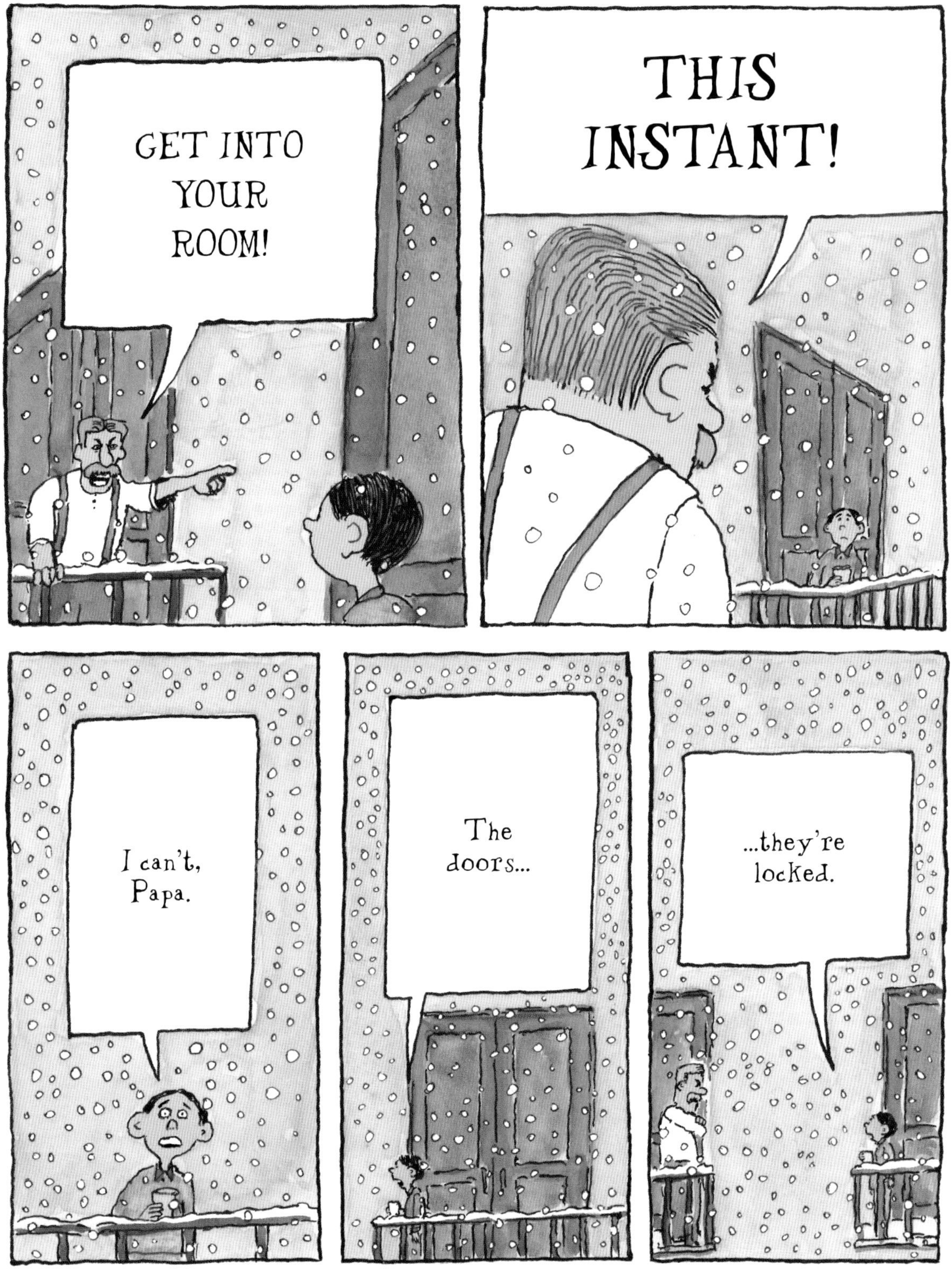
GET INTO YOUR ROOM!
THIS INSTANT!
I can't, Papa.
The doors...
...they're locked.

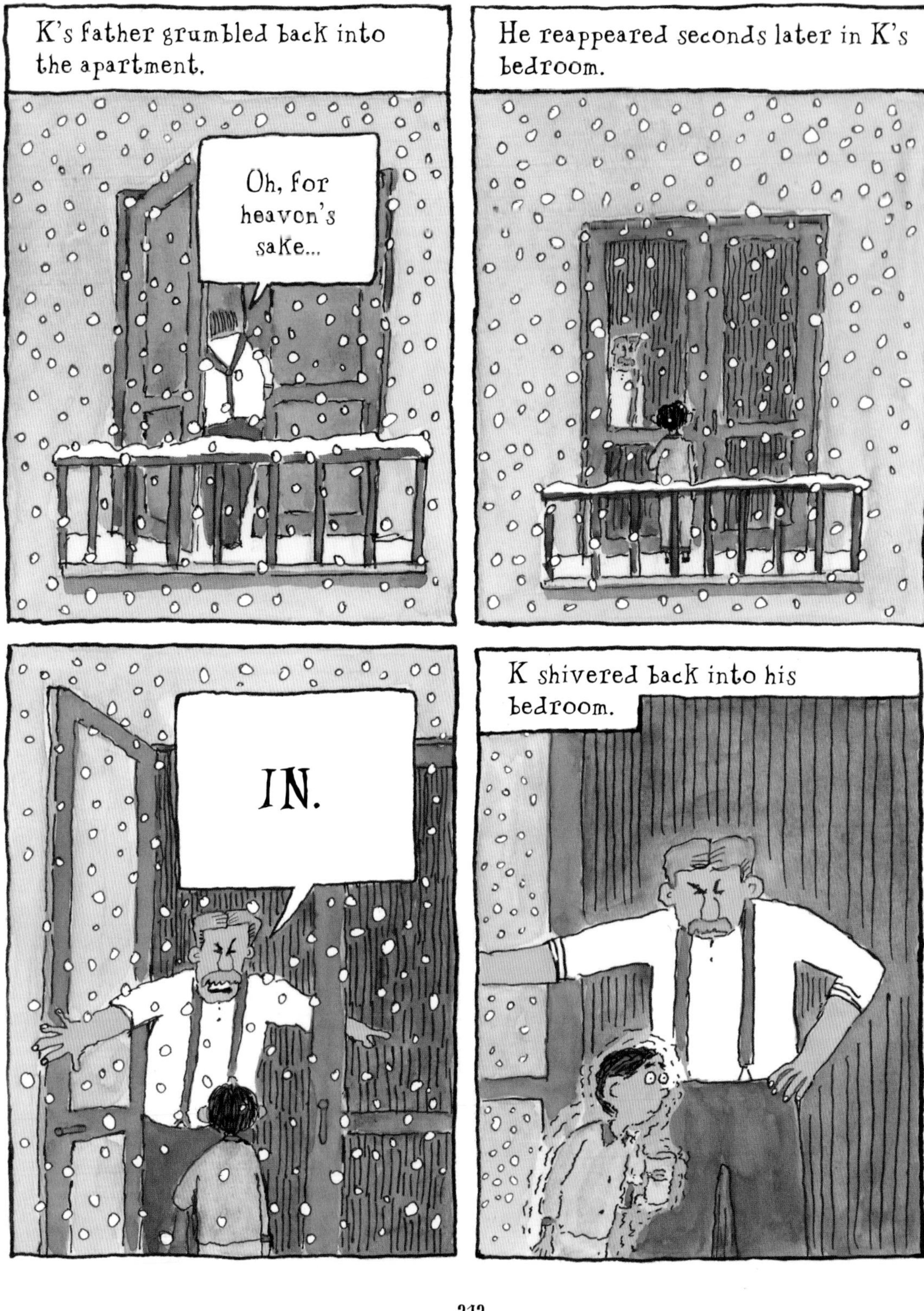
K's father grumbled back into the apartment.
Oh, for heaven's sake...
He reappeared seconds later in K's bedroom.
IN.
K shivered back into his bedroom.

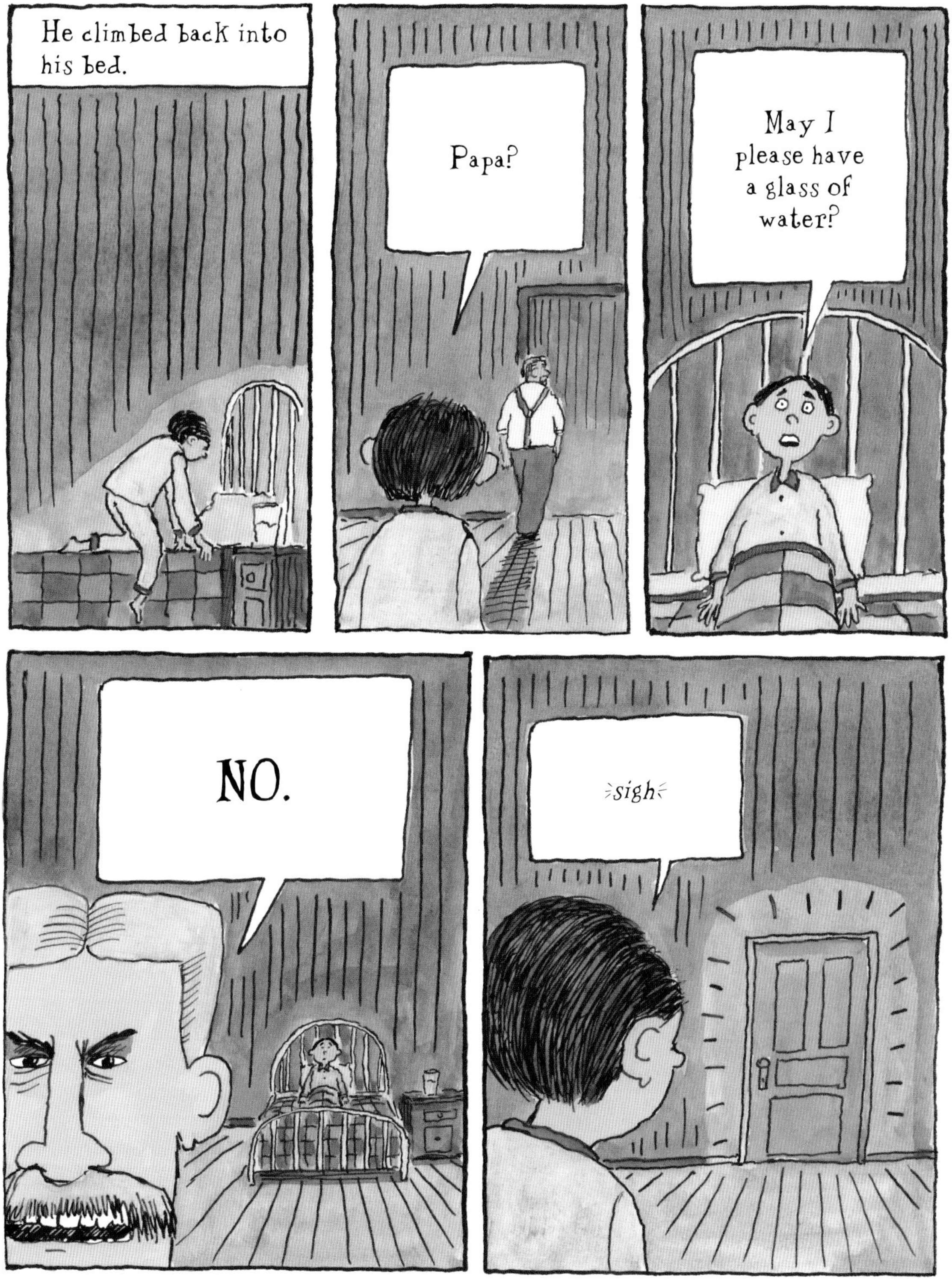
He climbed back into his bed.
Papa?
May I please have a glass of water?
NO.
sigh

K picked up his glass.

He scooped out a small handful of snow.

The snow felt cold and refreshing as it melted in his mouth.

He rested his head on his pillow.

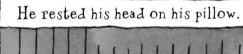

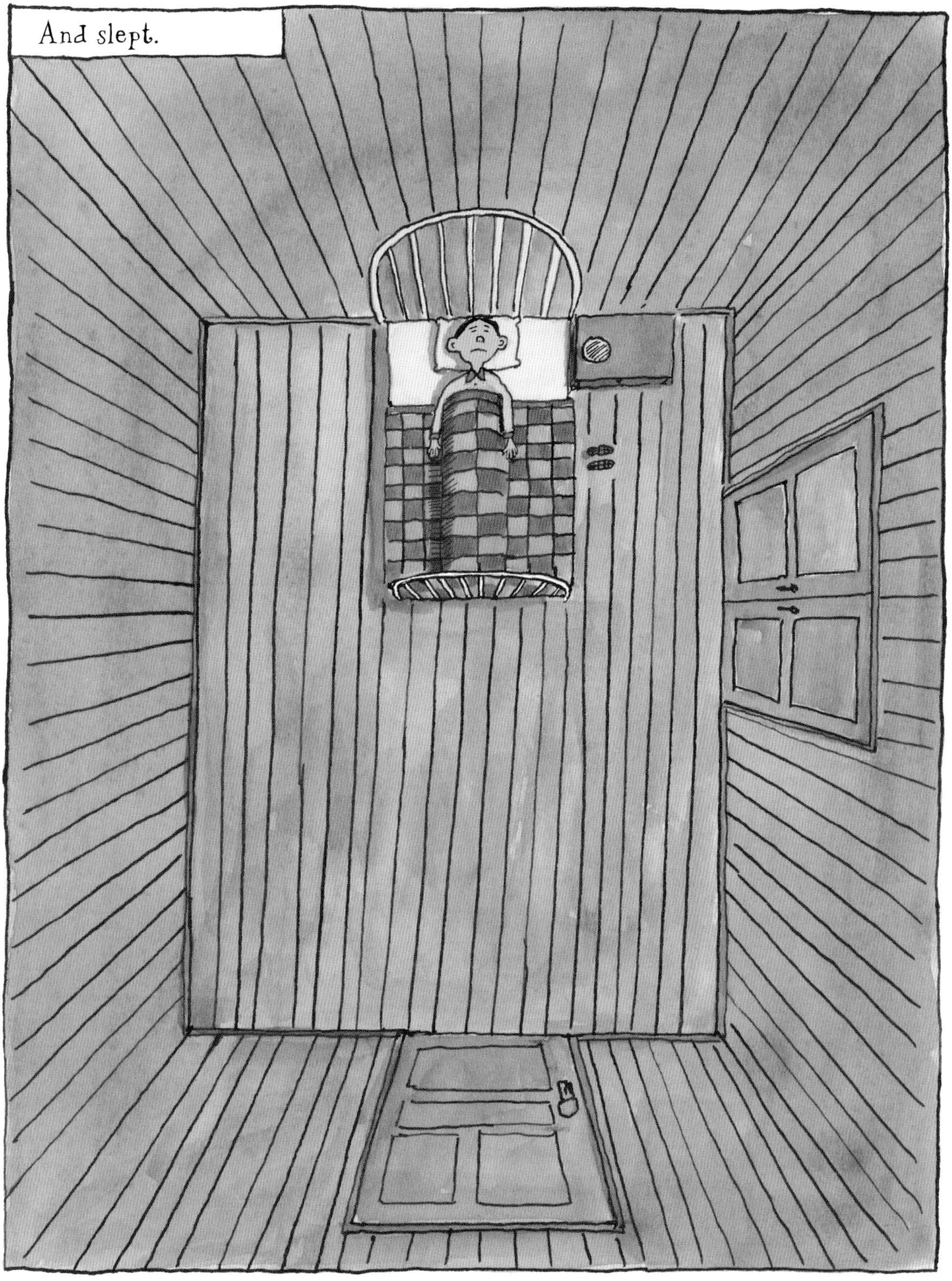
And slept.

Acknowledgments

It is my general belief that all things are in some way connected and that nothing is created in isolation. This belief has been positively reinforced with respect to the creation of this book.

If it hadn't been for the excellent people at PJ Library underwriting my brief residency at The Center for Cartoon Studies, I never would have had the opportunity to meet the magnanimous James Sturm, whose advice and encouragement were enormously helpful in the early stages of writing and drawing this book.

Without James, I would never have had the opportunity to work with Judy Hansen, whose vast experience and thoughtful input were crucial to this project's evolution.

I'm extremely grateful to Judy for finding K the perfect home, where I found the best editor I could have possibly imagined: Andrea Colvin. I value her unerring eye, penetrating insight, and always (really—always) helpful suggestions. She has made this book a better one in every way.

This book would not look the way it does without the tireless efforts of its designer, Megan McLaughlin. I owe her a debt of gratitude for her work and for making the many accommodations my feeble technical skills required. I must also thank her for introducing me to the term *workflow*.

Thanks also to Zara González Hoang for her camaraderie and her cheerful sharing of Photoshop know-how in the early stages. It is entirely due to her that I understand the concept of *layers*.

Sort of.

I reached out to Joe Ollmann, a perfect stranger and, as it turned out, gentleman, who very freely and generously offered thoughtful feedback at a critical moment in my workflow.

I am grateful as well to Patsy Aldana whose support, counsel, and friendship I value more than words can say.

I would be remiss if I didn't acknowledge the teachers of my youth…further proof of the connectedness of all things. They connect my past to my present in the form of this book, and they inspired me in ways that I'm quite certain were unintentional.

I thank and love my children, Sarah and Benjamin, for their unconditional support. Their enthusiasm for this book was a constant source of strength.

And finally, to Gill, my patient wife, my first reader, my wisest advisor, and my eternal love.

GARY CLEMENT is a Canadian artist, cartoonist, illustrator, and writer. He's the author and illustrator of several children's books, and his illustrations and cartoons have appeared in newspapers and magazines across North America. *K Is in Trouble* is his debut graphic novel.